Run With the Wind

Run With the Wind

To Ronald

Jim Cole

Colemines Publishing

Run With the Wind

Printed in the United States of America

ISBN: 978-1-7347678-0-3

Publication Date: April 15, 2020

To order additional copies of this book, contact:

Colemines Publishing
https://colemines.com
jim@colemines.com

Contents

Chapter 1

Early August 1938
51st and Strand, Galveston, Texas

There was no way Sarah Jacobs could have believed that within fifteen minutes there would be a dead man in her front yard.

She was on her front porch, fretting, waiting for her ten-year old son who should have been home by noon. She knew where he'd gone, pier fishing at Offats Bayou using a private pier owned by a family friend. It was nearly an hour past, and Sarah was anxious to return to her job as secretary and assistant manager of the Galveston Pilots' Guild, but she was reluctant to leave until Benji was home for the afternoon.

A freighter that had had an engine room fire was returning to port, and she hadn't yet done all that was needed to ensure a safe entry into Galveston's harbor.

She rose from her chair as she'd already done a number of times, and once again looked down the street toward Broadway, leaning outward into the sun, shading her wide-set dark eyes with her hand.

"Finally!" she said aloud.

Benji was still two blocks away, but her crippled boy was moving rapidly, his straw fishing hat bobbing as he limped awkwardly along, sunlight flashing off his aluminum wrist cane. Sarah waved, noting that he seemed to be moving faster than usual. "Good thing!" she thought. "He's late! He knows how busy I am!"

Benjamin spotted her on the front steps and waved back. Sarah's forehead crinkled as she thought he might have shouted, but if he had, the distance diminished any sound. She turned back to the porch shade, regained her seat in the rocker and picked up her glass of iced tea, rubbing the wet glass across her forehead. She wished the ancient creaking overhead fans could turn faster.

Sarah's thoughts briefly moved away from her anxiety about the incoming ship and her son's tardiness to the pride she had in the strong personality of her crippled boy, and the progress he'd made against infantile paralysis. Benji had begun walking at only nine months, and a half-year later the toddler was running all about the house. Then, polio had struck with devastating suddenness.

Doctors promised her he'd never walk again, but they had been wrong. He still needed a brace, on his left leg from the knee down, and he used a wrist cane; but he could walk. Sarah's son often told his mother that one day that brace, and the cane, would be stored in an attic room, to be forgotten along with other braces he'd outgrown.

Sarah once again rose from her chair and moved to the porch edge, leaning outward and again squinting against the midday brightness. There was rarely much traffic on the crushed shell 51st Street, and today she saw only one car, three blocks away, beginning a slow turn toward her, a block behind her son.

She saw Benjamin step off the curb heading to their side of the street just as a tour jitney turned onto 51st Street. It honked noisily and Benji scrambled back, dragging his rusty 'fishing' wagon over the curb as the jitney passed. Sarah heard the driver shout rudely, "Out of the way, Jew-boy!"

The tour jitneys, open-sided, gaudily painted buses, picked up tourists at the beach or along the seawall and for a few coins provided a "historic" tour through Galveston's residential areas. Sarah knew the spiels used by the jitney drivers rarely touched on anything remotely historical or accurate.

The car Sarah had seen earlier was now fully onto 51st but was still moving slowly. Benji shouldered his rope harness and again pulled his wagon into the street and headed across.

The tour jitney slowed, preparing to stop in front of Sarah's house, and she moved back to the deep shade and her rocker, hoping the jitney driver would not see her. She recognized this driver and knew that he always stopped and shouted about the "once-rich Jews" who lived here, adding in a sneering voice to derisive laughter, "Everybody knows that in Galveston the Eye-talians have all the sin and the Jews have all the money. Well this is one Jew family that ain't rich no more! Look at that old house! It's almost falling down! They don't even have enough money for a coat of paint! That old house is gonna fall down any day now; they won't have to wait for a hurricane!"

Sarah knew that had the driver seen her, his 'spiel' would have been longer and more insulting.

The jitney's gears ground and it began moving slowly. Sarah once again left her chair, this time walking down the porch steps. She opened the rusting wrought-iron gate as Benji pulled his wagon through, then reached down and hugged him, knocking his straw hat onto the walk.

The jitney completed its turn at the corner.

Benjamin breathlessly pulled away from his mother's embrace and pointed at his wagon. "Nothing today, mom," he said, his voice trembling. He spoke rapidly. "All I caught was hard-heads and piggy-perch. I gigged some crabs, but I lost my gig and the bucket turned over." Sarah looked down at Benji. "You didn't get your brace wet with saltwater, did you?" She silently reminded herself to make sure he cleaned and oiled the brace later, after supper.

Benjamin shook his head at her question and turned, looking back along the street, his brown eyes widening as he saw the car Sarah had noticed earlier, a dark sedan, less than a block away.

Sarah heard the sound of an accelerating engine, looked and saw the car begin to move rapidly toward them. Benjamin buried his head into his mother's skirt, his hands clenching and bunching the cloth.

Sarah, annoyed that Benji was hampering her movements, turned toward the porch steps, keeping her eyes on the suddenly accelerating sedan, pulling her son with her as the fishing wagon overturned, spilling its contents. Sarah stopped at the top step, still holding Benji. She looked back to the street.

The dark car sped through the intersection and turned sharply to the left, their side of the street. Dust and particles of shell scattered as tires sought purchase. Sarah pushed Benji farther onto the porch and he fell.

The car jumped the curb and, engine roaring, crashed through the wrought iron fence and turned toward Sarah and her son, lurching into a stop fully into her weed-strewn yard. Crushed shell dust floated around the car, settling in a fine patina on the car's polished blue surface.

Sarah stood resolutely at the top step, determined to face what might now be danger. She heard her son making a frantic scramble across the porch, noisily dragging his cane by its leather strap.

There were shouts from the jitney. The bus lurched to a stop. Gawking tourists began climbing out.

Sarah heard the rusty hinges squeal on the heavy leaded-glass front door and knew Benji had opened the door.

She remained on her old house's front steps, her fright turning to fascination as a man climbed from the car. He moved slowly, almost as if exhausted. He was hatless, tie askew, his suit jacket unbuttoned. He turned strangely staring eyes toward Sarah and her son, and they locked with Benjamin's as he stood at the opened front door. Sarah heard the door slam and knew Benji had fled inside.

The focus of the man's eyes moved to Sarah. He nodded to her in what could almost have been a greeting as he stood, weaving, holding onto the car's door, his left hand extended. His face contorted into what might have been a smile as his unbuttoned suit jacket suddenly gaped open. Sarah saw the man's shirt soaked dark red and knew it was blood.

The injured man moved slowly around the open car door, holding onto the doorframe with his right hand while his left remained extended. Sarah thought it might be an odd form of a greeting. The man staggered and fell sideways onto the fender.

A woman from the tour jitney, overweight, wearing tight, sweat-stained orange-colored rayon slacks opened Sarah's front gate. Others, behind her, began pushing and crowding into Sarah's front yard. There was excited chatter.

The man's lips moved once more as he pushed himself upright. His left hand was still extended, and his lips moved again, but Sarah heard no sound over the nattering of the tourists crowding into her yard, evidently assuming this was a show that had been arranged for their entertainment. Sarah saw one man bend down and pick up Benji's prized two-piece fishing rod, snug in its leather case. He slung the strap across his shoulders.

The man by the car shook his head in what appeared to be frustration as he tried to push himself off the fender. He fell to his knees.

Sarah now knew! The man needed help. Her thoughts swung from fascination to concern.

She raced down the steps, two at a time, as the man crawled toward both her and the gaggle of tourists flooding through her front gate.

Sarah pushed tourists aside, threading her way through them, shouting, "Get out! This is private property!"

No one listened. The orange rayon-slacked woman was ahead of Sarah and screamed as she watched the man collapse onto his face, then roll over onto his back.

Sarah reached the now prone man, shoved the overweight woman aside and knelt at the side of the stranger.

His dark eyes were blank, staring sightlessly into the brassy August sky. He was dead.

Chapter 2

Aftermath of a Murder

Sarah never knew who had telephoned for the police, but a number of them seemed to magically materialize within minutes. At least a dozen policemen swarmed about, corralling the tourists and insisting they remain seated on the jitney and wait to be questioned.

An ambulance had arrived, and attendants covered the dead man with a white cloth after police photographers snapped what seemed to Sarah to have been dozens of flash photographs of the body. They continued roaming about, taking photographs of her, the tourists, and her broken fence.

Sarah sat in her porch rocker while a policeman asked question after question, often repeating himself. Another man seated himself nearby and seemed to be taking notes.

"You have simply got to allow me to go to Galveston Pilots,'" Sarah told the policeman perhaps a dozen times.

"No, ma'am," he had replied each time.

She had explained: "I am the secretary and assistant manager of Galveston Pilots' Guild and there's a crippled freighter, needing tug assistance, on its way. The coast guard has already been alerted, but I have to arrange docking crews and a pilot."

After the last time she said this, he once more cut her off, but instead of a curt "No," he added, "Okay, lady. I'll tell you what. Let's go inside, you can make telephone calls, I will listen. Do you have an extension telephone?" She shook her head. "Then," he said, "I want you to hold the earpiece away from your ear so I can hear, okay?"

He and the note-taker followed her to the hall telephone.

Thirty minutes later, he permitted her to make one more call, to her attorney, so that he could meet Sarah at police headquarters where she was to be taken to give a formal witness statement along with all the jitney tourists and their bus driver.

The next weeks were hectic for Sarah; there were simply not enough hours in her day as she tried to respond to endless questions by the police and, at the same time cope with the needs of Galveston Pilots'.

After one harrowing meeting with an especially unpleasant police lieutenant, Sarah's attorney exploded. Words were thrown back and forth, and threats of a lawsuit were made. That unpleasant episode was followed by another, an acrimonious and lengthy meeting with Galveston's police chief.

As Sarah went through the weeks following what she had begun to call 'the incident,' Rae, her housekeeper, often mentioned Benji's behavior. Sarah scarcely noticed. One morning, two weeks after 'the incident,' Rae suggested that perhaps Benji needed to see a doctor.

Sarah looked up from her seat at the kitchen table, a ledger on her lap, a cooling cup of coffee before her.

"Rae, he seems all right to me. You said something the other day, and just this morning, I asked him if he was sick, and he said he wasn't. He'll be all right. Besides, I've paid enough money to doctors. He's only ten, and he's had a shock seeing that man die. He'll get over it. I've got to go downtown again. The police have more of their infernal questions; I'll have to bring Billy Bentley once more.

"Oh, my lord!" she exclaimed. "I thought doctor bills were high. But Billy's fees? They're out of sight!"

She rose from her chair and went to her bedroom and began gathering her things, worrying about money.

Sarah's job at Galveston Pilots' paid well but Benji's medical bills had been, from the beginning, overwhelmingly high. Her trust fund, established at her birth by her great-grandfather and thought sufficient for a lifetime, simply vanished into the ever-hungry maw of hospitals and doctor bills.

As Sarah thought about the early years of Benji's life, the image of his father protruded into her consciousness. Glenn Jacobs had been a gentle man, kind and loving, and Sarah had fallen in love the first time she met him. He was a Gentile and her marriage shocked the Jewish community in Galveston, but Sarah, young and headstrong, paid no attention.

Glenn was gone, having died in an accident at sea when his son was a little less than a year old. Six months after that, Benji was stricken with polio.

Sarah would never forget her baby's screams as she gritted her teeth and endlessly massaged his paralyzed limbs as directed by his doctors and therapists. Her jaw would eventually settle into a hard line, making her mouth straight as she lost her tip-tilted young-girl smile. The laughing playful dark-haired, brown-eyed girl that had been Sarah vanished during these years and was replaced by a slender, strong-willed and determined woman.

Benji at age ten was better but not well. He got about using a wrist cane and only one brace, but Sarah, like Benjamin, wanted more. She wanted him to be able to walk unaided; he wanted to run. Sarah remembered vividly the day when her boy was four and fitted with full leg and body braces. That day she and the medical staff surrounding him wept and cheered when, with crutches Benjamin took the first faltering painful steps he had taken since the onslaught of polio. Her little crippled boy, pain filling his eyes, his black hair wet with sweat, looked into his mother's eyes as the room rocked with cheers, and said, quietly, "Mama, someday I'm gonna go to the beach, and I'm gonna run with the wind."

He had never given up on his dream.

Sarah finished gathering her things and walked back into the kitchen and into the hallway leading to the side entrance of her crumbling old house. Rae followed her.

Rae had been brought to the twenty-two-room Weismann Mansion a few years before the 1900 storm when both servants and family were numerous. Most of Sarah's family and many of the servants joined the 12,000 who died in the Great Storm. Sarah was born five years later and, by the time she thirteen, she and her father found themselves left stunningly alone by the influenza epidemic of 1916-18. Rae was the only remaining servant.

"Miz Sarah," Rae called to Sarah's back as she opened the side door and trotted down the steps. Sarah turned, halfway to her car, and looked back. Rae was standing on the side porch, hands on her hips.

"Rae," Sarah said, irritation plain in her voice, "you talk to Benji after a while. Try and get him to go outside and play or something. I'll call around noon if I get the time and see how he's doing."

She turned and climbed into her roadster and slammed the door. As usual, the latch didn't hold, and the door swung open. Sarah slammed it again. She gritted her teeth and slammed the door, once more, harder. She looked up at the cloth top and saw pinpoints of sunlight. "One more thing," she told herself distractedly, "that I need to spend money on; this damn old car!"

An hour or so after Sarah left, Rae knocked on Benjamin's door. "Got some milk and cookies," she said brightly.

He opened the door slowly, looking about, seemingly nervous, "Thanks. Can I eat them in my room?"

"You know the rules," Rae said, shaking her head.

Benjamin shrugged and limped to the kitchen, avoiding the windows.

As he sat at the table she said, "Honey, sompin' has been bothering you for the longest, eva' since that man died. Ah has asked before. Y'wanna tell old Rae about it?"

He looked down at the plate of cookies for what seemed a long time. "No."

Rae was silent for a minute, busying herself at the sink. She turned to the boy. "Don' you think you needs to talk to someone? Ah been wonderin' iffen you wuz sick, but Ah don' think so. Ah think you worrying yourself about that man what died. Honey, that was a long time ago."

Benji had not touched the cookies, but as she spoke he picked one up, broke it in two, then placed both pieces back on the plate. He looked up at the skinny Negro, grizzled gray hairs protruding from under her head covering, which he'd heard her call a 'head-rag.'

When he finally spoke, he lied, speaking rapidly. "I don't know anything about that man or that day. Nothing that everyone else doesn't already know."

The boy shook his head as if to clear it.

Rae was thoughtful for a few minutes, holding and drying a dish, looking at the boy and recognizing the lie.

She said, "Ah allus thinks it's better to talk about sompin when there's sompin that's bothering us." She continued in a sing-song voice as she turned back to the sink, "You ain't sick but you act sick."

Rae shrugged and resumed washing the same dish. "I dunno why you act this way," she said, her back to Benji, her voice low. "Forever so long," she mused, "everybody in town's been talkin' about that day. I heard your mama say that they's gonna be an inquest next week, to make ever'thin' all legal but the po-lice," she finished again with a sing-song sound, "they don' know nuthin'!"

Rae continued, her dialect becoming more pronounced as her voice became more positive. "Yo' mama says they's gonna de-clare that man wuz murdered, but by someone they don' know who, and they don' know if they eva gonna learn who. Y'mama say the case gonna be closed. It's all just gonna go away."

As she talked, she occasionally turned slightly, watching the boy but not looking directly at him, seemingly focusing on the dish she was washing. He had been slumped in his chair when she began talking, studying the broken cookie as if it had something to say. As she went on, Benji straightened in his chair. Rae could tell he had begun to listen closely.

"Yeah," Rae continued, her voice brightening, still washing the same dish, "you know, eva' body when that man dropped dead, they all runnin' around, 'who done it?' they askin.' 'Who murdered this guy?' 'What was used to kill him?'

"An' then, you know what, then they say, 'No one know. So, we just gonna bury him, and eva'body gonna fo'get about it. An' we all just gonna go about our business.'"

Benji, with more interest than she'd seen said, a cautious sound in his voice, "Do they know what was used to kill him?"

"No, they don't. Y'mama tol' me they know he was stabbed, but they don' know if that wuz what kilt him or sompin else. Tha's just another thing they gonna fo'get about."

It seemed to her that Benjamin relaxed. He picked up a cookie and dunked it in the milk, then ate it, milk and cookie crumbles dribbling onto his chin and down to his shirt.

Rae picked up a dishtowel and went to the boy. She wiped his mouth and dabbed at the milk on his shirt. "Yep, tha's the way I unnerstans it. They are just gonna fo'get about eva thing, and we all gonna jus' go about our business like nuthin' eva' happened."

Benji dunked another cookie, this time being careful not to dribble milk or crumbs.

Rae returned to washing the dish. "Ah thinks, Mistah Ben, that the police and all, they worried. An'," she went on, "Ah don' think they's worried about who done what. No sir, lemme tell you what Ah thinks. That okay with you?" She looked back as Benji nodded. He felt a knot beginning to reform in the pit of his stomach.

"Wul," Rae said, "Ah wuz talkin' to mah preacher, you know, ova' at th' African Methodist Church here in Galveston. You know what Rev. Mumpford says?"

When Ben didn't answer, Rae continued, "He say we all gonna be in a war with Germany, real soon. He sez already they's German submarines out in the Gulf. He sez that sooner or later, they gonna be German spies all ova' Galveston."

Benji looked up with more interest than she'd seen in days. "Really?"

"Yassa, tha's what he said. He dunno for sure if the U-boats is out there, but he thinks they is. He said that he 'specs that man, the one who died, he one of the early spies. Checkin' things out, so when the war starts, they know who to watch. He says that y'mama is someone they gonna watch, because she's in charge of shipping, and the spies gonna need to know so's they can tell the submarines when to shoot at boats leavin' Galveston, tha's what he says."

"There are German spies here in Galveston?" Ben asked, wide-eyed.

"Wul," Rae said, "He don' know and Ah don' know, but mebbe the po-lice, mebbe they think so, and mebbe they think that whoever kilt that man done us all a favor, tha's what he thinks, and Ah does too!" She said this last with conviction.

Benji felt relief flooding over him. It fit, in a way. "Maybe he was a spy," he told himself, "That man asked about mama enough times that day. Maybe it's gonna be all right after all."

The knot in his stomach began to dissolve.

The boy rose from his chair. "I guess I might go outside," he said, going into his room. He limped out, wearing his metal brace, his cane hanging from his right wrist, a baseball glove in his left. "Maybe I'll find Aaron," he said. "Let him throw some balls to me." At the door he turned. "Rae, don't tell Mama what we talked about, okay?"

"You got it, honey, it's just between you and me. But, honey, lemme tell you one other thing." Rae kept her face and voice neutral, but inwardly was smiling as she said, "Ah thinks that mebbe one of these days you might ought to go an' talk to that preacher guy you and your mama go to once in a while, that Rabbi Cohen. Maybe just ask if you can talk, private, sometime when your mama ain't around. Then, if sompin is still botherin', you tell him. Okay?"

"Maybe he'd tell," Benjamin said as the worried look returned to his face.

"Noam," Rae said. "Preachers don' do that. Stuff people tells them, they kain talk about it. It's sompin about bein' a preacher. Th' law says preachers kain tell."

Chapter 3

Azzo Burkhardt

In May of 1938, almost two months before a stranger died in Sarah Jacob's front yard, Azzo Burkhardt moved into a two-room suite on an upper floor of the Galvez Hotel, overlooking the seawall and Gulf. He carefully went about becoming known in and around Galveston.

Azzo was urbane, friendly and outgoing, and wore expensive suits with a snappy gray fedora, his shoes always impeccably shined. He lunched almost daily at the business communities' favorite restaurant on 19th Street, joined the Galveston Rotary, attended temple on occasion, and was often to be found at the Rosenberg Library on Sealy Street.

Sarah's great-uncle Levi also lived in a two-room suite at the Galvez and had done so since his wife had died two decades earlier. It was his habit to have his breakfast and dinner at the hotel. Azzo only breakfasted there but used the morning occasions to study the banker intently. He sometimes spoke a greeting to the older man, but only in passing, and did not otherwise try to engage the patrician banker in conversation.

It was common knowledge at the Galvez that their newest long-term tenant traveled a great deal, sometimes staying away for a week or more.

Azzo was on the train, returning from New Orleans when he read with interest newspaper stories of the Galveston widow who'd witnessed the bizarre death of a man in her front yard. A reporter and photographer for the *Daily News* had arrived on the scene before the body was removed and Azzo studied published photographs of the event. One photograph on page three showed the widow as she was being led to a police car for transit downtown.

Some weeks later, Azzo attended the public inquest of the death. Instead of his usual business suit, he dressed in khaki trousers and shirt, his sleeves rolled up against the summer heat, his hat a shabby brown felt, his shoes scuffed. Sitting on one of the hard benches in the spectator gallery he daily studied Sarah, her attorney, and her great-uncle.

When the hearings were over for the day or during recesses, the man in khakis rarely talked or mingled with other spectators. He left when appropriate and as quickly as possible.

In the early twentieth century the island-city was known as the "Free State of Galveston," and Galvestonians considered that Federal and state laws regarding liquor sales, gambling, and prostitution did not apply to them. Therefore, before, during and after the years of the Volstead act, liquor in Galveston flowed freely and gambling was open. Prostitution was rampant, and both men and women were readily available for sexual services. Azzo was not known to have participated in any of Galveston's readily available vices.

Personnel at the Galvez knew that their newest long-term tenant loved surf fishing. He often brought a quantity of fresh fish to the hotel and asked the restaurant staff to prepare it for him in a special way, which, for a price, they did, and he offered the special dish to other guests as well.

Azzo's 'fishing jalopy,' as he called it, was an older and very rusty Ford Phaeton whose top had long ago been removed. It was kept in a rented garage not far from the Galvez, along with specially made extra-long sectional surf rods and other fishing equipment. Often, late in the day, Azzo could be found fishing on the beaches of Bolivar Peninsula, or on Galveston's West Beach, past the end of the seawall where Green's Bayou emptied into the Gulf. Sometimes he could be found further along the poorly maintained West Beach Road, nearer to San Luis Pass, preparing for a night of solitary fishing, removing the long sectional rods from their tubular carriers and mounting both the rods and gasoline lanterns into specially designed holders on the car's front or rear bumpers.

Often, once he deployed his fishing lines, Azzo ran along the beach, shirtless, bare-footed and in cut-off dungarees. He ran for the sheer joy of it, the salt-laden wind blowing his hair amidst the sounds of the crashing surf and the cries of sea birds. Others nearby, surf fishermen or picnickers, sometimes bathers, noting this strange behavior, shook their heads and decided the man had lost his senses.

One day shortly after the close of the inquest, Azzo, dressed impeccably in a business suit and tie, made an afternoon trip to Galveston's prestigious Weismann Bank. He opened a checking account, depositing $2,000 in cash, and arranged for a wire transfer from a New York bank in the amount of $18,000, and instructed that this amount be placed into a bank savings account which would be drawn upon as needed.

His deposits, as intended, earned him an introduction to Levi Weismann, president and founder of the bank.

The elderly banker found Azzo to be affable and witty, entirely friendly and open. He commented on the number of times they'd spoken at breakfast and remarked that he'd noticed Azzo in attendance at the inquest.

"Yes," the younger man answered. "My new book had just been submitted to my publisher and I was waiting for him to react, so I was at loose ends." Azzo grinned. "He reacted, and I'm now engaged in rewrites."

"You're a writer," the patrician banker said, leaning back in his chair and tenting his hands.

"Yes," Azzo answered. "I was trained as an architect and worked in that profession for several years. At present I make a good living with my writing, but I may be interested one day in returning to the practice of architecture, perhaps here in Galveston. I love the Gulf Coast, and I think Texas and I will get along famously."

"I certainly hope," the bank president said, "that you will stay in Galveston and make it your home. Galveston needs talent, both yours as a writer and perhaps someday your talents as an architect."

Azzo nodded without speaking. There was a long and pregnant pause.

"Sir," the banker finally said, leaning forward and breaking the uncomfortable silence, "I've noticed you in and around Galveston for several months now. When you first arrived, I became interested and began making inquiries. I hope you will forgive me for invading your privacy."

Azzo now tented his own hands, then folded his fingers together. "You could have stopped me any day at breakfast, invited me to your table and introduced yourself. Whatever you have discovered is what I would have told you." He opened his hands. "I have nothing to hide."

"I should have done that," Levi said, "and now I wish I had. I learned from the Galvez that your stay was paid by funds forwarded from New York, but through another Galveston bank."

"Yes, that's correct," Azzo said. "I presented the management of the Galvez with a letter of credit. Here it is, if you're interested."

The banker shook his head, then continued,

"I learned from a friend of mine in New York that you're quite a talented architect."

"I admit to practicing architecture in New York," Azzo responded, somewhat cautiously. "However, I'm a writer now." He emphasized the word "writer".

There was a long pause after which Azzo continued. "And I have other responsibilities, as do you."

"Ah," the old banker said, a triumphant grin on his face. "I thought so! Are you the man whom I am scheduled to meet?"

"Yes, I am," Azzo answered as his eyes met those of the banker, "We need to meet somewhere very private, soon, and discuss our continuing relationship and our work. Do you agree?"

"Yes, I do," Levi Weismann said, adding defensively, "This office is very private."

"Yes, it is," Azzo agreed, "but others have seen me go in as a result of my deposits. They'll wonder if we spend more than a few minutes. Besides, we need to meet regularly and often, as the months progress and we become more fully engaged in our business."

The banker paused and leaned back in his chair. Neither man spoke for long moments.

"Sir," the man across from Levi Weismann said, "I have a suggestion. Let's have breakfast together tomorrow, and then let's schedule a few sessions in either my suite or yours, where we can go into some of the necessary details and decide how and where we can meet regularly but in a way that would arouse no one's suspicions."

The old man was silent as he reached for an ornately decorated humidor box on his desk. He opened it and offered one to the man across from him, who shook his head. "I don't smoke. I never have."

"It's a nasty habit," Levi Weismann said as he took a cigar and spent long moments rolling it, lifting it to his nose, cutting off one end, and lighting it. Clouds of blue smoke curled about. The other man in the room coughed.

"I have an idea," Levi said. "My niece has, for a long time, been considering repairs to that old house she lives in, repairs that would allow her to rent out a few rooms. She needs extra money badly and believes the rental income will be a help. She has not yet said anything about how she plans to get enough money together to make the necessary repairs, but I've been a banker most of my life. I know all the approaches when someone is planning to ask for a loan."

He paused. Azzo Burkhardt said nothing.

"She says that all she wants to do is simply wallpaper and paint a few rooms and rent them out," Levi said. "I haven't responded, but I think it'd be good money after bad to plan on just renting a few rooms. I think she needs to rehabilitate the entire structure and convert it into a modern apartment complex."

"Is it that large?" Azzo asked.

"Oh, it has twenty-two rooms, maybe more; I haven't been inside for years. You'd need to study it."

"Me?" Azzo responded, surprise in his voice.

"Of course. You're an architect. I told you I looked into your background some months ago when I suspected you might be the one I was waiting for. It turns out the senior partner of the New York architectural practice you were in was a classmate of mine at Dartmouth, years ago. I talked with him. He said you were a brilliant architect, and your specialty was multi-family dwellings."

"But I left the practice when I was recruited and moved to the Carolinas. I tell people these days I'm a writer." He again emphasized the word "writer."

"And you actually got a book published," Levi said, almost proudly.

Azzo shrugged. "You have to know that we—your New York associates—paid the publisher: one of those vanity presses. I'm not making any money writing. It was and is a good cover for my real work."

"Here's my idea," the banker said, becoming bored with what he considered the recitation of unnecessary history. "When Sarah approaches me about a loan, which will be soon, I'll tell her that I'll think it over. Then, you go see her, convince her that converting her old mansion into apartments is a good idea, and recommend yourself to be her architect. When she hires you, you can take up residence in the old carriage house. Then, we can get together often, it'll appear as if her old uncle is simply looking after his niece's affairs."

"That seems convoluted," Azzo said doubtfully. "What makes you so sure she'll hire me?"

"Oh, you're a charming fellow. You can figure that part of it out," Levi grinned as he waived his cigar dismissively.

"Yes," the old banker finally said, rising and indicating more strongly that the meeting was over, "join me at breakfast tomorrow morning. We need to move forward. I breakfast at 7 AM sharp!"

As Azzo left the bank that day he was thinking he had just met a most extraordinary man.

Inside the bank, Levi Weismann watched from the door of his office as Azzo exited through the marbled lobby. Sarah's Uncle Levi was thinking that he had just met a most extraordinary man.

Chapter 4

September 1938
The Architect

"Hello," the stranger said quietly, his tenor voice smooth and well-modulated, standing just inside the front door of Galveston Pilots'. He was dressed casually in khaki trousers and shirt, sleeves rolled up. He removed a battered brown fedora, revealing a full head of dark hair, a touch of gray at his temples.

"Yes," Sarah said, surprised at the intrusion. She had not been expecting a visitor; he had caught her halfway to her office, a coffee mug in hand. "Our manager is not in," she added. "I'm the assistant manager. May I help you?"

The stranger smiled, showing dazzlingly white teeth, "I'm not here to see George Stein," he said. "I understand he's ill."

"Why, yes," Sarah answered. She turned and placed her coffee on a nearby table.

"Then you must be Mrs. Jacobs?"

Sarah nodded. "Yes."

"It is you I came to see," the handsome man said, still smiling. "May I introduce myself?" Without waiting for an answer, he said, "I'm Azzo Burkhardt and I'm an architect." He held out his right hand and she shook it, blinking at the unusual first name.

"Your uncle at the Weismann Bank asked that I drop by and visit with you. Is this a convenient time?"

Sarah nodded, wondering why her uncle thought she needed to talk to an architect, picked up her cooling coffee, led the stranger past the half-wall separating the waiting area from several desks and a large marine radio on a back wall, and into her office, motioning her assistant to bring coffee for her visitor. She indicated one of the two leather chairs in front of her desk and moved behind. "Have a seat, Mr. Burkhardt," she said, regaining her own chair and wishing that she had not had to put up with this intrusion into her day.

"It looks very natural for you behind that desk," the man said as he accepted a mug from Sarah's assistant. There was a cream pitcher and sugar on a small tray, but he shook his head. "I like it black, hot, and strong."

He turned to Sarah as her assistant left the room. "You have an air of command about you."

"I wouldn't know about that," Sarah replied, still irritated at this interruption in her schedule. She was busy; there was no time to visit with this stranger. She again asked in a formal tone, "How may I be of assistance to you, Mr. Burkhardt?"

"Well, to repeat my purpose," the man answered, "I'm an architect and I'm here at the invitation of Mr. Levi Weissman. Surely he mentioned me to you?"

"No, not at all," Sarah admitted. "Your visit is quite a surprise."

"Well," he answered, "for starters, I'd like us to begin on a first name basis. I know you're Sarah. My name is Azzo."

"As..." Sarah began, still irritated at his presence and puzzled over the intrusion.

"Azzo Burkhardt," he replied, using a hard "t-z" sound and stirring his coffee. "It's an old German name, and I'm told it means 'of noble birth', although that's unlikely. No one of my family seemed to me to have been noblemen."

Sarah was quiet for a moment as she studied the man sitting across from her while he sipped on his coffee. When he'd entered the building, she had noticed how tall he was, at least six feet, perhaps a little over. Now, she saw that his face and arms were tanned as if he spent a great deal of time outdoors. The rolled cuffs of his shirt sleeves covered only half his biceps, which seemed to fill the shirt cuff. Azzo Burkhardt was athletically built with liquid brown eyes, high cheekbones, and a slightly hooked nose.

"When you finish studying me," Burkhardt said, still smiling, "May we talk about why Mr. Weismann asked me to drop by?"

"Oh," Sarah said, taken aback by his frankness. "Yes, we need to do so. I have a very busy schedule today. Why did my uncle send you to me?"

She was silent for a long moment, waiting.

"Your uncle said you've been talking to him about repairs to your place at 51st and Strand," Azzo Burkhardt began.

"It's true that I've mentioned it to him," Sarah answered. "But you said you were an architect. I hardly think I need one of those. Uncle Levi said something about a contractor, and a contractor is more of what I had in mind. All I want to do is fix a few of the leaks on the roof and maybe paint and wallpaper two or three of the rooms that haven't been lived in for a while, and I need to know how much that will cost."

"Your uncle took me by your house yesterday, Mrs. Jacobs." A slight frown again crossed Sarah's face. "He said you were planning on renting out some of the rooms. He said you needed to increase your income."

"Mr. Burkhardt!" Sarah exclaimed, rising in her chair as she wondered again how much information her irritating uncle had shared, and why.

Her irritation increased as her visitor seemed to take charge of her office and motioned her to sit down. He continued talking, a bland expression on his face, "Sarah, that huge house of yours is a treasure! Historically, I mean. It's a splendid example of Victorian architecture and deserves something more than simply a new roof." He paused, then said, "And, it deserves more than simply becoming a rooming house. Besides, any cost-to-benefit analysis would show that the cost of roof and plumbing repair alone will be more than you could ever earn back by renting only two or three rooms."

Sarah, still angry that this intruder was taking control of her office, nevertheless thought this last statement made sense. She knew what room rental rates were in Galveston, having often arranged for pilots from Houston to stay in Galveston overnight as they waited for the next day's interurban back to their home base.

She nodded, despite her feelings, and allowed the man across from her to continue.

"Your uncle told me you have twenty-two rooms. After he and I visited your house, your uncle asked me to come here, meet with you, and perhaps arrange a time when you and I could reconvene at your house and discuss the extent of the work you're considering."

"Still," Sarah said, "I think I need to be talking to a contractor."

"Perhaps you do," the pleasant man said, smiling. "In any case, I certainly have a great deal of experience regarding multi-family residential construction. I practiced architecture for almost ten years in New York and won several awards for my work. I'm offering you free advice and counsel as a favor to Mr. Weismann."

"Oh," Sarah answered. "Okay, free is good." Another frown crossed her face. "Have we met before?" she asked. "You seem familiar."

He smiled again. "I see you have a good memory for faces, something you have in common with your uncle. You probably saw me at the inquest. I was in the public gallery. I went every day."

"Yes," she said. "I remember now. You sat in the back row. But why? The room was stifling, and the procedures boring, and the furniture uncomfortable. I certainly wouldn't have wasted my time if I hadn't been compelled to do so."

"I admit to idle curiosity," he answered. "I'm new to Galveston and I was bored."

"So," she said, puzzled, "you don't have an architectural office?"

"No, I don't. I may open a Galveston practice someday," he said, "but all that is beside the point. How about my offer for free advice? I can give you some ideas on total costs, which is what your uncle is interested in knowing, especially if he's to loan money to you."

"Well," Sarah said, "I haven't actually asked him for a loan but in any case..."

Her voice died away in embarrassment. How much, she wondered again, silently, had her uncle shared with this stranger?

"Sure," Sarah said, making up her mind as her earlier irritation faded. "You want to go to my house and look it over? When? When can you go?"

"I'm available right now, Sarah," he said in that pleasant well-modulated voice. She was once again jarred at his use of her given name. She remembered that he'd asked that they use first names, but she didn't remember agreeing.

"Well," Sarah said, rising again from her chair, "I'm not available right now. It will have to be tomorrow, after lunch."

This time he did not motion for her to sit down.

The next afternoon Sarah had to agree, as they walked around her home, that he projected an air of confidence and was seemingly knowledgeable about construction techniques and costs. She took him inside, to the closed-off second and third floors, and was appalled when they disturbed a large rat. "Oh!" she said as the rat scurried across a cluttered floor, "Nasty creature! I'll have Rae ask Wallace to set out traps!"

"I've seen worse infestations, Mrs. Jacobs," the architect said calmly, climbing out of a side attic. "Will you show me the carriage house?"

"Yes," she said. "My maid Rae and her husband live there now in two of the rooms. I haven't been inside for years."

Later, as they sat in two of the ancient wooden rockers on her front porch, Rae brought iced tea.

"Sarah," he began as Rae left. "Uh, do you mind? I asked before about first names. I'm sorry to be so informal, but it just seems…"

She did not let him finish. "And yours, Mr. Burkhardt. I'm sorry, but I'm having trouble with it. Uh…Matzo?"

"No," he said, smiling once more, and producing a card. "My given name is Azzo." He pronounced it with a hard t-z sound.

"You're German, Mr...ah, Azzo?" she asked, remembering his earlier comment that his name was of German heritage.

"Oh," he answered, airily, "I came to the United States many years ago, before the Great War. I was still a teenager when I began my architectural studies. I applied for citizenship as soon as possible, and later renounced my German citizenship."

"I can't identify an accent," Sarah said. "Your English is quite good."

He smiled his engaging smile again. "I worked hard to get any hint of German out of my voice," he said. "Twenty or so years ago anyone speaking or sounding German was..." He paused.

"Ostracized?" Sarah finished the sentence for him.

"More than ostracized, I'd say. Anyway, I cultivated what I believe is a midwestern accent."

"You've done well. What experience have you as an architect?"

"I told you I practiced architecture in New York for ten years. My specialty was multi-family dwellings. Are you interested in my qualifications? I can submit a formal proposal if you like. I told you before I've won a number of awards for my work, and my New York license remains valid. I'm sure Texas will honor it via reciprocity."

"Well," Sarah said, "I'm not yet sure I need an architect."

But despite her irritation the day before, Sarah found that she was enjoying her visit with this engaging and handsome man. "Why are you no longer in New York?" she asked.

"I discovered a few years ago," he answered, "that I could make a decent living writing. I moved to the coastal Carolinas and simply wrote for a while. I've only recently moved to Galveston."

"You're a writer?" Sarah asked. "What do you write?"

"Oh," he laughed, "nothing you'd be interested in, I'm sure. I write books on historic coastal residential architecture."

"And there's a market for that?"

"It's limited," he admitted, "but, as I said, I've made a living at it these last few years. Sarah," he interrupted himself, "may we return to the subject of your house?"

Instead Sarah said, "Tell me again why you attended the inquest?"

He did not miss the sidestep and wondered why she kept returning to the subject of his attendance at what she'd declared was a boring and unnecessary affair.

"I said I was interested, so I attended. I must admit it was a surprise, at least to me, that they closed the case, especially since the FBI had become involved."

"And that made a difference?"

"Oh, yes, the FBI almost never closes a case until it's solved. They're much like Scotland Yard that way."

Sarah had a sudden memory of the police questions prior to the inquest, and at one session a young FBI agent was present and asked questions. Later, at the inquest, he provided testimony. She tried without success to remember the agent's name, but soon forgot as her visitor returned to the subject of her old mansion and the repairs she had in mind. As they talked, other topics intruded into their conversation from time to time. As they did, it seemed to Sarah that the two of them were in the process of deciding whether or not to become friends.

She learned that, in addition to his love of the Victorian architecture that he said he described in his books, he was also an avid surf fisherman. He told her about his old topless car kept in a rented garage and used for his surf fishing expeditions. He laughed as he described the car, calling it a jalopy, and rusty, he added, "beyond all belief."

In another part of the conversation that long afternoon he told her some of his early life in Germany where his parents and a sister still lived. At one point she asked if he was thinking of becoming a permanent resident of Galveston.

"I may do that," Azzo answered. "I like Galveston. I like the way the people of Galveston show grit and determination. I like how, after the 1900 storm, 12,000 people dead, Galvestonians didn't do the expected. Others, with less strength and determination might have simply abandoned this low-lying coastal island which is so obviously an unsuitable location for a city."

"Galvestonians didn't abandon their city," Sarah said, with pride in her voice.

"No, they didn't!" the architect said, smiling again and showing his white, even teeth. "They could have simply picked up and left. After all, as I said, this low island is obviously unsuitable for a city due to tropical cyclones. But," he went on, emotion evident in his voice, "No! Galvestonians didn't do that! They rebuilt this island and raised its center and everything in it by almost twenty feet. And, in the process they constructed an enormous seawall. 'Take that!' Galveston seemed to be saying to Mother Nature. That took grit! And I like Galveston for its grit."

He seemed to be enjoying himself.

Sarah smiled, pleased with his passion for her city. "I like Galveston, too," she said. "If I hadn't been born here, I might have wanted to move here."

He seemed interested in her family history, and Sarah learned he was a good listener. She found herself sharing things that would have ordinarily remained private. She told him that her great-uncle was her grandfather's brother, and the two of them had arrived in Galveston from Germany in 1874. One brother established a shipping business, which became an empire, only to be destroyed by the Great Storm. The other brother established a bank.

She told about her father taking his own life at the onset of the Depression, and her son, crippled with polio as an infant. She also told about the day a four-year old Benji had vowed to one day be able to run. She added, "He says he wants to run on the beach; he calls it running with the wind.

She was both surprised and pleased when he said, his luminous dark eyes boring into hers, "We must find a way to make that happen."

Chapter 5

A Week Later
The Beginning

Sarah, sitting at her Galveston Pilots' desk, shook her head in frustration. She'd just put the telephone down after a difficult conversation with her uncle. Earlier, Azzo had telephoned and told her he'd completed his estimates and had furnished them to Levi Weismann. She asked for a total, and when he told her she gasped at the amount.

"Why so much?" she exclaimed, loudly enough for her assistant to hear through the closed door. Azzo's laconic response was that she should call her uncle.

When she did, the elderly banker told her calmly that the estimate included a complete remodeling of the mansion, converting the entire building into apartments, and included enough for her attorney's fees and a new car as a replacement for her aging roadster.

"Uncle Levi!" Sarah exclaimed, "I can't afford all that! I've said over and over again that all I want to do is fix the roof and paint or wallpaper a few rooms! And a new car is out of the question!"

"Sarah," Levi Weismann replied calmly, "come on down to the bank. Let's talk."

Sarah snapped back. "That means you talk, and I listen! I'm busy and I can't come now!"

In Sarah's mind, she could see the old banker shrug as he said calmly, "I'll see you later today then. Come down before closing time."

He abruptly terminated the call before she had a chance to hang up on him.

That afternoon, precisely one minute before 3 PM, Sarah walked through the bank's large double-glass doors just as the bank guard was preparing to slide the ornate brass-embossed outer doors closed. She marched peremptorily to her uncle's office, steeling herself for the lecture she knew was coming.

She was not disappointed. She knew he usually left his bank promptly at three for a brisk walk to the seawall, returning later after tellers had closed and balanced, and reviewed the day's business with his managers. She had deliberately timed her entrance to be an interruption to his schedule but, to her surprise, he ignored what at other times would have been an excuse for rudeness and sarcasm.

The old banker began his lecture calmly and without preamble and went on for a number of minutes. Sarah sat, grinding her teeth, realizing that she had provoked him as she intended, but the consequences were unexpected.

"And in addition," he continued in a pedantic tone as if speaking to a child, "you're going to need a new car." He stubbed his cigar into an ashtray and reached for another. "You might as well roll the cost into the mortgage, which is what we'd convert the construction loans into." He rolled the new cigar, unlit, under his nose, seemingly bored with the idea of lecturing his great niece. Even so, she could see a flicker of interest in his gaze, and she knew he was waiting for her to comment.

She kept quiet, watching him cut one tip off the new cigar and spend long moments lighting it.

"There's going to be another war," the old man said, unexpectedly changing the subject. He leaned back in his chair, smoke curling about, and added, "Maybe not next year, but war is going to come soon. When that happens, no one will be able to buy a car. The automobile companies will be making tanks and what-all. This next war is going to be bigger than the 1918 war, and it will last longer!"

Sarah remained silent, refusing to think about war and seething at her uncle's audacious assumptions that he needed to manage not only the old Weismann mansion, but her life. "Already," Uncle Levi resumed, "there are rumors of German submarines in the Gulf. At one point, I heard the German government admitted they were there, but since their mission was to protect Mexican tankers taking oil to Germany their presence was completely legal. Whether or not it's true that they're out there, it's making everyone nervous."

Uncle Levi was clearly enjoying the sound of his own voice. He reminded Sarah of the increase in Galveston's population due to both civilian and military construction. "Here in Galveston," he droned, "housing is at a premium." Sarah wrinkled her brow, realizing her uncle was repeating the sales pitch she'd given him weeks earlier, and wondered if he knew he was repeating her arguments.

One of the senior managers knocked and opened the door, ledgers under his arms. "Not now!" Levi Weismann shouted. The door was quickly closed.

Sarah's great-uncle's sonorous voice returned to the subject of Sarah's original plans. "Your ideas about providing housing to Galveston's growing population, Sarah, are good ideas!" She shook her head helplessly as he awarded noble attributes to her need to increase her income, and continued, "But I have a better idea and that architect fellow agrees with me! Convert the whole house into modern apartments! Add the carriage house to the plans. Sarah, you'll make money! Enough to pay me back and enough for my great grand-nephew's future medical bills and his college later on, too!"

"Uncle Levi," Sarah said, protesting, "the numbers that have been thrown at me amount to a fortune! I will never be able to pay you back."

He waved his hand dismissively, the lit cigar tracing the path his hand made. "Sarah," he said, "you wouldn't be paying me back. I already said the bank would provide a construction loan, and afterwards it can be converted into a mortgage."

"Which I just said I'll never be able to repay!" Sarah said, sitting back in her chair and realizing she was giving up. Her uncle and that architect, it seemed, had already made all the decisions for her. There was no doubt in her mind that the reason the architect agreed with her uncle was that he was going to make a lot of money off her. She, in turn, would sink into the shame of bankruptcy and ruin. She shook her head, biting her tongue and wishing for the courage to say aloud what she was thinking.

Uncle Levi signaled the end of this meeting. "Don't forget that old carriage house," he said again." It's big enough for two families, maybe three. And underneath, there's enough room for automobile garages: you use one, charge your tenants to use the others!"

The old man puffed at his cigar, releasing clouds of noxious smoke. Sarah knew he was ready for her to leave. Her suspicions about the architect's motives were confirmed when Uncle Levi added, "Sarah, that architect fellow, Burkhardt, is willing to work both as your contractor and your architect, rolled into one package."

She sat back in her chair, then stood, deciding to speak one final time, "Uncle Levi!" she said loudly, anger and frustration plain in her voice. "He's told me that, and I understand that's part of the deal you and he have cooked up! I'm not ever going to be able to repay the mortgage and you know it!"

Levi Weismann did not answer, but sat, shaking and then nodding his head, saying nothing, releasing more clouds of smoke.

Sarah shook her head, standing before her uncle's ornate walnut desk and leaned forward with both hands on the desk surface. She stared at the old banker and said nothing for perhaps a minute.

Uncle Levi rose from his chair and adopted the same stance as his great niece. They stared into one another's eyes as Levi said in a firm voice, "That architect fellow did a detailed market analysis. I asked him to share it with my managers and they said they were impressed at the work he's done. They went to a local realtor who verified his analysis. Then they took it to a banking house in Houston, meeting with their real estate banking expert. They all agree. You'll make money, Sarah! If my managers and the people they consulted with didn't believe it, my managers would have told me. These guys are one of the reasons this bank is as profitable as it is. They're young, smart as a whip, and I trust their financial judgments. Its why I made them stockholders!

"Sarah," Levi went on, sitting back into his chair and looking up at her, speaking with a calm voice, "I made a lot of money by myself in the old days, but times change. I recognized the need for younger blood, and that's what they've got! Sarah, if a project has *their* backing no one should be worried about its profitability!

"That fellow Burkhardt told me he's interested in renting an apartment in your carriage house," Levi said triumphantly, "He could live there while serving as your architect and general contractor."

"Uncle Levi!" Sarah exclaimed, still leaning forward, her knuckles on his desk. Her uncle swiveled in his chair and turned his back to her. He sat, looking out the large window behind him.

Sarah said nothing more. Her principal thought as she tiredly exited her uncle's office was that she was at last free from the smell of that incredibly bad cigar, imported from Cuba though it might be.

Chapter 6

Mansion House Luxury Apartments
13 months later, October 1939

The demolition and reconstruction of the only home Sarah had ever known began a week after contracts were signed in her uncle's office, following work on temporary quarters for Rae and Wallace. Azzo had then cleaned out the rooms they'd been using in the carriage house, as planned, and moved in.

The day heavy machinery and construction crews arrived at Sarah's home was also the day that the health of Galveston Pilots' manager, George Stein, took a sudden turn for the worst. He was not expected to improve nor recover; it was only a matter of time. With approval from the Board, Sarah assumed full management responsibilities, which she'd been doing for some time. Neither her job title nor salary was changed. She found herself busier than ever.

At the mansion, Azzo was in control of the organized destruction of the old Weismann mansion. At the end of each day, at supper, Sarah was presented with a report on progress made that day along with projections for the work which would be performed the following day or week. Usually, decisions were presented for Sarah, along with recommendations and alternatives.

Uncle Levi was present for supper at least once each week. Rae always seemed to know when he'd be present, and Sarah learned he was coming when she saw Rae set an extra place at the table.

No matter how diplomatically construction decisions were presented, Sarah always knew what Azzo, her uncle, and even her son wanted her to do. When she suggested something other than what these three felt was the better plan, alternatives continued to be discussed until she changed her mind. Sometimes she deliberately made the "wrong" decision and waited grimly for the discussion of alternatives to resume.

The first morning of heavy demolition, enormous machines arrived as Benji was leaving for school. He hurried home as soon as possible that day.

Benji had never before been around construction nor men who worked with their hands and was excited to see what they would do to his home. The first day, when Benji returned from school, his eyes widened as he saw cranes and men with ropes and pulleys working on the turrets. Benji ran into the yard, was met by Azzo, and guided out of harm's way as a turret crashed to the ground.

Azzo, khaki-clad and sweat-soaked, said to Benji, "Go change into some old dungarees or something. I need a helper."

Benji stammered, backing away slightly, "I-I don't know how to do anything."

"No problem, Ben," Azzo answered, a hint of impatience in his voice, drops of sweat dripping from the end of his nose. "I'll teach you! Go get those dungarees on! Hurry back! Homework can wait, just for today!"

The boy dashed off, excited, both because he'd been invited into the work and that this new friend called him "Ben."

By the end of the first week's construction, Azzo had moved a drafting table and a draftsman into his carriage house temporary quarters. There, detailed construction plans were made from sketches begun by Azzo. Ben was recruited to take measurements when he wasn't bringing tools to Azzo or the work crew.

The boy was more than excited the day Azzo handed him a handsaw. "Here," Azzo said, "cut this two-by."

It was the first time Ben had ever held a handsaw other than to bring one to a workman, and he struggled to make the cut. Azzo took the saw away, showed Ben how better to use it, and Ben quickly completed the cut. It wasn't as straight as it could have been, but Azzo said it would fit where it was needed, and assured Ben that the next time he'd be better.

Eight months into the project, as planned, Sarah released advertising brochures. Each of the new apartments was completed in sequence, and, almost before the paint dried, people began arriving and signing lease agreements. Others came, copies of the brochure in their hands, looked at drawings delineating the yet-to-be completed units, and eagerly joined a waiting list.

After the daily suppertime meetings, Azzo, with Ben at his side, often took Sarah on a tour of the mansion, reviewing once again the day's accomplishments and what was scheduled for the following. Every other week, Uncle Levi began "taking the tour" as he called it, and accompanied Sarah, Azzo, and Ben in their after-supper walk. Later, when she left for her apartment, usually to finish up work she'd brought from the Pilots' offices and Ben left for his homework, Azzo and Levi often sat and talked on a bench in the area she'd been told would be a rose garden, which, from the very beginning, she'd objected to.

The rose garden and gazebo became just one more of those items 'the men' in Sarah's life wanted, and she did not.

In the end, when the last nail had been driven and the last coat of paint had dried, Sarah had to admit she was pleased with the finished complex. Both the main and carriage house were now different, with a modern look, yet Azzo had somehow retained the Victorian grace and elegance of the original mansion.

The apartment interiors were thoroughly modern but enhanced by the mansion's past as Azzo cleverly incorporated selected Victorian features.

The grand sweeping staircase which once led to a second-floor reception hall and ballroom was relocated and now ascended to the second floor from the wide hallway at the front door. The massive leaded glass entry door was retained, but the door was rehung with additional hardware and now opened at a touch, gliding as if on velvet hinges, leading visitors and apartment-dwellers alike into a luxurious entry hall, overlooked by marble fireplace and an enormous grandfather clock.

An understated but elegant sign, *Mansion House Luxury Apartments,* was placed at the front gate. Another sign, at the newly paved drive, announced the *Carriage House Annex.* The garden and gazebo Azzo had insisted upon was used regularly without charge by tenants for outdoor gatherings. When a tenant invited others from outside the complex to attend an event or barbeque, Sarah charged a fee.

The entire project had cost more than the original estimates, but Uncle Levi always agreed with the plans and advanced the funds.

Sarah hadn't before realized her son needed the company of adult males as well as the company of his school chums. Perhaps, she thought, his relationship with Azzo and Uncle Levi was what brought him out of his fearful attitude after that terrible day, which by now had, for all practical purposes, faded from her memory. She knew that Benji had also spent time with Rabbi Cohen, who told Sarah the boy had opened up to him but provided no details.

In any event, it seemed to Sarah her son was once again the boy he'd been before the car crashed through the fence and a man died, and that was enough for her, as busy as she was with her work at Galveston Pilots'. As new refinery units in Baytown came on stream, channel traffic increased, and Sarah found herself busier at Galveston Pilots than she'd ever thought possible.

As part of the project, Azzo also rebuilt the old stables behind the carriage house and converted them into a woodworking shop, bringing in power woodworking tools and fabricating cabinets for all the new kitchens, along with beautifully polished wood bookcases which he installed into the walls of the larger apartment units, as well as in Sarah's office, an alcove off her living room. Her desk, handmade by Azzo and polished and buffed by Ben, gleamed as if from an inner light. When Sarah ran her hand over its surface, it had the satiny feel of fine silk.

One day Sarah learned to her horror that Azzo was teaching her little boy to use the shop's power tools. She went to the shop and protested.

"Azzo!" she exclaimed, "He'll cut off his fingers!"

"No, he won't," Azzo answered calmly, snapping off the lathe he was operating and removing his safety goggles, his liquid eyes appraising her. "I always insist he wear gloves and eye protection, and, never, ever, use the machines if I'm not around. Sarah, he's good at woodworking and has a natural talent for it. Trust me and trust Benjamin. He's very bright, understands the dangers, but enjoys the work. Don't make him stop, please."

Once again, annoyed, she returned to the office alcove off the front room of her apartment. "He just takes over!" she said to herself. "Always in charge!"

Several months prior to the end of construction, Azzo asked Sarah if he could take her son surf fishing, at night.

She looked up from a ledger before her, irritated at the interruption. "You go at night? Why?"

"You've got me busy during the day, remember?" Azzo said, grinning, his eyes wide.

"Oh, well, sure. You can ask Benji if he wants to go."

"I already did, and he does," Azzo said, smiling broadly.

"Not on a school night," Sarah said, frowning because Azzo talked to her son first, "Benji needs his sleep."

"There's something else he needs, Sarah." Azzo said softly as his face lost its smile. "He doesn't want to be called Benji."

"Really?"

"Sarah, he's eleven, and in a few months he'll be twelve. He's growing up. Your son wants to be called 'Ben,' or, better yet, 'Benjamin.'"

"Of course," she said, annoyed once more that this man knew things about her son that she did not. She shrugged, pushing her annoyance away and turning back to the ledger, "Benjamin it is."

Then, thinking of Ben in or very near the surf, she added, "And make sure he wears the old leather brace for his leg. The metal one, even though it's supposed to be stainless, will rust at the joints."

"Yes, ma'am," Azzo said, tipping his hat, a slight grin on his face.

Almost two years after the terrible day when the stranger collapsed and died in Sarah's yard, the police brought the car he'd been driving to auction. Sarah was talking with Azzo one day in the woodworking shop when he told her he'd won the bid. Sarah was horrified.

"I'd never be comfortable riding in that car!" she exclaimed.

At her statement, Azzo looked up from the jigsaw and snapped it off. He said, grinning,

"I haven't asked you to go riding with me."

Sarah's cheeks turned pink and she turned to leave. He stopped her.

"Sarah," he said patiently, still smiling and ignoring her embarrassment. "A car is simply a machine, like this jigsaw, or that lathe. So, here is a late-model car, almost new, and I got it at a *very* good price." He added, "I didn't really buy a whole car anyway. I bought pieces. The police took it apart, looking for clues or something, and they didn't put it back together. The car will have to be completely rebuilt, reupholstered and repainted. But after I pay to have all that done, the car is a bargain."

She didn't respond as he added, "I'm getting awfully tired of going up and down the coast in that old jalopy of mine. This car will be much more comfortable and faster."

Sarah had almost forgotten about Azzo's writing and research. His work on Mansion house had seemed to consume most of his time. Had he often been away on "research" during Mansion House construction? She couldn't remember. Maybe he had.

"I thought you'd put your writing aside," she said.

"Not really," he grinned. "I've been working for you during the day and writing at night—when I don't take Ben fishing or have to make a quick trip down along the coast, or across to Bolivar Peninsula. Sometimes, if the ferries aren't working, for one reason or another, I have to take the long way to Bolivar, through Winnie. That's a long way to be in an open car."

During construction, Sarah had often found herself watching the architect while he worked. On warm days he usually discarded his khaki work shirt early and went about wearing only his sweat-soaked khaki trousers and a sleeveless undershirt. She would watch as the muscles of his back and arms rippled and the sweat-soaked khakis outlined his muscular legs. She blushed when she caught herself thinking how those arm and back muscles would feel under her caressing hands while his full lips pressed on hers, opening them. She scolded herself for being foolish and turned away, sure that he had no interest in her, hoping he hadn't noticed her watching him.

The architect never indicated anything but friendly interest, and she told herself sternly that there was no future in her daydreams. One day, as she was covertly watching him, he suddenly turned and said, "This job is going to be finished in a few weeks. You need to tell your uncle and your attorney. We can have a formal closing of the construction loans, which, as we've discussed, can then be converted to a fixed-interest mortgage, and," he grinned, "you can finally pay me."

At her expression, Azzo added, chuckling, "As I once told you, I don't work for free."

Chapter 7

San Luis Pass

The morning after the first time Azzo took Benjamin surf fishing, the boy burst into the kitchen just as Sarah was pouring her first cup of coffee. Rae had left earlier for a day-maiding job.

"We got there just as the sun was going down," Ben exclaimed, excited and speaking rapidly. "Mama! It was so beautiful! The most beautiful sunset I've ever seen. Before we got there, we stopped at a slough Azzo knew about, and I threw my casting net. He has one, too, larger than mine. We caught a lot of bait. Then we put our lines out. I didn't think I could cast one of those long surf rods, but I did, and he said I did super!"

As she stood at her kitchen counter, stirring her coffee and listening to her son's happy chatter, his distraught face from a day almost two years earlier popped into her memory. She scolded herself as she looked at her now happy and once-again outgoing boy. "You only did super?" she teased, "Not super-duper?"

Ben smiled. "Azzo said I did duper. I just didn't want to brag."

As the boy's happy chatter continued, Sarah thought, "This is what my boy needed, a strong male presence in his life." A small voice deep within her added, irritatingly, "And how about you, lady? Don't you need a strong male presence?" She shook off the thought.

Azzo came in from the Carriage House, showered and shaved. He went to the coffee pot and helped himself, then poured a cup for Benjamin, laced with cream and sugar.

"Azzo!" Sarah said, as the older man placed the steaming cup before her son. "I don't let Benjamin drink coffee!"

"It's time you should," Azzo said calmly, paying no attention to her protest.

"Well, anyway," Ben said, sipping at the coffee while looking at his friend and smiling gratefully, "right after we put the lines out, I caught the largest redfish I've ever caught. I asked Azzo for help, that fish was so big, but Azzo said I must bring it in myself. And I did!

"Azzo built this fire, a big bonfire," Benjamin chattered on, his words running together, "he's got this little shield, a folded metal thing to keep away wind, and he put that up and scraped some coals over and we fileted the fish and he has this little grate thing and he put the fish filets on it, scale side down."

Ben was breathless, but he went on. "And he had some potatoes that he put in the coals to cook and we cooked that fish and those potatoes and it was so good Azzo says the very best a fish can taste is when you cook it as soon as possible after catching it and…"

The boy stopped talking, now completely out of breath. After a pause, he added, "Mother! I caught more fish last night than I've ever caught before! They were bigger, too!"

Sarah's brow wrinkled, her thoughts catching up to Benjamin's chatter. "You cooked the fish with the scales on? Who does that?"

Azzo, standing, coffee cup in hand leaned against the kitchen counter and chuckled. "Sarah, it's called redfish-on-the-half-shell. They cook it that way over in New Orleans, and also throughout much of the rest of the eastern Gulf Coast. The fish cooks in its own juices. You'll have to try it sometime."

"So, you had a good time," Sarah said, turning away from the thought of eating fish with the scales on. Ben nodded vigorously. "Did you sleep," Sarah asked, "or stay up all night?"

"Oh, I fell asleep, Azzo spread an old blanket on the sand, but ..."

He looked at Azzo.

"We caught a fair number of fish," Azzo said, still chuckling. "They've been cleaned and iced down in several storage chests stacked in my fishing jalopy. I thought you might want to ask your neighbors if they'd like fresh fish for their supper tonight. Free, of course, one of the benefits of being neighbors at Mansion House Luxury Apartments."

"I'll ask," Sarah said, still grinning at her son's excitement.

"Some of the fish are fileted with the skin and scales removed, but others have simply been half-shelled, for baking, if that's what they want. Your neighbors can have their choice."

As Azzo and Benjamin unloaded the ice chests into one of the Carriage House garages, Sarah studied the old topless car. The rear seat had long ago been removed and replaced with a system of floorboards, providing a flat, level surface, where ice chests and other equipment had been stacked. There was a cabinet fitted into the rear of the car, where a folded top would have been stored. Azzo noticed her studying it.

"I keep lures and hooks, weights, all sorts of gear in that cabinet," he said, opening one of the drawers to show her.

He then changed the subject, diverting Sarah from her study of the cabinet. "Last night Benjamin told me about his dream to run, as he said, with the wind. I often run when I'm at the beach, leaving my gear at the car and just for fun I run barefooted in the sand. Would it be all right for Benjamin to run with me?"

"Yeah, Mom! I've always said I want to learn to run!"

"Benji," she began and paused at the slight wrinkling of her son's brow. She corrected herself. "Benjamin, I don't think it's possible for you to run. That brace will get in the way." She turned to Azzo. "Why do you run?"

"Oh, its great exercise. I ran the track when I was in college, though I was never on the track team. Then, later in New York, I ran around Central Park. I started running on the beach when I was in the Carolinas. When I came to Galveston, the beach patrols thought I was running away from something or somebody, like maybe I'd done something wrong. But I told them no, I just like to run. They just think I'm crazy." He laughed. "But they've gotten used to me.

"These days," Azzo continued, "those German subs out in the Gulf have the Army on high alert, as if they might send saboteurs on-shore."

"I've heard there are worries about saboteurs. So, it's true? There are German submarines in the Gulf?"

"Well it's true that the Army and Coast Guard are worried. I don't know if any bad guys are actually out there, or if any spies have actually landed. The rumor mill is strong, and I've heard more than once that the subs are actually out there. Has the Coast Guard's Commander Carruthers told you they're there?" As Sarah shook her head Azzo shrugged. "No, he hasn't, and he won't. Nothing is out there.

"Even so," he went on, "the patrols are pretty serious about the potential, especially now that it appears soon all Europe will be at war. But as I said, all the patrols know me, and know I'm harmless, just some crazy Jew who likes to fish and, for no reason at all, likes to run.

"Which brings me back to my question. Would it be all right for me to work with Benjamin? Take him to the beach. Help him learn to run?"

"I know he wants to run," Sarah said. Ben was still at the table, coffee before him, looking up at the adults, his eyes darting one from the other. Sarah's moved away from her son and seemingly stared into a distance. She was remembering that long-ago day when a four-year old boy with crutches and in full braces looked up at her. His wide-set dark eyes were filled with pain as he said he someday wanted to run.

Sarah's eyes came back from the past. She turned to Azzo. "I don't want him to be hurt."

"Tell you what," Azzo said, smiling and winking, looking at Ben as he moved to the table and sat. Sarah had a sudden flash of annoyance, realizing that Azzo had once again talked to Ben before talking to her. She remained standing.

"Monday," Azzo said, looking up at Sarah, "I'll go over to UT Medical Center and talk with some of Ben's doctors, maybe his therapist. Sarah, this may be the perfect time for him to begin learning to run and, we can all hope, perhaps get rid of those braces."

"Yes, Mother!" Benjamin shouted, rising from his chair. "Let's get rid of this old thing, too!" He held up his left foot, still incased in the dirty sand-covered leather brace. "The metal one, too!"

Sarah gave Azzo the names of several doctors. "His main therapist's name is Ralph," she added.

"That sounds a lot like 'patterning,'" Ralph told Azzo two days later, "such as that Australian nurse did a long time ago. It has merit of course and was the basis for many of the exercises and massages Mrs. Jacobs used on Ben when he was younger." He shrugged. "You know we're planning a series of new exercises in anticipation of Ben's approaching puberty."

"I think it's beginning," Azzo said.

"Puberty?" Ralph asked. At Azzo's nod he said, "Okay then. There's no sense wasting time. Let me follow up with Ben's doctors. We'll begin moving our plans forward. I'll get back to you, later today or tomorrow."

The next afternoon Azzo met Benjamin as he turned into the gate, pulling his books and other school supplies in his old wagon, limping with his wrist cane and metal brace.

"Ben," Azzo said, "go and change into dungarees or something. Shorts? Do you have any short pants?"

Benjamin grinned. "I usually wear long pants—they hide the brace. I have some old short pants that I used to wear when I went fishing at Offats, but they may not fit. Why are you asking?"

"Go slip into whatever short pants still fit. If none of them do, bring me your oldest pair of dungarees and we'll cut the legs off. Leave your cane and the metal brace at home but put on the old leather one. We'll take it off at the beach. There's something I want to try."

Benjamin was excited as Azzo guided the old jalopy toward the west end of the seawall. "Did you talk to Ralph?" he asked.

"Yep." Azzo looked at Ben in the passenger seat. "You know what Ralph and I think?"

Ben shook his head as Azzo said "We think that since you're nearly twelve, things are going to be happening to your body. You know what I mean?"

Ben nodded, then ducked his head, embarrassed. "Oh, that. Yeah, Ralph told me."

"It happens to all guys, Ben."

"Yeah, I know," Ben answered, his head down. "You said something once before to me, and Coach at school told me and a bunch of the other boys one day." He looked up at Azzo and grinned. "Mom hasn't said anything. I don't think she'd be very good at it."

Azzo laughed and said, "Well, Ben, puberty, and the muscle growth typically associated with it, is one of the things that may help us get rid of your braces."

"Yep," Ben said, determination in his voice, "Let's get started."

Azzo had chosen a section of deserted beach miles past the western end of the seawall. Benjamin was excited as Azzo cut the legs off his oldest pair of dungarees with a filet knife and slipped off the old leather brace. As Ben pulled on the cut-off's, Azzo said, "Don't put the brace back on, today we're going to try an experiment that Ralph thinks is worth a try."

Ralph had given Azzo webbing straps and he used these to hold his and Benjamin's legs together, connecting his strong right to Benjamin's lame left. When he finished, both Azzo and Ben stood together, bare-footed and shirtless.

"Benjamin," Azzo said, "we're going to begin by trial and error. We have to learn a lot. First, we have to learn to walk together, then we'll work up to learning to walk fast. Probably, today, we won't get around to actually running."

The onshore winds that August day were strong. Surf was high, and the salt spray quickly coated Azzo's and

Ben's skin and hair. The two moved off, clumsily, each trying to coordinate his movements with the other, trying to achieve a joint rhythm, legs tied together, arms locked. They were less than ten feet from the car when they fell the first time.

"Wow!" Ben said, gasping as he and Azzo struggled to rise. "This is more work than I thought it would be. I can't keep my foot up. It's just dragging. Take the straps off so we can get up."

"Nope," Azzo said. "We have to learn to get up with the straps on. This won't be the only time we'll fall."

"Let's try again," Azzo said after they'd struggled to their feet. Going through a patch of soft sand, Azzo added, panting, "Our rhythms have to match. We have to learn, both of us, to anticipate the other." They fell again.

"Let's pull these straps even tighter," Azzo said, "see if that will minimize the foot drop. I'll begin lifting my right foot higher and make my stride longer, so when your foot comes down it'll hit toe first. We need to let those lazy muscles in your left foot and ankle know that they need to be earning their keep. Let my right leg take the lead. You try to follow my movements."

They tightened the leg straps. "Now," Azzo said, "let's head toward that driftwood!"

It was awkward as they struggled along. There were more patches of soft sand and they fell often. Once at the driftwood, sweating and wiping themselves with towels Azzo had placed earlier, they leaned against what had once been the trunk of a large tree.

"I don't know," Azzo said. "Ben, maybe we shouldn't…"

Ben cut him off, shaking his head. "No! That time was lousy as hell! But that was only the first time. We're gonna do it again, and again, and again! I ain't gonna quit! Not now! Not ever! I'm gonna beat that old polio! I'm gonna give it the ax! I need you to help me! Don't you even think about stopping now!"

"Yes, sir!" Azzo shouted back, standing, snapping a salute, surprised and pleased at Ben's spirit. "You got it! Ben! Back!" He pointed. "Back to the car!" Azzo pulled Ben, and they moved away from the old fallen tree, struggling, falling, getting up, struggling again. But after each fall, their stride became slightly more coordinated. They were each learning, struggling, beginning to match the other's movements. At the car, leaning against a fender, Azzo poured water from a large thermos into metal camping cups.

"Ben," Azzo said, "this is hard."

Gulping his water, Ben said, "You're not planning to give up on me?"

"No, sir! I'm not. Maybe, back at that driftwood tree, after our first time, maybe then I thought about it. But not now. I'm your man! You can depend on me. When I'm in town, I'll bring you here every day after work, and we'll do this. Ben, you're gonna beat polio and I'm gonna help you do it!"

"Together?" Ben asked. "Together? We're gonna beat it together?"

"Together!" Azzo exclaimed. "I'm your man!"

He pulled Ben off the fender, both dropped their cups into the car seat, and they began their hobbling, awkward, graceless march to the old tree, falling, struggling, falling again and again. At the tree, resting, breathing heavily, Benjamin studied the ancient tree as his hand traced aimless patterns in the encrusted salt.

"Where do you think this old tree came from?"

"I don't know," Azzo said. He turned, looked out to sea. Ben saw his partner's eyes focus into the distance. Azzo began talking, slowly and with a strange tone to his voice, as if he was seeing a long-ago past. "Ben, I want to believe that somewhere, along a large river, maybe the Mississippi, and maybe during a spring flood decades ago, maybe a hundred years ago, the riverbank eroded, and a large tree fell. It made its way southward to the Gulf of Mexico for perhaps a thousand miles, or more.

"And then the Gulf rejected this inland contribution and cast it up on this beach near Galveston Island's San Luis Pass. This is our gift from the Gulf of Mexico. We'll make it our place, our place to rest as we beat polio."

"Thank you, Gulf of Mexico!" Benjamin shouted.

"Now," Azzo shouted, grinning, "back to the car! This time, faster!"

"Kick the crap out of polio!" Ben shouted. "Run! Let's run!"

They didn't run as they again used the awkward three-legged race gait. And they fell more times, but not as many as before. At the car, Ben asked, "What about winter? Can we keep on doing this?"

"We'll keep our shirts on, and maybe long pants. Perhaps a jacket or a sweatshirt," Azzo answered. "But I want us to keep on. You were better this time than when we started. I was better this time. You're going to get better every day, and I am, too. Maybe next time we'll use the leather brace."

"Nope," Ben answered, "Not gonna do that. If it's in the cards for me to put those braces down, then I want to start now!"

"Okay," Azzo said. "Then let's do it again,"

Benjamin reached down and tightened the straps.

"From here to the driftwood, then back to here. I want to learn to run! I want to be your partner!"

"Ich braude enin partner!" Azzo said. At Benjamin's puzzled expression, Azzo said, "That's German. It means 'I need a partner.'

"Listen," Azzo said, "and repeat it after me." He repeated each of the German words and Benjamin mimicked them. After several tries Azzo nodded. "Pretty good. I'll teach you some more German words soon. Perhaps some French and Spanish words as well."

"You speak French and Spanish?" Benjamin asked.

Azzo laughed again, "Yes, of course. You can, too. I'll teach you some words." He bent down and helped with the straps.

One more thing," Azzo said, straightening up, "The therapist said your leg muscles are going to be really sore tonight. He recommended massaging them. He gave me this." He held out a tube of mentholated salve.

Benjamin didn't answer right away as memories flooded through his mind, memories of his mother's tireless hands endlessly massaging his limbs as he cried from the pain, When he finally spoke, his voice began in a low and steady cadence. "I know about massages and I know about pain. If those lazy muscles start to complain," his voice became loud and Azzo could hear a challenge, "I'll take care of them!" Ben put the tube down on the car's fender.

"Now!" Azzo shouted, pointing toward the driftwood.

Benjamin turned to his friend and shouted, *"Ich braude enin partner!"*

Azzo laughed. "We're going to have to work on that accent!" Then together, they shouted as one, "One more time! To the driftwood and back to the car!"

Benjamin shouted, "Run with the wind!"

Chapter 8

The Closing
Early November 1939

The closing, consolidating the construction loans and assorted fees into a fixed interest fifteen-year commercial mortgage, was held in the Weismann Bank's large conference room. It seemed to Sarah somehow anticlimactic and abbreviated.

There had been weeks of legal and accounting activities, but the final event itself was over almost before it had begun. Legal documents were signed and initialed, a check issued to Azzo, and Sarah found herself the owner of not only Mansion House Luxury Apartments and the Carriage House Annex, but the entire city block that surrounded the complex. She felt the interest Levi was charging her was usurious. She had hoped, since she was family, that he would have lowered his normal interest rates. He did not.

While signing document after document, Sarah did a little math and found, to her astonishment, that she could not even imagine her life in fifteen years. She paused in signing and wondered briefly about the far-away year of 1954. With a start, she realized that when the mortgage was paid off, she'd be forty-nine, and Ben, twenty-six.

"Why," she said to herself as she resumed initialing pages, "Ben might be married by that time! I could be a grandmother!" Her eyes widened at this last, and she paused again in her initialing, only to be brought back to the present by her attorney's soft and discrete "Ah-hem!"

Then, it was over. The men in the room rose and there were handshakes all around. Assistants gathered papers, checking to make sure all had the proper signatures or initials, and in the correct location. Sarah, too, rose from her chair as a secretary congratulated her. Uncle Levi gave her a quick and peremptory hug, muttered something she didn't understand, turned and headed to his office. Azzo touched her elbow and, smiling and nodding, guided her from the conference room. He paused at a bank teller, signed and deposited his check and placed his bankbook in his jacket's breast pocket. He turned to Sarah.

"I want to buy you lunch to celebrate this day. I've made reservations at the Galvez. Will you join me?"

She was surprised. All during construction Azzo regularly had taken his supper with her and Benjamin, but he'd never before suggested anything like a restaurant meal between just the two of them. "I'd be delighted," she answered, pleased at the invitation.

Sarah had, after many months, given in to Levi Weismann's concerns over her aging coupe, and ordered a tan Chevrolet station wagon, its price included in the mortgage. Azzo led her to the new car.

He opened the passenger door and ushered her in. Azzo then walked around the car and settled under the wheel, holding out his hand for the keys. Sarah felt a flash of irritation, which she quickly dismissed.

He pulled up to the front entrance of the Galvez and as an attendant took the car away Sarah looked at her lapel watch. "Azzo," she said, "it's nearly 1:30. Will the hotel's dining room still be open?" Azzo smiled as if he had a secret and led her through the magnificent entrance, past the ornate lobby and the adjacent dining room, with its few diners still enjoying their lunch, and into an elevator. To the operator, he said, "Fifth floor, please."

They exited and Azzo opened an unlocked door to a two-room suite.

"I lived here for many months," he said, "in these two rooms. The view, especially at dawn, is outstanding."

The room was furnished as a living room, but with a cloth-covered table by the windows, fully set with tableware for two.

A waiter, dressed in a white jacket with gloves, silently greeted them and led the way to the table, assisting Sarah as she sat. He poured water into their glasses.

"Wine, sir?" the waiter asked, turning to Azzo.

"Yes, please," As the waiter exited to the other room, Azzo added, "I've ordered a chilled California Chablis. I hope that's satisfactory?"

Sarah looked out toward the Gulf. "Azzo, the view is breathtaking. I've never seen the Gulf from this high."

Puffs of white cloud dotted the Gulf sky this warm November day. A bay shrimper had braved the open Gulf and was trolling near-shore. Farther away to the east, several cargo ships rested at the anchorage called Bolivar Roads as they waited their turns to enter port.

As Sarah admired the view, Azzo said, "I have a good friend who runs an airfield. Perhaps someday we can ask him to give us an aerial view of Galveston, Bolivar Roads, and an aerial tour of the Galveston and Trinity Bay systems."

Sarah didn't comment about the prospect of an aerial tour as the waiter poured wine, then placed the bottle in an ice-filled bucket and retreated into the next room. "Why,

Azzo," Sarah said as door closed behind the waiter and she picked up her glass, "What a treat!"

He lifted his glass. "Here's to the success of Mansion House!"

Sarah nodded and added, "And to the man who made it all happen!" she added, laughing softly.

"No, Sarah," Azzo said, his voice turning serious. "You're the one who made it happen. It was your courage and foresight. I was only an instrument to be used during construction."

Sarah nodded, smiling at the compliment. "We were a team, Azzo."

"Yes," Azzo agreed, nodding. "We were. We work well together, Sarah."

"We did," she agreed aloud while in her mind she heard that annoying voice in her head saying, "A team, but he was always in charge!"

As if to endorse her last thought, Azzo said, "I have already ordered. We're having a cup of oyster stew, a small luncheon salad graced with the Galvez' extraordinary wine vinaigrette, and braised fresh-caught Gulf yellowfin tuna in a light cream-and-vinegar sauce."

Sarah thought with irritation, "That's what I would have ordered if he'd given me the chance!" The nasty little voice inside her head added, sarcastically, "So, lady, what's your problem?"

Azzo was quiet for a few moments as they both sipped their wine. He seemed to be studying her. There was a disturbing intensity to his eyes.

"Sarah, I need to say something."

She smiled, uncomfortable under his gaze, and was completely unprepared for his next statement.

"I think I may have fallen in love with you. No," he contradicted himself, "I'm pretty sure that I have fallen in love with you."

"Why, Azzo," Sarah said, surprised and blushing, eyes wide, taken aback. "You've—you never said..."

She paused, annoyed at herself for stammering. The irritating voice within her once again intruded, "Caution, lady, you now know he saw you watching him, all those months, those muscles rippling under his sweaty undershirt, his biceps as he strained, lifting, hammering or sawing."

Sarah started over, determined to keep her voice steady. "You've never said anything like this to me before," she said, surprised at the sternness in her voice. She straightened in her chair and said, more formally than she intended, "I've always felt we simply had a friendly business relationship."

As she finished, she dared to look into those large, liquid eyes again. It seemed there was a light there, somehow, behind the eyes, enhancing the intensity of his gaze. A wayward forelock that she'd often seen during construction dangling across his forehead had once again fallen. She had often wanted to touch it, and did so this time, leaning over and pushing it into place.

"I was your employee," Azzo said in a calm voice, as she brushed back the forelock. "You were my client. We had a business relationship. And I wanted to be your friend." He paused, then added, "Sarah, our business is finished, but I want the relationship to continue and I want more." The light behind his eyes seemed stronger. "I would hope that someday," he added softly, "you might want more, too."

He reached for the wine bottle and refilled both glasses. Sarah gulped from her glass without answering as the waiter reappeared and placed the oyster stew in front of them.

As the door once again closed behind him, Sarah whispered, "Why have you said nothing before? All these months, we've worked together, and…"

Azzo interrupted, smiling and whispered back, "You don't need to whisper. The waiter will never repeat anything even if he should happen to overhear."

He paused. When she said nothing more, he continued in a normal tone. "Sarah, it would have been improper for me to say anything while Mansion House was still under construction."

"Improper?" Sarah said. "I never even thought…" She didn't finish.

Azzo smiled, wistfully, it seemed to Sarah. "Perhaps," he said, "I'm too—ah—continental in my relationships. If I were more direct, more American…" His voice trailed away as Sarah ducked her head and picked up the refilled wine glass. She drank some, then turned to her oyster stew. Both dipped their spoons into the succulent hot broth.

Sarah looked up from her stew into Azzo's eyes. His gaze was steady and unwavering, but he said nothing. "So," she said, putting her spoon down and trying to make light of the situation, smiling as she said, "do I understand it's your intention to wine me and dine me and then ravish me in the bedroom next door?"

"Not at all, Sarah," Azzo shook his head, grinning as the light in his eyes seemed to fade slightly. "I simply wanted us to enjoy a good meal, a glass or two of wine, and discuss a continuing relationship. One that I would hope might someday result in more."

"Oh, Azzo," Sarah said, becoming serious as the alcohol buzzed in her head. She put her spoon down and turned slightly in her chair, looking out at the Gulf. "I loved Glenn with all my heart," she said quietly, her eyes on the far-away shrimper. "I knew I loved him the first minute I saw him. When he died, I thought I'd never love another man." She turned back to Azzo. The strange light in his eyes had returned, as if he knew what she was going to say. "When you came along, all those months we worked together, somehow that began to change. I began to think—" she paused, then began again, speaking slowly, repeating, "—I began to think that I might love another man," she again paused. "Someday."

In the silence between them, the waiter discreetly reappeared, took the stew away and placed small salads, leaving again quickly.

She looked fully into his dark eyes and felt she could lose herself under their intense gaze. "Azzo, perhaps, someday, there could be something for us, but..." The tone of her voice changed, "but you irritate me sometimes!"

His eyebrows rose as she continued. "No! You irritate me often, not just sometimes!" She ducked her head, bent to her salad and worried she'd said too much. She added in a softer tone, "Will you give me some time?"

"Yes, of course," Azzo said, the light now completely gone from his eyes. "I irritate you?" One eyebrow was raised, his mouth twisted in a half-grin.

"Azzo, I never intended to say this. It's the wine talking. You and that waiter have given me too much. But," she went on in spite of inner alarms, "you're always taking charge! Oh, it's a little thing, but just today, you didn't let me drive the car. Azzo, it's my car! You just ushered me into the passenger seat and held out your hand for the keys."

"Is that it?" Azzo answered, eyebrows raised. "Sarah, I meant no disrespect. On the contrary, I assumed a gentleman would always drive a lady instead of the other way around. I'll start right away, today, letting you drive your own car. Mine too, if you want."

Sarah felt petty and irritated at herself. "It's not just the driving, Azzo," she tried to explain, "it's a whole lot of things. When construction was going on, you always led me in the decision-making process. And when I didn't make the decision you or Uncle Levi or—even Benjamin!—wanted, you continued to discuss alternatives. I could always tell what you men wanted me to do before you finished talking." She almost spat the word "men."

"Today, even before we got here you had ordered for both of us. You didn't even ask what I might have wanted."

He smiled, the quizzical eyebrow still uplifted, "Well, what would you have wanted? We can re-order."

Sarah ducked her head, her wide mouth over her strong jaw twisted in an expression half-way between irritation and laughter. Finally, she did laugh, her dark wide-set eyes crinkling.

"Oh, Azzo!" she exclaimed, "I'd have ordered exactly the same as you ordered, but that's not the point!" Both laughed in unison.

The waiter reappeared and removed the salad dishes and placed the main course in front of both.

"I shall begin immediately letting you have your own way," Azzo laughed as the waiter again disappeared. "Shall I call the waiter back? You can pay the check!"

"No, you silly. You're going to pay for all this. You can afford it, after what you collected at closing!"

"It was only what was due, Sarah."

They both sat quietly, enjoying the tuna, which was exquisite. Azzo broke the silence. "Sarah, I'm closer to

Levi's generation than you think. I'm ten years older than you, and I was raised in Europe by people who are only a little younger than your Uncle Levi."

She was briefly silent, thinking she'd gone too far, then said, hoping to lighten the situation, "You're not so old. Anyway, I just had a birthday. Now, there's only nine years between us!"

He didn't respond right away, but when he did, he ignored her comment and said, "Sarah, a man looks at things differently when he's in his mid-forties."

Neither said anything more as both turned and looked out the windows to the green-blue Gulf. There was silence for several long minutes.

"I think you have given me hope, at least," Azzo said, breaking the silence and turning again to his meal.

They finished their tuna, and Azzo called the waiter and asked for a dessert menu, handing it to Sarah. "You can order dessert," he said, laughing.

She took her time reviewing the menu under his watchful gaze, and ordered, asking the waiter how long it would take for the dessert to arrive. "Oh," the young man answered, grinning. "No time at all, Ma'am. I have the dessert in the next room."

Sarah looked down, a rueful expression on her face, then laughed outright. Azzo joined in, as did the waiter, proving he'd overheard everything.

With the mood lightened, Azzo said over coffee, "You accused me of wanting to sweep you off your feet and into a hotel bedroom. Of course, I want to do that." He said as he finished his coffee. He placed several bills on the table and stood, holding out his hand for Sarah.

They appreciated the view as the waiter reappeared, cleared the table and wheeled the food cart and all the table utensils out of the room and into the hallway. He left the door of the adjacent room open, and Sarah saw he'd thoughtfully turned the bed covers down.

As the waiter left, Azzo pulled her to him and she felt the strong muscles of his chest as his full lips sought hers. They kissed, his tongue parting her lips and entering, just a little. Sarah could feel Azzo's thighs pressing against hers, and a warm liquid feeling swept over her.

Standing in the embrace, she whispered into his ear, "Now to the bedroom?" To Sarah, her own voice sounded breathless and perhaps hopeful.

"No," he said, smiling and pulling away, "now we go to your car. This time you get to drive. We may do the hotel room and that ravishing business some other day."

As they climbed into the station wagon Azzo said, motioning her to slide under the steering wheel, "Do you need to go to Galveston Pilots' office?"

"Yes, for a few minutes, just to check on a few things."

"Drop me off at my car. It's parked a block down from Levi's bank. I need to go to Mansion House. Benjamin and I are planning another fishing trip." He raised an eyebrow.

"Would you like to come along? If not now, someday soon?"

Chapter 9

Two Weeks Later

It was a Saturday when Azzo returned from a trip to the East Coast that seemed to have come up rather suddenly. A telegram had arrived that morning giving his arrival time, and Sarah drove to Houston's Municipal Airport to pick him up.

"Welcome home!" she said as he crossed the tarmac and entered the fenced waiting area. "This trip was certainly shorter than many of your others." To her surprise, he bent and hugged her, giving her a quick kiss on the cheek.

"Yes, flying is so much faster," Azzo said. "When I took the train to New York, I had to allow a full day and part of a night just to get there and the same to return. The airplane can just whisk me there and back in jig time."

"How were your flights? Aaron's mother once told me flying is bumpy, air pockets, I think she said."

"It was smooth as glass, both ways." He was smiling. "You must come with me some time. New York is a grand place. We could see the sights, go dancing at Ciro's, perhaps see a Broadway production."

He tipped the redcap who'd placed his luggage in the rear of Sarah's station wagon and opened the driver's side door of Sarah's station wagon.

"You've heard," he said, changing the subject and ushering Sarah behind the wheel, "that the Soviet Union invaded Finland?" Azzo moved around the car and sat in the passenger seat.

"Yes," Sarah said, depressing the starter pedal. "I saw something about it in the *Daily News,* but I've been busy and haven't paid much attention." She frowned. "Russia? Are they on the side of the Germans?"

"No one is ever quite sure which side the Russians are on. And, of course, there's more.

"A bomb exploded in a Munich beer hall, twenty minutes after Adolph Hitler left. Jews are being blamed, and the Nazis are upping their persecutions. And while I don't understand the connection, the European newspapers say that Jewish persecutions were already accelerating following the Russian invasion of Finland. Now since the beer hall bombing, Hitler is claiming Jews were behind it. It's a bad time to be a Jew in Europe."

"How did you know all that?" Sarah asked.

"Some of it was in the New York papers," Azzo said. "But I also learn a lot from a good friend of mine. He works in the German Consulate. He's not Jewish, but we've been friends since childhood. Every time I go to New York, he and I have lunch, and he tells me news that the papers and radio don't."

Sarah didn't know how to respond and said, "The Coast Guard's Commander Carruthers came by the office. He said that war is inevitable, if not this year, then soon."

"He's right," Azzo said. "Britain, France, Australia, New Zealand, and Canada have already declared war on Germany. Roosevelt is under pressure to ask Congress for a declaration of war. But there's also a lot of pressure on him from many who say they want no part of another European war. Now, if one of those German submarines in the Gulf—if they're really there—should take a pot shot at one of our T2 tankers, well, war would be upon us overnight."

"Commander Carruthers said he's pretty sure there are U-boats in the Gulf," Sarah said, "but he also asked that I not say so to other Pilots' personnel. He doesn't want it to become public knowledge. He said he'd talked to Sam at the *Daily News*, and Sam had agreed to keep it quiet."

"Sam?" Azzo questioned.

"Yes," Sarah answered, "Sam Klein, the managing editor. I've known Sam since maybe forever. He's almost like family to me, though he isn't Jewish. Maybe he is to me much the same as your New York friend."

"Well," Azzo said as Sarah turned the car onto Telephone Road, accelerating smoothly and merging into traffic, "I'm sure Carruthers is going to be keeping in close contact with you.

"And," Azzo went on, "something else, and this was in all the papers: there was a Nazi rally in Madison Square Garden just a few days ago. My hotel was near the Garden, so I saw some of it first-hand. A Nazi rally in the United States!" he added with intensity in his voice. "An anti-Jew affair! Men shouting, 'Death to the Jews!' I'm more worried than ever about my parents and sister."

Sarah was surprised. Azzo had mentioned family before, but only briefly. She couldn't think of a proper response.

"You told me your parents were scientists, working for the German government."

"Yes, I did. You'll remember I said they were virtually prisoners. They were taken away from their home in Munich and from their work at the University and are forced to work at what the Germans call a secret laboratory, although everyone knows where it is."

Sarah slowed for a traffic signal in Webster.

Azzo shrugged, "Well, at least as of two weeks ago they were alive."

"What does that mean?" Sarah asked.

"I get letters from them. It takes about two weeks for a letter to reach me. I just got one before I left for New York. I'm reasonably sure that two weeks ago my parents and sister were alive."

"Ordinary letters?" Sarah asked. "Just through regular mail?"

"We're not at war with Germany, so yes, the mail comes through, although it takes several weeks. In addition, my friend in the German Consulate keeps me up-to-date about them."

He grinned, thinking of his lunch only two days ago. "My friend and I go to lunch—he's hooked on American hot dogs, and we always go to the same vendor in Central Park—my hot dog is kosher, of course—and he tells me about both my parents and my sister, and he tells me things they can't, because of Nazi censorship."

"Are they mistreated?" Sarah asked.

"Oh, no, not at all. For a Jewish couple, they're being very well treated, good food and good housing. They have their own apartment, furnished quite nicely, and they have their privacy.

"They're getting along in years now, but their work is quite valuable to the mission of the research facility. They can't retire, since if they did, they'd be immediately transported to a concentration camp, a one-way trip, with no way out, ever."

"I've never heard you talk like this," Sarah said. "I've never even been sure you were Jewish."

"Oh, yes, I'm Jewish," Azzo grinned. "Your Uncle Levi would never have let me get close to you if I weren't. I don't go to temple as often as I should, nor do much about observing our holy days, but my parents did. They don't anymore, of course. The Nazis frown on anything remotely Jewish."

"What work do your parents do?" Sarah asked.

"They're experimenting with rockets and jet engines. It was the work they were doing at the University. Hitler wanted the work to advance faster, and there are a number of scientists focusing on the same type of work, not all of them Jewish. He intends to send rocket-propelled bombs to England."

"Rocket airplanes?" Sarah interrupted.

"No, rocket-propelled bombs, launched over the English Channel. They'd be virtually unstoppable, would cause panic in the cities where they'd fall, and Hitler wouldn't lose any of his airplane pilots. They're also working on jet engines for airplanes that would, theoretically, be much faster and more maneuverable than propeller-driven aircraft. My sister works as an assistant to my parents."

They drove in silence for several miles.

"I fear for my family's lives," Azzo said. "I've heard that the Nazis execute scientists if just one of their experiments fails. I don't know if that's true, but it doesn't keep me from worrying."

Sarah sat, silent as the miles passed, not knowing how to respond.

"I heard something a few months ago," Sarah said, "about a ship full of Jewish people from Germany. I didn't pay much attention at the time."

"Yes," Azzo said, nodding. "That was the SS St. Louis, in May last year. The passengers were trying to get to Cuba and hopefully from there to the United States. My friend in New York helped me when I tried to book passage for my parents on that ship." He shrugged. "I didn't succeed, but it would have been useless in any case. The Cuban government turned the ship away and Roosevelt refused them entry to the United States, so the ship returned to Hamburg and most of those on board no doubt wound up in concentration camps."

"Why did Roosevelt turn them away?"

"I don't know. Probably the German government was exerting pressure not to let them enter the United States, no doubt afraid they'd tell the world about the Nazi's treatment of Jews.

"Anyway," Azzo went on, "I believe that the primary reason the St. Louis was turned away was our own government. It's well-known that the head of the FBI, J. Edgar Hoover, is almost rabidly anti-communist as well as anti-Semitic. He and politicians, congressmen, and some senators, were concerned that the passengers might have been communists or German spies, or both. Moreover, many politicians were squalling that you couldn't tell a Jew from a spy or a communist, and no one wanted a shipload of Jews, spies, and communists to enter the United States."

They rode in silence for a mile or two, each occupied with his own thoughts. As the car navigated the final turn of the highway, and the Galveston Causeway was in view, Azzo said "Oh! My first breath of salt air! How I miss Galveston! Has anything happened while I've been away that I should know about?"

"Oh, I was going to tell you, but we got involved with your stories of your parents. Benjamin found a key. A flat-looking odd little thing. It looks like a safe-deposit key."

"Really?" Azzo said. Sarah thought she saw a quiet change in his demeanor. There was the flicker of an eyelid.

"Yes," Sarah said. "Benjamin was riding behind Wallace on that noisy gasoline engine mowing-machine thing you had someone build for us, something I've told him never to do, by the way!" She frowned, remembering her many admonitions to Ben. "Azzo," she said, momentarily forgetting about the key, "I've told you before that mowing machine thing was going to cause trouble! Benjamin's been after Wallace for ever so long begging for a ride, when I'm not around of course. You know Benjamin! He wouldn't give up and Wallace finally gave in, and there they went, tearing around the yard, lickety-split."

"You saw them?" Azzo asked.

"No," Sarah said sharply. "Rae told me. Azzo, the next thing you know, Ben will be trying to drive that mowing machine and he'll wind up cutting his foot off or something."

Azzo laughed, proving to Sarah that he'd encouraged Ben to disobey. "What was this about a key?" he asked.

"Oh, yes. It was flung up from the grass right near where that man died. Benjamin thinks the man who died dropped it. There's a large oleander next to that spot now. I showed the key to Uncle Levi. He said it was nothing and I shouldn't tell the police, they'd get all, well, he said they'd get all 'hot-and-bothered.'"

"I agree," Azzo said. "Everything about that day is now history and it needs to stay that way." He shrugged. "And, anyway, that key is almost certainly not connected with that day at all."

He rambled on, making some of the points her uncle had made, and reminded her of the dozens of workmen that had been at mansion house all during construction, and that the lawn had been completely resodded during landscaping. "There's no way I can see that the key has anything to do with the man who died," he ended.

Sarah shrugged inwardly, deciding to say nothing more. As she did, a memory flashed before her eyes. She saw the man standing beside his car, holding onto the open car door with his right hand, his left extended. She'd thought at the time it was some sort of greeting. "But," she thought, "had he instead been holding something in his hand, something he intended to deliver?"

Azzo abruptly changed the subject as Sarah turned the car off Broadway onto 51st street. "How's Ben? Has he been keeping up with his exercises?"

"Yes, he has," Sarah said, forgetting about the key. "And his leg muscles have been cramping dreadfully. I've seen him any number of times massaging. I volunteered to help, but he said no, it was now his job. He said I'd done enough when he was a baby."

"Sarah, he's going to make a fine man. I hope you're proud of him."

She smiled as he said this.

"Do you suppose he'd want to go to the beach with me this evening," Azzo continued, "after supper? To run?"

"Do I suppose? Azzo, he's talked about nothing else after he found out you were returning today."

Chapter 10

December 1939

Azzo and Benjamin rested on the old driftwood tree trunk. Though the early December day was warm, the light breeze was producing a slight chill as they wiped sweat and salt spray from their bodies.

"Ben," Azzo said, wrapping the towel about his shoulders, "your mother tells me you've found a key of some sort."

"Yeah, I did," the boy answered. "I was riding behind Wallace on the mowing machine, and it pulled the key up from the grass. It's a funny looking flat thing. Mom said it looked like a key to a safety deposit box and she took it to Uncle Levi, but he said no."

"No, as in it wasn't a safety deposit key, or no, it didn't fit the boxes in his bank?"

"I don't know. Mom said he seemed irritated. Anyway, she brought the key back. I made a box for it..." His voice trailed away.

"Hmm," Azzo said. "You used the power woodworking tools which I asked you not to do unless I was in the shop with you?"

Benjamin looked down, embarrassed. "Yes, sir. I'm sorry—about using the tools."

"Me, too," Azzo said, not mentioning the mower.

"You said you built a box?" Azzo returned to the subject.

"Yes. I keep the key in it. Sometimes I take it out and look at it, wondering, well, you know…"

"I'd like to see it. Maybe when we get home tonight? Bring it up to my apartment before you go to bed."

The next day, Azzo visited Uncle Levi.

The old man studied the polished wooden box. The key was in an inlay, its shape carved into the floor of the small container.

"This is really fine workmanship," he said, indicating the wood box.

"Yes, Benjamin is talented at woodworking. He used the power tools without my permission, and I'm sorry he did that."

The old banker tried to pry the key from its resting place with his thumbnail and failed. He reached for a letter-opener. "Sarah showed me the key," Levi said, "when Benjamin first found it. I told her it was nothing, certainly not a key that would fit any box in this bank and that she should forget about it, but of course she didn't."

"I don't think anyone else knows about this key," Azzo said thoughtfully, "other than Wallace, who may have said something to Rae, but I doubt it. He knew Benjamin had been forbidden by his mother to ride with him on the mowing machine, yet he let Ben talk him into it. I'm guilty, too. I encouraged Ben to keep after Wallace for a ride. Anyway, Wallace is likely embarrassed and wants to forget about disobeying Sarah."

"I don't think we have anything to worry about," Levi said. "The police consider the case closed."

"On the other hand," Azzo said, a wry grin on his face, "we could certainly use that eight million of German government bearer bonds from that Atlanta S.D. box."

Levi Weismann chuckled grimly. "That's out of the question. We know that our friends must have learned who had stolen the bonds, and they're the ones who attacked our courier. We also know they don't know exactly where the bonds are, and we need to keep the news of that as well as the key under wraps."

Azzo replied, "The contents will be useless anyway if war between Germany and the United States is declared."

Levi nodded. "The bonds are as good as gone. We know where they are, but we can't get to them. Stop thinking of them. We have other financing, and more is on the way. We need to simply forget them. Give the key back to Benjamin. He seems to think it's some sort of talisman."

"It might be dangerous for Ben to have the key," Azzo said.

Levi shrugged. "I disagree. If anyone learns that Ben found the key, and we didn't do anything about it, that would more-or-less prove we know nothing, and neither does Ben."

"Well it solves a lot of things for us," Azzo said. "The man who died was, without a doubt, our man. He was no doubt bringing the key to you. We may someday learn that a German agent caught up to him, attacked, and that's when he got the stab wound. We know from the inquest that our man was carrying a pistol, and that it had been recently fired. What we don't know, and perhaps never will, is where and how he got the chest wounds."

"The other thing we don't know," Levi said, "is why the man was following Benjamin. If he was bringing the key to me, why didn't he just do it?"

"Maybe," Azzo said, "our man got himself stabbed, then, all bloody and needing medical attention was certain that there was no way he could enter your bank without drawing attention to himself. He must have known you had a niece and was following Benjamin to learn where she lived. But how did he know she had a son, and how did he know to follow just one boy? And as you've already pointed out, where and how did he get the second wound in his chest?" He sighed. "Parts of this will always remain a mystery."

Levi Weismann fiddled with lighting a fresh cigar, his face somber.

"You're right," he said, releasing a cloud of smoke and ignoring Azzo's slight cough. "And I'm right. The business of the bonds is over. We need to simply go about our business. As I said, we already have other financing, and more is on the way, as are more clients. You're not done with running up and down the coast. Keep checking your short-wave on the days and times previously scheduled."

Azzo nodded, then shrugged. "Well, that's what I signed on for. I plan to return the key to Benjamin. I don't see any harm in Ben having a souvenir of that day."

Levi Weismann nodded agreement as blue smoke from his cigar drifted around the room. "There is a bright side," the old banker said. "We can't get to the bonds, but neither can Hitler. Declaring war on the United States will cost him eight million. He can't be too happy over that.

"How about your parents?" Levi said, abruptly changing the subject. "How are they doing?"

"They're well as far as I know," Azzo answered. "Their letters are heavily censored of course, but we have a little code of our own that the Nazis haven't yet figured out, so I know that most of what I'm reading is accurate. If war is declared with Germany, I won't get letters through regular mails, and I worry about that.

"This," Azzo said, holding up the key, anxious to escape the cigar fumes, "goes back into the box and back to Benjamin." He turned to leave the room, coughing loudly. "See you at supper Wednesday night," he said between coughing spells.

As the door closed behind Azzo, Levi studied the lighted cigar in his hand and wondered about the coughing. He reached into the tastefully decorated box on his desk and withdrew another of the expensive Cubans, rolling it under his nose.

He thought it smelled like money.

Chapter 11

Mansion House Apartments 1940

As 1939 became 1940, Sarah found her life had evolved into a busy routine. She worked mornings at Galveston Pilots' offices, returning to Mansion House for lunch. Afternoons, she worked from the small alcove that served as an office, just off her living room, managing the apartment complex. Azzo had installed a direct line to Galveston Pilots' and staff there took advantage of the more or less constant contact with Sarah.

Prospective tenants came by almost every day, eager to join her waiting list, and Sarah explained the lease requirements and general rules of the establishment, and why she had a "no pets" policy.

Azzo was a flaw in what could have been a satisfactory routine. After the luncheon in the Galvez and his astonishing declaration, he was away from Galveston more often than not. When in town, he was friendly, but nothing more, except that he had begun taking all his meals in her kitchen. She couldn't quite understand his actions. Was he waiting for her to do or say something? Was he simply trying to annoy her? Was there ever going to be a follow-up to his declaration at the Galvez?

While Mansion House was under construction, Sarah had not charged him rent for the rooms he used in Carriage

House, as their agreement had stipulated. However, now that construction was over, she presented him with a lease agreement for what was now a studio apartment, and he signed it without comment.

She paid little attention to what Azzo did with his days now that construction was over. Her duties at Galveston Pilots', coupled with management of the apartment complex, consumed her attention. Once, she'd seen Azzo downtown, exiting a local restaurant where the Rotary met, and she guessed he had resumed attending Galveston Rotary.

She asked him about it one day after supper.

"Rotary's a great place," Azzo said, "to make business connections. I'm thinking more and more about opening an architectural practice here in Galveston. A number of my fellow Rotarians are encouraging me to do so."

"What about your writing?" she asked.

"Oh," he said airily, "I'll wrap up that book one of these days, and when I do, I think I'll return to architecture. If there's a war—and there's going to be one, you can be sure of that—when it's over this whole region is going to go bonkers with growth."

"Bonkers?"

"Oh, well," Azzo answered, smiling as he realized that British slang hadn't yet made it completely across the Atlantic. "Killer-diller then."

Azzo and Benjamin continued going to the beach often for their exercise routines, and Sarah was usually invited. Sometimes she took them up on it, and when she was being truthful with herself she knew she enjoyed the togetherness with her two men. It was almost as if they were a family during these times, joking, teasing, and simply enjoying one another's company.

For quite some time Sarah had been ordering her groceries by telephone using a list prepared by Rae. One day she realized it had been more than a week since she'd ordered groceries. She asked Rae about it.

"Oh," Rae said. "Mist Azzo, he says he guine take over the grocery shopping. He goes to th' new Piggly-Wiggly near downtown."

Sarah was astonished. That night after supper she asked him about it.

Azzo shrugged. "I thought that as long as I was eating all my meals with you, the least I could do was buy the groceries. Besides, Piggly-Wiggly is cheaper than Morgenstern's on 45th."

"But Morgenstern's delivers, and I never have to worry whether its Kosher or not," Sarah protested. Another thought intruded, and she frowned as she said sternly, "I'm not going to reduce your rent even if you are paying for groceries. No one asked you to do that."

He shook his head, wearily it seemed. Then he looked at her, a smile spreading across his face. "As long as you keep letting me eat here…" His voice trailed away, and he got up and left the room without speaking further.

Sarah's Uncle Levi had started attending most Wednesday night suppers, and afterwards he, Azzo, and Benjamin left for the rose garden. They always invited her, but she never stayed long after Levi unleashed his cigar. Ben usually left at that time, too, diplomatically referring to his homework.

After a few weeks, Sarah noticed a pattern developing. Azzo had begun leaving town after the Wednesday night suppers, usually for only a day or two, although there were times it was a week, sometimes more.

He announced his trips just after Levi left, peering around the corner of her office alcove where Sarah always went after leaving the garden. "Oh," Azzo said, speaking casually, "I've got to run down the coast tomorrow." Then he'd name a day he expected to return.

The routine changed a few weeks into the new year. Azzo announced at breakfast one morning that he was leaving again. When Sarah asked, "For how long?" she expected his usual answer, "Oh, probably a day or two."

Azzo said, "I don't know. Sometimes research takes longer than expected." He left later that day.

He did not return for several weeks. There had been no word. She learned of his return after a long day at Galveston Pilots'. There, in its Carriage House garage, was Azzo's Buick.

Walking to Mansion House's side entrance Sarah noted that Azzo's car was astonishingly dirty. She wrinkled her nose against the smell of cow manure. Dead bugs coated the front grill and were caked over the headlight lens. The windshield was smeared where the wipers had been used in an ineffective attempt to clear away dead bugs. "Where on earth has he been?" she thought. Were there no paved highways in towns near Corpus Christi?

She thought she'd ask him about it at supper, but when Azzo entered the kitchen unannounced, freshly showered and shaved, she forgot her questions in the midst of her annoyance. She was standing in the middle of the kitchen, a casserole dish in her hands. He bypassed her on his way to the table, saying, "Oh, hello."

He was wearing his usual khakis, clean and crisply ironed, and she smelled soap and after-shave. Ben jumped from his chair and hugged Azzo before he could sit.

"Welcome home, stranger!" Ben shouted. "Glad to be back," Azzo said, and sat in his usual seat.

Sarah moved to the table, put the casserole down rather hard, and, still standing, picked up a plate and filled it. Azzo looked at her as she sat and put the plate in front of him,

"I was afraid I'd be late for supper," he said. "I was getting my car washed."

Sarah didn't answer but reached for Ben's plate and filled it. "Chicken casserole," she said, looking at Azzo, her lips pursed. "It's one of Rae's specialties."

"Smells good," Azzo said, stirring his tea. The telephone rang. Ben leaped up from the table and ran to the office.

"That was Uncle Levi," Ben said, returning to the kitchen. "He said to tell you he couldn't make it for supper tonight. You should come to his office tomorrow."

"Great!" Azzo said with mock enthusiasm. "I'll get to enjoy his cigar smoke in a closed room!" He wrinkled his nose as Ben grinned. Sarah began filling her own plate as Azzo leaned toward Ben and whispered, conspiratorially, "Your mom is ticked off at me."

"Not at all," Sarah said, smiling as ice water dripped from her words. "I'm just glad to see you. I didn't know you'd be gone for so long."

"I didn't either," Azzo said. "I guess I should have telephoned."

"Nonsense," Sarah said, a tight smile on her face. "Save some room for dessert. Rae made apple pie and I bought ice cream. Do you like vanilla?'

Rae left, carrying a tray for her supper and Wallace's. Sarah and Azzo ate in an awkward silence, as did Ben, his worried eyes darting between the two. Ben left the table after only one helping of dessert, mumbling something about homework. Azzo rose and began clearing the table. When he started washing the supper dishes, Sarah interrupted.

"Rae can do that in the morning,"

"No, let's do it tonight. You dry."

Sarah picked up a dishtowel as she said, "I've got some things for Pilots' that I need to do."

"They can wait," Azzo said calmly. Sarah felt her annoyance increasing.

They finished the dishwashing in silence. As Sarah was putting away the last of the dishes, Azzo wiped the red checkered oilcloth covered tabletop, then the white-and-black tiled countertop. He rinsed the dishtowel, wrung it out and hung it on the rack to one side of the sink.

"Want to go for a ride?" he said, eyebrows raised as he pushed his wayward forelock back in place. "We evidently need to talk."

"Yes, we…" Sarah didn't finish. Azzo had already turned and walked to the living room. Benjamin was sitting on the couch, swing music playing softly on the radio, a schoolbook on his lap. "Your mom and I are going out for a while, buddy. You need anything before we go?"

Benjamin looked up. "I'm fine." He winked at Azzo.

The seven-minute ride to West Beach was in silence, broken only by the hum of the engine and the whisper of tires on asphalt.

They drove along the sandy beach for perhaps five minutes before Azzo turned the Buick so that its nose pointed seaward. As he set the parking brake, he said, "You might as well let me know how you're feeling. It's been pretty clear all through supper that you're not happy with me."

It was past sunset on a cold and cloudy late February day. A strong southeast wind, racing northwestward toward an approaching frontal system rocked the car while the headlights illuminated the crashing surf, and salt spray dotted the windshield. Azzo kept the engine running and operated the car's heating controls.

"I'm confused," Sarah answered.

"Most of the time," Azzo said calmly, with a hint of his former and annoying 'in-charge' demeanor, "when someone says they're confused, they often mean that they are upset and angry. It almost always means that they disagree with some action or lack of action."

"Well," Sarah said, a sarcastic tone to her voice, "if you want to talk about lack of action…you wine me and dine me in a private suite at the Galvez, tell me that you love me and then we just go around for days and days and don't say anything important to one another. Then, you go away to wherever. Sometimes when you come back, you act—oh, I don't know. I guess the word is timid. You've never been timid around me before! What's going on?"

Azzo said nothing, but he turned his body and looked directly at her. "Then," she went on, "two weeks ago you just up and leave again, this time with little more than a nod, and again you're off to who-knows-where and no word when or if you'd be back. No word, Azzo! No word for nearly two weeks! And all this after you declared that you were in love and I said I might be!"

"My latest itinerary," Azzo said patiently, "was Bay City, Palacios, Port Lavaca, Victoria, and Corpus Christi. I had planned on going no farther than Corpus Christi, but in fact I went farther."

Sarah interrupted. "And those towns don't have paved roads, is that it?"

"What do you mean?" Azzo asked, his eyebrows up.

"Your car!" she answered with an exasperated sound in her voice. "It looked as if you drove it into a swamp! Don't those towns have pavement? And I smelled cow manure. Do they let cows roam their streets?"

"Sarah," Azzo said quietly. "the towns are quite modern. There are construction detours on the Hug-the-Coast highway as well as the highways around Robstown and Kingsville, and those detours can be pretty muddy. Some of the old houses I was looking at were once ranch headquarters and some haven't been occupied in decades. One in particular, while there was a fence around the house itself, is located in a large pasture which was full of cattle waiting transport to auction. The ranch roads often leave quite a lot to be desired. My car got stuck when I left that house, and I had to walk almost five miles to a country store to find help.

"So, you're right about the cow manure. The cattle seemed to congregate around my car, and they pooped when they did."

Sarah sat quietly, not looking at him.

"I spent my time," Azzo continued, "taking photographs, making sketches, sometimes talking with current or past residents, crawling through attics. I even learned," he said, his enthusiasm rising, "about a coastal city, once a port larger than Galveston, at a place called Indianola. It was destroyed by a hurricane many years ago, but…"

Sarah cut him off. "Azzo, you know what I want to talk about!"

"Yes, Sarah, of course I do. I'm playing with you a little."

"Then stop it!"

"Okay," Azzo said, his voice taking on another tone, neutral, as if conducting a business conference. "First off, let's get the quotes straight. I said at the Galvez that day that I *think* I *may* have fallen in love with you." He added, "I amended my statement, if you recall. I said I was pretty sure I had fallen in love with you. Sarah, 'pretty sure' is not one hundred percent sure.

"And," he continued, "you have the quote accurately about what you said. You said you *might* love me."

"So, in effect we both said much the same thing that day at the Galvez."

She answered, "But when you came back from your latest trip this afternoon, I saw your car, but you didn't come down from your studio and say anything."

Azzo shrugged. "Sarah, I was storing and indexing my notes, sketches, and photographs. You could have come up. I saw you. You just stood by your car for a minute, hands on your hips, and then you went inside. I assumed you had business to attend. And, my car was dirty. I took it to Morton's Sinclair and had it washed and vacuumed. Even the floor mats were caked with dried cow manure. I had them washed, too."

He grinned. "I think it smells better now, don't you?"

She ignored the question and said, "Well, when you came in for supper, you just said, 'Oh, hello'. I expected more."

"What?" Azzo said, a grin now spreading across his face. "You wanted me to grab you? Give you a big 'Honey-I'm-Home' kiss? Sorry, I had an audience, Rae and Benjamin. I thought Levi was going to be there too, until he telephoned.

"Sarah," he went on, "Several times when I left it was because something unexpected came up. This last time, while I had business to attend and it took a while, was also because I needed time to think. This last trip came up suddenly but if it hadn't, I would have left anyway."

He paused, stared at the surf for a few seconds, then turned back to her.

"Sarah, all these months, building Mansion House, working with you, knowing that there was something beginning between us, I found that I was also coming to love your son. I've always liked him, from the very beginning, but now my feelings for your son were becoming stronger. Sarah, he's a special person, and I want to be part of his life as he matures. So, I wondered, was my declaration to you at the Galvez made selfishly so that I could be sure of a continuing relationship with a boy who will one day be a fine man? Sarah, I love your son almost as if he were my flesh-and-blood.

"And what about you?" he asked, a sudden change in his tone, almost angry. "You said the same to me. You said you *might* love me." He added, calmly,

"I simply believed we both needed time away from one another. Time to think. That's what I told Benjamin."

"You told Benjamin?"

"Yes, I did. That night before I left for my first trip after the Galvez luncheon, when he and I were at the beach, I asked him how he'd feel if you and I…"

"And?" Sarah said, her eyebrows arched. "Did you get my son's approval?"

"Sarah," Azzo said, not answering her question, but sliding a short way toward her, "Sarah, I now know. And I'm going to ask how you feel." He was staring intently at her.

She averted her eyes and stared out the windshield at the pounding surf. "I need to know," she said, almost angrily, "what is the business you say you have to do, this 'business' that causes you to leave suddenly and without notice."

"Well, Sarah," Azzo said, "when you want to spend several days inspecting some old house, many of which are still being lived in—not deserted—you have to go when those living there say you can."

He stopped speaking, turned away from her and, like Sarah, stared through the windshield. The silence between them became profound, broken only by the sounds of wind and surf.

"Sarah, let's go back to what I just said, a few moments ago," Azzo said again turning to her. "Remember? I said, 'I now know.'" His voice was strong and positive as he repeated, "I now know, and I know for sure!" he said. "Sarah, I love you!" His voice changed as he added, softly, "I hope you could love me."

She turned and looked deeply into the eyes of the man next to her. She saw, from the glow of the dashboard instruments, a pensive, longing look, and a strange expression in his face and eyes. It was almost as if there was a light behind them, the same light she'd seen at the Galvez luncheon.

Sarah did not respond for a long moment. She looked at the man in the car with her, his eyes fixed upon hers. Several times she turned away and stared outward. Finally, she leaned back against the seat cushions and turned toward the man beside her and looked deeply into his dark eyes. and saw once more that the strange expression had returned, and the light was again behind his eyes. She spoke, her voice soft.

"Azzo you're right. I hadn't thought of it before, but I agree that we both needed time to think." There was another long pause as they stared into one another's eyes.

Then she smiled and her expression softened. "Yes, my dear Azzo. I needed time. You needed time."

The silence between them became profound. His eyes never left hers as the wind howled and the car rocked. There was the sound of distant thunder from the northwest, behind the car. The approaching storm system was near.

"I too have come to a decision point," Sarah spoke, breaking the silence between them. "Just now. Just this very minute."

He leaned toward her. The strange look in his eyes seemed to intensify. Sarah suddenly wanted to be sure she would always remember this moment, the two of them, parked on the beach beyond the end of the seawall, the strange light in the eyes of the man in the car with her, the wind shaking the car.

She leaned toward him. "Azzo," she said, softly, "I do love you." Then, she straightened, and in her Manager-of-Galveston-Pilots' voice added, "Don't ever again do this!"

"Ah, do what?" he asked, his eyes wide, eyebrows raised, a half-grin on his face. "Tell you I love you? Leave on trips? Take time to think about our future?"

"Oh!" she cried. "Never mind!"

She reached for him as they moved together, feeling the warmth of his body. As he put his arms around her she noted as if for the first time the black hairs on his hard-muscled forearm. One hand rested just above her breasts. She moved it and he cupped his hand as they kissed, his tongue probed questioningly and she opened her mouth in invitation, but the probing tongue pulled back.

"Azzo," she said, pulling away from him, needing to say more, "sometimes you seem so distant. Other times, like now, you seem to be holding yourself back. Azzo..." she paused. She flung her arms around him and they again kissed.

As before, his tongue probed and this time she opened fully, and he accepted the invitation. His warm breath flowed across her face as his hand moved against her breast.

He pulled his mouth away before she wanted. "Oh," she said, longing for more. He turned slightly, switched off the engine and moved the floor-mounted shift lever to the reverse position, giving her room to move closer and she accepted the invitation. His left hand reached under her blouse and, one-handed, unclasped her bra.

Her eyes opened wide as he did. "How did he do that?" she wondered.

They remained together for long minutes, his hand now massaging softly as her nipples hardened. Sarah moaned as he opened her blouse and his lips and tongue found her breasts.

There was a metallic tap on the rear of the car. A face peered into the steamed glass.

Sarah squeaked a short scream and pulled away. Azzo rolled the window down. A soldier bent down and looked into the car. "Sir, the beach has been closed since eight o'clock!"

The young man suddenly straightened. "Oh, Mr. Burkhardt!" he exclaimed, embarrassed. "It's you. I didn't recognize the car. But, ah…" The young man paused and averted his eyes as he saw Sarah straightening her clothes, frantically buttoning her blouse.

"I didn't mean, ah…"

"Never mind, Larry," Azzo said. "It's okay. I didn't think the beach was closed until eleven."

"No, not tonight," the soldier stammered, still embarrassed. "I'm not supposed to say, but our C.O. said that radio signals have been picked up which indicate there might be a landing tonight. Saboteurs or something."

"Sorry," Azzo said, depressing the clutch pedal and placing his right foot on the starter. "We'll leave right away."

As they drove away, the car climbing the paved ramp to Seawall Boulevard, Sarah said, "Oh, he frightened me so! His face! Staring through the fogged window!

"Will he report us?"

Azzo laughed. "No, Sarah. He knows both me and Benjamin. He's seen us surf fishing and running often."

Azzo turned the car onto 61st and was silent, thinking not of Sarah but of a conversation he'd had with Levi Weismann before leaving on his most recent trip.

"When I return, sir," he'd said to the elderly banker, "I'm planning to ask Sarah to marry me."

"I'm not surprised," Levi had replied, lighting yet another cigar. "You've certainly taken your time. I'd hoped you'd get around to it much sooner although I've always been concerned about our business. Sarah can never know about it."

"I think I can keep her out of it, although at times it'll be hard. She's never questioned that I go along the Texas coast for research." Azzo shrugged. "I actually do a little, you know, just to keep my hand in. I'll finish that book one of these days if you and I are not caught beforehand and forced to spend the rest of our lives in Leavenworth."

Levi smiled. "I don't think it'll come to that. I have a crack team of lawyers in both New York and Washington working to ensure that we both remain out of jail. Our tracks are pretty well covered."

"Aren't our attorneys at risk, too?"

"No. There's something called attorney-client privilege. We can tell them anything. If we're caught, it'll almost have to be red-handed. And suppose some smart Federal agent figures it all out, so what? Our clients won't know our names or the names of all on this side of the Atlantic who've helped them. You've given a different false name to each, as do others who've helped them cross the ocean. I'm the only one who knows all the links, all the complexities of our operation. And if they catch me, I'll suddenly go *altar cocker,* an old Jew who wets his pants and drools and can't remember shit."

Azzo grinned in spite of himself.

Levi changed his demeanor. "You have *tefilah* from me, my blessings concerning you and Sarah, but one more word of caution, my friend."

At Azzo's raised eyebrows Levi said, "You will be lying to your wife every day of your lives together until this is all over, which may be years from now. I suggest you talk to Rabbi Cohen. Marriage is difficult under the best of circumstances. It may be more than difficult for you to have a marriage based on lies."

"It isn't a lie that I love her," Azzo said defensively. "And Ben, too!

"You've told me before," Azzo went on, "that the rabbi knows everything. So, yes, I did talk with him. He's concerned, of course. He agrees with you that Sarah can know nothing.

"It'll all come out one day, of course. I'm hoping that when it does, with the help of you and Cohen, that Sarah will understand and forgive."

"How about Ben?" the old banker asked. "He may feel betrayed."

"Yes, Ben might," Azzo replied. "But I don't know any way around it. If he ever feels that way, I hope that he can find a way to forgive me."

Azzo's mind returned to the present cold and windy night. Rain began, and he switched on the wipers. He had only driven a few blocks along 61st, but it seemed he'd been somewhere other than in his car. His thoughts of Levi diminished as he turned the Buick into Mansion House driveway and stopped the car at the side entrance.

He and Sarah had not spoken since they'd left the beach. "May I come in for a few minutes?" he asked.

"Of course. Want a cup of coffee?"

"No, I don't. Sarah, I have something to say to both you and Benjamin. Do you think he'll be asleep?"

"Maybe. I don't know. Sometimes he reads late." They exited the car, Sarah holding her coat over her hair as the rain poured, and they hastened to the side door accompanied by low rumbles of thunder.

They hurried down the main hallway of the complex, brushing rain off their clothing, Azzo shaking droplets off his hat. He whispered, "If Ben's asleep, don't wake him. But if he's awake, call him into your living room."

Benjamin was not in bed. As Sarah opened the door they found him reading on the living room couch, a crocheted throw across his lap. Ben put his book down as they entered and switched off the radio.

"What're you reading?" Azzo asked as he and Sarah removed their coats. "A schoolbook?"

"No. I found this in the Rosenberg library. It's a book about a boy who runs away with a circus. His name is Toby Tyler. He has a monkey named Mr. Stubbs."

"I've read that," Azzo said.

"When you were a boy?" Benjamin questioned.

"No," Azzo said, laughing, turning from the coat rack beside the door, "I came across it in a public library long after I'd come to the United States, and sat, one afternoon, reading. I had other things to do, but I got interested, and I just ignored my other work." He sat beside Ben and looked at the book. "This is a recent edition," Azzo said, handing the book back to the boy.

Sarah entered, carrying a tray with two cups of coffee. "I asked earlier and you said no, but it seemed to me, all this rain and cold, that coffee would hit the spot," she said to Azzo, "so I just assumed…" She poured cream into her cup and looked at Azzo, a question in her eyes.

He nodded his head as she sat in her rocker. "I see you've brought in cookies as well. For Benjamin?"

"And you if you want."

Azzo rose from the couch, picked up his cup and took a sip, returned it to the tray, smiled and turned to Sarah's eleven-year-old son. "Benjamin, I've come in with your mom to talk to her. I've something serious to say."

"You want me to leave the room?" Benjamin was grinning. Sarah noticed once again the annoying man-to-man look. She picked up her cup from the tray and sat, feeling irritated and, oddly, alone.

"No, Ben," Azzo said, " I don't want you to leave. You're pretty grown up. I want you to hear what I have to say."

He turned to Sarah, his eyes luminous. The light she'd seen before was there, but this time there was more. "Benjamin," Azzo said, still looking at Sarah, "I've told your mother that I love her. Not the way you love her. I love your mother a different way. I love her the way a man who wants to marry her loves her."

"You're gonna get married?" Benjamin said, an incredulous half-grin on his face.

"Maybe," Azzo said, "if she'll have me. I haven't asked her yet. I talked to you some on the beach weeks ago, you remember?" Benjamin nodded as a serious expression settled onto his face. Azzo knelt on one knee before Sarah. "Benjamin Jacobs," he said, still looking at the boy, "would it be all right with you if I asked your mother to marry me?" Azzo's eyes turned to Sarah.

"You bet!" Benjamin' almost shouted as his face split into a broad grin.

"Not so fast, Ben," Azzo said, his eyes still on Sarah. "Let me tell your mother and you a few things, and then I'll ask."

He remained on one knee in front of Sarah's rocker, and she put her cup down and leaned toward him, thinking he looked silly. "My dear Sarah," Azzo began, reaching for her hands, "we've talked. You know I'm almost ten years older than you. I've never married. I have never met any other woman whom I feel as strongly about as I do you. Sarah, I want to share my life with you." He paused.

"Marriage, Sarah, would be a new experience for me. I might be too selfish. I would hope not, but I can't guarantee."

Sarah's eyes glistened as she forgot her earlier thought that he looked silly on one knee. "Azzo, I've told you how I feel, but..."

He continued holding both her hands in both of his. "But you want to wait a while?"

"No, you silly! I want to marry you right now!" She reached toward the man before her. He released one of her hands and held his hand to her chest.

Azzo looked back at Benjamin, one eyebrow raised, a half-smile on his face. "Benjamin, man-to-man, it looks as if I don't have a choice. What do you think?"

Benjamin, showing maturity beyond his years, said, "Man-to-man, you better take her up on it!"

Azzo laughed and turned back to Sarah.

"Sarah," Azzo said, emotion now evident in his voice as well as his eyes, his laughter gone. "Will you marry me?" His hand left her chest, and he opened it before her. Inside, a small opened box rested in his palm. A diamond glittered.

Sarah slid off the rocker and onto her own knees, ruining her stockings. She threw both arms around Azzo. The box fell to the floor as his arms went around her and she kissed him. They remained together for long moments as Ben danced an awkward jig around them, favoring his crippled leg, which spasmed and caused him to fall against them. As all three scrambled upright, Benjamin, laughing, picked up the box.

"Wow! Mom! Get a look at this rock!"

Sarah turned and took the box from Ben.

"Azzo!" she exclaimed. "This is beautiful! More than beautiful. It's gorgeous!"

"The stone is not large," Azzo said, "but it is flawless. I think you'll find the workmanship more perfect than any available today. I had it resized in Corpus Christi," he added as he slid the ring on her third finger.

Benjamin looked up at the ceiling and shouted, "Hooray! I'm gonna have a Dad!"

As Azzo pulled her onto a chair, Sarah was studying the ring. "Where did you find a ring like this?" she asked.

"It's from the last century, Sarah," Azzo said. "Your uncle gave it to me. He had it made when he was a young man and about to be married."

"So, this ring belonged to great-aunt..?"

"Yes," Azzo interrupted. "When I told Levi my intentions he said it would give him the greatest pleasure if I would accept that ring for you and me to seal our promises, one to another."

Sarah burst into tears, her arms around Azzo.

Ben stood and said, "You two need some time alone. I'm going to bed." At the door, he stopped as Azzo said, "Wait."

Azzo left Sarah in her chair, stood and turned to Benjamin, taking the young man's hand.

As they shook hands, Benjamin Weismann Jacobs, standing straight and tall, looked into the eyes of the man he loved, and said, "Azzo, thanks for including me."

He looked at his mom, still in the rocker, and said, a wide grin on his face, "It's okay if you two go to the couch now. My room is two doors down. I won't hear a thing!"

"Ben!" Sarah shrieked, embarrassed, as Ben shut the door behind him and moved down the hall toward his room, laughing.

Chapter 12

Making Love

A smiling Azzo bent to Sarah, gently taking her hand and lifting her from the rocker. They stood together as his lips sought hers, and she felt once again the strength in his chest muscles as his arms wrapped about her. He broke the embrace and guided her to the couch.

Sarah felt her embarrassment diminishing as they embraced, kissing deeply as she and this strong, gentle and sometimes shy man tasted, touched, and felt one another, leaning into the other's body. Sarah succumbed to her emotions, held in check since Glenn's death, and her hands explored this man who had elected to love her. Azzo was surprised at her aggressiveness but gave in to the pleasure. Her hands moved to his belt and began working to loosen it.

Azzo pulled her hands away. "Not tonight, my dear. We have a lifetime ahead, but I want us to be truly married before we take one another." He sat up, pulling her with him.

As he did, Sarah whispered, "Azzo, it's 1940, not 1840. These are modern times. We don't have to wait. Ben can't hear."

Azzo pulled away and in a whisper said, "Sarah, I have to wait." He sat straighter and pulled her head to his shoulder. "And it has nothing to do with Ben."

She had a sudden thought and raised her head. "You said you'd never married. Does that mean you've never been with a woman?"

"No, of course not," he smiled as he bent again to her, kissing as he fondled her breasts.

"Have you ever thought of becoming married?" she asked.

He sat up, his left arm about her shoulder. They leaned back onto the couch cushions. "Yes," he said. "It was long ago. I met her in New York. She was not Jewish, but I was young. I felt that our not being the same faith wouldn't matter. I asked her to marry.

"But she had other plans. We drifted apart. We never spoke of marriage again, and after a while, she began seeing other men."

"Were you hurt badly?" Sarah asked.

He shrugged. "It was a long time ago."

"Were there others?" she asked.

He shook his head. "Let me say this: other than the woman in New York, I've never asked another to marry me. Sarah, I know now that I didn't truly love her. I was young. I confused sex with love.

"This time, though, it's different. Sarah," he murmured, his voice husky, "I've never before been with a woman for whom I cared enough to wait until God seals our union before we come completely together."

"Oh!" she breathed, wondering about this complicated man. "What," she thought, "am I getting myself into?"

Azzo pulled her to him and placed her head on his shoulder, his arm around her, his left hand on her breast. "Please, Sarah, understand that I love you." He kissed her neck and in a low voice said, "All these months we've worked together, rebuilding this old house, getting to know one another, I've wanted you and I want you now. But as I began to understand your ordeals with Benjamin, his polio, your courage and his grit, your grit—Sarah, that's a word I've used before with you. I like Galveston because its people show grit. You and Benjamin share the grit of other Galvestonians. I felt I needed to be careful, to be sure of my feelings and to be watchful for yours."

He dropped his arms and she buttoned her blouse.

"And," he went "as time went by I saw that perhaps you could love me. Perhaps we could have a life together. And, as you know I've talked to your Uncle Levi.

"No," she said. "I didn't know until tonight and you told me about the ring. When did this happen?" Sarah asked as she nuzzled into his shoulder.

"Some time ago," he answered. "It was really several conversations, over a period of months. The first time I mentioned my interest in you as a life partner was several months before our luncheon at the Galvez."

She pulled away, looking at him in surprise. "Azzo! For months now you've been pussy footing around? I can't believe it!"

"Well," Azzo said, "I wanted to take my time. And as I told you, until Mansion House was finished I was your employee. It wouldn't have been proper."

"Proper!" There was irritation and impatience in Sarah's voice. Azzo again pulled her to his shoulder.

"Then we had the closing," he said, "and I took you to the Galvez and made my declaration. Sarah, that scared me. It was a big step. I'm so much older than you."

Sarah leaned into him, dropping her cheek to his chest, her irritation fading as she thought about the dark mat of chest hairs just under the cloth of the shirt, and longing to run her fingers through them.

"Anyway," Azzo continued, almost lightly, "after that lunch, I had to go away. Several times, in fact. I had to be sure, not only sure that I loved you, but sure that I didn't love Benjamin more. I do love Benjamin very much as you know, and I needed to be sure that my love for you wasn't selfish, that it was only because I want, so much, to be part of Benjamin's future. Perhaps I should have said something to you. I'm sorry now that I didn't. It was unfair to you. But I couldn't help myself. I had to go away.

"And then, my dear," Azzo said, smiling, his voice becoming strong, "we found ourselves parked on the beach in a compromising position."

Sarah grinned. "And the soldier tapped on the window, thereby saving my honor." She looked into his eyes. He was smiling.

"Yes. And, Sarah, now I just want to talk. There'll be plenty of times, later, when we can do all the other things that we both want to do."

They leaned back onto the couch, each holding the other close, talking in murmurs, touching.

There were many things they talked about that night as the storm continued unabated and rain lashed the windowpanes. They quietly told things about their lives, families, and loves, things that lovers tell one another. When the grandfather clock in the hall chimed an hour past midnight, Azzo escorted Sarah to her bedroom next to the kitchen, kissed her at the door, and dashed through the rain for his studio apartment in Carriage House Annex.

The next morning the storm was gone; the frontal system had passed. Sarah woke late and saw a sunny sky outside her window. When she came into the kitchen, tying the sash on her robe, she found Rae waiting.

"Been wonderin', ma'am," Rae said.

"Wondering what, Rae?"

"When's you gonna be gittin' up. Mist Benjamin, he up a long time ago, already off to school."

Sarah looked up as Rae filled her coffee cup. "And Mr. Burkhardt? Have you seen him"?

"Yas'm" Rae answered.

"You have? What was he doing?'

"He tol' me to let him know when you gittin' up."

"When was this?"

"'Bout seven."

Sarah looked at the wall clock over the refrigerator. It showed 8:30.

"Are you going to tell him I'm up?"

"Noam, ah already did. I heard you when you started your shower. He tol' me to tell you he'd come and fix your breakfast."

Just then, the door opened. Azzo walked in, fully dressed in his usual khakis. "How about eggs and toast?" he said.

She sat as he refilled her coffee, then watched as he moved about, breaking eggs into a bowl and grating cheese. "How about an omelet?" he asked. Rae left, heading for the laundry room and the upstairs apartment she was to clean this day.

"I thought you might go to the beach for your run," Sarah said.

He nodded as he placed two slices of bread in the toaster. "I did," he said, almost casually.

"And you're already back?"

"I left early."

"Will you take me with you when you go running?"

"Do you mean next time or always?" he asked, placing a plate with a beautiful omelet and two slices of fresh-buttered toast.

"I always want to be with you."

"I can't promise to always be with you, running or otherwise," he said, sitting across the table from her. "When I'm running, sometimes I want to run alone. Sorry. That's just me. I often get my thinking done when I run, and I don't want to give that up. And I'm not going to give up my research, my writing." Sarah thought there was a flicker of an eyelid as he said this last, a moment's hesitancy. Then, she forgot it as he went on. "So, I'll still be away for that. And, no, I don't think you should take time off from your job and come with me. If you're worried that I'll be off meeting other women you can put that idea to rest my dear. That's not me. If you want me, as you say you do, then, Sarah, you've got me. Just me. I will always be true to you."

"It never occurred to me that you'd be off…" She paused, a hint of irritation in her voice as she realized he'd just confirmed that he knew what she had been thinking.

"Nevertheless, I thought it needed to be said." He rose from his chair, pulled her from the table and moved to kiss her. She pulled away.

"Oh, you're mussing my hair, and I taste like coffee and eggs. At least let me brush my teeth!"

"Nonsense. If you do that, you'll taste all toothpasty. I like coffee and eggs better. Come here!" He crushed her to his chest. His tongue probed and she opened to him. Again, she felt the strong muscles of his chest and arms. His thighs pressed against hers.

"Now," he said, releasing her, "when breakfast is over, let's go down and apply for a marriage license."

"Just like that?" Sarah said, surprised. "Azzo, I've got to go to the office. You've ruined my makeup. I've got to redo it."

"The office can wait. Go fix your makeup. I'll bring the car around to the side door."

As Sarah did a quick face repair she had a sudden thought. The Azzo who was always in charge was back. Did she like it? Or, she thought, did she want the man who was hesitant, unsure of himself and of her?

She decided quickly as she looked at herself in the mirror. "I want this man," she murmured. "There may be some battles ahead, but that's okay. This man is mine, and I want him!"

They were married five days later by Rabbi Cohen, with Benjamin, Uncle Levi, Rae, and Wallace in attendance, along with the Rabbi's wife.

The honeymoon was one night on an upper floor of the Galvez, in a two-room suite.

Chapter 13

Eighteen Months Later
Late September 1941

Azzo and Sarah were sitting in the station wagon parked once again on the broad sandy beach at San Luis Pass. The nose of the car was pointed toward the setting sun, away from the Gulf. They could hear the sound of light surf pounding the beach far behind them. Azzo, in his cut-off dungarees, sweaty and shirtless, was in the passenger seat, a dry towel across his shoulders, another spread on the rich leather underneath.

He, Sarah, and Benjamin had run together, arms locked, running as a team, Ben's left leg connected to Azzo's right with the webbing straps. The leather brace had been left in the back of the station wagon, as was often done as Benjamin continued to improve.

Benjamin was taking another run alone, unaided. Azzo and Sarah had seen him fall a number of times, only to get up, motion that all was well, and continue his somewhat awkward run. They knew it was hard for him to keep the left foot from dragging. He raised his left knee as he ran in an attempt to minimize the foot-drop.

The warmth of the day was fading. When they'd first parked, Azzo opened the station wagon's rear window, allowing the onshore breeze to flow through the car. But as the sun set into the coastal prairies across Galveston Bay, the day cooled, and he closed the window. Sarah was glad her dungarees were full length and not the very short cut-off slacks Azzo preferred. She pulled Glenn's old pea-jacket about her shoulders.

She remembered the first day she and Azzo had run together. He'd objected to her slacks that day, an old pair, and had pulled a filet knife from a cabinet in the rear of his old jalopy fishing car. She'd shrieked as he deftly removed the legs, making the garment much too short for, she said, decent women. When she said this, Azzo kissed her and said he liked women in short shorts and laughed at her reaction.

Gulls turned and wheeled in a late evening sky dotted with puffs of cloud, highlighted with color from the sunset. Pelicans cruised across the calm bay waters, occasionally diving headlong and sometimes emerging with a struggling fish in the expandable pouch beneath their beaks.

"I'm really proud of Ben," Azzo said, watching the boy as he fell again.

"Yes," Sarah said. "Me, too. I never thought we'd see the day when he could run as well as he is running now."

"He's getting better each time we come," Azzo said. "You can be proud of Ben's progress. You know he's told me over and over about all the massages, the nights when he couldn't sleep, and you were beside him, working those muscles. All that is finally paying off."

"Azzo, dear, you've played a big role in Ben's recovery. All those trips to the beach, the webbing straps that we used today, you and Ben falling, together, then getting up again, wrestling in the sand, playing like children."

Azzo chuckled as he remembered one special run. He, Sarah, and Benjamin had come to the beach that day, crowded together in the fishing jalopy's only seat. Like this day, it was an early fall day, almost a year ago, cool but not yet cold. All three had run, Ben and Azzo in their cut-off dungarees, Sarah in her short, short rayon cut-offs that Azzo preferred. Ben ran that day with his right foot bare, but they'd brought along on this day his old leather brace, which Ben claimed he didn't need and was awkward.

This time Azzo and Ben were running at the water's edge while Sarah rested in the car. Remnants of the crashing surf swirled around their ankles, water splashing, wetting them. Their arms were locked, Azzo's strong right with Benjamin's left. They'd left off both the webbing straps and at Ben's insistence, the leather brace.

Early into the run, Azzo could feel Ben beginning to falter and knew the left leg was weakening. He let go and Ben tumbled head-long into a wave remnant, two inches of salty sandy water.

Ben looked up, surprised and laughing, shaking saltwater from his eyes and hair. "You did that on purpose!"

"Not me!" Azzo sang in mock surprise as he bent over, laughing, and offered his hand to Benjamin.

Ben grabbed Azzo's hand, locked his right ankle around Azzo's left, and pulled just as the remnant of another wave rushed to them. This time it was Azzo who splashed headfirst into saltwater.

Sarah watched in amazement as the two, laughing and shouting, wrestled in the wet sand, wave remnants continually swirling about. When they finally returned to the car, thoroughly wet and covered in sand, Ben limping rather badly, Azzo said,

"Sarah, we're gonna wash off in the surf. Bring us as many towels as you can find."

"Wait!" she shouted. "The water's cold!"

Both her boys, turned, laughing. "Nah! It's not cold! The water's warmer than the air! Come on in yourself!" Azzo and Ben, their arms locked, ran headlong into the surf.

She shook her head, grinning, standing at the edge of the water, a towel about her shoulders, holding other towels, pulling at her too-short shorts, watching her husband and son play in the water as children, splashing one another, laughing.

"Yeah," Azzo said, both their minds returning to the present, "that day was fun. It was a good day. There have been others, Ben and I—and you, too, Sarah, we've had fun.

"All of us, you and me, Ben, his therapists, the coach at Ball High, well, we're all just helping, but only a little. The exercise he's getting helps his muscles to develop as his nerves recover. I want to believe that Ben's going to beat polio."

"Azzo, I've never seen Benjamin as happy as when he is at the beach with you."

"Yes, he always shouts, 'Run with the wind!' as he did today. He sometimes shouts, '*Ich braude enin partner!*'"

"What on earth does that mean?"

Azzo laughed. "It's German. I taught him to say it. It means, 'I need a partner!'

"Sarah," Azzo continued, "I love being here with him. And with you. We don't get to do this as often as I'd like."

"Well, your research," Sarah said. "It keeps you away. More than either of us, I might say, me or Benjamin, would like."

"Sarah," Azzo said, as a serious expression crossed his face, "I need to change the subject. I have to tell you about something I learned in my last trip to New York."

"That was over a week ago," Sarah said as a feeling of dread passed over her. "Is this bad news? And if it is," she added as a slight frown crossed her features, "why have you waited so long to tell me?"

Azzo did not answer. Sarah waited. It seemed to her that he was trying to collect his thoughts.

When he finally spoke, his voice was calm. The cadence of his speech was slow and deliberate.

"I've told you before about my parents and sister."

"Yes. Scientists, working for the German government."

"Jewish scientists. They are for the most part prisoners, forced by the Germans to work in a secret laboratory, in a place named Peenemunde, building rockets and jet airplanes."

"Yes," Sarah said. "You've told me about this."

"Now I need to tell you more. You remember I told you about my friend in the New York German Consulate." Sarah had never seen his face in such an expression of concern. She waited silently for him to say more.

In the distance, they saw Ben fall. The thirteen-year-old regained his feet, waved that he was all right, brushed the sand off, and resumed his run.

"Look at him, Sarah," Azzo said, ignoring his last remark, nodding toward Ben. "His muscles are filling out. His shoulders are widening. Sarah, he's going to be okay."

He put his arm about her shoulders as she leaned into him. "Azzo," Sarah said, "what did your friend tell you?"

Instead of answering, Azzo opened the car door, climbed out and moved to the front of the car. He leaned against the front fender. Sarah joined him as he stood, looking first across the bay at the sunset, then back to the distant green-blue Gulf, white foamy wave tops rolling toward the beach.

She waited, shivering under the pea-jacket, wondering why it was so hard for him to continue.

Azzo turned to her and said, "They've escaped!"

"Your parents?"

"And my sister. My friend met me in Central Park at lunchtime. We had our usual hot dogs and sat on a park bench. He told me that several men—German soldiers—were killed the night my family disappeared."

Sarah felt a chill run up her spine. "Where are they now?"

"No one knows. It's driving me crazy. When my friend told me my first thought was that they'd been caught and executed, and I asked him about that. He said it was unlikely. If they'd been caught, the Germans wouldn't have kept it secret. They would have been very publicly executed.

"He said the German government has instituted possibly the largest search in European history. Every traveler on every train or bus throughout not only Germany but the occupied countries as well must show identity papers, and even then are often interrogated, especially if they're elderly. My parents would stand out. My father is seventy-four, overweight and has a heart condition. He uses a cane. My mother is frail, thin and grey-haired. Both have medicines they must carry with them at all times.

Azzo paused, then said "Someone had to have helped them, but I don't know who that could have been or why. I'm almost sick with worry."

"But…" Sarah was at a loss.

"Anyway," Azzo continued, "what you need to know about this is that once the Germans become convinced my parents and sister have left Europe, they'll assume that they and whomever is helping them will head here, to me, in Galveston."

"Will they head here?" Sarah questioned. "How could they? How could they cross the ocean?"

"I have no idea."

Sarah had never seen Azzo in such a state. He leaned against the fender, head down, arms crossed. He looked as if he might cry. She couldn't think of anything to say.

He raised his head. She noticed his eyes were dry. "Maybe they've already made it to Switzerland," he said, his voice brightening. "I know they have good friends in Zurich who would help, who would hide them. Of course, the Germans also know about their friends and a little thing like Swiss sovereignty wouldn't deter the Gestapo. They'd be in constant danger."

He turned to Sarah, the stress he was experiencing clear in his eyes. "In any event, there's a strong potential that we're going to be watched by German agents, and that's my primary message to you."

Sarah felt a start of fear. "Should we tell Benjamin?"

"Let's don't tell him yet," Azzo answered. "I'll know if they start watching us. We can tell Ben then."

"Oh, my god!" Sarah exclaimed. "How will you know if we're being watched?"

"I'll spot them. I've been watched before, so I know what to look for. At first they'll be at a distance, possibly disguised as tourists, or maybe just as ordinary businessman. When and if I see them, I'll let you know."

"Will they hurt us? Will they hurt Ben? Should we send Ben away? To a school? I have a friend who sends her son to a prep school in North Carolina."

"They won't hurt Ben or you. They might try and take me somewhere to see if I know anything, but I don't know more than I'm telling you. We need to simply continue going about our business and be watchful of what we say and to whom we say it."

"We ought to go to the police!"

"No!" Azzo said, sharply. "The Galveston police aren't trained in anti-espionage. We might think about telling Commander Carruthers and through him the FBI, or maybe Army Intelligence. That FBI man McCuskey came by your office a few days ago, didn't he? What did he tell you at that time?"

"I told you before," Sarah answered.

"Tell me again," He grinned his wry grin. "I didn't really listen before."

The day had been so happy for Sarah, exercising on the beach with the two men in her life, secure and safe from the European war. Now it seemed as if an overcast had blotted the sun, though the sunset was as bright and beautiful as before.

She looked along the beach, eyes searching for her son. As her eyes found Ben, he saw her looking and waved, which caused him to lose his balance. He tumbled headlong into hard-packed sand.

"Oh," Sarah said, blinking and trying to remember Azzo's question while worrying that Ben was hurt. She saw him regain his feet and wave, signaling that he was okay. She turned to Azzo.

"It was a few days ago that I saw him, last Thursday, to be exact. You were out of town. Commander Carruthers came to the Pilots' offices and Agent McCuskey was with him."

"What did they do or say?" Azzo asked, eyes widening.

"Yes. Well, they came to my office and inspected the radio equipment. They said the government was going to give Galveston Pilots' a newer and better radio. They came out to Mansion House, too. They told me the radio you installed should no longer be used for Pilots' business."

"That's interesting."

"Yes. They said they wanted to take it back, and I let them. They said they had paid for it. Did they?"

Azzo nodded. "Yes, while construction was underway I asked the Coast Guard about installing a radio in your office at Mansion House. At the time they agreed and, yes, the government paid for the radio. They also paid for the antenna next to the woodworking shop."

"Azzo," Sarah said, "I'm cold. Can we get back in the car?"

As they settled in Sarah said, turning the crank to close her window, "They said they were planning to station a Coastguardsman in my Pilots' offices. Do you think there's a possibility the FBI and the coast guard know about your parents and that we may be watched?"

"Maybe," Azzo said. "But I think they're just taking ordinary precautions that they'd take during wartime. War is going to be upon us soon, maybe as early as next summer. It's a sure bet that German agents will be in Galveston once war is declared, and Galveston Pilots' will be a target for information about shipping schedules."

He paused, then asked, "Did they talk about security training? For you and your staff, perhaps even the pilots and dock crews?"

"Azzo!" Sarah said, sharply. "They didn't say anything about that. You're beginning to frighten me!"

"I expect some sort of training is being planned, at any rate. Tell you what," Azzo said, "tomorrow I'll go see the Commander. Tell him about my parents. He'll understand my concerns, I'm sure. He'll make sure the personnel he sends are to guard not only you but keep all the personnel at Galveston Pilots' safe."

Benjamin ran up to the car, opened a rear door, and grabbed a towel.

"Best run ever!" he sang out. "I only fell four times!" He spread a second towel across the rear seat. "I'm gonna run to the surf and wash off. Drive over and pick me up. I'll be done in a hot-shot!"

As they watched Ben dash to the surf, Azzo said as Sarah started the car, "Don't say anything to Ben or anyone else about the possibility of agents. Let's wait and see if and when security training is scheduled. That must be why McCuskey is in town."

Ben climbed into the car. "Thanks for coming over. That last run was swell! You could have left me here. I feel as if I could run all the way back to town! Let me out! Let's see if I can!"

Sarah shook her head and laughed. "Not this time, buddy!" Azzo said as she turned the car eastward onto the rutted West Beach Road.

Sarah glanced through the rearview mirror at the sunset, then stopped the car and opened her door, standing and looking back at the serene beauty of San Luis Pass, the bay waters shimmering in the last rays of the sunset.

Sarah wondered silently, "How could the bay be so calm when I'm anything but?"

Chapter 14

Six Weeks Later

Friday-Saturday, December 5-6, 1941

On Thursday of the first week in December a telegram was delivered to Sarah at Galveston Pilots'. It was from her husband, asking her to meet him Friday afternoon at Houston's Municipal Airport. When Ben learned of the telegram, he begged to go. Sarah picked her son up from school before his last class, and they took Azzo's Buick for the ninety-mile round trip.

"Let me drive!" Ben said as he climbed into the car, his books and notebook held under his arm.

"You're too young to drive," Sarah said, shaking her head.

"I'm thirteen," Ben protested. "I can get a hardship license at fourteen."

"Ben," Sarah said sternly, "you can only get a hardship license if I tell the judge you're needed for errands at Mansion House."

"Well, I am needed. I could pick up groceries, not only for us, but for the tenants, too, drive Rae and Wallace to church, go to the post office and pick up Azzo's mail."

Sarah didn't answer. After parking at the airport terminal, Sarah and Ben elected to climb the stairs to the observation deck. Ben wanted to watch for the plane carrying his stepfather.

As they climbed the stairs, Sarah noticed that Ben was not wearing his brace. He had his wrist cane but did not use it. She tried to think. Did he wear a brace to school today? She was unsure of her memory.

They looked down at a group of well-dressed passengers being led to a waiting airliner. Sarah was wearing more casual clothing and was glad they'd elected to come to the observation deck. She would have felt conspicuous in casual clothes, mingling with a crowd of fashionably dressed men and women.

As the passengers climbed the three short steps leading into the airplane, an engine on the wing opposite started with a throaty roar and a spurt of flame, followed by smoke.

Ben was beside himself with excitement. He had missed his stepfather for the past week and was now excitedly watching the plane below and the skies above for an incoming airliner.

"Look, Mom!" he shouted, pointing to the northeastern sky as the second engine on the parked plane caught. A uniformed young woman pulled the small oval-shaped airplane door closed. "That's him! I know it! That's his plane! Let's go downstairs!"

They arrived at the gated area just outside the main terminal as the departing airliner moved away, wind from the propellers of its twin engines blowing about them. Sarah now appreciated her slacks while women nearby held their skirts. Several men lost their hats, and Ben ran them down, limping a little but still not using his cane, and returned them to their owners.

Ben came back to his mother's side and pointed toward the end of the runway. "Look! Look! Oh, wow!" Ben shouted. "It's one of those four-engine jobs! I've heard they carry almost forty people. Imagine, forty!"

They saw the arriving TWA airliner line up with the runway as landing gear unfolded from the fuselage. The plane touched down with a puff of blue smoke and a half-second later they heard a distant screech of tires on pavement.

The giant airliner rolled up to the terminal and turned, engines roaring. Those standing near Sarah and her son were once again buffeted by wind.

"There he is!" Ben shouted as Azzo stepped off the plane. Once through the gate, he bent and kissed Sarah. He reached to shake Ben's hand, but the boy hugged him instead.

"Welcome home, Dad!"

Azzo noticed it was the first time Benjamin had called him "dad." He hugged Ben in return and kissed the boy's cheek.

"Thanks, son!"

As a porter gathered Azzo's luggage, Sarah whispered, "Is there any news of your parents?"

"No," Azzo whispered back. "My friend said he thinks they may have escaped Europe completely, but he's only guessing. The Germans still have patrols combing every highway and rail line throughout Europe. You've said nothing to Ben?"

"No," Sarah said as Ben raced ahead, directing the porter to the car. "We agreed to say nothing, and I haven't said anything."

"It's the dark blue Buick," they heard Ben say to the porter who stopped at the rear of the car and held out his hand for keys.

Azzo shook his head. "The trunk's full of stuff," he said. "Put the bags in the back seat."

Azzo tipped the redcap, then slipped into the passenger seat. Sarah settled under the wheel, pulling keys from her purse.

"What's it like to fly, Dad?" Ben asked, hanging over the rear of the front seat.

"Oh," Azzo answered, surprised. "Well, it's nice and smooth. Fast. Almost two hundred miles an hour. Just this morning, I was in New York. This afternoon, non-stop, well, here I am."

"Wow!" Ben exclaimed. "I want to go with you sometime! Could I?"

"Oh, Ben!" Sarah exclaimed, "It's much too expensive. Besides, you have to stay in school."

"I meant in the summer, when school's out."

"We could do that," Azzo said. "Sarah, we've talked about this before. Maybe we three could take a small vacation, fly to New York, see a play, have a nice dinner. Sarah, you and I could go dancing at Ciro's, maybe, or the Stork Club!"

"Mom!" Ben said. "That'd be great! Can I go with you to Ciro's or the Stork Club? I bet we'd see a movie star!"

"And all that would cost a fortune!" Sarah said.

"Maybe not," Azzo said. "My publisher always pays my air fare and hotel room, so we'd only have to pay for an air ticket for you and one for Ben."

Sarah shook her head. "I've got to run Galveston Pilots' as well as Mansion House. I can't be away. Anyway, airline tickets are much too expensive to even think about and I've heard those Broadway theatres charge as much as ten dollars for a ticket!" Her tone and expression cut off debate.

"Well, take just me someday," Ben said to his stepfather. "I'd love to go up in an airplane. Maybe someday I could be a pilot! Then, I'd fly both of you to New York for free! You can go to the Stork Club!"

Azzo laughed as Sarah grinned. Ben continued chattering "Dad! Didn't you tell me once you had a friend who runs an airfield? Maybe someday soon we could go see him. Maybe he'd take us up. I want to go up in an airplane, see what it's like!"

Before anyone could answer, Ben changed the subject again but continued in his excitement to monopolize the conversation.

"When are we gonna go to the beach? I'm doing better and better! I want to show you! I almost never wear my brace anymore. I brought my wrist cane to the airport today, but I didn't use it. The track coach at Ball High has started working with me a couple of times a week. He says if I keep on improving, when I get into high school I can be on the track team. Can you imagine that? Me! On the track team! I've got to get a lot better though. I'm getting good! I only fell twice at the track yesterday! Well, maybe three times. But I didn't have either brace on! I skinned my elbows. Those cinders are sharp!"

Both adults simply sat, silent and grinning, trying to keep up with Ben's chatter.

The next afternoon was as warm as the day before, and Benjamin begged Azzo for another trip to the beach. Benjamin drove the fishing jalopy under Azzo's watchful eye as they headed for West Beach Road and San Luis Pass. Passing S Road, Ben said, "I heard at school the other day that S is gonna be paved all the way to San Luis Pass."

"I heard that, too," Azzo said. "It'll make getting there a lot faster. And I know the Army patrols will like getting to the Pass faster."

Once they arrived at "their spot" on the Gulf side of Galveston Island, they shucked their shoes and Azzo took the webbing strips out.

"No," Ben said. "We don't need those anymore."

Azzo shook his head. "Humor me, just once more."

"We didn't use them last time, and that was almost two weeks ago."

"You had your old leather brace."

"No, I didn't. Anyway, I'm better now."

Azzo, on one knee, holding the webbing, looked up. Sarah's station wagon was bouncing toward them on the poorly maintained West Beach road. He stood, waiting for Sarah.

"Thought you had a 'ton of things' to do at work today," Azzo said as she exited the car.

"It turned out to be a pretty slow Saturday after all. I thought I'd join you guys for an afternoon run, that is, if you'll have me?"

"You bet, Mom!" Ben sang out. "I need your help reining this guy in. He's gonna make me use that webbing! Next thing you know, he'll be having me back in that old leather brace. And the cane!" Ben's voice was indignant, but then he smiled and sang the refrain from a popular song, *Don't fence me in.*

Sarah laughed. "Oh, Ben, humor him. Old men get stuck in their ways."

"Old!" Azzo cried in mock anger. "Sarah, I'll put this webbing on you! I'll show you old!"

He knelt as before, grinning and mocking Sarah, saying "Oh yes, kind master Ben. Humor this old Jew. Use the webbing just one more time."

Ben, laughing, reached for a webbing strap. "Stand up old man, I'll lash you to me instead of the other way around. I'll show you! You're being an old horse's ass!"

He bent over, fastening the webbing around both his and Azzo's leg.

"Ben!" Sarah said, shocked, "Don't call your stepfather names!"

"Never mind, Sarah," Azzo said, laughing as Ben tightened a strap. "I call him an ass sometimes, too. Especially when he's being one, like now!" He jerked the strap Ben had just tightened, making it even tighter.

"Ow!" Benjamin howled. "He's a slave driver! Okay, slave driver! This is gonna be the last time this slave uses the straps!"

The two locked their arms. "Now!" Azzo shouted. "Watch, Mom!" Ben said.

In unison, they sang out, "To the driftwood!"

Sarah leaned on the fender and watched her two men. Their three-legged gait was smooth and coordinated. Though they were lashed together, there was a freedom in their movements. It was not as if they were lashed, but as if they were running as one man, not two.

At the old driftwood, their normal half-way point, both breathing heavily, Azzo bent down to the straps on their legs and said, "Okay, Ben, I agree. You're your own man now. I won't bring the webbing strips along again. Run with me but run on your own." He nodded his head toward Sarah and the waiting cars. "Back to the car!"

They began, Azzo's right arm locked onto Benjamin's left, but this time they ran as individuals. Then, Ben faltered and thought he was going to fall. Azzo's strong right arm held him up. They ran a few more steps.

Azzo suddenly let go of his partner, and Ben faltered again as his left leg spasmed. He staggered for a few steps, recovered, and, catching up to Azzo, resumed running smoothly, separate from his stepfather, both running with freedom. Ben suddenly remembered the time when Azzo said running was addictive, and as the thought occurred he felt a surge of energy, a lightness in his whole body, and it seemed for that instant of time that he could run forever.

At the cars, both Ben and Azzo breathing heavily, the older man pulled Sarah off the station wagon fender and pointed again to the distant tree trunk prone in the sand. As he did, Ben shouted, "To the driftwood!" and Sarah echoed her son, "To the driftwood!"

This time, as they ran, Azzo and Sarah locked their arms, but Ben ran alone, his stride coordinated with theirs. All three realized this run was special. It was a first. Ben was running on his own, no brace, no webbing, and no strong right arm from his father. It was a realization of a dream. The addictive energy surge returned to Ben, and he felt as if he was effortlessly flying, soaring into the afternoon sky.

The overcast cleared as they ran, and Ben raised his eyes, looking skyward at the blue of the late afternoon sky. He did not fall as he, his mother, and Azzo ran together, a team, on this peaceful but windy Shabbat, on the sandy Gulf shore near San Luis Pass. On the return run to the cars, all three shouted in unison, "Run with the wind!"

And each knew, at that moment, that late afternoon, that Ben's polio was beaten. His left leg might still spasm on occasion, he might sometimes fall, but polio was beaten. His maturing muscles and nerves had taken over. Ben was free. He had won his war. Ben, Sarah, and Azzo, on that run, that late December afternoon, knew in their hearts the day was one of victory, and the victory belonged to Ben.

Later, resting at the cars, drinking water from tin cups, Azzo said, his voice serious, sounding choked, "I've got something I want to ask of both of you."

Sarah raised her eyebrows in surprise. "What?" She looked closely at Azzo. His cheeks, as hers, were streaked with tears.

Azzo handed towels to Sarah and Ben and took one himself. "I not only want to ask," He said. "I need to ask. This is something that's been on my mind for a long time."

He was silent as he wiped himself with the towel, then draped it across his shoulders, almost as if it were a prayer shawl. There was a serious expression on his face, "Sarah, first I want to ask you, then I'll ask Benjamin." She waited, said nothing, hoping for something, though she did not know exactly what she was hoping for.

Azzo took both Sarah's hands in his. "Sarah, would it be all right with you if I adopted Ben?" She felt her heart leap. Yes! Her heart sang.

"Don't answer right now," Azzo said, turning to Ben and reaching for the boy's right hand. "Let me ask Ben."

The thirteen-year old, on the cusp of manhood, so recently victorious, felt a surge of anxiety as he grabbed Azzo's hand with both of his. Azzo responded with his free hand so that they were joined in a four-handed grip. The dark haired, dark-eyed, fair-skinned Ben, tanned from the sun, hoped and wished as he and his stepfather locked eyes.

"Benjamin Jacobs," Azzo said seriously, his voice formal and strong. "I'm already your stepfather, because I'm married to your mother. But I want more. Ben, I love you. I want to be your father. Would you…" He paused. "Would you say yes if I asked to adopt you?" Ben's answer was to let go of Azzo's hands and hug the older man. "Yes!"

he whispered as tears cascaded down his cheeks. "Yes, a thousand times yes!"

Azzo squirmed partially out of the hug and kissed Ben's cheek. His eyes found Sarah's, and she saw a questioning look.

Through tears, she nodded vigorously as she joined the two, and all three stood, holding tight to one another. To Sarah, it felt at that moment as if love was a palpable force, which now surrounded and encapsulated the three standing together on Galveston Island's Gulf shore near San Luis Pass.

Ben turned his head. Through tears, he saw a brown pelican cruising through the clear evening sky above the churning surf. There was a splash, and the bird surfaced, arched its neck, and swallowed.

Ben looked at the deepening blue of the late evening sky. He could see three stars, the signal from God that Shabbat, the 6th of December 1941, was over.

Chapter 15

December 7, 1941

It was 1 o'clock Sunday afternoon at Galveston's prestigious Mansion House apartment complex. Azzo and Ben rose from their lunch, complimented Rae, and announced they were heading to the radio.

"Aaron's coming over, mom," Ben said. "There's a game on. The New York Giants."

Sarah did not care for sports but nevertheless asked, "Who are they playing?"

"The Brooklyn Dodgers."

She frowned as she finished the last of her iced tea. "Baseball? I thought baseball was over. Didn't they have a world series or something?"

"Mom," Ben said in a scornful voice, his mouth turned down. "This is football." He saw no reason to explain further.

"Well," Sarah said, rolling her eyes and mimicking one-half of a popular radio comedian team, "Excuse me!"

"You can join us," Azzo said, patronizingly. "We'll explain it to you as the game goes along."

"Never mind!" Sarah answered. She reminded her two men that she had three tankers coming down-channel today, two from Baytown and one from Texas City. It was going to be a busy day for her. "I need to go to the Pilot's offices, check on arrangements and be sure everything's going well. There are already people at the office. I won't be long."

"We'll miss you," Azzo chuckled as he tuned the console radio.

As she trotted down the hall toward the side entrance, irritated as always at signs of male superiority, she heard, *"This is WOR in New York, bringing you today's game..."* Climbing into her car, she quickly forgot the ball game as her mind began sorting details that needed to be checked to ensure the safe passage of tankers exiting into the Gulf one after another.

Almost a half-hour later, Azzo, Ben, and Aaron were leaning toward the radio, listening intently as the excited voice of a radio sports announcer gave the play-by-play: "*... he's heading toward the 25, now he's been hit hard at about the 27-yard line...*"

The radio went silent. Azzo glanced at the grandfather clock in the hallway through the opened living room door. It was precisely 1:26 PM. Ben's eyes and those of his stepfather widened as the radio crackled into life: "*We interrupt this program to bring you this important bulletin from the United Press! Flash! Washington! The White House announces Japanese attack on Pearl Harbor! Stay tuned to this station for further developments, which will be broadcast immediately as we receive them!*" There was another instant of radio silence, this time with a few crackles of static. The game narration resumed.

Azzo rose from the couch and twisted the radio dial, away from the forgotten sports event, pausing at a CBS affiliate. He and the two wide-eyed boys heard: "*This is CBS in America calling Honolulu. Go ahead Honolulu.*" There was no response other than static.

The voice resumed: "*We would now like to call Manila, the capital of the Philippine Commonwealth. This is CBS in America, calling Manila. Go ahead, Manila.*" Again, several moments of silence.

Azzo turned the dial again as Sarah walked into the room. "As I expected," she announced, "everything's okay..."

Azzo cut her off. "Shh!"

A voice came from the radio speaker: "*At this time each Sunday the National Broadcasting Company presents H. V. Kaltenborn, dean of radio commentators, who will today analyze and interpret the startling news from the Pacific.*"

"What on earth!" Sarah said as the unmistakable voice of Mr. Kaltenborn flooded into the room. She looked at the two boys, wide-eyed, their mouths hanging open. They had evidently not moved from the couch since she left. Azzo turned up the volume as Rae and Wallace came into the room.

"*Good afternoon everybody. Japan has today made war upon the United States...*"

"Oh, God!" Sarah said as the telephone rang. She went into her office alcove, picked up the handset, listened, then turned. "Aaron," she said, "your mother wants you to come home."

The news was bad, and it continued to get worse. At one point during that long afternoon the five people in Sarah's living room heard, "*Hello, NBC. Hello, NBC. This is KTU in Honolulu, Hawaii. I am speaking from the roof of the Advertiser Publishing Company Building. We have witnessed this morning...*" there was an instant of static, then the voice continued, "*...brief full battle of Pearl Harbor and the severe bombing of Pearl Harbor by enemy planes, undoubtedly Japanese...*" static interrupted, "*...it is no joke. It is a real war... the public of Honolulu has been advised to keep in their homes...there has been* *serious fighting going on…"* there was another interruption, accompanied by the sounds of explosions,

Sarah's telephone rang again. Ben picked it up, handed the handset to his mother.

"This is Sarah Burkhardt," she said.

After listening a few minutes, Sarah cradled the receiver. "That was the Coast Guard. I've got to go back downtown. The Galveston-Houston channel is to be closed. The Port of Galveston, along with Port Neches, Freeport, Corpus Christi, and Brownsville are to be closed immediately."

"Ben and I will go with you," Azzo said, then paused, a thoughtful look on his face. "No, I think it'd be better if Ben and I followed you in the Buick. You go on ahead. Ben, run into the kitchen and get my keys. We're likely to need both cars. It's going to be a long day."

He turned to the two servants. "Rae, it'd be a good idea for you to make a bunch of sandwiches. One of us will come back later to pick them up. Wallace, if Rae needs anything, go over to old Mr. Samuelsson's corner store. If he says he's closed, tell him what's going on and that Mrs. Burkhardt asks that he sell us what Rae needs. Tell him put the charges on a tab; we'll pay him later." He paused as a thought occurred. "Wallace, Mr. Samuelsson may not even own a radio. Tell him the Japanese have started a war in the Pacific. I'll come back later and take sandwiches and whatever back to Galveston Pilots.'"

Sarah, putting on her coat, turned. "Rae, I think we're going to need the old coffee urn, you know, the one we used to use when we still had a ballroom. Go to the storage room and get the old urn out, clean it up and Azzo can bring it to Galveston Pilots' when he comes back to pick up the sandwiches. Wallace," she added, "buy all the coffee Mr. Samuelsson has. We're likely to need it."

She turned and trotted down the side-door steps to her car. Azzo and Ben followed in Azzo's Buick, the car's radio bringing in still more news from the Pacific. At Galveston Pilots' they found a young coastguardsman waiting at the front steps. Sarah unlocked the door and ushered the young man inside and followed. Azzo and Ben entered as Sarah moved past the half-wall partition and snapped on the new marine radio.

Ben said, "How about I make start making coffee?" He turned toward the coffee kitchen at the rear of the Pilots' offices.

"Ben," Azzo said, "there are two coffee pots. The larger one is on a shelf in the big closet next to the coffee room. Get that and use both coffee pots until we can get the urn over here."

Sarah frowned slightly as she wondered how Azzo could have known about the larger pot.

"Uhh, ma'am," the coastguardsman said, interrupting her thoughts. "Who are these?" He had followed her behind the half-partition and nodded toward Azzo and Benjamin. "I'm not sure they should be here."

"Well," Sarah snapped, "I'm sure, even if you're not. This is Mr. Burkhardt, my husband, and this is our son Benjamin." Azzo shook hands with the young coastguardsman. Ben stopped on his way to the coffee kitchen, came back and did the same.

"Where's that coastguardsman who's usually here at the Pilots' offices?" Sarah asked abruptly.

"Ma'am," the young seaman said, stuttering just a little. Sarah was already at the radio, flipping switches and twisting a large dial. She looked at the young man with irritation as he said, "H-he's on Christmas leave. I-I've been sent to tell the m-manager of Galveston Pilots' t-that the Port of Galveston is officially closed, as of right now."

"Well," Sarah said, speaking briskly, "I've already talked to Commander Carruthers, and that's what he told me. I'm the assistant manager. George Stein, our manager, is ill. I'm in charge and have been for quite some time."

"Yes, Ma'am," the young man answered. "I-if Commander Carruthers has already talked with you, then I assume that you already know what I'm supposed to s-say."

"And that is..." Sarah said, a question in her voice.

"Ah, t-that there are complications."

"I'll say there are," Sarah said, looking at hand-written notes on the tabletop. She picked up one of the two telephone handsets and began to dial, "I've got three T2 tankers, heading down-channel, and at least two are underway right now. One of them should be nearly here. A third, in Texas City, is preparing to get underway."

"Those two c-coming down-channel will have to turn around r-right away," the young coastguardsman said, his voice cracking. Sarah shook her head, frowning as she thought, "He's just a kid!"

She stopped dialing and looked up at the uniformed youngster before her, a slight frown on her face. "It is not possible to turn those tankers around in mid-channel," she said, hanging up the telephone. "Commander Carruthers knows it and you ought to. The channel is too narrow. If they're where I think they are, they'll have to exit into the Gulf, then turn around and re-enter. They may have to go all the way back to Baytown for anchorage. The ship's owners are going to squall bloody murder. And, besides that, there are two merchant ships currently docked at the Houston Turning Basin which are scheduled to exit the port behind the tankers. We can hope they've not yet left their berths." She again picked up the telephone.

"Are those ships in G-galveston?" the Coastguardsman asked.

Sarah put down the telephone again and looked up at the young man, irritated by the redundant question. "You're pretty green, aren't you?" she said sarcastically, not really expecting a response. The young man ducked his head, embarrassed.

"Son," Sarah said, kindlier, "I just said that the freighters are currently docked in *Houston,* at the *Houston* Turning Basin. If they haven't yet gotten underway, it won't be a problem. But, as you see, I've got some telephoning to do." She again picked up the receiver and resumed dialing.

Once connected to the Coast Guard, she asked for the Commander and quickly explained the situation.

"Mrs. Jacobs," Commander Carruthers began, his voice crackling over the wire. She cut him off. "My name is Burkhardt now."

"Yes, of course," the Commander answered. "Please accept my apologies, Mrs. Burkhardt. It was a slip of the tongue. However, my orders are clear. The tankers have to find anchorage within the bay system. Moreover, those cargo ships that are now in Bolivar Roads will have to be brought into port. There's concern that there might be submarines in the Gulf and if so, they might try to sink one or the other of the cargo ships, block the channel and bottle up the entire Trinity and Galveston Bay systems, possibly for months. We're simply going to have to find anchorage."

"Well," she said, "the very first thing I've got to do is stop those freighters from leaving the Houston Turning Basin."

"No," the Commander said, "I've already called Houston. That's one problem you'll not have."

"Okay," Sarah answered, "I can find temporary anchorage at Galveston Wharves for the cargo ships now in Bolivar Roads. That operation alone is going to take four to six hours. I've got dock crews to mobilize. The cargo ships likely don't have a full crew on board. Those seamen will have to be located.

"Now, about the tankers. Commander, I know you know a loaded tanker's draft is a full thirty-six feet. These vessels use tug assistance all the way down-channel, since they often drag bottom. The channel needs maintenance dredging and is narrow, so the two that are on the way can't simply turn around without exiting into the Gulf. There will be costs involved." She paused while a responding voice crackled from the receiver.

"Yes, I know," Sarah said. "I know we've got a war on our hands—we didn't this morning, but this afternoon we do. Even so, the ship's owners will balk. The Port of Galveston doesn't have funds..."

"I can't tell you what to do," she heard the Coast Guard Commander say tiredly, "Because I don't know myself. Just do what you can, and we'll figure out how to deal with costs later."

Sarah put down the receiver. "I need someone to find Gus Morton for me," she said, naming her most experienced pilot. Then she added three other names while mumbling, not quite under her breath, "The pilot in the lead ship is not quite as experienced as Gus. That old gray-headed bastard better not be in a Bolivar bar!" She brightened and turned to Azzo. "It's Sunday. Don't Christians close bars on Sundays?"

Azzo grinned. "Usually, they do. However, Sarah, everyone knows there's a few of those beach dives that stay open all the time. There's no closing time on Bolivar."

"Twenty-four hours a day?" Sarah said. "Who can drink that much?"

"Ah, Gus Morton?" Azzo grinned. Among all Sarah's other irritations, here was her husband smiling, joking and maddeningly calm. She was hard put to see any humor, and anyone could see this was no time to be calm.

Sarah's two assistants arrived. After the situation was explained, both began frantically dialing their phones. Ben brought in fresh coffee, filled everyone's mug except Sarah's, then turned back to make more.

Azzo took a quick sip from his mug. "Good coffee, Ben!"

Sarah rose from the radio and followed Ben to the coffee room for her refill. When she returned, she found Azzo manning the radio. Sarah's eyebrows went up even further.

"Where on earth," she thought, "did he learn our radio protocols?"

An aide walked up and reported that Gus had been found, and was, indeed, in a Bolivar beach beer bar. "Don't worry," Azzo whispered. "Ben and I will go get him. I know which bar he's in. And he'll be sober when I bring him back. See you in about an hour."

"They won't let Ben into the bar, Azzo," Sarah said. "He's under twenty-one."

"Oh, they probably will out on Bolivar. But if they don't, they will when I tell them to." Azzo rose from the radio and called out to Ben.

"Ah," the coastguardsman said, "I overheard. The Highway Department's f-ferries have been shut down."

"Well, start them up again," Azzo said. "We need that pilot."

"Under the circumstances," the seaman said, trying to redeem himself after Sarah's earlier comments about his inexperience, "maybe the C-coast Guard can do better."

He seated himself before the radio and switched frequencies. "Excuse me," he said to Sarah as he adjusted the ear-phone headset.

After about a minute, the young man turned, removed the headset, and said, his stutter gone, "A cutter will be dockside here at Galveston Pilots' in about fifteen minutes. We'll get you and your son across the channel, sir, and have a jeep and driver waiting on the other side."

After several hours, it seemed the immediate situation was under control. Air patrols had been dispatched from Palacios and Navy Blimps from Hitchcock, patrolling the skies and searching for possible submarines lurking near Bolivar Roads. Azzo and Ben returned with Gus, sober and freshly shaved. As Gus boarded the Pilot Boat for transit to the first tanker, Commander Carruthers gave his grudging approval to allow both tankers proceeding down-channel to exit into the Gulf under tug assistance, turn around and re-enter the bay system to dock once more at Baytown. One of the coast guard's two new cutters would accompany the tankers as a precaution.

The third tanker remained docked at Texas City.

The ships waiting at anchorage at Bolivar roads had been brought into Galveston Wharves and would discharge their cargos there instead of Houston.

There were costs, and the ships' owners were angry, demanding reimbursement. To one, Sarah responded with sarcasm, "There's a war on. Everyone has to do their part."

Lawsuits were promised.

Sarah, sitting at the manager's desk, looked up from her latest telephone call, surprised to see darkness was falling.

"Everything okay?" Azzo asked, noting the surprised look on her face.

"Yes, I was just surprised that it's nearly dark. Tell Paul to bring the radio logs up to date," she said, naming one of her assistants.

"Already done," Azzo said.

"Oh, then I've got to have Eric complete the owner reports," she said.

"Finished," Azzo said. "You want to review them?"

"Ah, well…" She looked closely at her husband. He was seemingly unruffled, only the wayward forelock out of place as he calmly studied her.

"Ah, well…How about those sandwiches and the large coffee urn? Did you go get them?"

"No, Ben did. Sarah, he picked up the sandwiches and the urn hours ago. You ate one of the sandwiches, and you've been drinking coffee from the urn. Rae made two pies, and you had a slice."

"I ate a sandwich?"

"Yep, about two hours ago."

Sarah frowned. There was something that had just flown past. "Azzo, Ben can't drive!"

"Yes, he can. I've been taking him out practicing for weeks now." Azzo was still disgustingly calm, slouched in the chair across from the manager's desk, looking at her with ill-disguised amusement.

"Thanks for all your help," she said, a slight frown on her face as her mind still tried to catch up to events. "How did you know so much about how we work?"

Azzo chuckled, then shrugged. "You talk about it a lot. I listen."

"I do? I talk too much?"

Azzo ignored her, saying, "I've also been listening to KLUF Galveston. The attack in Hawaii appears to be over. There are fears that the Japanese will invade, either Hawaii or the West Coast, but there's no news. The president, tomorrow, is going to address the congress and will likely ask for a declaration of war. It'll be on the radio 12:30 tomorrow, 11:30 our time."

"Sarah," Azzo continued, "I telephoned Rae. Dinner is ready. Why don't you tell Paul and Eric to go home? I've already told the others. We don't have to keep the office open all night. Everything that you need to do, and the Coast Guard needs you to do, has been done."

Two hours later, the telephone rang at Mansion House. Sarah answered. Azzo heard her say, "Yes, but—well, we were just getting ready for bed." Then, after several minutes, "Okay, I'll get dressed."

"What was that all about?"

"We've got some more complications," Sarah said, tiredly. "The Coast Guard just received a distress signal from a crippled Argentine freighter. There's a cutter on the way, and Commander Carruthers wants tug assistance and a pilot. I've got to reopen Galveston Pilots' office."

"I'll go with you," Azzo said, pulling on his trousers. "Want me to call Paul and Eric?"

Sarah shook her head. "Not yet. Someone has to get some sleep tonight so the office can be open tomorrow."

Ben was in the kitchen in his pajama bottoms as Azzo walked in. "What's up?" he asked.

"A crippled freighter. Your mom and I need to go back downtown, arrange for a tow. A cutter is on the way and will stand by."

Ben's eyes were wide. "Was it a sub attack? Is it sinking?"

"Probably no to both questions," Azzo answered. "I don't think there's war in the Gulf just yet."

"I want to go downtown with you," Ben said.

"It's been a long day for all of us, Ben, and you'll need to go to school tomorrow. Get some sleep."

Sarah walked in, dressed in slacks and blouse, and noted Ben wearing only his pajama bottoms. A little irritated, she realized her son was copying Azzo, who also wore only the bottoms.

All his life Ben had worn both the top and bottom of his pajama's but once Azzo moved in, the tops remained in his bureau drawer. She didn't comment on her irritation but reinforced Azzo.

"That's right, Ben. You've been a great help today, and I'm glad you were along. But there's school tomorrow. This won't take long for us to get everything organized."

"Mom," Ben almost whined, "It isn't every day you get to see a war starting. I want to be able to tell my grandchildren about this day. It's history."

Sarah shook her head. "This freighter isn't about war. It's simply a crippled ship, needing a tow. Azzo and I will go downtown, make whatever arrangements are needed, then be back home quickly. You go to bed."

"And you think I could sleep?"

"I think you should try," Sarah said. "And don't even think about coming in Azzo's car later. I told him to put both sets of keys in his pocket."

At Ben's expression, his mother added, "Don't be so shocked. I know you and Azzo have been sneaking around, practicing driving. Also, I know you drove my car to pick up sandwiches and the coffee urn earlier today. We needed the help today, but I'm still peeved at both you and Azzo for sneaking around behind my back."

"Mom!" Ben said forcefully. "There's a war on, we all have to do our part!"

Azzo laughed loudly as he followed Sarah to her car.

Chapter 16

The Day After

Sarah, after only a few hours' sleep, awakened at her usual time. The empty pillow next to her attested that Azzo had arisen earlier.

She poked her head into Ben's room and found him awake and on his way to his bathroom. Sarah shook her head.

The terrible day before had saddened Sarah, but Azzo's reaction to the national danger was different. He somehow exuded a strange excitement. When they'd finally gotten to bed, she had not wanted an approach, but found herself not only allowing it but responding. Azzo knew precisely how and where to touch her, and his lovemaking raised her to heights beyond what she'd experienced with Glenn. The night of December 7-8, though, was different. During that tumultuous night it seemed to Sarah that she could have touched the stars. This morning, remembering, she felt embarrassment mingled with remnants of excitement.

Sarah finished dressing and heard Rae moving about in the kitchen and Azzo's voice, cheerful, unnecessarily complimenting Rae on her cooking. Her hand on the doorknob, Sarah knew what she would see when she opened the door. Ben was already at the table, fully dressed and ready for school, eating his cereal, a steaming cup of coffee before him. Azzo was leaning against the counter, holding out his plate to Rae as she served several slices of French toast.

The apparent normality of this day, following the overwhelming drama of the day and night before was unsettling. Before she could reach for the coffee mug Rae held out to her, the telephone rang. Sarah went into her office alcove to answer.

"What's wrong?" Azzo asked, concerned as he noted Sarah's face.

"George Stein has died," Sarah said, a catch in her voice. She slumped into her chair as she added, "About an hour ago. That was the Board Chairman, telling me that I am now officially Manager of Galveston Pilots' Guild."

Azzo rose and stood behind Sarah, putting his arms about her shoulders. Ben stopped eating, his spoon half-way, a look of concern on his face. Rae stood near, still holding the coffee mug. No one spoke for a long minute.

"Oh," Sarah said, putting her hands to her face and stifling a sob. "I wanted the job, but not this way. I always hoped he'd somehow get better, some miracle drug, anything. He was only sixty-two. He deserved comfortable retirement years, time to enjoy his grandchildren. Oh, God!"

Tears began as she remembered the kindly man who gave a down-on-her-luck widow with a crippled son a job and a chance. "I never even thanked him," she sobbed. "He gave me a job. I had no experience. He taught me everything. And I never even thanked him."

"He knew," Azzo said in a quiet voice. He bent down and kissed her cheek.

Sarah sniffled. There was another sob. "At least now," she said through tears, "at least now, I'll get full salary."

Azzo chuckled, shocking Sarah. This was no time for laughter.

He bent down to her cheek. "Spoken like the true Jewish mama you are!" he said as he kissed her cheek. "One more of the reasons that I love you!" He lifted her from the chair and hugged her as Rae and Ben grinned uncertainly.

"Let me go!" Sarah said, twisting away, regaining her composure, irritated at his good spirits. "I've got to repair my makeup and go downtown." She headed to her bedroom, stopped briefly and looked at Rae, who hadn't moved and was still holding the coffee mug. "Rae," Sarah said briskly, "wrap a couple of pieces of French toast in paper towels, I'll eat them in the car, and have coffee at the office."

"I'll come, too," Azzo said. "There may be a few chores I can help with. I'll come in my car."

Ben spoke. "Me, too, Mom. I want to go to the Pilots' offices with you and Dad."

Sarah turned back to her son. "No. Absolutely not. You go to school. I'll be fine."

Later, a crowd of about twenty people stood about in the offices of Galveston Pilots'. They were employees of Galveston Wharves, several tug company owners, and pilots who'd come to offer condolences and congratulations to Sarah. They stood about, smoking, drinking coffee, talking in low voices and waiting for the voice of the President of the United States to come over the radio.

Ben was in history class, but classes throughout the school had been paused in anticipation of the President's address to Congress and the nation. Ben's attention, along with other students in the room, was focused on the public address speaker. The room was extraordinarily quiet.

Wallace and Rae were huddled around the small Philco in their apartment.

Other radios in other Mansion House apartments, and indeed in homes, businesses, city and Federal offices throughout Galveston and most of the United States were tuned to history. It was a moment of national silence as radio announcers, in hushed voices, described the scene in the House of Representatives in Washington, D.C. The President was standing at a podium.

A CBS radio announcer said, "Speaker of the House Sam Rayburn is rising to speak."

"Senators and Representatives," the Speaker shouted, *"I have the distinguished honor of presenting the President of the United States."*

There was applause, a few cheers.

The President began speaking: *"Mr. Vice President, Mr. Speaker, Members of the Senate and House of Representatives…"* Across the nation all heard a brief pause in the solemn patrician voice of Franklin Delano Roosevelt, almost as if he had a catch in his throat. He then said, *"Yesterday, December 7, 1941, a date which will live in infamy…"*

The entire speech, including pauses for applause, lasted a little less than ten minutes.

When it was over, no one in Ben's classroom spoke, though several girls were crying. Ben's eyes were dry, but he was moved, not only by the words of the President, but by their extraordinary meaning. The horror of Pearl Harbor had seemed somehow to be make-believe, perhaps like a movie, even though he had heard the radio broadcasts as bombs fell and Ben knew that real people had died. He had even joked about it the night before, telling his mother, "It's not every day you get to see the beginning of a war." But today, it all was real and not a joking matter. Ben realized that his life, and lives of millions throughout the world, was now changed forever.

The principal's high-pitched voice came over the classroom speaker. "Teachers and students, school is dismissed for the remainder of this day. Before we gather our books and coats, I ask that we all bow our heads as I offer a brief prayer for our President and for our Nation, to the one God in whom we all believe."

Ben would never remember the prayer offered by his Jewish principal. When he finished, his teacher, overweight Mrs. Robertson, a devout Catholic, stood beside her desk and said loudly, somehow sounding defiant, "In the name of the Father, Son and Holy Ghost, Amen!" She crossed herself. A bell rang. School was dismissed.

The crowd in Galveston Pilots' offices, now silent or speaking softly one to another, slowly dispersed. Azzo, Paul, Eric and Sarah's secretary, Katie, began tidying the place, emptying ash trays, sweeping where cigarette butts had been carelessly dropped and stepped on, and taking empty coffee cups to the coffee kitchen in the rear. Azzo picked up a discarded copy of the *Daily News* and unfolded the front page. The banner headlines shouted, "BOMBERS ATTACK PHILIPPINE ISLANDS; PRESIDENT TO SPEAK TO CONGRESS TODAY."

Sarah, head down at her desk, heard the door open. She looked up. Azzo ushered four men into her office.

"I believe you've met FBI Agent McCuskey?" Commander Carruthers said, nodding at a square-jawed blond young man with a military haircut. They were followed by two uniformed Coastguardsmen and Azzo.

"We've met before," Sarah said, rising and moving around her desk, taking the proffered hand of the FBI man. "Agent McCuskey, good to see you again."

"Call me Josh," the FBI man said, smiling, showing even white teeth. Azzo motioned to Katie to bring coffee.

"Mrs. Burkhardt," Commander Carruthers began as he took his seat, "first, I want to offer you my condolences over the death of George Stein, and my congratulations to you in your new capacity as General Manager. Next, I'll wait and ask that you assemble all your staff. I want everyone to hear first-hand what I have to say."

"There are only three, besides me," Sarah said, "Paul and Eric, along with Katie,. I'll ask them to crowd in." The Commander nodded.

"Seaman Steve Cohen, here," Commander Carruthers began, speaking briskly as one of the two uniformed seamen rose from the couch, "is proficient in shorthand and will transcribe everything that's said here today." The seaman nodded and regained his seat, taking out a stenographer's pad and pencil.

"Both Seaman Cohen and Seaman Jacob Sullivan will be assigned to this office, on a rotating basis." The second Coastguardsman stood, nodded, and regained his seat. "They are both excellent typists, trained in all Coast Guard radio protocols. Your radio, after this day, will operate solely on Coast Guard frequencies. Ships that contact you on other frequencies will be directed to switch frequencies. Both these men are trained in anti-espionage and will be armed at all times."

Sarah raised her eyebrows. "Armed? Why?"

"Mrs. Burkhardt," the young FBI man interrupted, "it is expected that Germany and Italy will declare war upon the United States before the end of this week. The world will be at war. There will be submarines in the Gulf, targeting shipping, and schedules for that shipping will be information that enemy agents will be interested in.

"Spies will of course have visual information about when vessels are being made ready for departure but more detailed knowledge of pilot's assignments, tug schedules, and so on, will of course be useful to them. You can expect to be under surveillance."

Sarah sat back in her chair, wondering if she should be frightened. "Commander, the man who was here yesterday, will he be back?"

"No," Carruthers said. "That man will go back to sea duty. These two men will be here on a more or less permanent basis."

"Are they to be my bodyguards?" Sarah asked.

"Not exactly," the FBI man answered. "Neither of the Coastguardsmen will accompany you about town. They're here as a precaution, and they've been trained in counterespionage. They will work with you and your staff and schedule some counterespionage training."

"I suggest you put them to work," the Coast Guard Commander said. "You're likely to need help as this war progresses. Shipping has already increased, and it's going to increase further. Security at all Texas ocean ports is to be reinforced along with the Port of Galveston. The coast guard is beginning regular patrols up and down the entire intracoastal system to ensure against sabotage."

"Mrs. Burkhardt," Carruthers continued, "our actions are not limited to Galveston nor Texas. Every port throughout the United States will soon have military personnel assigned to manage radio transmissions and assist in port operations."

The commander changed the subject. "Agent McCuskey is in Galveston for an extended period of service. He will assist in counterespionage training, not only here at Galveston Pilots' but also the Galveston Police and the County sheriff's offices. He'll work out of our Coast Guard station and will also drop by your offices from time to time."

The Commander arose from his chair. "Well, that's about it for now, Mrs. Burkhardt. I know you have a number of owner reports to complete and file regarding yesterday's turmoil, so we'll be leaving now."

As the door closed behind the Coastguardsmen and McCuskey, Sarah noticed the elderly managing editor of the *Daily News*. He was in a straight-backed chair, off to the side and leaning against the wall. "Tough times," he said to Sarah, rising. "I heard about George. He was my friend. I stopped by his house, offered my condolences to his family and decided to come here. Been waiting for your meeting to end.

"Kind of interesting, ain't it?" the editor said. "I overheard everything, and these are the guys who are supposed to be helping you keep everything a secret."

"Come into my office, Sam," Sarah said.

As he took the chair so recently vacated by the FBI man, Sam said, "Sarah, don't worry. I'll not print anything I heard today. I came by to offer my condolences about George, and my congratulations to you."

"Thanks, Sam. We all knew this was coming, even though we had hopes."

"I know," the newspaper man answered. "At any rate, I'd like a statement from you. His death will be in the paper tomorrow, along with the announcement that you'll be taking full control—along with the US guv'ment, o'course." He grinned, reminding Sarah of a skinny, elderly gnome.

"You'll have it, Sam," Sarah promised. "It'll be sent over in an hour or so."

Friday morning, December 12, 1941, Sarah's kitchen tabletop radio told her and the rest of her family that Germany and Italy had declared war upon the United States of America.

Chapter 17

Four Months Later
April 1942

Sarah, Azzo, and Benjamin were in a conference room at Billy Bentley's office along with Commander Carruthers, Joshua McCuskey, and attorney Bentley. Rain pelted the windowpanes of the conference room. From time to time, there was a distant rumble of thunder.

The FBI agent was speaking. "Mr. and Mrs. Burkhardt and Benjamin, you've been invited here today because I have news that I'm sure you will want to hear. First, however, I have to ask you, Mr. Burkhardt, if you have shared information about your parents with Mrs. Burkhardt and Benjamin." His eyes sought out Sarah and Ben as he said this.

"I have told my wife," Azzo said. "We've only told Ben that they are scientists, forced to work for the Germans."

Ben had a confused look on his face. His eyes darted from his stepfather, to the FBI man, and back to his mother.

"He needs to be told," the FBI man said, "in order for me to complete what I have come her to say."

"They're dead," Azzo said.

"No, not at all," McCuskey said. "They're very much alive. May I simply tell everyone here what they need to know, beginning at the beginning?"

Azzo nodded, relief flooding his features.

Sarah started to say something. McCuskey held up his hand.

"Before I begin," he said, "Mr. Hoover, my boss, asked me to swear each of you to secrecy over what I'm about to say. It is a military secret of the highest order. Ben is young, and Mr. Hoover asked me if I could vouch that Ben, and indeed each of you, are persons of character who will stick to their oaths of secrecy. I've assured him that you are." The FBI man slid an English-language edition of the Torah across the table. "Will each of you stand, place your left hand on the Torah, raise your right, and repeat after me..." He paused. "You, too, Mr. Bentley."

"Yes, of course," the portly balding attorney said, rising, his hand on a Christian Bible.

After they'd all sworn, the FBI agent began speaking.

The story that unfolded for Ben that afternoon was remarkable in its detail. Ben knew a little of what was disclosed: Azzo's elderly parents and his sister were renowned scientists who'd worked on rocketry and jet propulsion at the University in Munich, but now worked at a laboratory on an island-city in the North Sea. Ben learned as McCuskey talked that they had been forcibly taken from their home to a secret laboratory at a place named Peenemunde. They, along with other scientists, some Jewish, many non-Jewish, had been forced to continue their work on behalf of the German government, racing to develop rockets that would fly across the English Channel and rain down on British cities.

An escape plan for Ben's step-grandparents and step-aunt, Azzo's sister, was developed and executed by a team of British and American Commandoes. They were taken, along with two other Jewish scientists, to England via submarine.

The Nazi government of Germany did not know where they were, and assumed they'd escaped overland into the occupied countries. There was currently a frantic search for the scientists throughout Europe in an effort to keep their knowledge and information from the Allies.

"Azzo's parents, sister, and the other scientists who escaped are," McCuskey said, "safe in England and have been for some time. They are continuing their work on rocketry and jet propulsion and our government, along with Great Britain and others, is pleased that they are doing so."

Azzo asked, "Where are they?"

McCuskey nodded. "They are in a secret facility in Great Britain, far to the north of London. I've wanted to tell you about them before now."

"I want to visit them!" Azzo said. Ben and Sarah said nothing as the FBI man shook his head and held up his hand again. "There's more you need to hear," he said simply. The slender young agent stood to resume his narrative. He moved about the room as he did so, and Sarah studied him. The shoulders under his suit jacket suit were broad and his hips narrow. It seemed to Sarah that his grey eyes rarely looked at anyone without seeming to study them.

"It has been imperative," the government agent said, breaking Sarah's reverie, "for the governments of both the United Kingdom and the United States that the Nazis believe the escaped scientists are dead.

"You said they are safe," Azzo said.

McCuskey nodded.

"There was a plan that was brought to fruition only a short while ago," the FBI agent said. "German agents were decoyed to a small village near the French Alps where they witnessed a small airplane taking off at dusk. Witnesses told the agents that there were three passengers on board, two elderly people and one younger, a woman. The airplane was headed east, to Switzerland.

"As soon as the plane was out of sight, the pilot bailed out and was recovered by French Resistance who'd been standing by. The airplane flew on, using autopilot, and later crashed into a rugged mountainside. There were four bodies, cadavers, on the plane along with luggage consistent with what the Burkhardt's would have been carrying. In fact, some of the luggage was actually luggage that had belonged to your grandparents. As planned, the crash was violent enough so that the bodies aboard were torn apart and burned beyond recognition. The terrain was rugged, and it took Swiss police, along with recovery squads and the pursuing Gestapo, a number of days to reach the crash site. Wolves had gotten to the site before them. Dental records from a dentist in Munich, and scientific notes similar to what your father might have been carrying were in the luggage, Mr. Burkhardt, and this confirmed to the Germans that three of the bodies were those of your family. The fourth body, of course, was presumed to be the pilot. The Gestapo took all the remains back to Germany where they were buried in a mass grave near a concentration camp.

"So," the FBI man concluded, "we believe we've convinced the Germans that your parents and sister are gone. In fact, as I've said several times," he added as he looked closely at Azzo, "they are not dead. They are safe and continuing their work to help the war efforts of both nations. But, Mr. and Mrs. Burkhardt, and Benjamin, we are now going to ask you to become actors."

"I don't understand," Sarah said.

"You know, don't you," McCuskey said, "that for the past several months you've been under surveillance?" Sarah, her hand to her mouth, gave a small gasp, almost a sob. Ben felt his excitement and being-in-a-movie feeling devolve into a knot of fear deep in his stomach.

"Azzo!" Sarah said. "You said you'd let me know if…"

"Don't worry, ma'am," the blond FBI man said, brushing his hand across his short hair. "For some time, now, we've been watching them watch you. From the first, Mr. Burkhardt, the Gestapo were certain that your parents and sister would head here, to Galveston and to you. None of you have ever been in any danger. We'd have been right there if they'd tried anything."

"You could have told us," Azzo said, a hint of anger in his voice, "that we were being watched by the Gestapo."

"No, we didn't want to do that. We wanted to convince the Germans that you didn't know where your parents were, and that your wife and stepson knew even less. You three did a good job of that. I must admit, Mr. Burkhardt, we were worried that many times you didn't outwardly display concern."

"Well, I certainly was concerned," Azzo said, "but there was nothing I could do. I did visit a friend of mine in New York…"

"Yes, we know all about that," the government agent said, his voice clipped, impatient to return to his narrative. "I like hot dogs, too, Mr. Burkhardt, though I don't eat the Kosher ones."

McCuskey grinned, though his eyes did not convey warmth. "I was less than twenty feet from you the last time you met. A tiny microphone had been hidden under the park bench."

He abruptly resumed his narrative. "We watched you lose them several times when you left on your frequent research trips along the Texas Coast. It almost was as if you knew you were being followed."

Azzo felt uneasy, wondering how much, if anything, the FBI knew about his and Levi's work. "There were times," McCuskey said, "when it was necessary for us to intervene when you left town. We did worry that if they cornered you in a remote part of Texas, they might try something, interrogation, intimidation, who knows? So, generally before you reached the end of the Galveston causeway we managed to, ah, intervene. Do you remember the fender-bender behind you in late November?" he asked.

Azzo nodded thoughtfully. "That was us," McCuskey went on. "One of our men, pretending to be a drunk, sideswiped their car."

"Dental records," Azzo said. "How did you manage to have dental records match phony cadavers?"

McCuskey grinned boyishly. "Yeah, that was tough. I'm trained in counterespionage, but we've got some guys who are experts far beyond anything I could do. Let's just say, 'They got it done.'"

A suspicion had begun dawning in Ben's breast. "So, Mr. McCuskey, you said something about our becoming actors. What does that mean?"

"Good question, Ben. I bet you've figured it out already." Again, Sarah noticed the FBI man's eyes. There was warmth in them when he talked with Benjamin. "Yes, indeed, the governments of the United States and the United Kingdom want the three of you to become actors."

"In what way?" Sarah asked.

"Mr. Burkhardt, your parents and sister have been in an airplane crash. They've been burned beyond recognition and buried along with several hundred others in a mass grave in Poland. Once you've been informed of this, what would you be expected to do?"

Sarah shrugged, "Nothing. Azzo's family isn't dead. We have nothing to do with those cadavers."

"Ah, Mrs. Burkhardt, but suppose it was real?"

Ben got there before his mother. "Dad and I would say a prayer of Kaddish, daily, for a year, as we mourn the death of his family. Is that it?"

"Exactly," Joshua McCuskey said. "The German agents out there," he motioned toward the street, "along with the German government, believe that at this moment we're telling you, Mrs. Burkhardt, that your husband's family is dead. It's a moment of grief. When you leave here, Mrs. Burkhardt, it'd be helpful if you could be seen crying."

"You mean German agents are outside this building right now?" Ben asked, excitedly as his mother turned worried eyes to the window.

"Come, I'll show you," McCuskey said, motioning to Sarah, but she shook her head. "No thanks. I'll take your word."

"I want to see!" Ben said, rising from his chair.

"Okay but wait!" McCuskey said. He rose from his chair and led Ben to the side of the window. "Don't look directly out, but just peek from behind this drape. Don't let the cloth of the drape move."

Ben did as he was instructed.

"Now," McCuskey said, "look carefully. See down there, underneath the awning at the drugstore?"

Ben could see a man's feet and trousers visible under the awning, and the lower part of a raincoat. Lightning flashed, followed shortly by a low rumble of thunder. "That's one of them," McCuskey said in a quiet voice. "The other is in a car parked three parking spaces to the left. See the man in the driver's seat, his hat pulled down over his eyes?" McCuskey laughed outright. "Don't they look like they're right out of Paramount's central casting? Really! They are clowns!"

"But dangerous." Azzo said.

"Yes, to be sure," McCuskey said. "Ben, never approach them. If you're with your school chums, don't point them out. All of this, Ben, including what I'm going to tell you next, is as we've discussed, a government secret of the highest order. It's why you were sworn a little while ago. Mr. Hoover, and the President of the United States as well, personally asked me if I felt that you, your mom, and your stepdad could do what I'm going to ask, and I told him I was sure that you could. You folks are quality. I told him I was sure you could be trusted."

"President Roosevelt?" Ben said, his eyes wide. "The President knows about all this, even knows my name?"

"He sure does. Mrs. Roosevelt, too. She said she's going to be in Texas in a few months for a war bonds drive and wondered if you could visit her in Dallas. I told her that wouldn't be advisable. We don't know how long we're going to have to keep the Germans fooled."

"Well, let's get back to that," Sarah snapped. "What's this acting part?" Even as she said it, she wondered at Azzo's quiet, strange behavior. He hadn't spoken for several minutes and had a worried frown on his face.

"Yes, let's get back to it," the FBI man said, leading Ben away from the window and back to the conference room table.

"Basically," McCuskey continued after they'd resumed their seats, "we want the Germans to believe, Mr. Burkhardt, that I'm telling you your parents and sister are dead. The commander and I will leave in a few minutes. We've been offering our condolences, and we want you to remain here with your attorney for a short while. Then, when you leave, we'll ask that you stop by 22nd Street and visit Rabbi Cohen at B'nai Israel."

"We-we'll need to bring him up to date," Azzo said.

"No," McCuskey said, "We've already briefed him. He is expecting you. Lordy! Does that man hate Nazis!

"Oh," McCuskey continued, "there's something the rabbi already told us, and we're passing it along, Mr. Burkhardt, that you and Ben won't be saying Kaddish for your parents but for all those who died at Pearl Harbor and the German concentration camps, and all those who will die at the hands of the Nazis and Japanese during this war."

Azzo nodded, confidence returning that the FBI knew nothing of his and Levi's operation. "Sure, Josh," he said, "and Ben and I won't be acting when we leave the Synagogue. Kaddish is a very emotional prayer, and all those lives lost, and those that will be lost, well, I get pretty emotional just thinking about it. Kaddish will bring it all home."

Chapter 18

Adoption

Two weeks had passed since the remarkable conference in Sarah's attorney's office. McCuskey had returned to Galveston and once again asked for a meeting in Billy Bentley's office.

"You mentioned, the last time I was here, Mr. Burkhardt," the FBI man began, "your desire to visit your parents. We can't allow that, but we have facilitated correspondence. When I returned to Washington, I discussed correspondence with Mr. Hoover, and then I left for Great Britain."

"You've seen them?" Azzo questioned.

"Yes, indeed. I've met them several times since their escape from the Nazis."

"You were along on the raid?"

"Oh, no. I met them later, in England. They know I'm acquainted with you, and I've told them a little about your current circumstances. I asked them to write, and the next day, before I left for the United States, they gave me this packet of letters."

He reached into a satchel at his feet and withdrew a package, tied with string.

"I'm sorry to say that these letters have been read by our security people, and you'll find some portions redacted."

He paused, waiting for the censorship issue to sink in.

"Now," McCuskey continued, "back to the issue of correspondence. I dislike telling you, and Mr. Hoover says he dislikes ordering it, but in addition to your parent's correspondence to you, anything you write back to them will be read and censored if necessary."

He went on. "We don't expect correspondence between you and your family to fall into enemy hands, but there's always that chance. I am sorry indeed. It's an invasion of both your and their privacy." He shook his head. "It can't be helped.

"I'm going to take my leave now," Josh McCuskey said. "These letters are to stay in your attorney's office, under lock and key. You can read them here and answer them here. Don't take anything home with you. If they send photographs, they, too, must stay here. If you want to send photos to them, bring the undeveloped film here along with your correspondence."

An hour or so later, after Azzo, Sarah, and Ben had read and reread the letters and looked at the photographs, Billy Bentley knocked on the door of the conference room and entered.

"How is it going?" the attorney asked.

"Right now," Azzo said, "we're planning our answers."

"Well, if you want, keep at it. This room is yours for as long as you'd like. However, Azzo, I thought I'd mention. It's been six months since I filed the adoption papers and you had your initial interviews with Judge Lawrence. I happen to know he's available this afternoon. If you want to complete everything today, it can be done." He looked out the window. "The rain has stopped. You can simply walk the two blocks over to the courthouse. I don't need to be there. I'll telephone Judge Lawrence that you're on your way."

Sarah frowned, thinking of something the attorney had said. "Azzo, it hasn't been six months since that day on the beach—has it?"

Azzo grinned sheepishly. "Sarah, I filed the papers some time before I got up the courage to ask you and Ben."

She sat back in her chair, unsure whether to be angry, annoyed, or happy.

After introductions in Judge Peter J. Lawrence's chambers, the judge brought in and introduced his secretary, who sat at a small table near the corner.

"Betty, here," the judge said, "will take notes of these proceedings. After they're typed up, we'll ask that you return and sign them, and they will be recorded in the official records of Galveston County. There are other documents you can sign today; returning to sign the others will simply be a formality."

He next proceeded with a lengthy explanation of what adoption means, and the legalities of actions to be taken on this day. The judge paused and asked Ben if he understood. Ben nodded, but the judge said, "I need to hear a verbal response from you, son."

Ben held his head up, sat straighter in his chair and said, "Yes sir, Your Honor. I understand what you have said."

"Good," the judge answered.

Everyone was sworn, using an English-language version of the Torah. There were a series of questions for both Azzo and Sarah, then the judge turned to Benjamin.

"Benjamin Weismann Jacobs, I am going to now need some very specific answers from you."

Ben nodded and responded, "Yes, sir."

"Benjamin, you do not have to agree with your stepfather's petition, asking that he be allowed to formally adopt you as his son. Do you understand that?"

"Yes, sir."

"Do you agree to be adopted by Mr. Burkhardt?"

Ben turned. He saw tears in his mother's eyes. There was a strange look on Azzo's face, and, it seemed, some sort of light behind his eyes. "Yes, Your Honor," Ben said. "I agree to be adopted by Azzo Judah Burkhardt."

Sarah was surprised that Ben knew Azzo's middle name.

The judge turned to Sarah. "Mrs. Burkhardt," he said, "this is a consent form. If you agree with the proceedings today, please sign this form."

"Of course," she said, leaning forward and taking the proffered fountain pen.

There were also papers for Azzo to sign.

It was all over more quickly than Ben would have thought, and to him it was anticlimactic. He felt there should have been more—more of something, perhaps a note of celebration. He found it hard to analyze his feelings.

Ben's last name would now to be the same as his father's. At Ben's request, the name Jacobs, his previous last name, had become his middle name.

On the way home, they stopped at Temple B'nai Israel and it was here, Ben realized, where his emotions could be calmed. "God," Ben thought, "is the One who understands, and it is to Him that I will offer my thanks for bringing all this about. I now have a father, and I honor him by taking his name." In the hallway outside Rabbi Cohen's office at B'nai Israel, Ben continued his reverie. "I also must honor my biology," Ben said to himself, "and this is the reason I am keeping Glenn Jacobs' last name as my middle one.

"So," Ben continued his silent soliloquy, "here at Temple is where I honor God for bringing Azzo to my mother, and thus to me, and I am now, and forever more will be, Benjamin Jacobs Burkhardt."

With Rabbi Henry Cohen leading, the family offered prayers of thanks to God. Ben, to Sarah's utter astonishment, unaccompanied by neither Azzo nor the Rabbi, sang his prayer of thanks to God from the Jewish Book of Tehilim. Afterwards, he rose, pulled his father from his kneeling position, and hugged him. Ben kissed his father, whispering, "Thank you for wanting me to be your son."

The next day, Sarah and Azzo headed downtown. The day had begun as the previous, with a light rain shower, though the sun was now shining brightly. As Azzo started his car, he said, "Sarah, for some time now I've been meaning to mention. Ben didn't have his Bar Mitzvah when he turned thirteen last summer."

Sarah shook her head. "It's just that I've been so busy," she said, irritated at herself for feeling she had to make excuses.

"I didn't even think about it before his birthday," she went on, "then, afterwards, well, I guess I just forgot about it. No one in my family has been very religious, anyway. I never had a Bat Mitzvah, and you know I almost never go to Temple."

"I know," Azzo said, turning onto Broadway. "Ben and I go more often than you." He paused, a thoughtful expression on his face.

"I never had a Bar Mitzvah, either," he said abruptly.

Sarah, surprised by the sudden change, said, "Really, why not?"

Azzo grinned ruefully. "Germany's been a tough place to be a Jew for a long time, even before Hitler came to power. When I turned thirteen, times were tough, and Bar Mitzvahs were often simply skipped. Moreover, I was preparing to come to the United States. I decided then that someday, when I was married and had a family, that I'd arrange to have an adult Bar Mitzvah."

Sarah was thoughtful. "Azzo, how old were you when you immigrated?"

Azzo answered as he turned the car to the curb at Levi Weismann's bank. "I was fourteen."

"Did you have a relative to stay with?"

"No," he shook his head. "A distant cousin arranged for me to attend a boarding school in Connecticut. I qualified for college in two years and entered the university when I was sixteen."

He switched off the engine. Sarah began opening the car door, fumbling with her umbrella, wondering at the courage of a young boy coming to a distant country, knowing no one, and applying himself so that he could enter college at an early age.

Before she could exit, filled with her thoughts, Azzo interrupted. "Sarah, I want Ben and me to have a joint Bar Mitzvah, an Adult Bar Mitzvah. We could do it on Ben's fourteenth birthday, coming up soon. How would you feel about that?"

Sarah stopped and turned halfway out the door, surprised and still somewhat annoyed at herself for not arranging for Ben to go through the rite at the appropriate age. She started to speak, but Azzo cut her off.

"Sarah," he grinned. "I'm married, and I have a son. A son that I feel about as if he were my own flesh and blood. And I know that Ben feels strongly about me. We need to have a joint adult Bar Mitzvah." Sarah leaned across the seat and kissed her husband.

Chapter 19

War Comes to Galveston

The radio and newspapers were full of news of far-away places where people were dying, places that Sarah had never heard of. There were death marches on the Philippines' Bataan Peninsula. Army flyers were making hazardous flights over the Himalayas, bringing supplies to China's Chiang Kai-shek. In Europe, British airplanes were bombing Hamburg and the Germans, in retaliation, were again bombing London. Axis and Soviet forces were barreling toward the Caucasus and the oil reserves so desperately needed for their machines of war. There were fierce battles being fought in North Africa, and Rommel's panzer divisions seemed to rule the deserts.

Daily, radio news reported that young men across America were enlisting by the thousands, and thousands more were opening letters from their local draft boards. Ben, on his way to school began seeing small flags with blue stars on a white-and-red background in windows all along his way. Occasionally, Ben would see that one of those blue stars had changed to gold, and he knew that whoever had lived in that house would not return from the war.

Newsreels at the Isle Theatre showed convoys crossing the Atlantic, and Ben learned from young Coastguardsmen he knew that these convoys were being accompanied by United States Navy Destroyers. Azzo had predicted, and Ben's coast guard friends confirmed, that Axis forces were moving even more of their U-boats into the Gulf of Mexico. It became routine for tankers loaded with Texas and Louisiana crude to engage in zig-zag maneuvers soon after passing the seaward buoy. Newspapers were full of news about around-the-clock work on both the "Big-Inch" and "Little-Inch" pipelines, to transport Texas crude to New Jersey refineries.

Around-the-clock work was also underway on new Texas and Louisiana refineries, and military defense construction efforts proceeded at break-neck speed. The population of Galveston County and the City of Galveston continued to grow.

Sarah visited with Uncle Levi and talked about the government's plan to institute national rent controls, and he advised that she increase her rates immediately. She did, tenants complained, but few opted to cancel their leases. Those that cancelled were quickly replaced.

Mansion House, from the beginning, had had long tenant waiting lists, and they became longer even after Sarah increased her rates. Both Azzo and Uncle Levi encouraged Sarah to construct additional apartment units, and she agreed. Azzo prepared the plans and acted as Sarah's construction manager. Work began that summer on a new twenty-four-unit complex located at the rear of the city block occupied by Mansion House, the part of Sarah's property where once was a paddock for her grandfather's carriage horses, prized matched black Friesians.

Azzo swore he would go crazy as he fought daily battles with the project's contractor, who felt that shoddy workmanship could always be hidden beneath a coat of paint. He sometimes succeeded in his efforts, but more often than not Azzo uncovered the shoddy effort and the contractor was given the option of re-doing the work or having his contract cancelled. Ben often worked as his father's assistant and inspector, and the contractor grew to dislike the fourteen-year-old boy as much as he disliked his father. There were many contentious conversations, and often Azzo simply turned to Ben, who calmly pointed out the mistakes and how they could be corrected.

The project was eventually completed ahead of schedule, despite all the delays, and the contractor applied for and was awarded his performance bonus. Azzo and Ben shook hands with the man and said they hoped there would be no lasting hard feelings. The contractor grudgingly told both that he respected them and their judgments, though Ben did not believe him. Ben was glad to see the last of the man.

With the completion of Mansion House West, Sarah hired a man-and-wife team, new to Galveston, to be managers of the complex. She offered free rent along with a modest salary, and spent an entire afternoon with the man's wife, explaining how she wanted the books kept, and the responsibilities of the management job.

That evening at supper Azzo asked about the new couple.

"I'm not sure how it's going to work out," Sarah admitted. "I'm worried that I wasn't as thorough as I might have been in checking their references."

"What's the problem?" he asked.

"Well," Sarah said, "the man, a Eugene McElroy, said he had experience operating a hotel and gave me the name of one in Shreveport. He said he's originally from Arkansas and he certainly sounds like he is. His voice is so nasally and whiney he may actually run off prospective tenants. His wife, Edith, though she seems nice, is certainly uneducated. Oddly, though, she seemed to understand about bookkeeping. You know, I watched her add a column of figures in her head. No paper nor pencil. I used the adding machine to check. She was right.

"Still, there's something about those two that is a little off. I can't quite put my finger on it."

Azzo asked, "Did you telephone the hotel in Shreveport? Ask about their work?"

Sarah shrugged. "I was going to, but the operator told me the long-distance charge would be three dollars. Imagine! Three dollars! I sent a telegram for only seventy-five cents."

"Did you get a reply?"

Sarah shrugged again. "No, Azzo, I didn't. I hired them anyway. I was tired of fooling with the issue. They'll be fine. If they don't work out, I'll run them off. Get someone else."

Azzo said, "Mansion House West is completely full now, isn't it?"

"Oh yes," Sarah answered, "one hundred percent occupancy, and I've got a waiting list as long as your arm."

"Well, I'd advise you to keep a close eye. I wish you'd have checked out the couple more thoroughly, but," he shrugged, "they'll probably work out just fine."

"The accents of those two!" Sarah exclaimed. "Arkansas! Imagine! They both sound like hillbillies!"

Azzo laughed and went outside to his wood-working shop. He was building a cabinet for his studio apartment in the Carriage House Annex, and, he told Sarah, getting ready for yet another trip southward along the coast.

As the days and weeks passed, Sarah continued her busy schedule, managing both Mansion House and

Galveston Pilots'. She postponed time and again visits to Mansion House West. Rent money continued to pour in, the ledgers the woman brought to her all tallied, and she heard no complaints from Mansion House West tenants. As time passed, she forgot about checking further on her new managers.

Chapter 20

May-October 1942

On a Wednesday Sarah telephoned from her office at Galveston Pilots'. Ben, returning from school, entered the living room as Azzo was hanging up the phone.

"I need to go to Galveston Pilots,'" he said.

"What's up, doc?" Ben asked, a grin on his face as he mimicked a popular animated cartoon character.

"I'm afraid Gus Morton has been lost," Azzo said, a serious look on his face. "Your mom just called. She needs me to come over."

"Gus?" Ben asked, regretting his flip attitude as a sinking feeling invaded his stomach. "How?"

"I'm not sure," Azzo said. "Want to come with me?"

At the office, a clearly upset Sarah told them, speaking calmly, "The Gulf Penn, 8863 tons out of Port Neches, carrying a cargo of fuel oil and traveling with her sister ship, the Gulf Prince, exited into the Gulf yesterday. The pilot that'd been planned for the Penn became ill before sailing, and the Port Neches folks called me. They needed a substitute. Gus was available. Both ships were attacked today by a U-boat. The Penn was sunk off the coast of Louisiana."

Sarah was sitting at her desk, a cooling cup of coffee before her. A damp handkerchief was in her hand.

"The Pilot Boat didn't pick Gus up at the seaward buoy?" Ben asked.

"Gus didn't get off. The ship's Captain asked him to stay. They'd been told a U-boat had been spotted. The Captain knew Gus and wanted his help in the zig-zag maneuvers they all have to do these days."

"Surely," Azzo said, "he got off before the ship went down. He's in a lifeboat, somewhere in the Gulf. The Coastguard will find him. They must have sent a cutter."

"There was a cutter all right, several in fact, out of New Orleans. Two lifeboats were launched, and twenty-six men got off the ship. Gus was not among them. Commander Carruthers called me."

Azzo walked behind the desk, knelt, and put his arms around Sarah as Ben stood by, the enormity of the tragedy plain upon his face. Ben knew and liked Gus and was looking forward to the day when he was the one who'd go searching for the old drunk, sober him up, and bring him into Galveston Pilot's offices.

As if she were echoing Ben's thoughts, Sarah exclaimed, shaking off Azzo's hug and rising from her chair.

"That old drunk!" she said loudly, her voice emotional. She walked around to the front of her desk and leaned against it. "They called from Port Neches, needed a substitute. I went to Bolivar, sobered Gus up one more time—oh, God! How many times have I sobered him up! Port Neches didn't want him, wanted to know if anyone else was available. I'm the one who convinced them to take him, to put him on that tanker. I even drove him over to Port Neches; Gus' old car was broken down! I took him to his death!"

Ben watched in astonishment as his mother slumped, held her hands over her face, and sobbed as if her heart was breaking. Azzo went to her, placed her head on his shoulder. Ben awkwardly patted his mother's arm, then turned and left the room.

"And then," Sarah said, pulling away from Azzo, "Carruthers called me! Would I contact Gus' next-of-kin? No! How could I? He had no next-of-kin that I ever knew of! You know what?" Sarah asked.

"Mom," Ben said, interrupting as he returned to his mother's office, "I've brought in some fresh coffee. Why don't you come over here?" He placed three cups on the low table in front of the leather couch as Sarah sat and repeated, "You know what? He called me his daughter! Me! That old drunk! Oh, God!" She sank back in the cushions. "He said Galveston Pilots' was the only family he ever had, and that I was his daughter!" Sarah broke into loud sobs, placing her head on Azzo's chest. "Oh, God!"

Ben quietly left the office and went to the marine radio in the next room, asking the Coastguardsman radio operator to ask that Commander Carruthers telephone. A few minutes later, he returned to the office and pulled a straight chair to the low table and picked up one of the coffees.

"There are two cutters from New Orleans still on the scene," Ben said, "but the battle seems to be over. The Penn's sister ship, the Gulf Prince, was hit but not sunk. It's heading to New Orleans, where it'll be off-loaded at sea, and then sent to a repair facility.

"The cutter dropped depth charges, but there's no debris field so they don't believe they got the sub. Hopefully, it's lying on the bottom, and those bastards inside are all dead." There was a steely tone to his voice.

Sarah wrinkled her brow. "You heard all this on an open radio channel?"

"No," Ben said, "I had your radio operator call and ask that Commander Carruthers telephone. He did, I talked to him, and he said he felt he could trust me and asked that we not talk to the newspapers or anyone from radio news if they call. But he told me everything, saying he was just about to call you with a final report. I told him you were pretty broken up at the moment."

Sarah grinned ruefully. "Yes, I was. I'm a little better now. I loved the old coot."

"We know, Sarah," Azzo said, as Ben added, "Mom, we all did." Azzo glanced sideways at Ben, impressed by his son.

The next day the *Daily News*, in a subdued notice on an inner page, simply reported that a member of Galveston Pilots' Guild, August Sidney Morton, had died in an accident at sea.

Two days later, as the sun rose out of the eastern Gulf, coloring the dove gray of the morning clouds with highlights of gold and red, a small crowd gathered on Galveston's West Jetty and, led by Rabbi Henry Cohen, prayed a prayer of Kaddish for those lost at sea, as gulls shrieked, wheeled, and turned in the morning sky.

As the year 1942 progressed, Galvestonians turned worried eyes to the Gulf of Mexico. The beaches were closed nightly and patrolled as rumors of landings, saboteurs, and spies ran amuck throughout the island-city. Bathers and picnickers were discouraged from venturing far past the western end of the seawall.

Azzo, well-known to Army patrols, moved many of his nighttime fishing expeditions to late afternoons. Often, though not always, he invited Sarah and Benjamin. Her work usually caused her to decline, but Benjamin was eager to accompany his father. They brought back fewer fish than earlier days, since usually both Ben and Azzo concentrated on running instead of pulling fish from the warm Gulf waters.

When Ben turned fourteen in the summer of 1942, and he and Azzo had their joint Adult Bar Mitzvah, Sarah marked a turning point in her son. His strength had improved to the point where, going about town, he never used his cane nor his braces. He was rapidly becoming the man she wanted him to be, although there were times when she selfishly wished to hold him, stop him from growing and keep him always her boy.

Sarah and Azzo often overheard Ben late that August as he rubbed and massaged truculent leg muscles with medicated salves, most often after a run on the beach. To himself, Ben grumbled, "High school only weeks away now, and, dammit! You guys are not gonna stop me from getting on the track team!"

Sarah called out once, "Ben! Don't curse!"

Both heard Ben answer as he massaged his leg muscles even harder, "I'm not cursing, Mama, I'm cussing! And Azzo says it is okay for me to cuss!"

She turned accusingly to Azzo. "You're corrupting my son!"

Azzo grinned. "If I can't teach my son to cuss, who can I teach?" He took another tube of salve to Ben.

That summer, Azzo and Ben often stayed on the beach until after sunset, running or fishing, usually both. Sometimes, after they'd returned to Mansion House, Azzo returned to the beach alone but there were no fish added to Mansion House's refrigerators on those nights. And, these solitary beach trips were often followed rather quickly by what he called a research trip southward along the coast, toward Corpus Christi.

One day, Sarah asked Azzo about the beach patrols.

He laughed and said, "Oh, all the patrols know both me and Benjamin, and have for a long time. We've been going fishing or running for so long, we're a common feature. There are a few other fishermen that the patrols ignore, but I have a secret weapon!"

At her frown, he added, "I use my secret weapon against the patrols. You see, I always have a few bottles of beer iced down—which of course they're not supposed to have, and I always hand out a few. When they stop and tell me it's time to leave, I ask them, 'Boys before I go, would you like to have a Coca-Cola?' When they say yes, and they always do, I show them one particular ice chest and I say, 'This is where I keep my Cokes,' and they reach in and pull out a bottle of beer. They always say, 'This is an Azzo Coca-Cola' and laugh. I usually tell them that I'll leave in a few minutes, and they finish their beer and go on to the next fisherman.

"Also," he chuckled, "quite a few of the officer's wives seem to appreciate a gift of fresh fish from time to time, which the patrols take back."

Sarah shook her head, wondering about Azzo. Sometimes he seemed playful, and these times she compared him to Glenn in her first marriage. Other times he seemed a stranger, somber, deep in thought. She had learned that she could predict, from his moods and the solitary night-time beach trips, when either another trip down the coast or a trip to New York would occur.

There was no comparison, however, to Azzo's lovemaking. Her first husband had been gentle, slow, and caring. She never doubted that Azzo cared for her, but his lovemaking contained a power—an aggressiveness and a hint of violence—yet she was raised to heights she'd never before known. She found her passions matching his and she gloried in it as they reached the peak of the mountain, not as two blended bodies, but as one. Then on the way down from that mountaintop, Azzo became more like Glenn, stroking and petting, guiding, leading her, murmuring things that meant nothing and everything.

One cool September morning, a young man dressed in a business suit appeared at Sarah's Pilots' Guild office.

"Mrs. Burkhardt," he said upon entering, removing his hat and exposing his short blond hair, cut military style. He extended his hand.

"Yes," Sarah said, stepping from behind the half-wall that separated the entry area from several desks. She held out her hand. "Come in, Mr. McCuskey. I haven't seen you in months. How may I help you?"

"May we go into your office?" the FBI man said. "What I have to say to you is extremely confidential."

Sarah smiled. Joshua McCuskey was such an engaging and clean-cut young man. "Please do sit down, Mr. McCuskey. May I ask my secretary to get you a cup of coffee?"

"Yes, that would be great. Thank you."

A young man brought in two mugs on a tray and left, closing the door.

McCuskey smiled. "I remembered your secretary was named Katie."

Sarah smiled. "Yes, and she was a good secretary. However, an Army man from Ellington courted her, they married, and she became pregnant right away. She could have remained my secretary, of course, at least for a few months, but her young man got transferred to Pensacola and she followed him. Anyway, after she left I needed a secretary and Oliver applied. He's quite helpful, and not subject to draft due to some sort of kidney issue. So, he'll be around for a while, and I need consistent help."

"Mrs. Burkhardt," he said, shuffling about in his chair, "I didn't come here to discuss your employees."

"Of course not," Sarah nodded, enjoying the young FBI man's discomfiture. "Let's start over. Welcome back to Galveston."

"Okay," McCuskey began, again smiling his engaging smile. "Starting over, I want to remind you about the key that Benjamin loaned me some time ago. We believe that this key was dropped by the foreign national who died in your front yard a few years ago."

"I didn't know that Ben loaned you the key," Sarah said.

"Yes. I met him once coming home from school. We went to Schultz's Ice Cream Parlor over on Seawall Boulevard, and I bought him an ice cream soda."

"You questioned my son without my knowledge?"

"Yes, I did. I broke a few rules but not all. Your attorney knew I was going to talk to Ben."

"And…?" Sarah questioned.

"We talked about the key he found. He loaned me the key, and I promised to return it one day."

Sarah retreated, studied the FBI man a few seconds before answering. He wasn't as tall as her husband, but nearly so. Slender, a look about his eyes—she thought for a moment—a look about his grey eyes, she decided, as if he had seen many things that he regretted seeing.

She returned to an earlier comment by the FBI man. "I never knew it was firmly established that the man who died was either Jewish or German."

"I didn't say that he was either, only that he was a foreign national. The autopsy noted the man could have been Jewish, but at the time there was no proof. In fact, he was Jewish, and he was German. Since the inquest, the FBI followed through on the dental records."

Sarah interrupted. "I thought after the inquest the matter was closed."

"Not, Mrs. Burkhardt, from the Bureau's point of view. It was closed from the point of view of Galveston County, but not from Mr. Hoover's perspective."

"Um," she murmured, remembering Azzo had once said almost the same thing.

Agent McCuskey went on. "After the inquest we worked with French and German police, interviewing dentists. War had not begun at that time and, though it was a tedious process, we got lucky. Our man used a French dentist."

"Really?" Sarah said, interested, as images from that terrible day flashed unbidden through her mind.

"Yes. Incidentally, your attorney knows I'm here today and what we are discussing."

"Should your visit concern me, Mr. McCuskey?" Sarah said.

"It shouldn't, Mrs. Burkhardt. Neither I nor the Bureau is a threat to you. You may call your attorney to confirm, if you want."

"No, I'll trust you."

The young man nodded and, smiling, continued.

"Mrs. Burkhardt, you've seen the key that Benjamin loaned me?"

"Yes," Sarah said, cautiously. "He found it over a year after the inquest closed. I took it to my uncle and to Billy Bentley, but, by then the entire affair was over, and no one could imagine that if the man had dropped a key that it wouldn't have been found much earlier. You know the police roamed all around that day looking for clues or whatever."

"Yes," McCuskey said, "we know all that. I saw Benjamin running on the beach one day, and he told me about finding the key. Later, at the ice cream parlor I asked him to loan it to me. I promised to one day return it, and now I'm going to have to break that promise."

He reached into a pocket and held out his hand. A key rested in his palm. "This is not the key Benjamin gave me but a copy. The one he gave me is in Washington and tagged as evidence."

"So," Sarah said, "you know what the key was for and what it fitted. Apparently, you have connected it to the man who died. How much are you going to tell me?"

"Not much more," McCuskey said, again with his engaging boyish smile. "We are interested, however, in why the man would be bringing the key to you.

"Well," Sarah said, "I certainly don't know. I never saw the man before in my life until he died in my front yard."

"Yes," Josh McCuskey said, "that's confusing to us, too."

A memory stirred as Sarah remembered a conversation with Azzo. "Mr. McCuskey, you've established that the key belonged to the man who died? Remember, there were tourists all over that day. Then, Mansion House was under construction for almost two years, and during that time the lawn was resodded. A year after that, Benjamin found a key. It could have been dropped by a workman, one of the tourists, a policeman, or maybe fifty years earlier. Who knows?"

"Yes," the FBI man said, "the time element is confusing. But, once we learned the dead man's identity and the political entity with which he was affiliated, and then after Ben loaned us the key and we found the SD box that it fit, well, then, we knew the key was dropped by the man who died in your yard. We are still confused about the circumstances surrounding the event, him crashing through your fence, staggering toward you, it's almost as if he was bringing the key to you as the final desperate act of his life."

Sarah sat, silent, her eyes wide as she wondered if McCuskey was going to make some sort of accusation.

"Of course," Josh continued, "while we believe he was delivering the key, we have no way of knowing to whom he was to deliver it. Somehow, perhaps, he perceived his injuries were more serious than he'd originally thought, and he decided to seek medical attention and was in the process of searching for a hospital. His crashing through your fence might have been a way to ensure emergency crews would arrive quickly. That's possible."

McCuskey paused, then continued. "Those two small chest wounds he had. They are among the things that are confusing. We know that the two sets of wounds, the knife wound in his side and the chest wound were inflicted at different times. He was stabbed first, and we know, from the gun powder residue on his hands, that the man who died fired the pistol we found in his pocket. Additionally, there was a dead man found in the woods around Winnie, with a bullet hole in his chest and a bloody knife in his hand. The bullet that killed him came from the gun the man who died in your yard had in his pocket, and the blood type on the knife matched his blood type."

"Winnie?" Sarah said. "Up in Chambers County? None of this came out at the inquest." Sarah's brow wrinkled as she tried to remember events she'd put out of her mind years earlier.

"No. We learned all this months later. The case by then was closed in Galveston County, but, of course…" His voice trailed away.

"The timeline fits," McCuskey continued, "based on when the murder in Winnie is known to have occurred.

He could have driven to Bolivar, taken the ferry across to Galveston, then…and here's the odd part. Somehow he received a second wound, those two mysterious holes in his chest, each of which are a little more than an inch apart.

"We're still trying to figure that out. The local police, here and in Chambers County, well, as you know, they've declared both cases closed. The FBI, however, has kept the case open. And then Benjamin found that key."

"Mr. McCuskey, why are you telling me all this?"

"I talked with our Director before coming here. Mr. Hoover and I want Benjamin to know why I can't return the key he found. He made me promise, you know, to return the key to him. And now I can't. That's why the key I just gave you is a copy, and I want you to tell Benjamin."

"You can tell him yourself," Sarah said.

"Yes, I could, but Ben's in school today, and I've got to leave Galveston on another assignment. I visited with Billy Bentley before coming here, to let him know that I was going to leave a duplicate key with you. Later today, or tomorrow, you can give Ben the duplicate key and tell him why we can't give him the original."

Sarah started to speak, but McCuskey held up his hand. "Mrs. Burkhardt, I need to tell you, at your attorney's insistence, that neither you nor anyone in your family is under suspicion for anything connected with this whole affair. Both the Bureau and your attorney think it's important for you to know that."

"Thank you, Mr. McCuskey," Sarah said. "I appreciate your consideration."

Later, as Sarah's car turned into the main drive of Mansion House, she saw Azzo walking from Carriage House. He met her at Mansion House's side entrance.

"I'm through for the day," he said, walking down the wide hallway with her. "Do you think Ben would be up for a run? How about you?" Without waiting for an answer, he turned toward Benjamin's room, calling, "Hey, Ben, ready for a run?"

Benjamin shouted over the transom, "I'm always ready! Let me pull on my shorts."

Azzo looked at Sarah, a question in his eyes.

"Sure!" she said, nodding, thinking that this delay would give her more time to digest all the FBI man had told her earlier. She and her husband went into their bedroom to change. Ben was already behind the wheel of the jalopy, honking the car's 'ah-oogah!' horn, anxious to be on the way.

She stepped into Ben's room, dodging the model airplanes he'd built and had hanging from the ceiling, and placed the key that Joshua McCuskey had given her into the small box Ben had built, thinking, "I'll tell him all about it later tonight."

Benjamin continued honking the jalopy's horn as they, laughing, exited Mansion House and climbed into the car's front and only seat. After Ben's birthday and his and Azzo's joint Bar Mitzvah, Azzo had taken Ben to the driver's license bureau, where he was given a "hardship" license. Ben had decided at that time that the jalopy was now his car.

"Mom, I've told you all my life, I'm gonna run with the wind," Ben said, steering the car toward the beach, "and I'm getting really close thanks to Azzo."

Azzo chuckled. "And thanks to your therapist, your track coach, your mom, and to your own perseverance, my friend."

"I'm already working out with the track team, Mom," Ben added with a note of pride. "Coach says I'm improving. I'll never be good at the hurdles, but this little Jew can run, and Coach damn well knows it!"

"Ben!" Sarah said, "I've told you before! Don't curse. Don't call yourself a Jew!"

"Why not? Azzo says it's okay. I'm proud to be a Jew. Everyone knows I'm a Jew; it's no secret. Rabbi says it's okay to be proud of who you are. And I'm especially proud to know and love another Jew, this man in the car with us, my dad!" Ben said this last with emphasis. He looked at Azzo and winked. "And you too, Mom!" Ben said over the wind noise.

They discovered the beach was almost deserted. Ben parked and excitedly climbed out, beginning a few warm-up exercises.

Winds were light this early fall day, and the weather warm. The afternoon sky was dotted with cloud which foreshadowed highlights of color later. Sarah, though, found the beach to be cooler than she'd thought back at Mansion house and wished for heavier clothes. She soon abandoned the run and returned to the car, leaving her two men to run without her. She huddled behind the windshield, a heavy towel across her shoulders.

Ben and Azzo, finishing their run early, came to the jalopy and reached into the rear for towels and an old blanket. They wrapped themselves in the towels and spread the blanket across the seat. Sarah moved under the wheel as Azzo said, "You're gonna have to be our chauffeur. We're all wet and sandy."

That night, preparing for bed, Azzo said, "Sarah, I can't say it enough. Your boy is all the son that I could ever have wished to have. He makes me so proud when he calls me his dad."

She looked at her husband. "The reason I married you was that my son needed a father," she said, turning back to the dresser, brushing her hair.

"What?" he teased, leaning over, nuzzling against the back of her neck. He murmured, "I thought you married me because you wanted to get me in bed with you."

"Well," she said, reaching for him, "that, too. Come here, boy, and be my lover."

"I'm not a boy," Azzo whispered as he picked her up and carried her to the bed, "but I am your lover."

As he stood beside the bed, holding her, she once again and for the briefest of moments thought about the key and her conversation with the FBI agent. "I'll talk to Ben tomorrow," she told herself as Azzo placed her gently on the bed and turned toward the bedroom door, closing it and snapping off the light.

Sarah forgot everything about the key.

Chapter 21

Mansion House West
November 1943

Ben was sitting in the gazebo, his English-language version of the Torah open on his lap. His *talit*—the prayer shawl from his adult Bar Mitzvah—was across his shoulders, his *yarmulke* upon his head. It was late on a Sunday morning, nearly noon on a cool late fall day. Ben could hear church bells, to him a sound of peace, calling his Christian friends to their services.

He was not reading. Instead, as he listened to the Christian bells, he was thinking about his life and how his earliest memories were of pain. He remembered blaming his mother for the pain, but later, gradually, he had come to realize that the massages, though they hurt, were designed to one day relieve the pain. That was when he knew his mother had loved him enough to hurt him, and to work tirelessly so that someday the pain would be gone.

Ben did not actually remember the time when he was four and declared his intention to someday run, but he'd been told the story so often that he felt he remembered. And now he knew the declaration he made that day was done to reassure his mother that all she was doing was working. Ben somehow believed, even at the young age of four, that the day would come when he would be free of pain. And now that day seemed to have arrived, or nearly so. His left leg sometimes cramped and muscles still spasmed, but the pain he now felt was so minor he could put it out of his mind. He heard footsteps on the graveled walk and looked up, hoping it was his father, who was away once again. A clearly distressed Aaron entered the gazebo, his face a mask of worry and concern.

"Hey," Ben said, glad for company as his earlier meditations faded from his mind.

"I gotta talk, Ben," Aaron said in a low voice, almost whispering.

Alarm bells rang in Ben's head as he closed his Torah. "Have a seat."

"I think what I have to say might be worth interrupting your studies," Aaron almost whispered.

Ben put his Book down and looked at his friend.

"Ben," Aaron began again, "I did something awful yesterday."

"What?" Ben said, a grin beginning to spread across his face. "Did you tease Mrs. Godwin's old cat again and she caught you?"

"Stop it, Ben!" Aaron said. "This is serious!"

The boy paused as if deciding what to say, then blurted, "I went to a whorehouse yesterday!"

"Whoa!" Ben said, astonished at the announcement. "Man, if you did something like that you better get to a doctor! You can catch stuff in one of those places that'll rot your dick off! At the roots!"

"I didn't *do* anything," Aaron said almost angrily, looking around as if fearful someone might overhear. "I just went there. It was awful, and Ben," his voice dropping to a whisper once again, "it was in what you and your mom call Mansion House West!"

The world for Ben seemed to tilt. He had the feeling that he might slide off the gazebo bench. "Mansion House West!" he exclaimed as the breath went out of him.

Mansion House West! His mother's pride. The new twenty-four-appartment unit built in the part of the city block that had once been a paddock where his great-grandfather's matched carriage horses pranced. The new unit that had enhanced his mother's income and reputation was in danger of ruin!

He shook his head, whispering, "No, no, it can't be!"

"It is true," Aaron said almost calmly, his normal voice returning. "Ben, something's gotta be done."

"I'll say!" Ben answered. "This will ruin our reputation—Mom's, mine, Dad's...everyone! Yours too, if anyone ever finds out you went there!" He paused for a minute, thinking.

Turning to his friend, he said, "Start from the beginning. Tell me everything. Even if you—ah, did something, you tell me!" He paused, looking his friend in the eyes, and added sternly, "And you tell me the truth!"

Aaron held up both hands palms out, chin up, defiant. "I swear, Ben, I didn't *do* anything! I'll tell you everything."

Ben nodded, his eyes boring into those of his friend. "You better!"

"Well," Aaron began, "Mom came back from Mrs. Kaine's, across the street from the apartments you call Mansion House West. She'd been over there for a party or something, maybe they played bridge, I don't know. Mom likes her bridge games. Maybe it was mah jong, she likes that, too."

Ben, becoming agitated, suddenly stood, looking down at his friend, hands on his hips. "Aaron, get to the point!"

"I'm trying, Ben," Aaron said, stress clear in his voice. "You told me to tell you everything. Besides, this is hard! I'm telling another guy that…"

"C'mon, Aaron," Ben said, calming himself and returning to his seat. He placed his arm across his friend's shoulders. "We're buddies. You can tell me anything."

"Okay, Ben," Aaron said, looking at the floor. "Here's how it was. Mom came back from that party, and she was talking about how Mrs. Kaine was complaining about loud music that came from your mom's apartments. She said it came both from the manager's office and the one right next to it. They're both right up front. Mrs. Kaine said it sounded like the music from one of those bars on Post Office Street. You know," Aaron looked at his friend, "everyone says those bars are nothing but whorehouses, and all those ladies that walk up and down Post Office are whores…"

"Who was your mom telling?" Ben interrupted, removing his arm from Aaron's shoulders and rolling his eyes.

"Oh, it was just one of the maids, not your maid Rae but one of the others that come in. Rae's so busy at your apartments, she's stopped day-maiding in the neighborhood."

"Why did she tell her?"

"Mom didn't talk to Rae," Aaron said, shaking his head.

Ben let out a long breath. "Aaron, I meant, what did your mom say to the person she was talking to, just after the party. And why?"

"Oh, that's just Mom's way. She knows I don't listen to her when she comes back, and my dad never listens and she always feels as if she has to talk about everything."

"Um," Ben said, cradling his chin in his hands.

"Anyway," Aaron continued, " I overheard what she said, about it sounding like a whorehouse. So, last evening, it wasn't even dark yet, you know, this wartime daylight savings they call it…"

"Aaron!" Ben almost shouted. "Get to the point!"

"I'm getting to it," Aaron said defensively. He looked into his friend's eyes. "Last evening, I rode my bicycle over. There was a guy sitting on the porch. He offered me a cigarette."

"You're smoking now?"

"Ah, no, well, just a little. Ben, it's no big deal. Everyone does it."

"It'll kill you," Ben said in exasperation, "but not, I hope, before you finally get to the point of all this!"

"Okay, okay," Aaron said. "Well, I sat on the porch with him. There was music coming from inside. He asked me if I wanted to go inside. Hear the music better, he said. Ben, you know what he did?"

Ben shook his head, waiting for Aaron to answer his own question.

"Ben, he put his hand on my leg. Way up. You know what I mean?"

"God!" Ben said, gagging.

"So, Ben, when he put his hand there I got up as quick as I could, just to get his hand away, you know. And then he grabbed my hand and took me inside. You know what I saw?"

"Well, I hope you're going to tell me one of these days!"

"Ben, there were four ladies in there. They weren't wearing very much. One of them said, 'Oh look, fresh meat!' Ben, they meant me! I was fresh meat to them.

"I started backing away, back toward the door. Then, this guy who gave me the cigarette—he said his name was Eugene, I think—well, this guy said, 'Oh, Jews don't like girls? How about boys? Do Jews like boys instead of girls?'

and, just then, two guys not much older than you or me, Ben, they came out from a hallway or something. One of them had lipstick on, and not much else."

Aaron's face was red. Ben noticed sweat on his forehead. Then, Aaron began crying.

"Ben," Aaron said through sobs, "this guy told me that I could have anyone I wanted, a boy or a girl, or both a boy and a girl at the same time, for only three dollars! That's the way he said it! Only three dollars! He called me a 'clip-cock Jew.' Ben, I turned and ran out the door. That Eugene guy, he followed me out onto the porch, laughing. He said, 'Come back little Jew! We can have some fun!' I ran to my bicycle and went home."

Ben let out a long sigh. "Oh, my god!" A feeling of disgust almost overwhelmed him as gorge rose in his throat. Ben stood and shouted "*Shtik drek!* Piece of shit!"

"Ben, what are we going to do?"

"We?" Ben said, eyebrows up. "Right now, this minute? Nothing! You don't tell anyone! Go home!"

"Ben what are *you* going to do?" Aaron asked.

"I don't know, not yet. I've got to think a minute."

"Tell your dad!" Aaron said. "That's what I think you should do!"

Ben rolled his eyes and looked skyward. "Not a chance. Dad would—well, there'd probably be bloodshed." Ben was silent as he thought. Then, his ideas crystalized into a plan. Ben turned to his friend and said, calmly, "Aaron, I'm sorry I shouted at you. I think the first thing is that you and I ought to go over there a little later, about the same time as when you went yesterday. I want to see for myself."

"You said for me to go home," Aaron said, shaking his head. "I'm not going back to that place! Nuhh, uh!"

"Yes, you are," Ben said, standing again, his voice now strong. He looked at Aaron and for the first time realized he was taller than his friend. "You come back here after supper. We'll walk over together. That guy will recognize you, think you're bringing a buddy, so both of us can—well, you see what I mean. Aaron." He gave his friend a stern look. "You're going to go with me!"

The next morning Ben walked into the kitchen as his mother was sitting at the table, eating her breakfast and reading the *Daily News*. "Got hotcakes and eggs for you," Rae sang out to Ben. "They're almost ready."

Afterward Ben followed his mom into her office alcove.

Sarah turned and looked at her son, eyebrows raised.

"Mom," Ben said, "we gotta talk."

"Ben," she said, beginning a protest, looking for a way to delay. Ben could tell that his mother was irritated and thinking about her upcoming day at Galveston Pilots'.

"You've got to go to school," she said.

"No, Mom," Ben said calmly, "you need to sit down and you need to sit down now! You need to listen to me! Please have a seat," he smiled, indicating her office chair. "You may be a little late for work this morning. I may be a little late for school."

Sarah suddenly sat, open mouthed as she thought, "My son is telling me what to do!"

"Ben, I'm in a hurry," she said as she sat. "We can talk later. After school. It can wait. You don't need to be late for school."

"Nope," her son said, standing tall and straight, looking down at his mother. "What I've got to say won't wait. It has to be now. Right now!"

Sarah sat and listened. As she did, her face changed. By the time Ben had finished, Sarah was no longer concerned either about Galveston Pilots' or Ben's being late for school.

She said, "So, as far as you know, only you and Aaron know about this?"

"Well, Mom, I don't know anyone else who knows, but apparently this couple in the manager's office have been at it for some time, so, you know, there have been customers..." His voice trailed away, his eyebrows up.

"Well, we've got to get them out of there! Azzo said I should have done more checking! Have they turned the whole complex into a—" She couldn't complete her sentence.

"I don't think they've taken over the entire complex," Ben said, "at least not yet. But it seems to me that since they have the manager's apartment and the one next to it, surely there are tenants who must be complaining. Of course, they'd be complaining to the manager, and the manager's the one making all the noise. The neighbors are surely beginning to notice. And, I just remembered, didn't two of the tenants break their lease last month? Mom, there may be more."

"I'll tell your dad. He'll be back in town in a day or so!"

"Not a good idea, Mom," her suddenly adult fourteen-year-old son said. "There might be bloodshed, and it wouldn't be Dad's; it'd be that couple and the police might call it murder."

That thought scared Sarah more than she would admit. "Yes," she told herself, "Azzo would go crazy."

She sat at her desk, biting a thumb nail and musing, partly aloud, mumbling to herself. Ben remained standing, waiting, seemingly knowing her thoughts.

"You can't go to the police," Ben finally said. "In the first place, everyone knows Sam Klein has a police radio on his desk at *Daily News* and you don't want reporters running around. Bad for business. Not only bad for that couple's business but bad for your business, too. Also, that manager couple just might have been paying off someone at the police department. I've heard that those on Post Office Street do."

Sarah wondered briefly how her innocent little boy had learned so much about the world. There was a momentary feeling of sadness.

"Mom," Ben said, "any publicity about this would be bad. You're probably going to lose tenants as it is."

Sarah made up her mind.

She stood in front of her son, her back straight, her shoulders squared. "I know what to do, and who to tell. I'm going to go there right now!"

Ben smiled and named a name, a question in his eyes.

"Yep!" his mother said, no longer the shrinking widow but the determined woman, the same woman who'd worked with aching fingers to beat her son's polio, who'd turned a dilapidated Victorian mansion into a profitable apartment complex, and who managed the waterfront dock crews and channel pilots with an iron hand.

"He and his gang," she said, "are responsible for all the prostitution in this town and I'll bet dollars-to-doughnuts he doesn't know about Mansion House West operating right under his nose!"

She smiled a grim smile. "I'm pretty sure he doesn't like competition."

"Go for it mom!" Ben said, his mission complete.

Four days later, on a Saturday morning, Azzo and Ben walked through the shambles of what had once been a luxury apartment. Both the manager's apartment and the adjacent one had been incorporated into the operation, and a rough-cut interior doorway connected the two. Rough unpainted plywood partitions separated each bedroom into two. Furniture was spare and ragged, couches had plastic sheets thrown over them, and underneath were covered with dirt and stains. Mattresses were the worst of all, some on the floor, all of them stained and dirty beyond dirty. Cigarette butts, empty beer and liquor bottles along with used condoms littered both apartments. Floors were scarred and tile was missing from kitchen and bathroom counters. The door of one refrigerator sagged and water dripped onto the linoleum floor. A third apartment, adjacent to the first two had had walls removed in preparation for expansion of the illegal activities.

At one point, Azzo stopped and picked up something. Ben looked over. "What's that?" It looked like a roll-your-own, whereas most of the butts scattered about were "tailor-made."

"Dope," Azzo said with disgust. "Marijuana. Loco-weed. I've heard it grows wild a little farther south of Galveston, but this stuff," he paused, sniffing at the roll-your-own, "isn't local. It's imported."

Ben just shook his head. "Looks as if we've got some painting and carpentry to do."

"Can I count on your help after school?" Azzo asked.

"Well," Ben answered, "I've got track, but after that? Sure. And, Thanksgiving is coming up. We'll have a four-day weekend then."

Chapter 22

Two Years Later
Saturday Evening, August 1944

Sixteen-year old Benjamin rested part-way into his run, sitting on the ancient driftwood tree trunk, missing his friend and father. The sun was low in the western sky and the day's blistering late summer heat was beginning to fade. Ben was shirtless, sweaty, and coated with both salt and sand.

He looked seaward. The surf was high, but Ben could see mullet schooling just beyond the breakers. Redfish were probably there now, or else would show up soon, and he needed to check the lines he'd deployed earlier. He arose from the driftwood, and began a light jog toward his fishing jalopy, the old car that had once been Azzo's.

Ben's jog soon became a run, and half-way to the car he felt the now-familiar lightness, the freedom that a run always brought, the feeling that he could run forever.

Reaching the car, he ran past, noting that his lines were not stretched. Reds had not yet found the bait, Ben decided, thinking that he could continue his run. He jogged on but stopped as he heard one of the reels begin to sing. He wheeled and took up battle with a bull red desperate for life. Soon, the gasping fish was placed in an ice chest, and as Ben rebaited, he noted that the evening had deepened, and three stars shone. Ben paused, still holding the fishing rod and heard, in his mind, Rabbi Cohen reciting Havdallah prayers at the ending of Shabbat. He cast the line out, saw the bait and weights drop satisfactorily just past the second line of breakers, tightened the drag and replaced the rod in its holder on the car's front bumper. He leaned back onto the fender, deep in thought.

Always, prior to heading to the beach, Ben dropped by the Coast Guard Station. He always chatted with his friends, picked up his pass, winked at a reference for Azzo Coca-Colas, and knew he had assurance that he could stay the night.

Beach patrols had become less frequent since the D-day invasion of France, though submarine attacks on Gulf tankers continued. Usually, his Coast Guard friends told him, the attacks now occurred far into the eastern Gulf, not near Galveston.

He looked seaward as he lit the gasoline lanterns, fitting them into lantern-holders built into the old car's front bumper along with rod holder sockets. He both heard and saw a splash as mullet scattered. The redfish had shown up in numbers. He'd fill his ice chests tonight, he was sure.

He took another swallow of water from the Mason jar beside him, turned and looked at the last remnant of the sunset beyond the dunes. The beauty of the calm waters of San Luis Pass, reflecting the final rays of the setting sun always seemed to touch his soul.

He decided to reel in the two lines that had not been disturbed by the recent battle. He did, and found they needed re-baiting. He moved about the tasks methodically, and as he did his mind turned to Gus Morton and the day the tanker he had been piloting was sunk by U-boats. Since that day it seemed he and Azzo had come to the beach fewer and fewer times, and he wondered why.

On this evening he was lonely, missing having company and missing his dad. He had asked his friend Aaron, but Aaron had other plans.

Within three short weeks, Ben would begin his third year of high school. While still only a sophomore, he had been named captain of the junior cross-country team, and this year, as a junior, he hoped to again be named captain. He excelled at relay and cross-country, and Coach continually expressed amazement at Ben's speed. He and the Jewish boy had developed a strong admiration for one another. These days when Coach shouted and called Ben "Cripple!" it was a compliment, and even the high school cheerleaders echoed Coach's call with the cheer, "Go! Crip! Go!"

'Cripple' had become Ben's high school nickname, and he hoped it would follow him to college and beyond. He was proud of his progress against polio and he was proud of his nickname. To Ben, it was synonymous with victory.

Everyone in Galveston, it seemed to Ben, knew of his fight against polio. Even the prisoners behind their fence at 53rd and Seawall called him 'Crip' as they waved and shouted when he passed by. Ben was a volunteer at the camp, teaching English, and found he was learning German in the process. Azzo had complimented him on his improving accent.

Benjamin again reeled in his lines, replaced two of the baits, and cast all three out again. He looked up. A dark-colored sedan had turned off the new road and was bouncing along the beach toward him.

Joshua McCuskey, in a business suit, stopped the car and exited. "Hi! I heard the fellow everyone calls

'Cripple' was out here fishing. Thought I'd see how he was doing."

Ben tried unsuccessfully to hide his disappointment.

"Hello, Mr. McCuskey."

Ben wiped his hands on his shorts, and held out one to the FBI agent, who took it. "I thought you were someone else," Ben said as they shook hands.

"You thought I was your dad, right?" McCuskey said, holding tight to Ben's hand.

Ben nodded, embarrassed, then said, "Welcome to San Luis Pass."

"Well, sorry I'm not your dad," McCuskey said, letting go of Ben's hand. "But may I join you?"

"Sure," Ben answered, resuming his seat on one rusty fender and motioning the FBI man to the other. Josh McCuskey looked at the rusty fender with distaste.

"Hmm," he said. "I think I'll change into my khakis. They're in the car. Back with you in a minute."

"Do you ever go fishing Mr. McCuskey??" Ben asked as the FBI man returned. "Or are you too busy catching spies and stuff?"

"Call me Josh, Ben," McCuskey said, laughing. "And no, I don't often go fishing. In fact, I've never been."

"You've never been fishing?"

"No," Josh said. "I grew up in D.C. and was raised by a single mom. Fishing was something I guess I missed out on."

"Well," Ben said, "Stay here with me then. Ole 'Crip', here, would be excited to teach you. And," he ducked his head as he added, wistfully, "I was wishing for company."

The evening deepened, and Ben poured a little gasoline on a number of driftwood logs he'd collected earlier and began a fire. Soon, it was blazing nicely, offsetting the early evening coolness.

Ben nodded at the fire. "We need to let it go for a while," he said, "and it'll develop a good bed of hot coals. When it does, I'll scrape some of them out, put up a windscreen and a grate over the coals, and we'll cook some fish. I've got boiled potatoes wrapped in tin foil, and we'll put them into the hot coals to bake."

"Sounds good," the FBI man said. "How many fish have you caught?"

"Only one, so far," Ben said, grinning, as he settled into place on a fender. "But our supper is still out there, and we've got to catch it." He nodded toward the surf.

As Josh settled on his fender, Ben said, "Want to run? I feel like another run while we wait to catch supper."

"I don't have any shorts or proper shoes for running," Josh replied. He held up his feet, encased in dress shoes, now dirty with damp sand.

"I usually run bare-footed," Ben said, "but I have some old rubber-soled high-tops. They might fit. I've got an old pair of Azzo's cut-offs, too. They'd be better to run in than those khakis." He left his fender and reached behind the jalopy seat.

"Here," he said to his new friend, "see if these will fit. They're a little dirty," he added, apologizing but grinning, "just shake the sand out before you put them on."

"J. Edgar, the man I work for," Josh said as he removed his khakis and pulled on the shorts, "is a nut about his agents maintaining fitness. I go to the gym every chance I get, but, what with traveling and all, sometimes I miss more than a few days."

"Run with me now," Ben said. "I need to run again."

It was a challenge, of sorts, and to McCuskey it seemed Ben was saying, "If you want to be my friend, run with me."

Josh finished pulling on the ragged high-tops and stood before Ben in the cut-offs and a sleeveless undershirt. "Meet your approval, Crip?" he asked.

In response Ben leaned over, grabbed the FBI man's left arm with his right, locked the arms together, and said loudly, "C'mon!" He added, shouting, and pointing, "To the driftwood!"

They ran. The FBI agent found synchronizing his stride with Ben's to be easier than he thought, then realized that Ben was the one synchronizing their stride. Sooner than he thought possible, Josh McCuskey, an FBI agent from Washington, D.C. was running smoothly, arms locked, with Cripple Burkhardt, a high schooler from Galveston, Texas.

Half-way to the driftwood tree Ben shouted, "Run with the wind!" He picked up their speed.

As they reached the driftwood, McCuskey found himself gasping for breath. As Ben handed him a towel that had been placed earlier, he said, "That wasn't as hard as I thought it'd be, except the last part. I thought I was going to fall. Do you always shout like that?"

Ben laughed, then while using his own towel told McCuskey the story of coming up with that phrase at age four.

"You're in pretty good shape," Ben finished, "better than I thought you'd be."

"I haven't run in a long time," Josh answered, feeling the need to apologize.

"Oh, I could tell that," Ben said, "but I locked our arms together. That's the way Azzo taught me, and that's the way we like to run, together, father and son, arms locked.

"Let's go back," McCuskey said, nodding toward the cars. "Oh! Look! One of those rods is bent over!"

"Here!" Ben shouted, handing Josh the towels, "You come along and bring the towels, I'm not gonna wait on you this time! Follow me!" He took off running toward the bent rod. Josh was quickly left behind.

As McCuskey, panting and sweating, came up to the jalopy, he saw Ben wade into the surf and in a practiced motion, holding the rod high with one hand, using the other to slip under the exhausted redfish and lift it free of the water by its gill plates.

"Supper!" Ben said, wading back to the shore, holding the fish and surf rod high.

Later, as the fish cooked over hot coals behind the wind screen, Ben asked, "How about a beer?"

"You have beer?" Josh asked.

Ben laughed. "No, I have Azzo Coca-Cola's. Dad gives them to the patrols when they come by. He asks if they'd like a beer, and they always say no, they can't drink on duty. Then he says, 'Okay, have a Coca-Cola, an Azzo Coca-Cola,' and he points to that chest, the one that's mounted on the passenger-side front fender.

"Go ahead," Ben urged, "reach in." The FBI man pulled out an icy bottle of Southern Select Beer.

"Hmmm," Josh McCuskey said. "An Azzo Coca-Cola? Is this a local brand?"

"Well," Ben answered, "Southern Select is brewed near Houston, in Pasadena, over on Genoa Road. So, I guess it's a local brand. We call them Azzo Coca-Cola's for the obvious reason."

Ben took the bottle from his new friend, snapped the cap off on the bumper, and handed it back to the FBI man. He reached for a bottle for himself, opened it, and took a long, practiced pull.

Later, Josh McCuskey said, "That was, without a doubt, the best meal I've ever eaten in my life!"

Ben had spread a ground-tarp next to the jalopy and in front of the fire. He and Josh were sitting cross-legged on dry towels. The old jalopy had been moved to serve as a windbreak.

Ben grinned. "Dad says that the very best a fish can taste is when it's cooked as soon as possible after it's been caught. The fish I cooked tonight is called 'redfish on the half-shell', and it's cooked over hot coals, skin-and-scales-side down. No seasoning, other than lemon, salt-and-pepper, and butter. It cooks in its own juices."

"Rationing…" Josh began.

"I don't always have butter, that's true," Ben admitted, "and that stuff you get now-days, that oleo-margarine, well, you can just forget it. When I can't get butter…," his voice trailed off. "Mr. Samuelsson, over at the corner store, he sometimes gets real butter from a farmer he knows. We used Mr. Samuelsson's butter on our baked potatoes tonight."

"And the beer?" Josh queried, draining the last of his second bottle.

Ben laughed. "Yeah, that too. I buy it from him, I tell him Azzo sent me, that I need it for Azzo's Coca-Cola. I think everybody in Galveston knows about Azzo's Coca-Cola."

Ben rose from his cross-legged position and walked to Azzo's Coca-Cola chest. He opened it, pulled two more bottles from the chest and turned.

"You're a cop, Josh," he said. "Are you gonna arrest that old man for selling beer to a minor? You gonna arrest me for drinking it?"

Josh shook his head. "I'm a Federal cop, Ben. The drinking age is a state and local matter." He smiled. "Ben I wouldn't do that anyway. I'd like to be your friend."

"Well," Ben said, "that settles that. You want another, friend?" He handed a beer to McCuskey, first removing the cap on the car's bumper.

Ben popped the cap for a third beer for himself and sat on the car's fender, looking out to sea. McCuskey swiveled his seat on the tarp and looked up at Ben.

"Did Azzo teach you to fish?"

"No," Ben answered, staring out to the dark Gulf, talking as if he had something else on his mind. "I kind of taught myself. But I never went surf fishing before Dad came along, so I guess he taught me how to do that."

"And he taught you to run."

"Oh, yes indeed." Ben was silent for almost a minute, alternating his gaze between the sea and his new friend. As he turned to look seaward again, he frowned, arose from the fender and walked to the edge of the surf. The wind was increasing. Ben saw a dark line just at the horizon and knew a storm was coming. He walked back to the jalopy.

"You know," he said casually, "it took three of us, me, my mom and my dad, but we beat polio, and running is what did it. Coach helped, and all the folks at Texas Medical in Galveston, but we did it! *Toda lal!*"

"I agree," Josh said, "thank God!"

"You know your Hebrew," Ben said, eyebrows raised. After a pause, he added, "You're not Jewish." It was half-question half-statement.

"No, I don't guess I'm anything," Josh said, "I once had a good friend who was Jewish. She was someone I thought I would marry, and I studied some about

Judaism." He shrugged. "But she died." It was a simple statement of fact.

Ben said nothing but arose and waded into the surf. He washed the metal plates and other utensils used in their meal. As he returned, stowing everything in a small wooden chest, Ben said, his voice strong, "Josh, I keep waiting for you to tell me the real reason you're here, and maybe, just maybe, for you to tell me why you never returned the key I loaned you."

"I returned a copy," McCuskey said. "I gave it to your mother. I asked her to tell you."

"I certainly found the copy right away," Ben said, taking another slug from his beer, "but Mom never told me anything. I wondered about that. It's not even a very good copy."

"Ben," McCuskey protested, "it was perfect."

"No, it wasn't. The original key was a tight fit into the inlay at the bottom of the box I built. The copy didn't fit right. Only the original would have been a perfect fit."

"Josh," Ben said, looking deep into the FBI man's eyes, "want to tell me what's really going on?"

Chapter 23

A Day Remembered

Josh did not answer Ben, but instead rose from his cross-legged seat on the ground tarp, went to the "Azzo Coca-Cola" chest and took out another beer, then put it back. Ben slid off the fender and reached behind the jalopy's front seat. "Here," he said, pouring water into a camping cup from a large thermos.

Josh took the cup without drinking and walked around the jalopy as Ben stood, watching. "You know," the FBI man said, "I've never before looked closely at this old car. You've got quite a fishing machine. What's this?" He reached in and held up what looked like a broom handle, except with steel prongs.

Ben frowned. "It's a gig," he said cautiously.

McCuskey drank a little water. He stood quietly, holding the gig and looking at Ben.

"Azzo and I," Ben said, showing a sudden nervousness, "sometimes, we go to the bay side of Galveston Island, in calm shallow water and gig flounder."

"Hm," McCuskey said.

"Yeah," Ben went on, speaking too rapidly, "we go at night, use the lanterns. The flounder are just lying there on the bottom and we gig them. They're good eating."

"Well, Ben," Josh said, holding the gig. "I think I'm getting close to figuring out at least part of the story."

Ben turned away from Josh and again walked to the water's edge, looking out over the dark Gulf. There was no moon nor clouds. Stars shone brilliantly. Wind tousled his hair. The dark line on the horizon, larger now hid part of the night sky.

McCuskey walked up behind him. "I'm surprised your mother never told you anything I said when I returned your—ah—the copy of the key you found. May I tell you what I told her that day?"

Without waiting for an answer, Josh began to talk while Ben stood, not looking at the FBI man, instead continuing to look toward the horizon. He saw intermittent flashes of lightning; the storm was approaching faster than he'd thought. Gusts of wind whipped Ben's hair.

"So, you see," Josh finished, "we've puzzled for years about those two holes in his chest. They, along with the stab wounds in his side, are what killed him. How did he get them? What was the instrument that made those two holes?"

Ben turned to the FBI man. He was looking down at the gig in his hands, studying it. Then Josh looked up; his eyes locked with Ben's. Both men stood, silent. Then, almost simultaneously both turned toward the Gulf as a low-pitched rumble of distant thunder could be heard over the noise of the wind and surf.

Ben turned back to the FBI man. "You know what I'm going to say, don't you?"

"Maybe," Josh answered. "Were the holes in the man's chest made by a flounder gig? This gig?"

"No," Ben said, "not that gig."

Water from a spent wave washed over their feet.

"There's a storm coming," Ben said calmly. "We need to move the cars to higher ground, or they'll get stuck in the sand. Let's move them now." Josh realized that Ben was deciding what and how much to tell.

The storm was upon them quickly. There was an efficiency of movement as Ben broke down the fishing rods, folded the tarp, and stowed gear in the jalopy, silently motioning from time to time for the FBI man to help.

Later, both cars safely behind the dunes, shielded somewhat from the wind, Ben arranged a shelter, using the ground tarp guyed from the opened doors of the rented sedan across to the jalopy. Another, smaller tarp was spread as ground cover and, it seemed to McCuskey, almost as the last knot was made to the tie-downs, rain began pouring. Thunder crashed while the wind howled, and the tarp shelter snapped against its moorings. It suddenly seemed cooler than before; the storm had brought a chill with it.

Ben lit the two gasoline lanterns, then reached into the rear of the jalopy and pulled two old plaid flannel long-sleeved shirts out of a small chest. He donned one and handed the other to the FBI man. Ben sat cross-legged on the tarp and looked up at the FBI man sitting on the running board of his rented car. Ben stared without speaking for long minutes at this man who'd said he wanted to be his friend.

Then, Ben began talking about a hot August day in 1938, his speech sometimes faltering, emotional, often with a choking sound as he searched for a word. It seemed to McCuskey as Ben talked that the two cars, the nearby dunes, the twin lanterns hissing, the storm crashing about them, the tarp shelter snapping in the wind, all seemed to vanish from sight and sound. All at once Josh could clearly see Benjamin Jacobs at age ten, sitting on an old pier on a very hot and still day with a tattered straw hat on his head.

The day was one for disappointment. The southeast sea breeze had fallen silent and the broad waters of Offats Bayou were still and smooth under a brassy, hot midday sky. A few gulls wheeled about, and occasionally a brown pelican swooped low over the surface.

It was close to noon and Benji remembered his note saying he'd return home by lunchtime. But he delayed, thinking that he needed to bring home at least something even if the fish were not biting.

Benji decided to gig a few crabs. But before doing so, he methodically packed his gear onto the old fishing wagon, slid his new two-piece rod apart and placed it into its leather case. He carefully stowed his new reel, then cut several pieces off a hard-head catfish he'd caught earlier and left to die a gasping death in the sun. He tossed the pieces of rotting fish into the shallow marshy water near the shore end of the pier, and sat, legs dangling over, the hated straw hat on his head. He had worn shorts, and the steel of his brace flashed in the sun.

It did not take long for the bait to attract a hungry blue crab. Benji quickly impaled the crab on the tines of his gig and swung it to the bucket, partially filled with water. The mortally wounded crab did not know it would soon be dead and so did not easily relinquish the piece of baitfish that Benji pulled away with pliers, wary of the claws. Ben decided to try and gig two or three more before leaving for home and lay on his stomach, holding the gig at ready, his face peering over the pier's wooden curb.

Benji heard a car door slam and looked up. A man was exiting a dark sedan parked near the entrance to the pier. Benji's focus returned to the bait, and he watched two more crabs as they seemingly raced one another for the bait. There!

Benji quickly gigged one and dropped it into the bucket. The second crab quickly followed. Ben heard gate hinges squeal and looked up as a man walked slowly onto the pier.

"Having good luck with those crabs, I see."

Benji saw a man dressed in a heavy business suit, hat low over his eyes, tie askew, leaning against a piling.

"Yes, sir. The fish weren't biting, so I thought I'd take a few crabs home for lunch."

"Do you know Sarah Jacobs?" The voice now seemed harsh. The man spoke loudly, almost shouting. His dark eyes stared.

Benji got up, using the gig as a cane, and turned to the man. "Yes, sir," Benji said as he backed several steps toward the roofed end of the pier, wishing he hadn't left his wrist cane in the wagon.

"Do you know my mother?"

"I got something for her," the stranger said too loudly, his voice guttural, gagging. He moved toward the now frightened boy. "Take me to her!" He kicked the bucket and crabs off the pier into the water.

"You made me lose my crabs!" the frightened boy shouted angrily as all three crabs escaped and the bucket sank.

The man staggered, and this time fell against a second piling. The jacket gaped open, and Benji saw that one side of his white shirt, just above the belt, was darkly wet with red.

"You're hurt!" Benji said, still backing away, alarm bells ringing in his head. He felt as if he was in a rapidly descending elevator. It seemed the man did not hear him.

"I'll go get help!" Benji shouted, looking toward the shore for a way around the man.

"No!" the man answered, now shouting. "There's no time! Take me to Sarah Jacobs!"

"She's not at home! She's at work!" Benji lied, shouting, looking toward 61st Street, looking for help. He was using the gig with both hands, tines pointing skyward. Ben moved toward the sheltered end of the pier, to his wagon and wrist cane.

"Take me to her!" The man staggered forward as Ben took more steps back.

"Go!" the man again shouted. "Get in the car!" He pointed to the dark car parked on 61st Street.

Benjamin was now thoroughly frightened.

Never enter a stranger's car!

This shouting stranger was menacing, staggering as if he were drunk.

"No!" the boy shouted as tears of fright began. He reached the roofed end of the pier, stumbled over his wagon's rope harness and fell, sobbing, as the man rushed toward him. Benji, on his knees, turned and faced the oncoming stranger, holding the gig, trying to regain his feet. The butt end of the gig slid on the deck and came to rest against the wood curb as the man lunged.

Benji's eyes widened in horror as the twin steel tines slid with agonizing slowness into the man's chest. The world stopped. It seemed everything was frozen, nothing moved. There was no sound. Then, time and sound resumed but jerkily. The stranger's wide dark staring eyes locked onto those of the now-terrified boy as his mouth opened. He straightened and in what seemed one motion pulled the gig out of Benji's hands and the tines from his chest. He slung the gig away.

Benji heard the splash as he watched in disbelief the twin spurts of blood erupting from the two holes in the man's chest and cascading down the white shirt. The man slumped onto one of the two benches.

The boy's only thought now was to escape this horror.

Home!

Benji grabbed his wrist cane and, sobbing, slipped the rope harness over his head and began limping shoreward, pausing only to pick up the battered straw hat. Once at the gate he stopped and looked back at the man who was now standing, holding onto an upright and shouting "Stop! Come back!"

Benji pushed the gate shut and fumbled with the padlock, which slipped its hasp and fell into the marshy water. He left the pier and limped to the street, past the dark car, moving as rapidly as possible. He was afraid to look back.

At the street, Ben wondered for the briefest of moments if he should try and stop a passing car, but the thought vanished as he heard more shouts from the pier.

"Stop! Stop I say! Come back! Take me to your mother!"

"Oh, God! No! What have I done?" Benji murmured to himself. "I've got to get home! I've got to get away!"

His mind was a jumble. This had to be a dream. He would wake up soon. Neither his crippled leg nor his good one seemed to be working right.

Run! Run! Get away! Faster!

He crossed the street. A car narrowly missed him, honking, its driver shouting, "Crazy kid!"

Benji barely heard. He limped alongside the street and turned at the corner, heading to his home at 51st and Strand, now only eleven blocks away.

Oh, still so far!

Benji's feet were not working right. He fell, scrambled up, tried to move faster in the thick mud which existed only in his mind. At the next block, Benji crossed catter-corner into the tall hedges that bordered Mrs. Swenson's property.

He rounded the house, hidden from the street and entered the alleyway. Now that he was out of view from the dark car, it seemed he could move faster.

Cane flashing in the sun, sweat pouring in rivulets down his forehead, joining the tears that cascaded down his cheeks, Benji kept going.

"Faster! Faster!" the boy said aloud. "Oh, God!" he prayed. "Let me run, just this once, please!"

The nightmare continued unabated and Benji wondered why he could not wake up.

"Rae!" he called out. Rae usually woke him for breakfast. Why wasn't she waking him now?

He came to 52nd, exited the alleyway and turned, moving along the street. There were no more hedges to hide his movement. He felt exposed and dared to look back.

Two blocks away the nose of a dark sedan edged out into the street.

Ben fell.

He scrambled once again to his feet.

Only two more blocks! Home!

Benji could see his mother, standing on the front steps.

"Mother!" He thought he might have shouted, but his mouth couldn't move properly.

He again looked back. The car was still there!

The dark sedan, now an evil thing with a life of its own, was no longer hiding.

"It's coming to get me!" Benji tried to shout, but it was a whisper.

The Gulf was once again calm as the sky lightened, foreshadowing the oncoming dawn. The squall had abated as Ben talked and told his story, tears streaking his cheeks, intermittently sobbing as he relived the horror. At times,

Ben's voice was a whisper, hesitant, faltering; other times it was clear and steady.

Josh had remained transfixed, sitting on his car's running board while Ben talked, often sitting cross-legged and staring directly into the FBI man's eyes. Other times he moved about, looking from under the shelter at the wind and rain as he searched for a word or phrase while thunder crashed. When Ben finished, he was again sitting cross-legged and looking up. Neither spoke.

Ben went to the sand at the edge of the ground tarp and emptied his untouched beer.

"The sun will be up soon," he said, not looking back at the FBI man. "I'd planned to spend the night anyway, though I thought I'd catch more fish."

"Ben..." Josh McCuskey began, standing behind Ben. The younger man held up his hand.

"Let's don't talk for a minute," Ben said. "I can make us some coffee. I brought eggs. I'll make breakfast."

Neither spoke as Ben took the gasoline camp stove from storage in the jalopy, placed it on the tarp and knelt. Soon, water was boiling for coffee and eggs were frying in a skillet. Josh discovered he was very hungry.

After the meal, Ben moved about, clearing things away, wiping the skillet with a cloth. "I'll wash everything later today," he said, then turned to Josh. "Unless, of course, you plan to arrest me." Ben's eyes were steady, looking at the man who had said he wanted to be his friend.

"Not gonna do that, Ben," Josh said.

Ben bent to the lanterns, extinguished them, folded the ground tarp, stowed it and other gear in the jalopy, and began taking down the shelter tarp. He looked at Josh.

"Want to help me fold this thing?"

As they folded, Ben said, "Not gonna arrest me?"

"No, Ben. It was self-defense. You were only ten. But I'm glad you told me. It clears up a lot of things."

Ben put the shelter tarp into the jalopy. "I thought maybe you thought my father had done it, murdered the man."

"I never thought that," Josh said. "We've known from the beginning that Azzo was in New Orleans that day.

"Also, Ben," McCuskey continued, "it's not clear and it never will be whether the man died from the knife wound in his side or the gig wound in his chest. While it was probably a combination of the two wounds, I do not think you committed murder.

"Tell me, Ben," Josh asked, thoughtfully, "did you ever tell anyone what you've told me?"

"I told Rae a little," Ben answered, "And I told Rabbi Cohen. I told the rabbi everything."

"Everything?"

"I told him everything that I told you, and I told you all there is to tell."

"What did the good rabbi say?"

Ben paused, looked to the east. There was a tinge of bright orange at the point the sky met the sea. He turned to Josh and said, "Sun's gonna be up in a minute. It'll be a beautiful sunrise. Come over here. This is one of my favorite things to do, watch the sun as it rises out of the Gulf of Mexico."

He turned to Josh as he walked up and together the two men stood, watching the sunrise. "The rabbi told me," Ben said after long minutes, "what you told me. Self-defense. He said it would be best though for me to not tell anyone. So, I didn't. I didn't tell mom, and I haven't told Dad. Do you think I should?"

"Yes," Josh said. "Ben, while I agree with Rabbi Cohen that the story needs to stop, your Dad needs to know it.

Then, it'll stop with you, the good rabbi, me and your Dad. The story clears up a lot of things but will never be in any report I submit."

"Why not?"

"Because it doesn't bring us any closer to the truth."

"Josh," Ben said, "what do you mean? What truth?"

Josh turned from the sunrise to look at Ben. "What I'm trying to do," he said slowly, "is fit a puzzle together. An enormous puzzle. I needed a key to unlock the puzzle."

"The key that I found?" Ben asked.

"No," the FBI man shook his head. "I think the last part of the puzzle, the key, is your story, this jalopy and those surf rods you stowed earlier."

Josh got up and walked around the car, inspecting, thoughtful. "This old car," he said. "I've thought before that it must be part of the answer. If I'm right, then I know the whole story. I'll then know everything. Proving it will be a little difficult, and I hope I never have to even try.

"Ben, get one of those rod sections out of storage, will you?"

Holding the rod, Josh said, "Look. The ends of these sections, the connectors that you snap together when the rods are assembled, they're electrical. That same connector is built into the rod handle. Now, if there was a metallic rod or wire inside the bamboo, connecting the two ends, don't you see that these long rods, when assembled, could be radio antenna?"

Ben took the rod section from him and broke it over his knee. The bamboo splintered, and a thin steel rod glinted in the sunrise. Josh simply looked at the broken rod in Ben's hands; then he turned to the jalopy. He walked to the front and dropped to one knee, looking into the rod holders welded to the car's bumper. "You see," he said, "there's an electrical connector at the base of each rod holder and wiring leading toward the rear of the car."

He arose from his knee, brushed the sand off his khaki trousers, and walked to the rear of the car.

"Interesting cabinet, here, in the very rear," he said, indicating the varnished wood cabinet that was fitted into the space where a folded top would have been.

"Yeah," Ben said. "I keep lures and hooks in the drawers. Dad did too when he used the car."

"I bet he did," the FBI man murmured, running his right hand over the smooth varnished wood of the cabinet. His hand stopped, slid to the rear.

"And what did your Dad keep here?" Josh asked as he pushed a hidden latch at the rear center.

The cabinet popped open, the front fell away, making a flat surface. Behind was a jumble of what looked to be electrical cables.

Ben turned and ran to the Gulf shore. The sun was now above the horizon; spent waves washed around Ben's bare feet. He bit his lower lip, trying unsuccessfully to keep from crying.

Josh McCuskey had run behind and stood a few yards away, on dry sand.

"My father's not a spy," Ben said, his voice tight as he turned to the FBI man. "Not my dad! I know! He was born in Germany, but he's an American citizen! He loves this country! He's my dad!"

"I never said he was a spy," McCuskey said, "only that he's been up to something and has been doing it for some time. The cabinet, Ben, those surf rods, the electrical connectors in the rod sections and in the holders on the bumpers. You have to know what that means."

Ben looked at Josh McCuskey through his tears. "I thought you said you wanted to be my friend," he said.

"Ben!" Josh said, loudly, speaking sharply. "I do want to be your friend! Trust me! I am being your friend at this very moment!"

Ben turned away and looked again at the sky, at the morning sun, shielding his eyes.

"Ben," Josh McCuskey said, softly, "what I'm about to do could cost me my job if anyone ever finds out. I never said that Azzo was a spy, I only pointed out that the surf rods make excellent radio antenna, and that the electrical cables we saw when the cabinet popped open clearly indicate that once there was a short-wave or marine radio installed in that cabinet. And," he went on, "Ben, I said that he needed to stop doing what I think he's been doing. If I'm right, he's been doing it for years."

"And what's that?" Ben questioned.

"I don't yet have enough proof for an arrest," Josh said, "and frankly, I don't want to arrest your father at all."

"You're not gonna tell me?"

"No."

"I don't understand," Ben said.

"You don't need to," Josh said. "You already now know more than I think is healthy for you to know."

He paused for a long minute, both looking into each other's eyes, silhouetted against the spectacular sunrise, the calming sounds of a light surf forming a backdrop. "Ben," Josh said, his voice soft and kind, "you need to tell your father three things: First, tell him that I admire what he's been doing. I think he's an unsung American hero."

Ben's brows wrinkled in thought. "But..." he began. McCuskey held up his hand.

"Ben," he began, "I think not only is your dad a hero, but also whomever it is that's working with him. My Jewish friend who died, she would think so, too.

"Now, my boss," McCuskey said, "Mr. J. Edgar Hoover, that's a different matter. My boss is an almost rabid anti-Semitist. He, pardon the expression, hates Jews. Communists, too, but that's another matter."

He paused, waiting for Ben to respond, to make the connection. When he didn't, Josh McCuskey continued, "I don't hate Jews. Had the young lady I told you about lived I might have converted to Judaism; I cared that much for her. But, had I converted, I would not have had a career with the FBI. And Ben, you need to know that I admire your father. I admire him so much that I'm breaking several dozen FBI regulations. I'll be fired quicker than you can believe if anyone in my agency finds out what I'm doing."

Josh paused again, then went on. "After you tell your dad that I admire what he's been doing, I want you to tell him next that we've been intercepting radio signals for some time, years really, and have only recently broken the code. So, we know. We just don't have enough proof that Azzo Burkhardt is the one sending them. The hidden radio compartment in your car told me not only who has been sending the radio messages, but how he's been sending them."

"No," Ben whispered. "There's no radio in my car."

"No, not now. I suspect it's in his car. At first, he was using those sectional rods as radio antenna. I suspect that today there's some sort of hidden telescoping antenna in Azzo's car, probably operated hydraulically. I know the car he's using was the one used by the man who died in your front yard, and that it was almost completely rebuilt after he bought it. I suspect that he's moved the rear seat forward, and, behind it, if we look, we'll find a hidden radio. I could go to a judge and have the car impounded, and then we'd know for sure."

"So, you believe my father has been sending secret radio messages?"

"Oh, yes, I'm pretty sure. Let me ask you another question. Did you ever look into the rear compartment of Azzo's car?"

"The Buick?"

"Yep. Where a spare tire is kept."

Ben didn't answer for a few minutes. Then he said, "I never did. Once at the airport the porter tried to put luggage into the trunk, but Dad said it was full, use the rear seat. I never thought about a spare tire. The Buick has fender wells, there are spare tires on each side of the car, in the front fenders."

Josh McCuskey nodded, saying nothing, letting Ben draw his own conclusions.

As Ben's mind continued working, sorting the logic, he said, "And the messages were sent in code?"

The FBI man grinned, "Yeah, that's the third thing I want you to tell your father. I wonder now why it took us so long to break it, it was so obvious, kind of like being hidden in plain sight. Tell your father that. Tell him the key to the code was hidden in plain sight, just like Poe's *Purloined Letter*. Tell him I said it was really clever. But we've broken it, and he needs to know."

"Hidden in plain sight?" Ben asked.

"Yeah," McCuskey said, "truly brilliant."

"I just figured it out," Ben said. "The code was based on Yiddish, not German nor English."

Josh was silent for a few moments. "I'm telling you too much. I want you to tell Azzo Burkhardt that there will be others who won't feel the way I do. If I were being left in Galveston, I promise you I'd do everything I could to protect your father. But I'm being assigned to another case. The others who come after me will not feel the way I do."

"You told me you didn't have proof."

"I don't," Josh said, "and none of this will be in notes I leave to my successors. But they'll eventually follow the same trails I did and if Azzo keeps on doing what he's been doing, they'll catch him, and he'll be sent to Leavenworth."

"Leavenworth?"

"It's a Federal prison in northeastern Kansas, near Kansas City.

"Ben," the boyish-looking FBI agent continued, "I can't tell you enough times how much I admire what Azzo Burkhardt has been doing. He is a hero. But don't you see? He's got to stop!" There was a pleading sound in the FBI man's voice. "Tell him everything I said. Tell him everything that you told me about the man who died in your yard and that I know what the key was for, and that I now know that he—or someone close to your mother—was the intended recipient. Tell him that I don't know—and I don't—who the intended recipient was, but I can guess." He nodded, almost to himself, a grim expression on his face.

"Others who come after me won't just guess," McCuskey added. "They'll arrange for a subpoena and search warrants, then the cat will be out of the bag for sure. Azzo, and maybe whoever his partner—or partners—are will go to jail. The agents who come after me will figure all this out in a heartbeat!"

"Who's my father's partner?" Ben asked. "It's not mom, is it?"

"Oh, lord, no!" Josh laughed. "Ben, your mom's a great lady. Tough as nails, hard-headed as any Jewish woman I've ever met. It's no wonder all those old salts in the Pilot's Guild that she bosses around all day respect and obey her. But she's not tied up in this business.

"Ben, I've told you several times I don't want you to know more. You don't want to know more. Stop asking questions and just tell Azzo! Tell him, for God's sake, to stop!"

Josh paused for a long while. Just beyond the breakers, a brown pelican suddenly dove headfirst into the water for his breakfast.

"Ben," Josh said, his voice now quiet, just a whisper above the light onshore breeze, "Make the case for me, my friend. Ben," Josh seemed to take a deep breath, "please make the case!"

Ben had stood, his back to McCuskey, looking out to sea during the FBI man's final impassioned pleas. When Josh had finished, Ben turned. "You're being transferred?"

"Reassigned," Josh answered. "There's a couple in San Antonio who've been swindling Uncle Sam big-time. Other agents will be assigned to Galveston. It's up to you to tell Azzo to stop what he's doing, otherwise they'll figure it out."

"Who are the men who are coming?" Ben asked.

"I suspect they'll introduce themselves soon enough, but I can't tell you more than that. Ben, I told you I want to be your friend. I want to be Azzo's, too. Tell him that! Tell him everything!"

Josh turned, walked to his car while Ben remained at the water's edge. Ben heard the engine in the rental and turned to look at his new friend.

Josh McCuskey put the car into gear and drove away, leaving Ben standing on the lonely beach in the sunrise.

Chapter 24

A Month Later
A Change of Plans

"I can't," Azzo said.

"Josh said you must. If you don't, he said, you're going to get arrested! Azzo—Dad—I'm scared. I don't know what to do. He said you could be sent to someplace called Leavenworth. I don't want to lose you."

Azzo had been away for weeks, and there had been no opportunity for Ben to talk to his father. Then, a telegram arrived, giving Azzo's arrival time at Houston's airport. Ben left school early and drove to Houston.

They were parked in Azzo's Buick in the airport parking lot. Ben was at the wheel. After retrieving Azzo's luggage and stowing it in the rear seat, Ben at last had the opportunity to tell about his night with Joshua McCuskey.

Azzo smiled at his son. "Ben, I agree with Josh McCuskey on one thing for sure. You don't need nor want to know more. If you know more, it is possible that someday you could be charged as an accessory.

"And," Azzo continued, his voice lighter than his feelings, "You've skipped school today to tell me all this nonsense."

"I only skipped after lunch. I told Coach. He said it'd be all right," Ben said defensively.

"Ben, you need to listen to me," Azzo said. "I appreciate what McCuskey told you to tell me, but I can't. I can't stop right away. There's only one more thing left to do. Just one. Then I'll stop."

Ben was silent for a few seconds. He turned to this man who'd become his friend first, then his father and said, "Is there anything I can say that'll convince you to stop now? Before you get arrested."

"No, you can't," Azzo said sternly and with more confidence than he felt. "Cheer up. They haven't caught me yet. I'm a slippery soul. I'll see to it that they don't catch me."

"I'm so scared!" Ben said.

"Ben," Azzo said, "it's awfully hot, just sitting here in the car in the parking lot. Get the car moving; get some air coming in." He had already put his suit jacket in the rear seat, now he loosened his collar, removed his tie and rolled his shirt sleeves partly up.

As Ben started the car Azzo said, "Turn right onto Telephone Road. I'm hungry. There's a new drive-in restaurant near the Eastwood Theatre. Go there. We'll get something to eat. We'll talk some more.

"Josh McCuskey told you that he was being a friend?" Azzo continued as Ben exited the parking lot and turned the car toward downtown Houston. "Okay, I agree with him. He was in fact being a good friend, not only to you but to me as well. He was giving me what I've heard people call 'a heads-up.' Okay, message received and understood, roger-and-out. I appreciate the heads-up, but I'm sorry he felt he had to do it through you. He could have come directly to me."

Ben answered, "He told me he'd thought long and hard about that.

"One more thing," Ben added as he pulled to a stop at Telephone and Griggs. "Josh said he truly admires you not only for what you've been doing, but also how you tamed mom."

Azzo laughed and shook his head. "I'm glad he thinks your mom is tamed, but there's no way anyone is going to tame her. She's one tough Jewish mama! Its why," Azzo added softly, "I love her."

"That's exactly what Josh called mom, 'a tough mama,'" Ben said. "I remember his exact words. He told me that it was no surprise that I beat polio, 'because she scared the shit out of it!'" Azzo laughed as Ben added, "He talked about how mom bosses around all those—he called them 'salts,' and he meant the dock crews, the tugboat crews, and the pilots."

Azzo said, "Never tell your mom what he said."

"You got it, buddy," Ben said.

Ben turned the car into the parking lot of Prince's Drive-In Restaurant and parked under the awning. He found himself calming down but still uneasy. It had somehow been helpful to tell his dad, though he remained anxious and concerned.

With an attempt at humor Ben said, "Okay, Dad, now it's time for you to do some thinking. Me, I'm gonna watch the carhops."

Azzo smiled as a shapely young woman in very tight clothing, red rayon slacks and a creamy white satiny blouse, approached the car. "Your old man's not dead, son. I can both think and admire the female form, at the same time."

They were silent as they waited for their orders to be delivered and the tray fastened onto the driver's side car window. Ben passed the food to Azzo and started to tune the car radio but stopped when Azzo shook his head. They ate mostly in silence, although Ben occasionally commented on the shapely carhops, hoping for a bantering response from his dad. There was none.

Azzo remained silent: reviewing, thinking, planning. He only nibbled at his sandwich.

It finally came clear. There was action that could be taken. It was simple idea but would be complicated to implement. Yet it would be something the Federal agents might not suspect. Could this new action be set up quickly enough? Bring in the last clients and leave no trace? It would all depend on how quickly Levi Weismann could react.

"I've got to talk to Levi," Azzo thought. "If we do it right, it could work. And it's only for just this one last time. Then, we're done. The war will be over soon. There's no need for anything more."

He brightened and took a few bites from his sandwich as Ben ordered another, plus a malted milk. "Do you want anything?" Ben asked, turning from the waitress, looking at his dad.

"Yes," Azzo answered, putting down his hamburger, and indicating Ben should return it to the tray. "Tell the young lady to bring me a black coffee."

The next afternoon Azzo was ushered into Levi Weismann's office.

"We've got trouble," he said.

"You mean that guy McCuskey?" Azzo wasn't surprised. The old banker was almost always ahead of everyone.

"Yes," Azzo answered. "He talked to Ben. Told him that he was being assigned to a case in San Antonio and that someone else is going to take over in Galveston. I think he said two men were coming."

The banker raised his eyebrows. "Are you telling me McCuskey brought Ben into all this? Put Ben into jeopardy? What did he say to Ben?"

"I'm not sure about the exact words. He said he was being a friend, not only to Ben, but to you and me as well."

"He gave Ben our names?"

"No," Azzo answered, "He gave Ben my name, and then said that he could guess who my primary associate was. Ben didn't mention your name, but Ben's a bright boy."

"What else did he say to Ben?" the old banker asked.

"Not much more," Azzo answered. "Ben said that McCuskey said he was telling Ben too much, and what he was saying could cost the FBI man his job as well as put Ben into some sort of legal jeopardy."

"That, at least, has a ring of truth," Levi said. "How did Ben react?"

"I wasn't there, and I don't know exactly," Azzo answered. "Anyway, the important thing is McCuskey said he was trying to be a friend. I believe that. McCuskey's a smart guy. I think he thinks Ben's smart enough to keep his mouth shut about whomever my associate—" he paused, looking at the elderly banker—"might be. I think Ben's already figured it out, but he's not letting me know it. I believe we can be confident Ben will never mention your name in connection with the program."

Azzo leaned back in the large leather chair across from the banker. "Whatever we do," he finished, "we need to do it fast, just for this one last time, and then we need to shut everything down."

The old banker nodded, sitting quietly, thinking. Then, he reached for a cigar and began his routine of holding it under his nose, clipping one end, and reaching for the silver lighter on the massive desk. Azzo knew that Levi had come to a decision and stood, suddenly anxious to exit the office and escape the clouds of smoke that would soon fill the room.

At the door he turned. "Slim and I are still good friends. Want me to talk with him? Bring him back into our program?"

"No," the banker said as smoke curled. "Don't do anything. I know what I need to do."

Ten days later, Levi and Azzo resumed their conversation. They were in a private compartment on the Southern Pacific's Sunset Limited, somewhere between San Antonio and El Paso.

"I have to hand it to you," Azzo said, "Your sudden trip to Los Angeles surely caught everyone by surprise. Have you ever been there?"

"Oh, yes," Levi answered, "I've been there any number of times. I invested in a motion picture company a number of years ago, and these days I'm on the Board of Directors. This is a regularly scheduled Board meeting that's been on my calendar for months.

"You followed my instructions?" the banker asked.

"Yes, precisely. I left my car in Beaumont in a public garage near the Blue Bonnet Hotel. From there I made several different bus and daycoach train connections, ending in Dallas where I was met by a man whom I did not talk to, and who spoke to me only to confirm the assumed name you gave me. He delivered me without comment to a run-down gasoline station in a suburb of Fort Worth where I was given the keys to an older car. I drove it without incident to San Antonio where I bought a day-coach ticket on this train to Midland-Odessa. I've talked with no one on this train, and I'm sure no one has paid the slightest attention to me. At the time you specified, I left my seat and came directly to this compartment. I do not believe anyone saw me enter."

The banker nodded. "Good."

"You'll never see your car again," Levi added. "I've been worried about that radio and telescoping antenna for a long time. By now, your car is in pieces in a Pasadena junkyard. The pieces will be sold off individually, the radio smashed and scattered into Trinity Bay.

"This train will stop at Midland-Odessa in about two hours," Levi added. "We've got until then for me to outline your next steps, and for you to commit a number of things to memory."

Levi Weismann talked almost non-stop as the Southern Pacific's streamliner roared through the West Texas desert. Azzo was amazed, not only at the plan, complicated and extraordinary, but at the details necessary for him to commit to memory. Each contact along the way was someone that had never before been used. Azzo would be a stranger to them, and they a stranger to him. Even if, someday, anyone tried to follow-up, there'd be no way to trace it back to either him or Levi.

"After our clients are safely delivered, you return to Beaumont, using public transportation much as you did to get here," Levi said. "Once there, go to the public garage, where you'll learn your Buick has been stolen. Report it to the police and your insurance company, rent a car, and drive to Galveston. You're done. I'm done. It will all be over."

"And we can then be scot free," Azzo said, "and live happily ever after."

"That's the plan, my friend," Levi answered, chuckling grimly as he lit a cigar, seemingly oblivious to Azzo's wrinkled nose.

"I want to keep both of us out of jail," the banker said, handing Azzo a large manila envelope. "For the next hour, commit the details you'll find in this envelope to memory. I will shred it after you leave."

Sooner than he wanted, Azzo felt the train slowing. A conductor knocked and said outside the door, "Midland-Odessa, next stop."

Azzo rose and donned his suit jacket. He picked up his suitcase.

Levi Weismann held up his hand. "Oh, wait," he said. "There's one more thing I need to tell you before you get off the train."

Azzo waited, his hand on the door handle.

"Several businessmen in Galveston have approached me, asking that I encourage you to open an architectural practice in Galveston."

"Really?"

"Yes. People are beginning to wonder about your writing. No one has seen anything you've produced. It might be time for you to get a book published; then announce your retirement from writing to establish an architectural firm. I know a number of potential clients who were impressed beyond measure with what you did to that old house of Sarah's and the new annex as well. The Chevrolet dealer has talked with me; he wants a new showroom. With the growth Galveston ought to have after the war, you'll have a client list a mile long."

Azzo laughed. "The problem is that the so-called next book doesn't exist. I have not actually written anything since that first book, and that book was published simply to provide cover. You know about the vanity press, and I don't think anyone has ever bought a copy. I've not done any real writing for years, though I've kept up the charade of course."

Levi laughed along with Azzo. "You certainly had a lot of people convinced!" he said.

"Tell you what," Levi continued, "simply re-publish your earlier book. You can donate several copies to the Rosenberg Library, and then announce your retirement to establish an architectural practice."

"That'll work," Azzo said. "I'll revise some of the stuff from the Carolinas. I actually did some research here in Texas, and I'll add that. We can go back to that vanity press, get it published, put a press release in the *Daily News*, and that will be that."

"Okay," Levi said. "We've got sufficient funds left for whatever your vanity press costs."

The train came to a full stop at the station.

"Sir," Azzo said, "you have my admiration. You've done some good work reorganizing and planning, and I hope there's no way anyone will ever learn that you are part of this operation."

As Azzo again turned toward the compartment door Levi rose and shook the younger man's hand, saying, "I hope I never have to visit you in Leavenworth."

"Me, too," Azzo agreed. "And I hope you're never my cell-mate! Those cigars, Levi. They're terrible!" He exited the compartment and stepped off the train just as the conductor was crying, "All aboard!" The train began moving slowly, pulling out of the station onto the open rail line to El Paso.

Chapter 25

March 1945
Preparing for Peace

Ben was excited when Azzo announced at breakfast that he planned to end his writing career. "I'm now planning," he said, "to open an architectural practice."

"For real?" Ben had questioned, while Sarah sat opened-mouthed.

Her mind caught up to what her husband had just said. "No more research trips?" Sarah asked.

"Nope," Azzo said confidently. "You're going to get mighty tired of having me underfoot all the time."

Sarah frowned, wondering what had brought about the change. She decided that, whatever it was, it was good. She rose from the table, bent over her husband and kissed him.

"I taste like coffee and eggs," he whispered.

"Oy vey!" she said loudly. "Already now he's getting all prim and proper!"

She laughed, gathered her things, and left for Galveston Pilots'.

Ben sat, silent, hoping that this was the end of whatever it was that the FBI man had warned about. His father was safe. But he had to know. He needed to hear his father say so.

An hour or so later, Ben went to the woodworking shop. Azzo was putting the finishing touches on a new desk for Sarah's office at Galveston Pilots'.

"I thought you'd left for school," Azzo said, removing his goggles and putting the electric sander to one side.

"No," Ben said. "I just drove around for a while. I came back here. I need to ask," he said.

"Sure. What?" Azzo said.

"Are you out, for sure? Out of whatever it was Josh was trying to tell me?"

Azzo pursed his lips. "Yep. I'm out. It's over."

"You're safe? I'm not ever going to lose you?"

"I'm safe. It's all over. There's no more for me to do. We can forget it all except for one thing; we can never talk about it. Not between us nor anyone else."

"Don't worry about me," Ben said. "I'm good. I haven't said anything to anyone but you, and now I will never mention it again, to you or anyone else."

As he left the woodworking shop, he stopped at the door and turned. "Ah, one more thing. I'm gonna need a note to take to school."

That night, after Azzo and Sarah had gone to bed, Ben placed his prayer shawl about his shoulders, and in his pajama bottoms and yarmulke went to the gazebo. He prayed as he wept in the starlight and thanked God for answering his prayers and leading his father to safety.

As the days passed, Ben mused about a career in architecture and imagined what it would be like to work alongside his father on exciting new buildings—skyscrapers, airports, and more. Everyone said the war would soon be over. Returning soldiers would come back to wives and sweethearts left behind. They'd start their families. They'd need homes and he and his father, a team, could build whole new cities for the soldiers!

But as these thoughts occurred, a small voice intruded, reminding him of his struggles, the desperation he had so often felt as he and his mom, his doctors, therapists, Coach, and even his father worked to overcome the arch enemy of his life, Infantile Paralysis. Ben nodded at the voice in his head. "Yes," he silently told the voice, agreeing, "I know. My destiny is medicine, not architecture. Someday, I know that science will wipe polio from the face of the earth! I want to be part of that! I've beaten polio and I want to be part of eradicating it from the face of the planet!"

There was still a war on, but Ben could see few signs of it in 1945 Galveston. The prisoner-of-war camp at Fort Crockett remained, and Ben knew that ships traversing the Gulf continued their zig-zag defensive measures, but there'd not been a U-boat attack in months. Galveston had long ago ceased the city-wide black-out when a ship exited the channel at night.

As Ben thought about his life he also thought about girls he'd grown up with, gone to grade school with, and who'd laughed and teased about his brace and cane. He didn't have either anymore and the girls who'd once teased him seemed to have forgotten and wanted to be friends. That seemed to Ben to be a good idea.

Ben asked his dad about getting a job.

"You've got a job," Azzo said. "Your schoolwork. Working around here helping Wallace. I give you money whenever you ask."

"That's just it," Ben said. "I don't want to run to you or mom every time I want to take a girl for a malt, or to the movies, or whatever."

"Um," his father said, eyebrows raised, "Any particular girl?"

"Not yet," Ben answered, ducking his head.

Azzo nodded, understanding. "Okay, let me think about it."

That Saturday Ben was painting one of the benches in the garden. Azzo walked up.

"You nearly finished?"

"Yep," Ben said. "I was just about to go clean the brushes." He placed a Wet Paint sign on the bench.

"Leave the brushes in cleaner; you can finish them later," Azzo said, "Go change out of your painting clothes. I know a man who'll give you a job, and I want you to meet him."

"Who?"

"A friend of mine. Go get cleaned up and we'll go and see him today," Azzo said. "Let's take your jalopy."

"Where are we heading?" Ben asked later as he pressed the jalopy's starter pedal.

"It's between Hitchcock and Santa Fe," Azzo said. "Nearly all the way to Alvin. After the causeway, take the turn onto Texas Highway 6."

There was a small but well-maintained sign adjacent to the highway, "Bichler Aviation." As Ben turned onto a wide graveled drive, he saw a number of small tee-shaped buildings and one larger, standing close to a residence. Ben pulled to a stop in a parking area near the rear porch, and a man came down the steps and walked to the car. Azzo exited and the two shook hands.

Arthur Bichler was over fifty but nevertheless slim and fit. As introductions were being made and handshakes passed around, the tall blond man said, "Call me 'Slim', everyone does, even my wife and daughter." A shock of straw-colored hair fell across his forehead, and he brushed it back, smiling. His cornflower-blue eyes were wide and welcoming.

They walked around the small airport and Slim led them into the large hangar, its sliding doors fully open. Ben saw six airplanes parked inside as if on display. "Are all these airplanes yours?" Ben asked.

"Yes," Slim nodded. "My business is charter. Businessmen from around this area, Galveston, Texas City, even parts of Houston, when they need to travel, say, to New Orleans, Dallas, sometimes Corpus or San Antonio, instead of going by train or car, they come here and I fly them to wherever they need to go. Sometimes they telephone, and I go pick them up in Houston or Beaumont and fly them to wherever they need to go. Their time is money, and they need to shorten their travel time as much as possible, so they pay me to ferry them about."

"Why don't they just fly out of Houston's airport? Eastern or Pan American?"

"Some do, but airline schedules and their schedules don't always match. So they call me or come to Galveston. Others have their own planes; they keep them here and I see to it that they're well-maintained." He nodded at the long line of tee-shaped hangars.

As they walked about the larger hangar, going from plane to plane, Slim named the different makes of airplane, opening their doors so Ben could look inside.

The airplanes that comprised Bichler Aviation were not the giant airliners Ben had so often seen when meeting his father at Houston Municipal, but were relatively small, four- and six-passenger craft. One was a twin-engine airplane that, Ben was told, could carry ten passengers. Another, a small yellow airplane, was, Slim said, "A piper cub. This is Diane's plane. A little two-seater."

A strange and unbidden thought crossed Ben's mind: "Would these planes be capable of landing on a sandy Gulf beach?"

He shook his head, annoyed for thinking about something that he needed to forget.

The apron in front of the main hangar was paved but the taxiways and the single runway were grass. "That's what I need someone to do for me a couple of days a week," Slim told Ben, "keep the runways mowed along with weeds around the hangars. I've got one of those golf-course mowing machines, and we keep the runway grass really short. Around the hangars, well, you'll have to swing a scythe."

"Lots of people," Ben said, "have the prisoners do work like that."

"Yes," Slim agreed, "and I've used them. But the war is going to be over soon, and those guys will be going back to Germany."

"I've heard that the government may let them stay," Ben said. "Offer them a way to become citizens."

"Yeah," Slim said, "I've heard that, too. But, still, I want someone from the local area. I'm comfortable with you if you want the job."

"Sure enough," Ben said. "I'd be glad to work for you."

"It's a deal," the genial owner of Bichler Aviation said, holding out his hand to Ben.

"How about an airplane ride to seal the deal?" Azzo said, grinning.

"Thought you'd never ask," Slim said. "I'm always ready!"

Ben wondered if the two men had planned their conversation as he helped Azzo and Slim push the bright-red airplane he'd been told was a Staggerwing from the hangar, and his face became a mixture of astonishment and excitement as the plane with the gold lightning flash on its side lifted from the ground, engine roaring. Slim had him sit in the right-hand seat while he piloted from the left. Azzo sat behind.

That ride reignited in Ben a desire he'd long ago told himself to forget.

The flames in Ben's heart leapt higher when Slim Bichler, as they cruised smoothly over the coastal prairies, told Ben, "Take the yoke."

Ben would have called it a "wheel," though it was only a partial-wheel sort of affair, mounted on a shaft that swiveled between the left and right front seats. Slim rotated the device so the yoke was in front of Ben.

"See what it's like," Slim said as he guided Ben's hands and pointed out the altimeter and turn indicator. "Keep the wings level, watch the altimeter, and keep our flight steady, on this compass heading." He tapped each instrument as he mentioned them. "If you pull back on the yoke, the airplane will rise. If you push it away from you, we'll lose altitude. If you turn the yoke one way or the other, the airplane will change direction and the wing will drop. A little goes a long way. Let's try a gentle turn," Slim said, adding, "Just move the yoke a little. Not too much."

As Ben felt the airplane respond to the slight movement of his hands, his soul soared. Ben's interest in aviation, ignited during his many trips to Houston Municipal when Azzo left or returned from his frequent trips to New York, had dropped to a small flicker as time passed. But now, Ben felt, flames had returned.

Ben suddenly knew, at that moment, that instant of time, that flying was going to be in his future. He didn't know how, and he knew he'd never abandon medicine, but this passion was strong. Maybe, Ben thought, medicine and flying could somehow be blended. He had no idea how that could happen, but as he struggled to keep the flight steady and smooth, Ben decided God knew, and God would guide the way.

Later, as Ben steered the jalopy on the return trip to Galveston, wind whipping both his and Azzo's hair, he couldn't stop talking about flying.

"That was a gas! A killer diller! Cooler than cool! I always wondered what it would be like to fly a plane! I'm really going to like working there!"

Azzo looked at his son. "I don't think Slim is gonna take you up every time you go over there to mow down his weeds."

Ben ignored his father's remark. "I got to fly it! Killer! He let me fly his f-ing plane!" It was almost a shout.

"He let you steer it for a little Ben," Azzo said, "and don't let your mother hear you say f-ing."

"Well, I didn't say—" Ben said and spelled the word.

"Trust me," Azzo said. "Don't say the whole word in front of your mother, and never say 'f-ing' either."

Azzo returned to his subject. "There's a lot more to flying than simply steering and keeping your wings level. You have to maintain altitude, and you didn't do that very well if you remember.

"And besides," Azzo added, "you've been talking for a long time about a career in medicine."

"Yeah, I know," Ben said, the voice inside his head agreeing with his father. "Still, it was a gas! No doubt!" He paused for a minute, breathless. "I'm gonna be a doctor. That's for real. That's established. But I don't care what you say. I'm gonna learn to fly, too!"

"Flying lessons are pretty expensive."

"I'll do it! I'll find the money!"

Ben paused as the car left the causeway and cruised along Broadway, the oleanders in the esplanade in full bloom. He turned to his dad and added, "I don't know how I'll get the money, but I'll figure it out! I'm gonna learn to fly. I'll work flying into medicine some way, somehow." His thoughts turned to something that had caught his attention earlier. As he turned the car onto 51st he said, "Who was that on Slim's back porch as we were driving off?"

"You mean that girl who waved?"

"Yeah," Ben said.

"Slim's daughter," Azzo answered with nonchalance in his voice. "His only child, I might add. Tread lightly around her, my friend. Slim's mighty protective."

Ben shrugged. "I guess I'll get to meet her when I start work next Saturday."

"Yeah," Azzo said, looking fondly at his son. "I wouldn't be a bit surprised."

Chapter 26

V-E Day

Ben had just suited up for track. He and his teammates left the locker room and trotted toward the cinder track as Coach called for warm-up calisthenics. "Crip!" he shouted, "warm them up."

Ben assembled the squad and took leadership. "Okay, you lazy bums, Jumpin' Jacks! One! Two! Three! Four!"

They were on High Knees when, out of the corner of his eye, Ben saw the school principal approach Coach. They talked briefly. Coach turned toward Ben as the principal walked away, toward the gym.

"Shut them down, Crip." There was a strange look on Coach's face.

"Okay, fat heads!" Ben shouted to the sweaty boys. "Crowd around. Conference time!" Soon, a circle of boys surrounded Ben and Coach.

"Come into the gym, boys," Coach said, a serious expression on his face. "The principal's got an announcement." Ben saw other students heading toward the gymnasium. There were automobile horns honking on Broadway. Ben felt a burst of anxiety, a knot deep in his stomach. He'd felt this way on a number of occasions since the war had begun; the most recent few weeks earlier when their principal had announced that President Roosevelt had died.

When all were assembled on the side-bleachers, Principal Branfman held up his hands for quiet.

"Members of the student body of Ball High and teachers," he shouted, "I have an important announcement. The war in Europe is over!"

Cheers erupted across the gymnasium as Ben felt his knees go weak with relief. The principal added, "School is dismissed!"

There were celebrations across America on V-E Day, the 8th of May 1945. Automobile horns blew, people shouted and waved, hugged and kissed one another, went to their houses of worship and wept and prayed. Times Square in New York was mobbed. Dealey Plaza in Dallas was overcome with throngs of celebrating citizens. Main Street in Houston was filled. The war in Europe was over! Our boys will be coming home, thought Ben!

Azzo had been in Houston both Monday and Tuesday, meeting with prospective clients. That afternoon, as he turned his Nash automobile into Mansion House, Ben ran to meet him.

"You've heard?" Ben excitedly questioned. "The war is over!"

Azzo exited his car and hugged his son. "I heard it on the car radio. It's V-E Day. Victory in Europe. There are people driving up and down Broadway, honking their horns.

"However," Azzo went on, "I'd like to point out that there's still a fair amount of unpleasantness going on in the Pacific."

"Yeah, I know," Ben said, casting his eyes down. "Maybe the Japs will give up."

"I don't think that'll happen," Azzo said, his face serious. "I think there'll likely be an invasion of Japan, and that'll cost thousands of lives, maybe millions, American and Japanese."

Ben shook his head, then brightened. "Anyway, it's over in Europe!" He hugged his father again as Sarah turned her station wagon into the drive, stopping behind Azzo's car and joining the two.

"I need a hug, too," she said, throwing her arms around Azzo.

"I've been away too long," he murmured as she pressed her body to his, knowing and expecting a physiological reaction from him. "Much too long," she whispered into his ear, pressing her body even closer. "I need my Jew lover!"

"I heard that!" Ben said loudly, grinning as he said, "Get a room!"

Azzo pushed Sarah away, laughing and whispering, "Later."

The next day, Azzo was meeting with Levi Weismann talking about the results of his meetings in Houston when a secretary knocked on the door. "Yes!" Levi barked. Everyone knew he disliked having meetings interrupted.

"I'm sorry sir," a newly hired young lady said. "But there's a man from the FBI here. He said it is most urgent that he meet with Mr. Burkhardt. I explained that you and he were in a meeting, but…" She spread her hands helplessly. "He insisted, and he's from the FBI."

"Who is it?" Azzo asked, rising.

"A Mr. Joshua McCuskey," she answered.

"Send him in!" Levi Weismann barked.

"Uh, sir, he said he wanted to see Mr. Burkhardt."

"I said…" Levi shouted and stood. "Yes, sir!" the young secretary said, fleeing from the wrath of the founder, president, and chairman of the board of the Weismann Bank, hoping she would still have a job by the end of this day. She trembled as she ushered a blond military-cut Josh McCuskey into the room.

"Hello, Mr. Weismann," McCuskey said casually, shaking the hand of the banker. "My mission is to talk to Mr. Burkhardt, but I expect it'd be okay with him if you sat in on the conversation."

Levi's anger reached a pitch, and he found himself unable to answer. He sat rather heavily in his chair, breathing hard. Azzo glanced worriedly at the elderly banker.

"It's certainly all right with me," Azzo said, taking the FBI agent's hand. "Will you have a chair, Mr. McCuskey?"

"Thanks," the young agent said, seating himself. "Mr. Burkhardt, I've been with your parents for the past several weeks. I've been on loan to our State Department, helping your parents close down their work in England and relocate to the United States.

"They asked that I be the one to come to Galveston and meet with you. I went by Mansion House, but a really nice lady named Rae Telar told me that you were here."

"Are my parents okay?" Azzo questioned. "My sister?"

"Oh yes, everyone is fine. We've also been in Los Angeles. I've helped them with house-hunting. I think you're going to be very pleased with the home they've selected. They're going to be working at the California Institute of Technology's Jet Propulsion Laboratory."

Azzo was still catching up to what he was being told. "You've been in England, with them?"

"Oh, yes. I met them any number of times during the war. They're great folks," McCuskey answered. "I first met them right after they'd been transported to England and fell in love with them right away. Several times during these past couple of years, I've personally carried your mail packages to them, keeping them up to date and all."

Azzo was completely taken aback. "Why didn't they let me know?"

"They told me they wanted everything settled before disrupting your life. They asked me to travel to Galveston and give you the news," the FBI man concluded, "as a friend."

Azzo raised his eyebrows at the term, knowing that Josh had told Ben that he wanted to be a friend, while at the same time telling the boy to warn his father about the possibility of arrest and punishment.

"Are they already in the United States?" Azzo asked.

"Oh, yes," McCuskey nodded. "I thought I'd made that clear. They've been in the United States for about three weeks now. It's been a busy time, first in Washington, then, later, Los Angeles. There was a side trip to Boston, to MIT. Your folks decided on Cal-Tech."

"My sister? Is she going to live in Boston?"

The boyish-looking FBI agent smiled, "No, she's planning to continue as your parent's laboratory assistant. She'll live with them in Los Angeles for a while. She told me she may get a place of her own sometime later."

"Why didn't they let me know?" Azzo said.

"They wanted to surprise you. Have everything settled," McCuskey said, grinning broadly. "It seems to me they've succeeded."

"I've never heard of the…what did you call it?" Levi said, losing his anger and developing interest in the news. "The Jet Propulsion..?"

"The Jet Propulsion Laboratory in Los Angeles," Josh McCuskey said, "It was formed in 1936, and is managed by the California Institute of Technology. They and your parents and sister wanted to meet, since your parents want to continue their research and both they and the Caltech folks want them to come to California. I must say the compensation they've been offered is rather generous, as was their appreciation bonus from both the United Kingdom and our government when they concluded their work in England."

"So they're in California now?" Azzo asked.

"No, they've been in California, but right now they are in an airplane, and expected to land in Houston in about two hours."

Azzo bolted from his chair, heading for the door. He turned to Levi. "I've got to find Sarah and Ben, and we've got to go to…"

Josh stood. "I've got a car waiting," he said, grinning broadly. I went to Ben's school and talked to the principal. Ben and I found your wife at Galveston Pilots'. She and your son are waiting outside."

"You're not going without me!" the elderly banker shouted.

"No," McCuskey said, still grinning, "and in fact there are two cars in front of the bank. Mr. Weismann, with your permission, I'd like to ride to Houston in the car with you."

The almost 17-year old Benjamin Jacobs Burkhardt had seen an airplane as large as the United States Government's C-75 aircraft, a converted-to-VIP Flight 4-engine Boeing 307 Stratoliner, but only once. He stood open-mouthed as the monster airplane taxied to the transit terminal at Houston's airport.

Four people exited, three of them waved at the five people standing at the terminal entrance, and a flight steward escorted them from the airplane to Azzo, Sarah, Ben and Levi Weismann. There were hugs all around with everyone talking at once. Joshua McCuskey moved unobtrusively to one side of the tarmac and stood there quietly, smiling, watching the reuniting of a family.

Words flew about as the group moved into the transit terminal.

Ben looked back at the airplane. Luggage was being unloaded; a redcap was placing the bags onto a cart. The engines on the giant airplane started. Ben looked around, suddenly concerned, wondering where his friend had gone.

Ben sidestepped the terminal entrance and moved toward the side of the building. The government's airplane, engines now roaring, began moving away from the transit terminal. Wind from the propellers blew Ben's hair. He walked around the corner of the building.

He saw Joshua McCuskey walking rapidly toward a sedan parked just at the edge of the pavement, some sort of emblem on its side. Ben shouted over the noise of the departing airplane. The FBI man turned, saw Ben and gave a silent wave. He opened the door of the parked car. Ben ran after his friend. "Wait!" he shouted.

McCuskey paused, holding the car's door open. Ben shouted, "Don't leave, Josh! I want to talk!"

"Ben," the FBI man said, smiling as Ben ran up, "this part of my job is over."

"You'd be welcome to stay," Ben said, breathlessly. "Join us for dinner tonight at Mansion House." It was almost a plea. "Rae's cooking up a feast."

"I know, Crip," Josh answered, standing at the open car door, "and it sounds like fun, but I've got another job."

"Are you going back to San Antonio?"

"Nope. El Paso this time. There's a government plane waiting for me over at Ellington. It's not a VIP plane like the one your grandparents qualified for," he grinned, "but it'll get me there." Ben studied McCuskey's expression. He couldn't decide whether his expression was one of sadness or longing.

"I wanted to tell you about Dad and..." Ben began. The FBI man cut him off. "I know what you're going to say," he said, "and I'm glad. I'm glad for you, and for your family. Ben, go back to them. Enjoy them. They're great people. Live your life."

Ben impulsively hugged the government man. "Is this goodbye? Will I never see you again?" he asked. There was a catch in his throat, incipient tears just behind his eyelids.

"Sure, you'll see me again. But right now, I've got some bad guys to catch. I'll be around, from time to time. Maybe one day I can come back to Galveston and go fishing with you and we'll run on the beach. Have a few beers. Enjoy some of that redfish-on-the-half-shell. We'll plan on it. Next summer. I'll write."

"Thank you for everything," Ben whispered, hugging the FBI man tightly, tears now wetting his cheeks.

"Goodbye, Crip."

The man who'd told Ben that he wanted to be his friend and proved it by his actions entered the waiting car which pulled rapidly away from the terminal. Ben watched as it merged with other traffic on Telephone Road and was soon out of sight.

Chapter 27

Summer 1945

Benjamin knew that he would never forget the summer of 1945, when he came to know and love his grandparents and aunt.

Ben turned seventeen that August, and there were long walks on Seawall Boulevard with his grandfather, talking and hearing stories of his father's childhood. Ben spent hours with his grandmother and aunt, telling about teaching English to the German prisoners while they taught him German. When the school year ended, all his family were together and watched from the stands as Ben and his track team competed in their final event. Ben thought he could hear their individual cheers—"Go, Crip, Go!"—and he thought that was probably the best birthday present he ever could have had.

Samuel Klein, the *Daily News'* elderly managing editor sauntered into Sarah's office at Galveston Pilots' two days after the arrival of Azzo's family.

"It's time, Sarah," he said, sitting without being asked in one of the two leather armchairs in front of her desk.

"I thought you might show up, Sam," Sarah answered, grinning.

"Yep," the newsman said, slumping a little farther down. "I remember Pearl Harbor Day, the government trying to keep your operations secret, and I also remember Azzo's and Ben's year-long efforts saying Kaddish for his 'dead' parents. Ben's grandparents, who, by the way, seem to not be dead after all. You've got them settled in now?"

"Yes. They're at Mansion House, in one of our furnished units, the one with a screened porch overlooking the garden and new pool."

You owe me a favor, Sarah."

He paused while Sarah's assistant brought in coffee.

Stirring sugar and cream, Sam raised his bushy eyebrows. He took a sip.

Sarah smiled at the newsman and said, "You're right Sam, I owe you. I'm not sure about photographs, though."

"Well, Sarah, ask them. If they're going to mind, I'll back off of photographs. But, you know, their story will be quite a coup for the *Daily News*. I've had radio reporters from New York calling me. They want me to ask them if they could do an on-the-air interview."

Sarah nodded thoughtfully.

"How about a movie camera?" Sam asked. "Warner Pathé has called, too. They're mighty interested."

"Sam," Sarah said, "come to Mansion House for dinner tonight and meet Azzo's parents and sister, and after dinner we can discuss arrangements. I can't agree on my own for what you ask; they'll have to be comfortable, and conversation during dinner tonight will have to be off the record. Sam, bring some of the questions you'll be asking if they agree to an interview. Tomorrow or the next day, or next week, whatever, you can return for the interview. If they agree, perhaps that'd be the time to bring your photographer."

"And Warner Pathé?" Sam questioned.

"I'll let the Burkhardt's decide all that," Sarah said, adding "We'll set up the interview in what was once the grand ballroom. It's smaller now; Azzo used some of it for an apartment. Our tenants use it now for small get-togethers, parties and especially Christmas."

Sam again raised his eyebrows. "So, it's true," Sam said. "I've heard about you letting your tenants celebrate their Christmas in what was once the ballroom."

Sarah grinned. "Well, as long as they don't decorate their trees with angels or crosses, and as long as they don't disrespect our menorah. We set the menorah at one end, and they put their tree in the other. It's become a sort of Mansion House tradition. We have Jewish tenants too, Sam, and they as well as we have our Hanukkah celebrations in the old ballroom. Uncle Levi sometimes gets a few wrinkles in his brows, but Azzo just laughs." She nodded her head. "I've softened."

"Azzo's been good for you, hasn't he?" the newspaper man said kindly.

"Come to dinner," Sarah said. "Meet Azzo's parents and his sister. I promise you're gonna love them."

"Sarah, every news organization in the country is looking forward to interviewing Azzo's parents and sister next month in Pasadena. This'll scoop them all, put the *Daily News* into the national scene, and give Mansion House Luxury Apartments national publicity. Sarah, it'll be good for you and your business. I've heard Azzo is planning an architectural practice. We could slip in a plug for his new business, and even a plug for the Port of Galveston as well. Good for business overall."

Sarah nodded and said, "Okay, Sam, just don't bring Warner Pathé or your photographer to dinner tonight. Let's let Azzo's parents decide."

The weeks of the Burkhardt's visit were much too short for Benjamin. There were runs at San Luis Pass with his aunt and both parents while his grandparents watched, and redfish-on-the-half-shell beach dinners. His grandmother listened when Ben tried out some of the German the prisoners had taught him, and later she worked to help with his pronunciation.

Slim Bichler assured Ben that he was still needed during that summer for mowing and maintenance at his air strip near Alvin. Ben brought up the subject of flight lessons.

"Why do you want to learn to fly?" Slim asked.

"I don't really know," Ben said. "That ride you gave me, oh, months ago now. It was—well, I just had this feeling."

"Tell me exactly," Slim said.

"Well," Ben said, ducking his head, "I don't know exactly how to say it. But, you know, back when you gave me that first ride, in the Staggerwing, when you let me put my hands on the yoke and steer, I knew, right then, that minute. I knew! I knew for sure!"

"Well, Crip," Slim said, "That's what I felt the first time I went up."

"Truly?"

"Truly. But you can't take lessons from me."

"No?"

"I'm not a licensed instructor. I took you up once, and I'll take you up again from time to time and maybe teach you a little, but when you decide to get serious about a pilot's license, you'll need a licensed instructor."

"Where do I find one?"

"Over in Houston." Slim looked at Ben's crestfallen face. "Tell you what, you forget about the weeds around the hangars this day. It wasn't news when you told me you wanted to learn to fly. Diane told me you'd told her you wanted to learn. Let Diane take you up in the Piper today. She'll see if you've got what it takes. She'll let you do a little more than steer, and maybe show you a little touch-and-go. You come back tomorrow for the weeds. That all right with you? For now?"

"Sure!"

Slim added, "You know the Piper is Diane's plane. I gave it to her when she completed her pilot's training last year. She's been flying with me since she was a baby and began her ground training at thirteen. I told her about letting you have the controls of the Beech for a few minutes, and I said I thought you might make a pilot. She doesn't think so. She said she thought you'd be lousy at flying."

Ben did not notice the grin on the face of owner of the airfield.

One day Slim took Ben, Sarah, Azzo, Grandpa Abe and Grandma Miriam in the Staggerwing for an aerial tour of the Gulf Coast. After reaching cruising altitude, as Ben held the plane steady under Slim's watchful eye, he told his grandparents about San Luis Pass and the many night-time fishing excursions throughout the war years.

Later that night, after dinner, Grandpa announced that for Ben's seventeenth birthday his gift from his grandparents and aunt would be formal pilot training by a licensed instructor.

For Sarah, the bumps of life had smoothed. Her job in peacetime was far less stressful than it had been when war rocked the world. Her husband was reliably at home. Sarah liked her new in-laws and thought that Adelheit—Azzo's sister, whom Sarah called Adel—was especially pretty. Sarah commented more than once that after Adel settled in

Los Angeles she should investigate a career in the movies. Adel just laughed and said no, she was more interested in high-speed data manipulation, such as had been developed during the war years at MIT. Caltech, she said, was also interested in the new technology.

As Sarah heard for the first time in her life the word "computer," she immediately dismissed it as just another nonsense promise that people were making about what the post-war years would bring. Ben had even shown her a comic strip in the *Daily News*, about a detective who had, of all things, a two-way wrist radio. What nonsense!

Sarah now had two assistant managers and one secretary. Mansion House, the Carriage House Annex, and Mansion House West continued to have high occupancy. Sarah had doubled-up on the mortgage payments and soon the facility would be debt-free.

August 15, 1945, the day Japan surrendered, was also, and only coincidentally, the day when Benjamin's grandparents left for California. Ben drove the station wagon with his grandparents and Aunt Adele, while Sarah and Azzo followed in Azzo's Nash automobile, heading to the Houston airport.

"The government's not giving you a free ride this time, are they?" Ben asked.

"No, that plane is reserved for government VIP's—Very Important People—and we no longer qualify," Adele said. "We're flying to California just like ordinary people."

Ben winked at his Aunt. "Fickle folks, our government, right?"

"Yes," Grandpa Abe answered from the back seat, "but it's the best government around, and don't you ever forget that!" Changing the subject, he added, "The war has been ended by the atomic bomb. Did you know that Adolph Hitler was also developing a nuclear device?"

"No, I didn't," Ben answered.

"Well, he was, and I assure you had he gotten one he would have used it. Against New York if possible, and if not, London for sure."

Ben was silent for a minute. "It's hard to believe that one bomb could wipe out a city as large as New York. But I've seen the newsreels of Hiroshima and Nagasaki, so I guess it's possible."

"Well, it is most certainly possible," his grandfather said. "Future wars will be even more dangerous. Larger bombs will be developed. And, heaven help us if others—Russia—for example, get the bomb."

"Maybe that won't happen," Ben said.

"We can all hope."

Ben turned the car into the terminal area, pulling up to the front. A redcap came out. "I'll park after your luggage is taken care of," Ben said. "See you in the terminal."

As the plane was loading, Ben thought he might cry as he saw tears forming in his father's eyes as he hugged Grandpa Abe and Grandma Miriam, who whispered as she hugged Ben, "When school winter break comes this year, you are all coming to California for two weeks. We'll celebrate Hanukkah on the beach at Malibu."

"You're going to live in Malibu?" Ben said, his eyes wide. "Where all the movie stars live?" Grandpa laughed. "They don't all live there, but some do. Our next-door neighbor is a movie star."

"Who?" Ben asked.

"Some lady I never heard of. Our realtor said her last name was Jones. You ever hear of her?"

Later, as the DC-4 Pan American lifted off the runway, Azzo said, "Ben, leave the station wagon where it is and come with your mother and me. Your grandparents and aunt have left an early high school graduation gift for you." He led the way to the Nash.

Across the airport, Azzo stopped at a hangar near the transit terminal. He said, "Ben, both the British and American governments have been quite generous with your grandparents. They can easily afford what you're now going to see." He and Sarah led a puzzled Ben to a side door. "Ben," Azzo said as he unlocked the door, "they've given it a name, but you can change it you want."

"What..?" Ben began, as Azzo and Sarah led him to a shiny new blue-and-white two-passenger Cessna 140. Emblazoned across the engine cowling in large gold script was the word "Crip", and beneath that, in smaller script were the words, "Fly with the Wind".

Chapter 28

1946
Post-War Galveston

Burkhardt and Associates, Architects, had come into being with fanfare in late September 1945, cumulating months of planning, calls on potential clients, and the remodeling of a small single-story building at 43rd and Broadway that had once been home to an insurance agency. Commissions began almost at once as businesses across Galveston looked to the future with enthusiasm.

Azzo was pleased with the rate of incoming business. The book that was intended to be his last cleared the vanity press publishing process and, to Azzo's and Uncle Levi's astonishment, was eagerly purchased by schools of architecture and architectural historians. Azzo's reputation increased dramatically when New York's Columbia School of Architecture invited him to be a guest lecturer in the spring of 1947.

Sarah was pleased that Mansion House and Mansion House West remained at full occupancy. Her days remained far less stressful than the dark days of World War II. She had accompanied Azzo to New York for meetings at Columbia and he had done as he once promised, taken her to Broadway shows and dinner and dancing at prominent New York clubs.

It was in late April of 1946 when Sarah and Azzo decided it was past time to formalize Ben's plans after high school. He'd talked for years about medicine, and they knew he'd recently been sending letters of inquiry to a number of colleges.

"I'm way ahead of you, Mom," Ben said to his mother.

They were in the large living room of Sarah's apartment. Much of the wall opposite the office alcove was a large window—Azzo called it a "picture window"—overlooking the garden, gazebo and pool, where Ben's high school graduation party would be held within weeks.

As the discussion continued, it was clear to both Sarah and Azzo that Ben's dream of becoming a doctor was still strong.

"I've been talking to the counselors at Ball High," Ben said, "and a bunch of the doctors at UT here in Galveston. I've got Pre-Med applications almost ready to send to the University of Texas in Austin, SMU in Dallas, and Tulane. There are parts you'll need to complete before they're sent. I'll have them ready for you tomorrow or the next day."

"You've still sure about medicine?" Azzo asked.

"Oh," Ben said without hesitation, "there's no doubt. I want to be a doctor; specialize in infectious diseases. It'd be keen if I could be part of the ultimate defeat of polio all around the world. The time element might work against me though. The doctors at UT tell me there's some cutting-edge work being done in Pittsburgh that's showing a lot of promise. I wish those guys God-speed, but if they're not done by the time I finish my residency, I'll make joining them a priority!"

"Mom," he said, turning to her, his dark eyes luminous, his face serious. "I beat polio, with your help and dad's, and ton of other folks. It's pay-back time. I want to help others as I've been helped."

Ben grinned broadly as Azzo said, "You certainly sound sure!"

"I am sure," Ben said. For an instant a mischievous look came across his face as he said, "Well hell no, I'm not sure! A lot of the time I think that what I really want to do is marry Diane and lie around all day making babies!" Sarah's jaw dropped; her expression one of horror.

"Ben!" she shrieked. "You're only seventeen!"

Azzo howled in laughter.

Sarah began to rise from her chair as Ben, serious once again, looked at his mom and said, "Mom, I don't think making babies all day will pay very well, and I bet you and dad aren't going to support me in that sort of life-style."

Sarah sat back in her chair. Azzo, still laughing, said, "I didn't know you and she were that serious!"

Sarah found her voice. "Who is Diane?"

Ben ducked his head, turned away from his mother and looked toward the window.

He walked over, stood looking out, and said to both, "We're pretty serious. We know we're young. She's got college ahead, too, and we know we're likely to be separated a lot. Maybe we can hold together when we're apart, and maybe we can't. Right now, though, we feel as if we can hold together and marriage can wait."

Ben turned back to his mom and dad and stood, silent. Azzo rose from the couch and put his arm about Ben's shoulders, speaking in a low voice, "You've thought this through carefully?"

"I think so," Ben answered quietly. Sarah rose from her chair and moved to stand beside her men.

"Where is Diane planning to go to school?" Azzo asked.

"She hasn't decided," Ben murmured. "Baylor's starting a new nursing school in Houston, but she's been thinking about Tulane."

"In any case," Ben continued, "if my college fund can stand the fuel cost I'll use the Cessna, and we'll get to see one another several weekends during the school year." He shrugged, "We really didn't intend to get serious so soon, Dad." He looked into his father's eyes. "It just happened." He shrugged.

Azzo clapped his son on the back. "Sounds to me as if the two of you have thought things out pretty well," adding in a quiet tone, "Son, I know what it's like to be serious with a young lady. But—" He paused, "you and she haven't—"

"No, Dad," Ben said, speaking in a low voice, almost a whisper as Sarah strained her ears. "But don't think we haven't thought about it. We talked. We both agree that it's too early in our relationship for more than we have right now."

The three stood together, framed by the garden view. Ben added, "I can't promise that we'll wait until we're married, but neither of us want a pregnancy. We know there are things we can do. Dad, and Mom, trust me and trust Diane, we've got our heads on straight."

"You'll know when it's time," Azzo said.

Ben changed the subject, and as he did, his face changed again. "I want to spend a lot of time on the beach this summer, as much as I can. I love this island so much," he added wistfully, "and I won't get to come home often when I'm in college."

"Speaking of that," Azzo asked, "it's a nice day. How about a run?"

"Thought you'd never ask," Ben answered.

"Me, too!" Sarah piped up.

Azzo kissed his wife. "Run," he whispered, "let's go with our son and run with the wind!"

Six weeks later a small blue-and-white Cessna cruised over the blackland prairies south of Dallas. Ben struggled to keep the flight smooth as updrafts from heated columns of air rose from the prairies below and buffeted the airplane.

"Sorry, Mom," Ben said, noting his mother's tension after one particularly strong bump. "This little plane's sturdy; a bump or two isn't going to bother us."

Sarah was not sure she would ever become comfortable in an airplane but was impressed at her son's handling of the machine. He looked every inch the professional pilot in his sunglasses, headphones over his ears, one side jacked up. She watched his legs as they operated the pedals on the floor he'd told her were called rudder controls. She was thinking, as Ben put the plane into a gentle bank, that he might never have learned to fly if Azzo had not come into their lives and taken Ben to the beach.

Her mind drifted as she remembered Azzo and Ben, arms locked, legs strapped together, stumbling along as wave remnants washed over their feet, sometimes falling, but always moving. She'd cried when the day finally arrived when they could run, and she cried again as Ben later learned to run alone. She treasured the memory of her two men wrestling in the surf, laughing, and being men who loved one another. How she loved both the men in her life!

Shortly the plane settled gently onto a runway at Love Field and taxied to the transit terminal. She walked inside as Ben talked with an attendant, giving directions for overnight services.

A tall, slender young man with striking dark auburn hair came up to her.

"Excuse me," he said, "you must be Mrs. Burkhardt." Sarah found herself looking into the bluest blue eyes she'd ever seen.

"Hi," Ben said as he walked up, smiling and taking the astonishingly good-looking young man's hand. "You must be Drew Neilan; SMU Admissions told me you'd be here to meet us. I'm Ben Burkhardt. This is my mom, Sarah."

"Glad to meet you," the man, about two years older than Ben answered, smiling and showing straight white teeth. "You're right, I'm Drew Neilan. I'm to be your guide in your tour of the campus today."

"So, you're the man with all the answers," Sarah said in a joking manner as she continued to be captivated by this man's eyes. They weren't exactly blue, she decided, but more blue than blue. "Cobalt," she said to herself in a whisper.

"Yes," the stranger chuckled. "I've been told I have cobalt-blue eyes."

"And great hearing," Sarah said, embarrassed.

Drew shrugged. "I didn't mean to embarrass you. At any rate, I hardly have all the answers, but I know where many of the answers are and how to find the answers that I don't know. C'mon, do you have luggage?"

"Yes," Ben answered, "I have a duffel and Mom an overnight. They're still in the plane."

They stowed them in the rear of an older blue Ford, and Sarah climbed into the rear seat as Ben held the back of the front seat for her. Ben joined Drew in the front.

Drew nodded to his car. "She's an old bus, but dependable. My wife and I are planning to keep her a few years longer."

"Your wife goes to college, too?" Ben asked as the car pulled away from the transit terminal and turned onto Lemmon Avenue.

"No," Drew answered, "she's a secretary for an oil company. But you'll find a number of married students on campus. They'll be GI's, home from the war and going to school on the GI Bill, and no doubt their wives are working girls. I've heard some of the wives joke that their degree will be PHTC, that's for 'Putting Hubby Through College'."

They laughed.

"The registrar showed me your high school records, Ben," the charming young man said. "A number of your references have been contacted, and I've read what they wrote about you. You're an impressive guy."

Ben smiled, not sure what response to make.

"I mean," Drew continued, "you've beaten polio, become captain of the track team, kept your grades up, volunteered at the German prisoner camp, all at the same time. And you were valedictorian of your high school class."

"In Galveston," Ben said, "they call me 'Crip'. It's my nickname, and I kinda like it."

"If you decide you like SMU, Crip," Drew said, "I can guarantee that SMU will like you."

"I was afraid," Sarah said from the backseat, "that Southern Methodist wouldn't let Ben in because we're Jewish."

"Not at all, Mrs. Burkhardt," Drew said, briefly turning his head and looking at Sarah, "I'm Methodist, but we have many students of different faiths. Personally, Mrs. Burkhardt," the engaging young man continued, glancing over his shoulder from time to time, "if you'll permit, I don't think Jews and Christians are really that far apart. Much of your Torah can also be found in what we Christians call the Old Testament, so we have a common religious background at the very least. Some of the greatest thinkers in history have been Jewish, and the man we Christians call The Son of God was born a Jew. You'll find very little anti-Semitism at SMU," he concluded, turning the car into the impressive campus in north Dallas.

At the conclusion of a long afternoon, Sarah and Ben climbed into Drew's car for the ride to their hotel.

"You'll find accommodations at the Adolphus to be quite comfortable," Drew said. "For dinner, though, I'd like to ask a very personal favor, and invite you for dinner at our house. I'd be pleased to pick you up, say, around 6:30?"

"Oh," Sarah exclaimed, "We wouldn't want to impose…"

"There is no imposition at all, Mrs. Burkhardt. I admit, this is beyond what SMU asks when I meet prospective students, but I'm very impressed with you both; I'd like to know you better." They were stopped at a traffic signal and Drew turned to Sarah, now sitting in the front seat. "Mrs. Burkhardt, I've read that during the war you were in charge of Galveston Pilots' and those pilots faced danger at any time from German submarines. I've read about Ben, his battle against polio, and, Mrs. Burkhardt, your battle against Ben's polio. Also, I've read about Ben's grandparents, and their escape from Nazi Germany, and their contributions to the war efforts of both England and the United States."

He looked back at Ben in the Ford's rear seat. "Ben," Drew said, "how you beat polio is a fascinating story. A really good friend of mine, when I told him whom I'd be meeting, said he knew you, and that you and I might become good friends someday even if you don't select SMU."

"Oh," Ben said, "I don't think you should have any doubt, this visit to SMU sold me on where I want to be for my pre-med. Who is this good friend of yours?"

Drew pulled the car to a stop at a traffic signal and turned to Ben. "Joshua McCuskey."

Ben and Sarah were astounded. "You know Josh?"

"Oh, yes," Drew answered, turning back to the road as the light turned green, "I haven't known him a long time, but he's known me for…oh, I guess practically forever. Ah! Here we are!" A uniformed doorman opened the car door for Ben and his mother, led them to the astonishingly ornate lobby, and a bellhop followed with their luggage. Ben was still wondering at the odd way Drew had answered about knowing McCuskey when he heard Drew calling after them, "I'll pick you up at 6:30!"

The June air was smoother on their return flight, and the Cessna cruised quietly. It seemed that the little airplane's spirit somehow reflected the mood of its pilot and passenger, both of whom were quiet, conversing only occasionally as they thought about their day at SMU and the evening at the Neilan's in Dallas' Oak Cliff.

They had found Drew's Hawaiian-born wife, Kowanda, to be as charming as her husband, and the meal as excellent as the company. There were two other guests in the home that evening, a retired Dallas judge and his wife, Kowanda's mother Mitsui, who whispered to Sarah that the food was completely kosher, using recipes given them by a Jewish friend.

At Drew's invitation, Ben offered a Jewish blessing prior to the meal. Afterwards, they gathered at the piano and Drew played and sang for them, accompanied by Kowanda. For one selection Mitsui sat at the piano and played; the dining room table was moved to the opposite wall and Drew and Kowanda performed a brief but thoroughly professional soft-shoe.

"That was an Eddie Mackenzie song, wasn't it?" Ben asked when they finished, impressed at the performance.

"Yes," Drew answered, "Eddie and I have been friends for a while."

"You know Eddie Mackenzie?" Ben asked, impressed once again.

"Yes," Drew said, modestly, "at the end of the war I was in a USO war bonds show, and Eddie Mackenzie and his band were part of the same show."

The conversations over dinner, and coffee and desert after, ranged from present-day issues to the 1930s turmoil of the Great Depression, to the promise of post-war America and finally to Ben's astonishing victory over infantile paralysis.

"That's a fight that's not yet over," Ben said, steely determination in his voice. "There are hundreds of thousands who haven't beaten polio, and millions more who may come down with it. Many in Galveston's UT Medical Center are working with other teaching and research hospitals to find a vaccine, now that it's been determined that polio is caused by a virus. In fact, there's a doctor in Pittsburgh who's doing some astonishing research. I just hope I can get through medical school in time to get in on that part of the fight, maybe as part of my residency. I want to be able to put in my two cents' worth. I beat polio and I want to have a hand in eradicating that stuff from the face of the planet!"

Sarah was not surprised by her son's passion. She told the old story of when Ben was four, fitted with braces and took his first steps, and how he'd vowed at that young age to someday run with the wind.

Later, as Sarah was saying her good-byes in the kitchen, and Ben and Drew were waiting on the front porch, Drew took the opportunity to say, quietly so as not to be overheard, "Ben, I invited Josh McCuskey to be here tonight, but he couldn't for a number of reasons. But he told me to tell you that if you ever need him, for any reason, he's your friend and he'll do everything in his power to help."

"What does that mean?" Ben asked.

"I don't know," Drew said, "But I know Josh. He's steady as the Rock of Gibraltar. If you do ever need him…" Drew paused, reaching into the breast pocket of his suit jacket, "He gave me his card and asked me to give it to you. The telephone number on the back is my number. He wants you to know you can call him at any time, day or night, though you'll have to call me first, and then he'll call you back."

At Ben's expression, Drew explained, "I have ways to contact him that don't involve going through the FBI's telephone system."

"Thank you for telling me this," Ben said. As he slipped the card into his wallet, he wondered if the evening had been arranged by Josh in order for Drew to deliver that specific message. And if so, why?

Chapter 29

Late October 1946
Indictment!

Two men in business suits entered the architectural offices of Burkhardt and Associates at ten o'clock on a Friday morning. The young receptionist looked up from her typing and smiled a greeting. One of the two, in a stern voice, announced they were looking for a Mr. Azzo Judah Burkhardt.

"Yes, of course," she answered, still smiling, but now curious about the attitude displayed by the strangers. "He's in the drafting room. I'll go get him."

Without speaking, the two brushed past her, moving down the hall toward the rear of the building. She followed, her curiosity turning into concern.

Azzo was in shirtsleeves, leaning over a drafting table, talking earnestly with his young delineator, pointing out details of the new Chevrolet showroom that needed to be modified.

He looked up at the interruption, frowning as the two men rushed into the drafting room, followed by his receptionist. She said, almost shouting, "Mr. Burkhardt..." The two visitors ignored her. One of them barked, "Azzo Judah Burkhardt!"

"Yes?" Azzo said, annoyed at the sudden intrusion.

"This," one of the two men said, still speaking loudly, "is FBI Special Agent Carter. I am Special Agent Johnson.

Here are our credentials!" Each man held out a small card case.

Without looking at the documents, Azzo said in a tight voice, "May we go to my office?" He turned on his heel and moved past the two.

Several minutes later, an ashen-faced Azzo, now wearing his suit jacket, walked from his office, his hands before him in handcuffs. The two stern-faced strangers followed. The receptionist stood, her face now a mask of fear as Azzo was led out the building and toward a waiting automobile, a third man behind the wheel.

Azzo looked back over his shoulder as he was being shoved into the waiting sedan's rear seat. "Catherine," he called, his voice calm, "call Billy Bentley. Tell him to meet me downtown. Tell everyone in the office to go home, the office will be closed for the rest of this day. Lock the doors when you leave. Do not call my wife."

The sedan's rear door was slammed in his face.

As the car pulled away, Azzo turned and looked back. Catherine was standing in the doorway, weeping.

Several hours later, the door to a small interrogation room in the Galveston County Jail opened and Azzo, handcuffed and wearing gray prison coveralls, was ushered in. Billy Bentley and the two arresting FBI agents were in the room.

"I insist that I be allowed to visit with my client in private," Billy said to the two, "and I insist the handcuffs be removed. I will file a protest over your treatment of my client."

Neither man responded verbally. One reached into his pocket, produced a key, and unlocked the handcuffs. Azzo rubbed his wrists as the two left the room. Billy said, "You haven't said anything to anyone?"

"No." Azzo shook his head. "They started questioning me in the car, even before we got here, then resumed shortly after the rigmarole of fingerprinting and photographing. I didn't respond in any way in the car, but once here, I said no questions without my attorney present."

"Good. I've read the indictment against you. It was filed in a Washington Federal Court. I have already gone to Judge Pennington and luckily found him in his office. I told him I was going to file a protest along with a Writ to get you out on bail. He said there was no need, agreed with my protest, and said he was going to issue a reprimand to the Department of Justice. He will grant you release on your own recognizance. You may have to stay overnight, but I'm hoping not. Your preliminary hearing, unfortunately, will be in Washington, in thirty to forty-five days. In the meantime, you are not to leave the City of Galveston."

"I need out of here as soon as possible," Azzo said. "I need to shut down Burkhardt and Associates, make several dozen calls to clients and so forth, tell Sarah what this is all about and get my life organized so I can be away for years."

"They haven't convicted you," Billy said, "at least not yet. Azzo, this is too big for a country lawyer like me. We'll need to bring Washington attorneys on board. I talked with Levi. He'll handle all legal fees. Have they read the charges to you?"

Azzo nodded. "Human trafficking, importing illegal immigrants and suspected communists into the United States before and during wartime, and being a communist agent."

The two men who'd arrested Azzo abruptly reentered the room. "Gentlemen," Azzo said, "following my attorney's advice, I choose not to submit to questioning at this time."

"It'll go easier on you if you do," was the FBI man's response.

Billy stood. "The answer is no. Gentlemen, I'm on my way back to the courthouse for another meeting with Judge Pennington."

"If he's innocent," one of the two agents sneered, "why is he afraid to answer questions?"

"That question is one more item I'll add to my protest!" Billy snapped.

It was dusk when Billy's car turned into the drive at Mansion House. Sarah ran to the car as he opened the door. She climbed in and said, "My God, Billy, I've been waiting hours. I don't understand what's happening. I don't understand anything."

He started the car without speaking and began backing out. Halfway down the drive, he stopped and turned off the engine. "Sarah, my dear," he said, turning toward her. As Sarah looked at him under the wheel, just for a moment she did not see an overweight, balding, married father of five in his early forties, but instead saw a young brown-haired slender seventeen-year-old Billy. The memory of being with him and a group of other young people at a beach bonfire party in 1922 flooded into her mind. She remembered, vividly, leaving the fireside as the others began roasting their pork sausages. She and Billy had walked behind the dunes, and she let him kiss her several times. He'd wanted to go farther, but she didn't and stopped him. They hadn't dated again after that night.

Sarah snapped back from the memory as Billy said, "Don't pepper Azzo with questions tonight."

"But I don't understand..." She began crying.

"I know," he said, pulling her toward him. She placed her head on his shoulder, sobbing. He said, "I don't know all the details myself, though I know more than perhaps I should. I've told you a little over the phone. Let me tell you as much as I think you need to know for tonight. Later, you'll learn much more, as will I. You and I will go downtown and bring Azzo home to Mansion House. Have Rae cook up a nice dinner, though I'm sure neither of you will be hungry. Still, eat something. Have a glass of wine with dinner. If you've got something stronger in the house, have a cocktail before dinner. Perhaps several. Relax. Do not be judgmental. I can't ask any more of you at this time."

She nodded, dried her tears, straightened her shoulders, and listened. Fifteen minutes later Billy started the car and they left to pick up Sarah's husband.

Chapter 30

Crime and Punishment

Weeks and then months seemed to fly past. In what seemed no time at all 1946 was gone and 1947 itself was racing toward history.

Sarah's life, tumultuous during the war, but so ordered and calm afterwards, became once again a life of anxiety and turmoil, full of fear. The peaceful but exciting days before Ben's graduation, attendance at track meets, weekends at the beach with her two men, all was gone.

In September, Ben had gone away to school. And a little more than a month later her husband was arrested, and Sarah's life cascaded into an unbearable turbulence and the blistering knowledge that her husband had been lying to her for years.

Upon learning of the arrest, Ben telephoned Drew Neilan and visited with him and Judge McGowan, at Drew's home.

Afterwards, the elderly retired jurist telephoned Billy Bentley, and, with Levi's concurrence, they selected the team of Washington attorneys that would be needed.

Ben dropped out of SMU at the end of his first semester. He flew his little plane to Alvin and parked it more or less permanently in one of Slim Bichler's rental hangars.

Slim advised him to sell it and use the money to help in Azzo's legal fees, but Levi Weismann flatly rejected the idea.

"I'll take care of the legal stuff," Ben's uncle said. Neither Ben nor his mother were provided further explanation.

Ben insisted on being allowed to accompany his mother on the numerous trips back and forth to Washington, and begged Billy Bentley to be allowed into the Washington attorney conferences. He and Sarah were allowed to attend only those conferences that did not include Azzo, at Ben's father's insistence.

Sarah and Ben were told by Billy Bentley that prison for Azzo was becoming more and more of a possibility. They knew Azzo never admitted guilt in the courtroom but had been astonishingly candid with his attorneys. Ben once asked Billy, after asking him to join him in a hallway for a private conference, if Azzo ever mentioned Levi Weismann. Billy shook his head but disclosed to Ben that Azzo's many trips to New York had not been to meet with a publisher but instead were made to pick up a suitcase stuffed with cash.

At one public hearing, Ben and Sarah heard the government's lawyers shout and insist that Azzo disclose the number of European Jews he'd brought into the United States after they'd crossed the Atlantic. Azzo remained silent to shouts about communist agents infiltrating the United States.

Ben and Sarah, on their visits back to Galveston, heard radio reports and recordings of politicians as they made speeches on the floor of the Congress, declaring with no information that the numbers of people smuggled into the United States were in the thousands, and most were surely communists, who by now had infiltrated all levels of US Government. Democracy, the politicians shouted, was in peril.

Beginning in late 1945, Ben had often seen newsreels and heard news reports unravelling the extent of the Nazi holocaust. Later, war criminal trials in Nuremburg were regularly featured in newsreels at the Isle Theatre. Billy Bentley told them that many in Congress worried the public would become sympathetic to those who escaped Nazi persecution by entering the United States illegally. The rush to convict Azzo accelerated.

At one Congressional hearing, Azzo's parents and sister were subpoenaed. Television screens across the country featured an eminent Jewish scientist as he and his daughter upbraided and chastised the United States government. Benjamin's grandfather told the government, over objections by the government's lawyers, that he and his family experienced persecution in Nazi Germany, and therefore were experts on the subject, more so, he added, than fat politicians shouting nonsense to foster their own political ambitions. He concluded his testimony with a ringing endorsement for the heroism of his son.

Sam Klein, one day, visiting with Sarah, told her the positive publicity about Azzo was bringing a shift in public opinion away from the narrative being promoted by the communist-baiting politicians. It was, he said, now becoming imperative for the government to convict Azzo quickly so as to remove him from public view.

The government ransacked Mansion House, the Carriage House Annex, and Mansion House West, desperately looking for documentation that would provide irrefutable evidence. Sarah and Ben watched helplessly as government agents invaded apartments and smashed walls with sledgehammers. Tenants private records were seized while the *Daily News* published scathing editorial after editorial, condemning government overreach.

The government's agents touted success when they found a secret cabinet concealed in the walls of Azzo's Carriage

House studio apartment, but their publicity campaign fell flat when it turned out to be empty.

Sarah's and Ben's world swirled with lies and counter lies, train and airplane trips to and from Washington. Expenses escalated, but Levi stepped in to avoid Sarah dipping into Ben's college fund.

Sarah was ricocheting from denial to horror as piece after piece of exculpatory evidence was exposed along with the extent of the lies on which she and Azzo had based their marriage.

In time, Sarah came to believe that her marriage could not continue, whether or not Azzo was convicted. She visited with Billy Bentley, who argued against divorce, telling her that Azzo's lies had been for a noble purpose. However, for Sarah, Billy's arguments did not mitigate the fact that her and Azzo's life together was based on lies, lies told with a straight face while Azzo professed his love for her and her son.

She thought about the lovemaking she'd experienced in the marriage. Azzo's unbridled passion had the power to raise her to incredible heights, far beyond anything Glenn had ever done. But if their life was a lie, was not his lovemaking a lie? When he took her to that mountaintop where two people experienced ultimate communion with one another, was it only she who had stood there, alone and bereft of the man who'd taken her there?

And, she thought, what about Ben? It didn't seem possible that Azzo's love for her son could also have been a lie, but perhaps it was. The man she married was so consummate a liar that he enticed a boy to love him, knowing that if the boy loved him, the boy's mother would surely surrender. Azzo's and the boy's trips to the beach were only to endorse his lies, as proved by the hidden short-wave radio the government said existed but were unable to find.

Azzo took her boy night fishing only as cover for his use of the radio while the innocent boy slept on a blanket next to the car! The fact that this might have implicated Benjamin in some way and could yet implicate him caused her even more distress.

Sarah was not particularly religious. To her, Friday evening services and prayers had always somehow seemed perfunctory, not the deeply moving communion with God that her son seemed to experience. And Azzo, too, she thought, though his religiousness was surely a lie, a lie to God!

As the trial roared through newspaper headlines and Sarah continued to contemplate divorce, Levi Weismann came to Mansion House one day. Without preamble, he strode into her living room and roared at her. He demanded that Sarah talk with Rabbi Henry Cohen.

Shrugging, irritated, and believing no good could come from such a conversation, Sarah agreed to go when Levi said that a meeting with the rabbi was the minimum that Benjamin would expect.

Sarah Weismann Jacobs Burkhardt met with Galveston's B'nai Israel's Rabbi Henry Cohen in his office at ten o'clock on a humid, windy late summer morning.

The elderly rabbi, born in England in 1863, was in his eighty-fourth year of life and his fifty-ninth year of service to B'nai Israel congregation when he agreed to meet with Sarah. He had never lost his English accent, nor a stammer which had begun in childhood. He welcomed Sarah that day dressed the way she had always seen him: black suit coat, white shirt, starched cuffs and collar, and a white bow tie. She knew he often took notes on his starched cuffs.

Before they began their talk, the good rabbi asked if they might pray first. She nodded, irritated that religious leaders always brought prayer into the conversation, knowing as she did that God never answered any prayers, especially hers, and this time she wasn't sure what answer she wanted. Nevertheless, she nodded to the good rabbi, her pessimism obvious.

Rabbi Henry Cohen began by telling her his prayer was *Mi Shebeirach* and would be a prayer for strength and healing. It was a long prayer, and Sarah began to fidget as the rabbi's stammering reedy voice recited the English version of words older than time. After what seemed to Sarah an eternity, Rabbi Cohen paused in his recitation, and announced he was nearing the end.

Sarah breathed a sigh of relief that the prayer would soon be over. But the rabbi had a surprise for her. He switched to the ancient words, words of Sarah's and the rabbi's ancestors. He intoned the last two stanzas line by line; first in Hebrew, then he recited the same line in English.

The Hebrew words flowed over her, beyond her understanding, yet they were somehow uplifting. When the English followed, it enhanced the prayer. The rabbi's stammering reedy voice had a unique quality now, and the thousands-of-years-old words had new meanings, and she felt her heart soaring with an emotion she could not analyze.

A portion of the ending contained the words "show me that you are near." Without realizing she was speaking aloud, she said, softly, involuntarily, eyes tightly shut: "Yes, God. Show me. I need help. I need You to be near. I need to know the way."

"Yes," Rabbi Cohen said, the reedy British accent now sounding stronger than ever, the stammer temporarily at bay, "Sarah, all those years when Ben was so sick, God was near. He was helping you even then, though you did not know it."

"No," she whispered, head down, eyes still tightly shut, denying the rabbi's words. "Sometimes I prayed, but there was no answer. I said, 'God, help me. Help my boy. Release him from pain.' But God never did. God never answered. Many times, I wondered if there was a God, and if so, how could he be so cruel to a child." She was crying, tears flowing down her cheeks.

The rabbi contradicted her. "There is God, Sarah, and He did help you. He gave you to Benjamin, and you helped your son. God led you to George Stein, who gave you a job. God brought Azzo Burkhardt into your life, and Azzo not only created Mansion House, he worked with Ben to overcome polio, and he strengthened you so that you and your uncle could restore your family relationship, a relationship that God intended you to have. None of that was George Stein's nor Azzo's nor Levi's doing, it was God working through those men. It was God who directed Levi Weissman to bring Azzo Burkhardt to Galveston and into your life."

Sarah had never before experienced the feelings that cascaded through her consciousness. She was confused and frightened by the strength of her feelings.

Sarah spent nearly three hours in the rabbi's office that day, and when she came out, she knew that God had in fact been near and had been near all her life. She knew now that Azzo loved her and she need never have doubted that he had been beside her on that mountaintop. Azzo loved her son. And Azzo loved his people, the Jews of not only Nazi Germany but of all the world.

She learned that the rabbi himself had been responsible, many years before, for bringing thousands of Jews from Russia and eastern Europe into the United States through the Port of Galveston, even before the years of the first World War.

These people came, and Rabbi Cohen helped them enter the United States, and helped them settle in Texas and throughout the southwest. They and their descendants were scattered, living in thriving cities and prosperous farms. They were citizens, and, while the rabbi admitted he did not know for sure, he felt that the descendants of those the rabbi brought in were those who had now bravely accepted the Word War II refugees–illegal immigrants—brought to them by Azzo Burkhardt. They were the ones who helped the people Azzo brought in establish identities and often set them up in business. And these people knew if it all came to light, there would surely be reprisals and possible deportations from the Jew haters in the United States Government.

When Sarah rose to leave, her tears finally gone, the rabbi said, "Once more, Sarah, before you leave, let us pray: Sarah, my dear," he said, holding both her hands, looking into her eyes, "there is defeat to overcome and acceptance of living to be established and always there must be hope."

She now knew what the next line would be and said it in unison with the good rabbi: "To know healing is to know that all life is one. Amen."

When Sarah left the rabbi's office she knew her husband loved her, her son loved her, and God loved her. The lies Azzo had told had been of necessity, to protect her, her son, and hundreds more across the southwest.

She climbed into her car and drove to the seawall, parked, exited her car, and walked to the Gulf edge of Galveston's incredible seawall.

Sarah stood there looking out at the treacherous and beautiful Gulf. The wind blew her hair about, and as it billowed around her shoulders, she silently praised God.

Sarah knew, then, and had known at the rabbi's office, that she would stand by her man to the end of her life.

In Washington, Azzo was offered a deal: plead guilty and serve only six months in a minimum-security prison in Beaumont, and Azzo, against the advice of his attorneys, took the deal.

Afterwards, the judge announced that he was setting the deal aside. He sentenced Azzo to ten years in the United States Medium Security Prison at Leavenworth, Kansas.

Chapter 31

October 1947

Six weeks after Azzo Burkhard became Prisoner Number 2137, Sarah and Ben were permitted their first family visit to Leavenworth. It did not go well.

After they'd settled into the family visiting room, given the rules about touching and conversation, Azzo was ushered in. Both were surprised as they found an Azzo Burkhardt who now seemed older than his fifty-three years.

They had been in Washington and accompanied him to the dilapidated Washington City Hall building when he entered the Federal Prison system to begin his sentence. Reporters shouted questions as television cameras recorded the scene. At the time, Azzo seemed upbeat, joking with reporters about an appeal.

To Ben and Sarah, he whispered, grinning, "I'll be out quickly on good behavior if nothing else! I'm gonna be a very good boy!"

Now, the gray-faced and worn man before them smilingly assured them he was being well-treated. "They allow me exercise time," Azzo said, "so I'm keeping up with my running." Ben knew the statement was a lie.

Then, with an attempt at humor, Azzo added, "They kind of frown on cross-country though. Narrow-minded folks, these jailers. They think I'd just keep on running all the way to San Luis Pass." Sarah burst into tears.

"And you," Azzo said to Ben, "you get yourself back in college! You'll never get to be a doctor by traveling all over the countryside to visit an old man at Leavenworth."

Sarah was still in tears as she and Ben left the massive gray stone fortress northeast of Kansas City, and Ben's eyes were moist. As he guided the rental car toward a privately operated airfield, Ben said, "I'm sorry dad had to see us both break down. I thought I could keep myself in check, but when he started making cracks about the food, I lost it."

Sarah, between sobs, said, "I lost it long before you did. I should have—oh, Ben! What are we going to do? I don't think I can live with him in that place! Ten years!" She held her hands to her face as renewed sobs racked her body.

Ben pulled the car to the side of the road and switched off the engine. "Mom," he said, "before we left Galveston, I telephoned Drew Neilan."

"Oh! Long distance! Ben, that's so expensive!"

Ben shook his head at his mother's focus on minutiae, then resumed. "You remember I told you that Drew once said that maybe a time would come when he could help. So, when I called I said, 'Drew, it's time. I need help.' I told him we were going to visit Dad today and he said for us to stop in Dallas on the way home. I need to refuel there anyway. We can overnight the airplane. Drew said he and Kowanda wanted us to have dinner with them, and that he'd make arrangements for us to stay at a hotel nearby."

"A hotel!" Sarah said. "Ben, we can't afford…"

"Well," Ben thought, "at least she's no longer sobbing." To his mother, he said, "Mom, you know Uncle Levi's still handling expenses. Don't worry about the cost of a hotel."

However, in the end she and Ben did not stay in a hotel. Sarah wound up sleeping on the single bed in the rear bedroom of the Neilan's small house. Ben and Drew, along with Judge McGowan, talked long past midnight. After the kindly Judge and his wife Mitsui left, Ben slept on the living room couch. Everyone slept late the following morning, but plans had been made. That morning, Drew's telephone rang, and he and Ben talked to Joshua McCuskey.

Three weeks later, Benjamin Burkhardt and his mother, together with attorney William Bentley and Sarah's uncle returned by train to Dallas for another meeting. They arrived late in the day and taxied to the Adolphus, where they spent the night. Levi Weismann continued to pay, while Sarah agonized about repayment.

The next day they met in an Adolphus conference room. Ben began the meeting with a short prayer, then turned the session over to Drew Neilan.

"Both Judge McGowan and I have read the trial transcripts you sent," Drew began, nodding to Billy Bentley, "and I've had lengthy conversations with Josh McCuskey and several of my law professors. Josh said he would be summarily discharged from the agency if anyone finds out what he's shared with me. I'm not going to share everything he said, but he strongly believes we have a chance."

"For an appeal?" Levi Weismann interrupted.

"No," Drew answered. "Please, let me continue. I'll explain as I go along."

"You see, as I've told Ben, I have a good friend who is the wife of the Arkansas Democratic senator, Senator Browning. I have loved his wife since childhood. Catherine Browning was my teacher in elementary school. A long time ago, when I was lost and alone, she led the search for me. I was lost for quite a while, but Catherine never gave up. So, you see, we've known one another for a long time."

Sarah interrupted. "How old were you when you were lost?"

Drew ducked his head slightly before answering. Then he said softly, "I was ten."

"But..." Sarah said, her eyes wide. Drew held up his hand. "We don't need to get into all that, Mrs. Burkhardt. Another time, please."

Sarah nodded as Drew continued.

"Catherine Browning," he said, "is a close friend of Eleanor Roosevelt's. And, oddly enough I've also met Mrs. Roosevelt."

"You know Eleanor Roosevelt?" Sarah almost shrieked.

"Mother!" Ben said loudly. Sarah realized she'd made another mistake, and as she did, she also realized that Ben was in charge of this meeting. Her son was no longer a child. Her little boy was gone. He was nineteen now and was a man.

"At any rate," Drew continued, picking up the thread, "as Ben and I have discussed, Josh believes that if we visited Catherine, share with her what Azzo has done and that we believe the Government wrongfully abrogated a plea deal, and, in fact, should never have raced to convict in the first place, that she would agree and would help us set up a meeting with Mrs. Roosevelt in her townhouse in New York."

"And then what?" Levi asked in a demanding tone.

"And then," Ben said, rising, "I ask Mrs. Roosevelt to ask President Truman to issue a presidential pardon for my father."

There was stunned silence for a full minute. It was Billy Bentley who broke the silence. "It's been a long-standing practice for presidents to issue pardons at the end of their terms. Truman is going to stand for re-election next year and may win. That would mean Azzo wouldn't be pardoned until the end of 1952. By then he would have served five years."

"Yes," Judge McGowan agreed, "but there's a strong chance Truman will lose next November. If that happens, the pardon could be much sooner."

Drew answered, rising and standing beside Ben. "It really doesn't matter. Josh believes that there's concern at high levels of government that Azzo should never have been prosecuted in the first place. The newsreels of the Nazi concentration camps, the Nuremburg trials, and all that come into play. Josh says a presidential pardon will give the government a way out of an embarrassing misuse of power, and he believes the President will act on it sooner rather than later. He believes the President won't wait until after an election."

"It's a wild scheme, Mr. Neilan," Billy Bentley said, "but the longer I think about it the more I like it, if nothing else because of its audaciousness. If it doesn't work, we'll go to plan B."

"And what," Levi Weismann demanded, "is plan B?"

"Petition the court for a reduced sentence," Billy answered, "on the grounds of the plea deal offered, which the Judge by-passed."

Drew added, "If we have to do that, Mrs. Browning has assured me that she and her husband will formally support our petition. We might get Mrs. Roosevelt to do so as well. But going back to court will take a while. There'll be delays."

"Josh has told me," Ben said, "about his boss's extreme prejudice toward Jews, but that's information he asked us to keep private. He said that's one of the reasons Truman is displeased with his FBI Director."

"J. Edgar Hoover's anti-Semitism is well known," Judge McGowan said, "but still, we need to refrain from mentioning it outside of this room."

"And there's this," Ben went on, "we can offer the government something they've wanted for a long time: Azzo's ledgers. He kept detailed notes about who was brought in, where they are supposed to be living, and so forth. It's what the government was looking for when they ransacked Mansion House. It's our bargaining chip, the only one we've got."

"What assurances do you have that the FBI won't deport every single person listed in the ledger, accusing them of being communists, and renege on a pardon?" Uncle Levi asked.

"We have Joshua McCuskey's word," Drew said. "I think we can get Senator Browning's word as well. Then, we'll ask Mrs. Roosevelt, when she talks to the President to get his word."

There was silence around the room.

"And," Ben added, "there's a twist. When we offer to disclose all who are on the ledger, I'll tell them that I'll do it only one person or family at a time, and then only if they agree, and then only to Josh McCuskey, and Josh will interview each. And he will then provide a report to the Department of Justice that these people are not communists."

"That's a tedious undertaking, Ben," Billy Bentley said.

"Yep, it is. And I'll have to delay returning to college. But Josh is committed, and I am, too. I am doing this for my dad. Josh is doing it because he once said to me, 'I want to be your friend.' He may lose his job."

"Ben," Drew said, "I think it's time for us to begin working on a time when we can go to Fayetteville, Arkansas." He smiled broadly. "Ben, you're gonna get to meet a great lady. If she can make a visit with the former First Lady happen, then you'll have met two great ladies."

Chapter 32

Three Weeks Later
Early December 1947

Sarah and Ben were in attorney William Bentley's third-floor office of the Weismann Bank building. Levi Weisman was present. Ben was speaking. Outside, a cold rain blanketed the city.

"As I've already reported," Ben said, "our meeting with Mrs. Browning went well. She's written to Mrs. Roosevelt who has agreed to meet with us three days from now in New York.

"Slim said I could use the Beech Staggerwing," Ben continued, "but December weather in New York can be rough. We'll fly commercial. I'll take Trans-Texas to Dallas, meet Drew, and we'll fly direct to New York from there.

"There's a small hotel off Times Square where we'll spend the night; then we'll taxi to Mrs. Roosevelt's townhome, in what's called the Upper East Side. We're to be there for tea. Mrs. Browning is already in New York."

"Afternoon tea?" Billy questioned.

"I guess," Ben said, shrugging. "It's at four, so I guess it's afternoon tea."

"High tea?" Billy asked. Ben shook his head, smiling. "Mr. Bentley, I don't know. Until this moment I didn't know there was both a 'Tea' and a 'High Tea.'"

"You'll do fine," Billy said. "That fellow Neilan is pretty impressive too."

"Anyway," Ben went on, "the hotel room has two beds and we'll bunk there."

Levi Weismann, sounding angry, interjected, "I'll pay for your rooms! You're going to let me pay for the airplane tickets, too!"

Ben smiled at his uncle. "Sir, with all due respect, you have paid more than enough. But I'll take you up on your offer to pay for the tickets."

Levi was angry, his mood reflecting the weather. Lightning flashed outside the window, with a roll of thunder a second later. Rain pelted the window and obscured the view.

"You need to tell that Roosevelt lady to tell Truman to issue that pardon right now!" the old banker said loudly. " I don't think we should let Truman leave Azzo in jail!"

"Uncle Levi," Ben said, "I disagree completely." Sarah was surprised. Ben almost never spoke in any sort of confrontational way to his uncle.

"Why?" Levi Weismann asked, his voice loud, his face red. "Why do you disagree with me!" It was an accusation.

"Drew's a friend," Ben answered calmly. "He did us an enormous favor by introducing me to Mrs. Browning, and he's going to go with me when she introduces me to Mrs. Roosevelt. Drew is the one who volunteered that we bunk together, and I think the thing to do is take him up on it. You know, both he and Mrs. Browning have gone above and beyond, as has that FBI man, McCuskey. This isn't their fight. Mrs. Browning has interrupted her schedules to be in New York with us. Mrs. Roosevelt has interrupted hers to meet with us. We just need to stick with the plan. Tell Mrs. Roosevelt what we ask, and why, offer our bargaining chip, and then wait and see. She may not take any action at all. And if she doesn't, we'll then go to what Billy calls Plan B.

"Mom," Ben continued, turning to Sarah, "I know we talked about telling dad about all this when you go to Kansas next week, but I think now that it'd be better if we don't. Maybe Truman will issue a pardon next year. Maybe he won't. We have no way of knowing if or when, and I don't think we should get Dad's hopes up."

"I don't think much about this pardon scheme anyway," Levi said in an angry voice. Ben turned and looked closely at his great uncle. As he did, there were more lightning flashes outside the window, quickly followed by ear-splitting thunder.

"Let's just go ahead," Levi said, his breathing heavy, "and call the FBI, tell them they've got the wrong guy, that I was the one they wanted all along. We'll give them the damn ledgers, let them deport everyone, that's what they want!"

Ben turned to his patrician ninety-three-year-old uncle and spoke softly. "And do you have those damn ledgers?"

Levi was silent for a few moments, flustered. "No. But you've got them! Do what I tell you!"

"Uncle Levi," Ben said patiently, "you're right. I've got the ledgers. I've had them all along. But I'm not going to do what you say. Please, sir. Let's remember, the FBI ransacked the entire Mansion House complex, every single apartment, and we lost tenants because of it. They almost tore Azzo's work studio in the Carriage House apart, but they didn't find the ledgers, and the reason is I found them first and they were behind the seat of my little Cessna, in plain sight all the time Mansion House was being torn apart. I'm not going to give them to anyone if the bargain is you go to jail in the process. So, the answer my dear Uncle is, no."

Levi was breathing heavily.

"Uncle Levi," Ben said, as a kind tenor entered his voice. "There is no need for you to turn yourself in, go to jail, your reputation in shreds. Dad did what he did because he felt loyalty to you. He is in jail now because he protected you and many others. We don't need to breach that loyalty, to make everything he's gone through worthless. And who knows if all that would work anyway. They just might put you in jail along with my father and throw away the key.

"Uncle Levi," Ben went on, "you, Dad and all the others who were connected with this set-up are heroes, doing what you did, and at enormous costs both financially and emotionally. Everyone connected with this is a hero, but most will likely remain anonymous to history.

"Only you and my father and the sacrifices you both have made will be known," Ben continued, "and they'll be known because I'll tell. I'll tell everyone. I'll wait a few years, but I'll tell. My father knew that he was risking what may be the last years of his life to do what he did. Yet, under enormous pressure he chose to plead guilty and remain silent. He, and you, are the ones that history will remember. You and he are the ones Jews around the world will come to know as their hero. And you and he are the ones I'll tell my children about, and they can tell their children, and they'll know that the name Burkhardt and Weismann are heroic names, and the middle name of my first son will be Weismann.

"So, Uncle Levi, for now we do what we can. If the plan doesn't work, then we'll do something else."

Levi Weismann sat silent. It was slowly dawning on the old man that Ben was no longer a boy, but a strongly principled man. He felt a surge of pride, proud of his nephew, proud of Sarah for raising such a fine man, a man who had promised to give the Weismann name to his son. The Weismann name would live on!

The old man's breathing became more labored than before. No one in the room moved. All eyes turned to the last surviving male member of a family begun by two brothers who arrived in Galveston from Germany in 1874.

Thunder, louder now, crashed outside.

"I seem to be a little out of breath," the old man said. "It's all this dampness in the air." He breathed heavily a few times.

Ben looked closely at his uncle. There was a strange expression on his face.

"You didn't climb the stairs again, did you?" Billy Bentley asked.

"I dislike elevators," Levi snapped. "You're only on the second floor!"

"No," Sarah thought, "this is the third floor."

Levi looked about the room, breathing even harder. Ben stared intently at his uncle, his eyes wide. Sarah held her handkerchief to her face, mouth opened. It seemed to Ben that his uncle was looking at someone standing at the closed door, someone who hadn't been there earlier, and who couldn't be seen by others in the room. Outside, the rain continued in torrents. There was another clap of thunder, and then, astonishingly, the rain stopped. A profound silence enveloped the room.

Levi's eyes widened as they moved, seemingly tracking a being who crossed from the door to the window. Ben felt the hairs on the back of his neck rise.

Levi began to rise from his chair, as if to follow whomever or whatever he had seen, then slowly the elderly banker sat back against the leather, his arms dropped from the armrests, his eyes fixed just to the side of the window.

It seemed to Ben as if someone or something was standing beside the window, beckoning. There was one final breath and a long sigh as the old man's eyes closed for the last time and his head slumped over, his chin on his chest.

Levi Weismann, patrician banker, civic leader, and one of Galveston's last remaining survivors of the Great Storm of 1900, was gone.

Simultaneously with Levi's head slumping forward, the sun broke through the rain clouds and amidst the silence of the room light flooded across the carpet.

No one moved for a long minute.

Ben stood from his chair, crossed to his uncle and fell to his knees as he hugged the old man. "Goodbye, my dear uncle," Ben said as tears flowed down his cheek, "*ch am aloaim,* Go with God."

Sarah, sobbing, joined her son, kneeling on the floor in front of the corpse, her arms around Benjamin.

A week later, Sarah again sat at a visitors' table at Leavenworth Prison. Unlike other visits, Azzo was allowed to sit across from her, there was no reinforced glass panel between. He was holding Sarah's hands across the table.

"How I'd love to hold you tightly at this moment," he said.

Sarah was crying and pulled one hand away, wiped her face with her handkerchief, and reached again for his hand, feeling the warmth, knowing and remembering how those hands once caressed her body, touching as his lips followed.

She straightened. "They should have let you come to the funeral."

He shook his head. "Not allowed."

"I appreciated hearing you tell about it though" Azzo said, "and Ben sent me a most moving letter, describing the circumstances of his death, and how, to Ben, it seemed as if God had sent *mal'akh*—the messenger—to lead Levi in his final passage."

"Yes," Sarah said. "He told Rabbi Cohen about it as well, and Rabbi spoke of it at the funeral. Ben said he actually saw the messenger, but when I asked him what the messenger looked like, he said he didn't know." She was silent for a brief moment. "How could he not know if he saw him?

"Azzo," she said, "I miss Uncle Levi, the old fool!"

"He was no fool, Sarah," Azzo answered. "He was a great man."

Sarah changed the subject. "Azzo," she said, "do you know that Uncle Levi left everything to Ben?"

"I suspected he might," Azzo said, "if in fact there was anything left after all my legal bills."

"I think the money for that came from..." Sarah began. Azzo cut her off, shaking his head. "No, don't say aloud what I think you're going to say. I also suspected that's what he might have done, of course.

"So, Ben's going to become a banker?" Azzo changed course, smiling as if to hold back tears.

"No," Sarah shook her head. "Azzo, there was a great deal of money. Apparently, several months before he died, Levi had begun proceedings to transfer the bank ownership to investors and convert all his holdings into cash. That cash is to be managed jointly by Billy Bentley and a Galveston accounting firm until Ben reaches twenty-five, then it all goes to him. Uncle Levi also arranged to pay off all remaining mortgages on Mansion House and Mansion House West, and I was awarded a lump sum of $50,000 cash. Some money went to B'nai Israel, but I don't remember how much. All the rest went to Ben. Azzo, it's a great deal of money, over ten million."

"So, Ben's college and medical school is now assured." Azzo was smiling.

"Oh, much more than that. And one other thing, I almost forgot. Right away Billy arranged for Ben to have an allowance from the principal—rather generous, too, I might add. Ben's planning to buy a new and larger airplane, a four-seater."

"Oh, what kind of plane?" Azzo asked, eyebrows raised.

"You mean who makes it?" Sarah answered, "Oh, I don't know. I think he said Beech-something. But then he said a Bonanza was a six-seater, and he wants a four, and then he said Cessna, and I don't know if Bonanza is the name of an airplane or someone who makes airplanes or a candy bar."

"You're not much help, my dear," Azzo said, smiling.

"Well, I can't help it if I don't understand airplane talk," Sarah said, a little testily. "and he doesn't have it yet, anyway." She changed the subject. "Azzo, I love you. I need you back in Galveston."

"Well, that's a shift," Azzo said. "I love you, too, my dear, and time goes by pretty fast for me here. I'll be out and home before you know it. I've long thought I could get out on good behavior, and I'm being a very good boy."

"Ben," Sarah said quickly, afraid she would blurt the potential for a pardon, "said for me to remind you to exercise. Don't just sit around. The first day you get back he said, you and he are going to the beach."

Azzo smiled, a little wistfully. "And we're going to run with the wind?"

"That's what he said."

"Tell him I'll keep exercising."

"What do they have you doing every day?"

"I started in the laundry when I first got here, but I probably didn't do a very good job. They gave me another;

I run the library these days. Easy work for an old man. I get to write a little. I type letters for some of the other inmates. There are some here who can't write, or read for that matter, and I send letters home for them. I'm teaching a couple of them to read, but many others aren't interested."

"Azzo, can I kiss you?"

"Well," he said, "that's a change of subject! And no, you can't, you know the rules. I'll be out one of these days, and Ben and I will go to the beach and run, and you and I will spend our nights—and maybe even some days—in bed. That's when I'll wear you out with this kissing business!"

He grinned and rolled his eyes, looking down, a gesture which she knew meant he was feeling a change in a lower part of his body. She winked in response, smiling a smile she did not feel.

A bell rang. The visit was over.

Chapter 33

Dallas Union Station

It was early February. Sarah had visited Leavenworth once more and was returning to Galveston. She was between trains in Dallas, waiting for the express to Houston, and had just left the Western Union desk, where she'd telegraphed Ben her arrival time.

Now as she remembered her visit, tears returned. It had been hard at the prison to act cheerful when what she wanted was to fling herself into the arms of her husband and cry. Azzo, too, seemed to be working at remaining calm and unemotional, when she knew he was struggling, quailing what was becoming more and more a reality to him, a reality of what a ten-year sentence actually meant. She ached to tell him the prospects of a pardon but kept silent.

As she sat, she heard the train she was to board entering the terminal area. A loudspeaker blared, "Now arriving, Track 4…" There was more, but she stopped listening when she saw Drew Neilan approaching, walking rapidly. He smiled across the huge vaulted waiting room, waved and began running. Waiting passengers stared.

"Glad I caught you, Mrs. Burkhardt," he said breathlessly, catching both her hands in his as she stood to meet him. "I came to tell you that my friend Catherine called. There's very good news! The pardon is going to be signed."

Sarah shook her head in confusion. "What? Who's Catherine? The pardon has been signed?"

"Let's sit down," Drew said, still smiling his engaging warm smile, "and I'll tell you everything." He drew her to a sitting position and added, "The pardon has not yet been signed, but the President has promised Mrs. Roosevelt that he will be sign it! Next Thursday! Not next December. Can you believe it? Next Thursday!"

"Oh!" Sarah said. "Ah…does Ben know?"

"Yes," Drew said, nodding and still smiling broadly. "I spoke with Ben long distance. He gave me your travel information. When I realized you must already be at Union Station, I rushed right over. I wanted to tell you in person!"

"But—"Sarah began, stammering, staring into Drew's intense but caring cobalt-blue eyes, "but I thought it might not be signed at all, and even if it was it wouldn't be until after the election, and then only if the President lost. And the election's not until November." It was almost a question, but not quite.

Drew looked around, making sure no one was in earshot. "You remember that Catherine Browning is the wife of the Arkansas Democratic senator," he said, his voice low. "You remember she's the one Ben and I went to Fayetteville to see. Catherine met Ben and me in New York and went with us for tea with the former First Lady."

"Oh, yes," Sarah said, frowning as she tried to catch up with his excited, rapid speech. She repeated herself, "I thought that President Truman wouldn't sign until after the election, and then only if he lost. What changed?"

Drew smiled. "Well, from what Catherine said, it was Ben's eloquence when he met and talked with Mrs. Roosevelt that made things swing our way. I was there and I have to agree, Ben truly was eloquent! And that caused Mrs. Roosevelt to insist that the President act sooner than later! She's been telephoning him daily. Catherine said he got really irritated, cussed a little when talking to Mrs. Roosevelt, and that grand lady fussed right back at the President of the United States, telling him to mind his manners about his language! Can you imagine?"

No, Sarah couldn't. "Really?" she said, disbelieving and wondering whether to frown or smile.

"Ben's sometimes a pretty good talker," she went on, "but he's not that good, and..."

She was interrupted by the station's announcement system. "Now boarding, Express to Houston, with stops in Corsicana and Huntsville, all aboard, Track 4, express to Houston."

"Trust me," Drew Neilan said rising, still holding both Sarah's hands, "Ben was wonderful! He's a great guy. I wish I knew him better. He talked about polio to Mrs. Roosevelt, how he'd beaten it, and how President Roosevelt was his hero and how he wished that the President could have beaten polio, and he talked about his plans to study medicine, infectious diseases, and maybe someday there'll be a preventive for polio. He called it a vaccine.

"He talked about Azzo being his adoptive father, but he loved him as if he and Azzo were flesh-and-blood. He told how it was Azzo who'd worked with him to overcome polio, and that neither he nor I nor you nor anyone who knew felt that what Azzo had been doing was a crime, saving Jewish refugees from certain death at the hands of a criminal regime. Ben said his father was a hero, and should be decorated, not imprisoned!

"He told about Azzo's parents, now his grandparents, and how the U.S. and British commandoes had raided a

German rocket facility and brought them out, and they'd been commended as heroes, and ever since Ben's scientist grandparents have been working for our side, helping to develop better rocketry, first in England and now working on jet engines and rockets at the Jet Propulsion Laboratory in Pasadena. Moreover, Ben said, that since the U. S. Government, when the war was over, gave the German prisoners-of-war who were encamped on this side of the Atlantic the option to stay in America with a path to citizenship and that action sort of decriminalized what Azzo had been doing and…" Drew paused, breathless.

"I am sorry," Drew said. "I get carried away sometimes. Mrs. Burkhardt, your son Ben was wonderful and Mrs. Roosevelt, Catherine said, left for Washington the very next day. Catherine met her in Washington and was present during the first meeting with the President. It was a luncheon in the family quarters in the White House. Mrs. Truman was there. Afterwards, Mrs. Roosevelt called the President or his First Lady at least once each day, demanding action!

"And there's more," Drew continued, still speaking rapidly, "but we're running out of time. Where's your bag? I'll take you to your seat, and I'll leave before the train begins rolling." He picked up Sarah's bag and cosmetic case and led her to the station platform.

"No one can know about this," Drew said as they moved through the crowd, "not even Mr. Burkhardt. Truman wants very badly to keep it all quiet. Catherine said he said, 'Keep those jackass-communist-baiting jackals in the congress at bay!' I'm not sure what that meant, but Catherine said Truman doesn't want the newspapers or radio to learn about any of this. He's going to quietly sign the necessary documents on Thursday, next week. White House staff will fly to Kansas and personally deliver the documents to the warden in Leavenworth the next day, Friday, and Saturday you can pick up your husband. The warden will have instructions for confidentiality. It usually takes about thirty days to process, but all that will be waived, and Mr. Burkhardt will be summarily released. He probably will not know what's going on until thirty minutes or so before he exits the gate."

"Whew!" Sarah said. "That's a lot to digest. Next Saturday? Azzo will be free next Saturday?"

"Yes," Drew answered grinning triumphantly as he assisted her up the steps and into the railway carriage. "I've told all of this to Ben, too. Not even your attorney is to know, but Catherine said she'd call me, to confirm, and I'll telegraph you, and you and Ben will need to be in Kansas at Leavenworth's back gate on that day. It's all going to happen quickly. You'll get to pick up a surprised and, I hope, happy Mr. Burkhardt, with no press nor cameras around. No information is to be released to the press until after the election."

The conductor's final call interrupted. "All aboard!"

"I've got to go!" Drew said, leaning over and kissing Sarah on the cheek. "They took our deal about the ledgers, including the twist Ben put to it," he said as he picked up her bag and placed it into the overhead. "Ben can tell you all about it. He, of course, agreed to comply."

"How can we ever..." Sarah began, looking up from her seat, trying to think how to best thank the tall young man with the incredible eyes. But Drew was gone. The train was moving. She saw him enter the vestibule at the end of the carriage, and she turned to the window.

Drew Neilan stepped off the now moving train and was soon out of sight.

Chapter 34

Saturday, February 21, 1948
Leavenworth, Kansas

Sarah opened her eyes as Ben knocked on her bedroom door. "Time to get up, Mom," he said. "Today's the day!" She thought she hadn't slept, excited as she was over what the day was to bring. But she must have slept some, she told herself. The last time she'd looked at her bedside clock it had read 2:45. Then, suddenly, Ben was knocking. It was four o'clock.

Instead of the telephone call they'd been told to expect, a telegram had arrived early Friday. All it said was, "Azzo Judah Burkhardt will be released at noon, February 21, 1948." The day before, a special delivery Justice Department letter had provided detailed instructions on where to pick up a prisoner, adding that the Justice Department would provide no transportation, either for the prisoner or for whomever was to meet him."

They took off at five o'clock, with Ben piloting Slim Bichler's newest, a four-passenger. It had still been dark, but Slim had arranged for a number of automobiles to line the runway, their headlights and the airplane's wing-mounted landing lights providing enough illumination for a pre-dawn take-off.

They landed in Kansas at half past ten, at a small private airfield operated by a friend of Diane's father, who'd arranged for a rental car. They had driven directly to the waiting area, a small graveled parking area adjacent to a paved highway.

It was bitterly cold in Kansas and Sarah's light winter coat was no match for the below-freezing temperatures. She knew she would have been uncomfortable without the rental car's heating system operating full force.

The road they were instructed to use took them past the impressive front entrance to the massive gray stone fortress that was the Federal prison, with its park-like entrance and expansive lawns, now brown and sere with patches of old snow scattered about. As instructed, Ben guided the car over a route that seemed circuitous to a rear entrance. He parked. Sarah was having a hard time controlling her emotions.

Then, she saw the personnel door at one corner of a gate for large trucks open and Azzo, in gray overcoat with a gray scarf about his neck exited, almost as if he were shoved. Someone stepped out the door behind him and placed a satchel and a large brown paper string-tied package on the ground, then turned and re-entered. The door closed as Sarah burst from the car and ran across the highway, toward her husband.

"Azzo! Azzo!" she screamed, then stumbled. She stopped, kicked off her high heels, and disregarding the cold ran in her stockinged feet up the long narrow walkway toward the man she loved. He, too, had begun running, ignoring the satchel and package. They met half-way.

Ben climbed from the car, picked up his mother's shoes, trotted past his embracing parents, retrieved the satchel and bundle and returned to his parents, putting his arms around both. "Dad," he said, kissing his father on the cheek, "It's colder than heck out here. Let's head to the car."

Azzo picked up his wife and carried her across the highway. Diane stood by the rear door, holding it open, and Azzo leaned over and deposited Sarah in the back seat.

Diane hugged her father-in-law and said, "Welcome back to the world." Azzo backed from the hug and looked at the blonde young woman. He said, "Diane Bichler?"

She hugged him again and said, through tears, "No, I'm Diane Burkhardt. Ben and I were married two weeks ago. We're so glad you're out of that place!"

Azzo, overwhelmed, nodded but said nothing and allowed himself to be ushered into the rear seat. Ben stowed the satchel and paper bundle in the rear of the car, closed the lid and went to the front passenger-side door as Diane slid behind the wheel.

Ben reached across the back of the front seat and grabbed both his father's hands. He pulled the older man toward him and they sat wordlessly in a four-handed grip. Tears streamed down the cheeks of both men as their eyes communicated their love.

Ben released his father's hands as Diane put the car into gear, released the parking brake and turned onto the paved roadway.

In the rear-view mirror, Diane saw Azzo turn and look back at Leavenworth Federal Prison.

"Taking a last look?" she asked.

"Yes. I'm just not sure I believe the last forty-five minutes."

"Believe it," Ben said, again looking over the back of the front seat, "You didn't know anything until forty-five minutes ago?"

"No, nothing at all," Azzo answered, wiping his face with a tissue Sarah handed him. "I was as usual working in the prison library when the warden for my section and two guards came in." He paused and took a few breaths, struggling with his emotions as Sarah put her arms around him.

"At first, no one said anything," Azzo continued. "Then, the warden told the prisoners present to leave. I was handed this suit and told to strip and put it on. After I did, they silently motioned me to follow, and I did, one guard and the warden in front, the other guard behind. I was escorted to the gate, where I was handed this overcoat and scarf and told to put them on.

"They showed me the satchel and that bundle. The warden gave me a clipboard full of papers and a pen and told me to sign each of about nine pages, without reading them. He said there were copies in the satchel along with belongings I had with me when I entered prison. Other items I had with me when I entered prison, including the watch I was wearing and the shaving gear I had at the time are supposed to be in the paper bundle. They said that I was free to go, Then, one of the guards unlocked the door and I was literally pushed out.

"I would not have been surprised to see a firing squad waiting. As it was, you were there."

He paused and grinned wryly. "Does anyone want to tell me more? I'm kind of interested."

"There's plenty of time for that," Sarah said. "But Ben did it. You'll never believe it all. Ben even went and talked to Eleanor Roosevelt and she talked to President Truman. Imagine! You've got an unconditional Presidential pardon."

"What does that mean?" Azzo asked.

"It means, sir," Ben said, "that your full rights of citizenship are restored. You can go about your life from here on as if none of this ever happened. You can vote. You can do anything you want. You're eligible for a passport and a driver's license." He grinned. "You can even get a library card, and the librarian at the Rosenberg has one waiting. The only thing you can't do, Dad, for the next year, or four more years if Truman is elected to a new term, is grant an interview to anyone in the news media. The past seventeen months—the trial, the testimony, the lawyers, the demands for disclosure of all those brought illegally into this country—all that never happened."

"It still seems pretty vivid to me," Azzo said, "and I've got the gray hairs to prove it."

"It's only salt-and-pepper," Sarah said, "and I think it makes you look distinguished and handsome!" She brushed back the wayward forelock and smoothed her husband's hair.

Ben was silent for several miles as his mother and father talked, occasionally embracing, and Sarah told her husband about life-changing and improbable events.

Diane turned the car into a small airport. "Time to ditch the car," she said.

"You flew up?" Azzo asked. Then, looking at the red-and-white airplane with tricycle landing gear, said, "Is this your new airplane?"

Ben shook his head. "No. This is Slim's new airplane. He's gonna use it in his charter business. This baby is his fastest plane, cruising speed: 162 knots, range 940 miles. It's on loan, free for this occasion. We left Galveston before dawn today."

Ben and Diane went into an office at the side of a hangar, built as a lean-to. Sarah and her husband waited in the car.

Ben came down the steps of the office to the car. "Why don't you guys come into the office and have a cup of coffee, use the restroom or whatever, stay warm. Freshen up a bit. Dad, we brought your khakis and a jacket if you want to get out of that prison-issue. I'm going to spend a few minutes checking out and looking over the airplane before we take off for our trip home. We can continue catching up during the flight. We'll all get brought up to date about everything that's happened." As Azzo exited the car, Ben hugged him again.

"Dad," he said choking. "Oh, God! Dad, I love you so!"

Azzo returned the hug to his handsome, slender, dark-haired and once-crippled son in return. "I love you, too!" he said as he felt tears again forming.

"Okay," Ben said, pulling away, "enough of this hugging. I'll be bawling again in a minute, and we'll have Mom bawling, too. Diane and I have some checking to do, weather and so on. Dad, I'll put your stuff in the plane. We need to take off pretty quickly if we're to make Alvin before dark."

Later, after Ben and Diane spent a few minutes with the fixed-base operator, reviewing weather data, paying for the rent-car and refueling services, Ben turned to his family, noting that his dad had changed into the khakis and jacket they'd brought.

"I put the suit, that overcoat and scarf into the trash," Azzo said. "They smelled."

"Time to go, folks," Ben said, "there's a weather system from Canada on the way, and we gotta beat it to Texas."

Diane pushed the airplane to its cruising elevation in a cloudless winter sky, and the airplane settled into a smooth flight. Azzo thought his son looked dashing, sitting in the airplane's right seat as the plane's co-pilot, in his leather jacket, aviator sunglasses and earphones, one side jacked up so as to hear conversation. Diane, as pilot, was wearing her own set of sunglasses and earphones.

Azzo looked at the ground below, seeing the broad flat landscape, the brown winter cornfields dotted with patches of white. Diane had banked the aircraft after takeoff, turning southward, and as she did, Azzo saw the sprawling gray stone prison where he had spent a little more than sixteen months. He kept watching as the prison faded into the distance.

Ben turned to his parents and discovered them once again embracing.

"Hey, you two," Ben said. "Plenty of time for that!" He was grinning. "Mom put fresh sheets on the bed before we left. As soon as we get home you two can stay there and muss them as much and as long as you like."

"Ben!" Sarah said loudly, too embarrassed to say more.

"First order of business is a bath for me," Azzo said. "I tried a spit-bath in the lavatory back at the airfield, but I still smell like Leavenworth."

Ben turned back to the instrument panel, noting that Diane was about to burst into laughter at his mother's discomfiture. He thought about adding to his mother's uneasiness but decided against it. "Back to business," he told himself.

Ben again turned to his passengers. "We've got great cruising weather. No ceiling, smooth air and unlimited visibility. We'll be passing into Oklahoma soon. Mom, it seems to me that now is a good time to tell your lover-boy here everything that has happened during these last few months."

"Wait," Azzo said. "Before you start, tell me about Levi."

Ben's face took on a momentary sadness. "Yeah, I guess that does need to be the first on the agenda. I wrote you; I watched him die. We all watched him die." Ben removed his aviator sunglasses and wiped his eyes. "Dad, we were in Mr. Bentley's office—well, Diane wasn't there—but I was, and Billy and mom. We were talking about our plans to try and get you out of that place. Uncle Levi had climbed the stairs instead of using the elevator."

"Climbed the stairs! Can you believe that!" Sarah exclaimed. " At ninety-three years old he climbed three flights of stairs!"

"I'm not surprised," Azzo said. "Years ago, when I first met him, staying at the Galvez, I noticed he climbed the stairs every day. I asked him about it once."

"What did he say?" Ben asked.

"He just shrugged," Azzo answered. "All he said was, 'Exercise.' I don't think he liked elevators very much."

Ben chuckled. "That's exactly what he said to Mr. Bentley. He was breathing pretty hard. It was raining cats and dogs. Water was hitting the window so hard you couldn't even see out. Then, some of the things we talked about, well, they made Uncle Levi rather emotional, but—but you know we were all emotional. And then, Dad, it was so strange. I was looking straight at him. Mom was making some point or another, I don't remember exactly, when it seemed to me that Uncle Levi straightened up and looked at the door. It was closed, of course, but the way he looked at it was as if he was seeing someone who had entered and was standing beside the closed door. His eyes, dad. I couldn't believe it, but Uncle Levi's eyes seemed to follow someone, someone or something. He could see who or what it was, but the rest of us couldn't." Ben paused.

"Whatever or whomever he saw seemed to cross the room and Uncle Levi's eyes followed. It seemed to me that it was a man—but I didn't actually see a man. It's hard to explain. It was like looking at a photograph, and part of the photograph was out of focus." Ben shook his head. "No, that's not quite right either. Anyway, the man—I guess—seemed to go to the window. It was still raining. And then..." Ben's voice broke. "And then the rain stopped! Oh, God! It was incredible how quickly the rain stopped. All at once! Then, just after the rain stopped, Uncle Levi closed his eyes and almost deliberately lowered his chin onto his chest. When he did, his arms dropped off the armrests. He took one last breath and let it out. It was like a long sigh." Ben again choked. "And then the room was full of sunlight, and Uncle Levi was gone.

"I believe," Ben continued, his voice strained, "and I will believe this all of my life, I believe we witnessed mal'akh, the messenger of God, who came that day for God's servant, my great, great uncle, Levi Weismann."

Ben turned in the seat, put his head down, his hands covered his face. "Excuse me," he said. A loud sob escaped.

"Ben," Diane interrupted, her voice brisk, "weather report coming in."

Ben straightened up, tears suddenly gone, turned and slid his headset over his ears. "Back in a minute."

Later, Azzo listened in amazement as Ben told, along with his mother, the improbable story of release from prison. He could see in his mind's eye a young good-looking stranger meeting Sarah and Ben and taking them around the SMU Campus. He wondered at the number of coincidences that had to have occurred over more than a decade for all that took place to have happened. This remarkable stranger, a resident of Dallas and only two years older than Ben, had sometime in the past happened to have had an extraordinary meeting with the then First Lady of the United States. Somehow, FBI Agent Josh McCuskey had known of this meeting which also included the wife of the Democratic Senator from Arkansas. Then, later, with a retired Dallas judge in attendance—a man of apparent substantial political clout—Sarah and Ben had dinner at this young man's house, and the plan emerged to present the situation to Mrs. Roosevelt, who would be asked to ask President Truman to issue a pardon.

"I can't believe any of this," Azzo said.

"It's true," Diane said, turning from the yoke as Ben took control. "I couldn't believe it myself as it was all unfolding. That was when I dropped out of Tulane and returned to Galveston. I wanted to do everything I could to help."

As she talked, Azzo studied her as if seeing her for the first time. The blonde-haired young woman that his son had chosen was beautiful. Slender, obviously athletic, every inch the aviatrix in her aviator sunglasses, with one earphone cocked away from her ear. He remembered the young woman when she was a child and was thinking how she'd grown and how much her father must appreciate her.

"How's Slim?" he asked.

"Dad's fine," she answered, smiling and showing straight white teeth. "and mom, too. They both send their best."

Then, turning serious, Diane said, "I don't know if my dad was involved in any of your and Levi's business, and Ben and I don't want to know. We all owe you a debt of gratitude for refusing to divulge…" She paused as if waiting for confirmation.

Smiling broadly, Azzo said, brightly, "You can call me Dad along with Slim."

Diane's dazzling smile returned as she realized she'd just had her answer. "Okay, Dad, but Ben's and my children are going to call you 'Pops.'"

"Pops!" Azzo said in mock surprise. "Why…?"

"Because," Diane said, laughing, "Slim has dibs on Paw-Paw."

"We're about twenty minutes out," Ben said, interrupting. "And there's one more thing that needs to be told before we land. There was a condition concerning your release. We dangled a carrot and the government snapped at it!"

"But Ben did it!" Sarah interrupted. "Ben complied. Azzo, dear, it was so amazing."

A slight frown crossed Azzo's face, as if he knew what the condition was.

"The condition, Dad," Ben said as Diane again resumed piloting the airplane, "was that the government be allowed to contact each of those brought in to confirm that none were communists. I agreed but offered a counter-condition. I told them that I wanted to be the one to contact them and, only if those I contacted agreed would I permit one and only one special FBI agent to confirm their status, and that he would be the one to confirm to the government that these people, refugees from Nazi terrorism, were, for crying out loud not members of the f-ing communist party!"

"Ben!" Sarah said.

"And I got them to agree!" Ben said, ignoring his mother's concern about his language.

"But it was Ben who did it!" Sarah broke in. "He and that FBI man McCuskey! Together they visited each of the people you brought in."

Ben nodded. "Yeah. I insisted it be McCuskey."

"All 350? How did you know where to find them?" Azzo asked.

"Dad," Ben said, "I had your ledgers. They're quite detailed, you know. You wrote them after all. When I learned the government was searching I knew there would only be one place for them and, sure enough, there they were."

"How did you know?"

"I watched you build it!"

"But you were so young, and you couldn't have known what that cabinet was for."

"Oh, Dad, I was just a kid, but I knew a secret cabinet when I saw one. The government boys tore the place apart. I watched them. They at first went right past your cabinet. The ledgers weren't there by that time anyway, but the existence of the cabinet just blew right past them until they busted down the wall.

"The ledgers were behind the seat of my tail-dragger, in plain sight, all the time they were tearing your work studio to pieces. After they'd left," Ben shrugged, "and the wall and cabinet were rebuilt, I put them back. They're there today. The government only has photocopies.

"Oh, Dad," Ben went on, "a lot of the help we needed came from Drew Neilan and Judge McGowan, and, oh, this remarkable lady, Catherine Browning. Dad, none of these people are Jewish, but they were all dedicated to our cause. Mrs. Browning even wrote a scathing editorial which appeared on the front page of a Washington newspaper!

"Oh, look," Ben said, changing the subject and pointing, "there's Houston and in the distance you can see the Gulf. If you have more questions, they'll have to wait until later." He nodded at Diane and took over the airplane's controls. "Can you guess the first thing we'll do?"

"Buzz San Luis Pass?" Azzo answered.

"You got it!" Ben said.

The red-and-white airplane lost altitude. At 700 feet Ben banked the plane and as the sun set, all aboard saw the blue

Gulf, the tan sandy beach, and the green bay waters as they met the surf. Surf fishermen looked up and waved.

The sun was below the horizon as Ben brought the airplane into a smooth and flawless landing, settling softly onto the grass runway of Bichler Airfield.

There were still many things that needed to be talked about, but at the end of the remarkable day, on the drive to Galveston, Sarah knew that Azzo wanted nothing more than to see Mansion House. She also knew, by the look on her husband's face, that he was remembering numerous sunsets, the orange globe of the sun riding in a clear blue and gold sky, settling into Christmas Bay across from the surf and the dunes of San Luis Pass.

Chapter 35

Six Weeks Later Saturday afternoon

It was mid-afternoon, a warm spring day in April. Azzo and his son were sitting in the gazebo next to the pool at Mansion House gardens. Winter was at bay and even with the light overcast it seemed as if summer might be just around the corner. They were both in their shirtsleeves, each with a bottle of beer. Wallace was on the mowing machine, its racket making conversation difficult as he occasionally passed the gazebo.

They had talked about many things over the last weeks. It seemed to Ben that his mother was happier than he'd ever seen, and he realized that she was accepting Azzo for who he was instead of the man she thought he should be, and Azzo in turn was falling in love all over again. Ben knew that they had at last become the partnership that defines every successful marriage. Any rivalry between them was gentle, teasing, and ultimately loving.

"Levi left everything to you," Azzo said. It was almost a question.

"No, not everything," Ben said. "We've talked about this before. Let me tell you the details. He must have had some premonition, because for months before he died he began the process of liquidating his holdings in the bank. Some of the bank officers got quite lucky, for he gave several of them more of their share of the bank than they'd earned. He liquidated all his holdings. He forgave Mom the remnants of her mortgages, both for Mansion House and Mansion House West and the loan to take care of repairing all the damages the Federal agents caused when they searched the place. He awarded her $50,000 to boot.

"Anyway, what he left me was money, not the bank. I guess he figured I could make my own investments or whatever. It's quite a lot of money. I don't yet know the actual total, but, after inheritance taxes it's going to be something around ten million.

"I'm currently," Ben said, "getting a generous allowance. I won't come into my majority until my twenty-fifth birthday. Billy said he'd advance enough for a new airplane."

"But you haven't bought it yet."

"No. Cessna's coming out with a four-seater version of my two-seater, and others are bringing out new models as well. I'm still shopping."

"Are you planning to return to college?" Azzo asked.

"Oh, sure," Ben said. "I took a leave after only one semester, and later Diane left Tulane." He turned to his father. "We had things to do. Even so, we managed to take classes at Alvin's new Junior College, so when we return we can enter as juniors instead of returning freshmen."

"I'm still amazed about how it all came about." Azzo said. "Tell me again about your visiting those I brought in?"

"I visited all 350," Ben said. "It was quite a job even to locate many of them. They'd moved, some leaving no forwarding address. When I found them, I telephoned if possible and flew to wherever they were in my little Cessna.

"A lot of times Josh flew with me. And each and every one, Dad, when they understood, agreed to come forward. There was no hesitation.

"Many times, I'd leave Josh waiting outside and when I got the common reaction, I'd simply go onto the porch or into the driveway, or wherever, and motion for him to come in. All are resuming their true identities. One woman—Oh, God, Dad, I love her to pieces—she was quite old and had escaped a concentration camp before becoming one of your refugees. She said, in one of the heaviest German accents I believe I've ever heard, "Ya, you joost bring dot Eff-Bee-I man right into dis house. You joost bring him into dis house now! I tell him! I show him my tattoo! I show also to dot Truman guy! Bring him into dis house! I show! I not a communist. I not a Nazi. I am an American!"

Azzo laughed. "I'm pretty sure I remember that lady. That time, an inflatable was used, and it capsized in the surf. She swam and waded, ignoring my attempts to help. Once on the beach, she turned to me. 'God Bless America,' was all she said."

Wallace passed by again, and Azzo waited until the noise subsided. "Her name was Ursula, wasn't it?"

"Exactly!"

Ben paused for a long time.

"Dad, I'd never have gotten you out of prison without the help of Josh McCuskey and Drew Neilan."

Ben was thoughtful for perhaps another minute and took a long pull on his beer, now becoming warm. "But Dad, while Drew was important, it was McCuskey all the way. He put his whole career on the line. It was he who arranged for me to meet Drew Neilan when we first visited SMU."

"It all seems so improbable, " Azzo said.

"Well, trust me, it happened," Ben answered. "And you're out of jail, which proves the point."

Then turning to his dad, he said, rising, "I need another beer. How about you?"

"You're not yet twenty-one," Azzo said, smiling because he knew what Ben was going to say.

"Dad," Ben said, his mouth turned down, mocking with a scorn he didn't feel, "I've been drinking since I was fourteen, and you know it! You're the one who gave me my first beer."

He left for the kitchen refrigerator. "So, Dad, here's the way it was,' Ben said, returning with two opened bottles of Southern Select, both wet with condensation. "It was all McCuskey, pure and simple." Ben paused as Wallace again passed on the mowing machine.

"Josh came to the beach one night. I remember it rained, and we pulled the cars up into the dunes so they wouldn't get stuck. That was the night I told him about…oh! I don't think you know…"

A frown crossed Azzo's face. "Know what?" he asked.

"About the day…" Ben paused. "Oh, my God! Dad, that was the day it all began," he said.

"What?"

And Ben told his father about being a frightened ten-year old, fleeing from an unknown menace, and how that menace must have been a courier who was to deliver a key to Sarah, who in turn was to take it to Uncle Levi.

Azzo nodded. "Yes, Levi and I wondered many times about that. The man was a courier, of course, bringing the key to Levi. Much later we learned that a German agent caught up with him. He managed to kill the agent but got himself stabbed in the process."

"Yeah, over in Winnie," Ben said.

"He must have known that Levi had a niece," Azzo continued. "When he realized he couldn't simply enter Levi's bank with blood dripping from his wound, he decided to go to Sarah."

"He asked me, Dad, two or three times, to take him to mom. I was afraid, especially when he shouted for me to get into his car. Uh-uh! I was only ten, but I knew enough to know never to do that!"

"It is curious," Azzo said, "that he found you. How did he know? Was it the wrist cane?"

"We'll probably never know," Ben said. "I was sitting on the edge of the pier when he started shouting at me. I could be seen from 61st Street. I don't think my cane was anywhere in sight, but I had the metal brace on my left leg," Ben shrugged. "Maybe he saw that. I was wearing short pants that day. It was hot. The sun was really bright. Maybe the brace flashed in the sun. I don't know and I don't think we'll ever know. I really don't care anymore. Once I told all this stuff to Josh, I kind of just put it away. I don't even think about it anymore." He paused. "Well, I don't think about it much anymore. Someday, maybe it'll go away forever." He turned to the man who'd become his father.

"You're getting stronger. All those trips to the beach since you've been back, they've worked their magic."

"Yes," Azzo agreed. "I feel good. Almost my old self."

"How about another run, Dad? Let's go now. A run is always guaranteed to clear my head." Ben turned, poured out the remnants of his beer. Azzo did likewise.

Ben and his father, along with Diane and Sarah, ran that day at San Luis Pass.

Sarah looked about as she climbed from the car in her cut-off dungarees. The light overcast, to Sarah, gave the day a dreary feel. "It's as if this day is an end of something," she said to herself, "but I don't know what it could be."

She puzzled about her feelings while the others pulled several large thermoses from the car.

And as Ben and his family ran, the rays of the setting sun broke through and colored the remnants of the overcast, making the calm waters of Galveston Bay shimmer with color. The blue of the Gulf had come far inshore, turning the near-shore waters bright green upon which foamy whitecaps shone bright and sparkled in the newly released sunlight. Gulls swirled and turned overhead with raucous calls.

Ben shouted, "To the driftwood!"

The three with him called out, in unison, "Run with the wind!"

Later, as darkness was falling, the overcast vanished completely. Ben and Azzo poured fresh water over their heads and shoulders from a thermos, dried themselves and placed yarmulkes upon their heads, their adult bar mitzva prayer shawls across their shoulders. They knelt in the sand, their women with them, and sang a prayer of *Havdallah* as three stars became visible, marking the end of Shabbat.

And, Sarah decided, that was the end that the day and the overcast had been forecasting, and now the stars and the prayers were telling her it was also a new beginning.

THE END

Epilogue

Run With the Wind is fiction. While the story takes place in Galveston, Texas, I have deliberately confused many geographic locations. For example, there is a 51st Street in Galveston, Texas as well as a Strand Avenue. However, the two do not intersect. There was never a historic Victorian mansion owned by a family named Weismann.

It is historical fact that Fort Crockett on Galveston Island became a prisoner of war camp in 1943 when the first group of 165 POW's arrived in Galveston. The compound was located from 53rd Street to 57th Street and from Avenue Q to Seawall Boulevard. The compound fence went across the Boulevard, down to the beach and across the beach into the water. A total of 650 POW's were detained at the camp until it was deactivated in 1946.

In the story, Sarah Jacobs works for an organization called Galveston Pilots' Guild, and it is she who is responsible for scheduling pilots for ocean-going vessels entering and leaving the Houston-Galveston Ship Channel. There is no such organization and never was.

A number of the events related to World War II described in the story are based on actual happenings. Several times I deliberately misstated the timeframe. Readers that are interested are directed to Google.com.

There was a real person named Henry Cohen, rabbi of B'nai Israel, born in London in 1863. He attended Jews College and graduated as a "Minister", one who was a Torah Reader, a Hebrew teacher, a schochet (ritual slaughter) and a mohel.

Cohen's first pulpit was at the Kingston Synagogue in Jamaica. In 1885 he accepted a position as rabbi of Congregation Beth Israel in Woodville, Mississippi. In 1888 he accepted the pulpit of Congregation B'nai Israel in Galveston, Texas, and served there until his death in 1952.

The words that my fictitious Rabbi Cohen speaks in this story are my words, not words spoken by the real-life Henry Cohen. I apologize in advance if my fictitious Henry Cohen in any way distracts from the legacy of the real-life person. It was not my intention to do so. Run With the Wind is in a small way based on some of Rabbi Cohen's experiences. Between the years 1907 and 1914 he assisted some ten thousand Jewish refugees fleeing Russia and Eastern Europe to enter the United States legally through Galveston. My fictious Azzo Burkhardt also assists Jewish refugees to enter the United States, though not through Galveston. Rather, Azzo brings them in via various unoccupied locations along the 600-mile Texas coastline. They, even though fleeing Nazi persecution, are nonetheless illegal immigrants.

In the final one-third of Run With the Wind the reader will find that I introduce Ben and Sarah to a 21-year old Drew Neilan and a few others from my first book, Never Cry Again.

This story, Run With the Wind, is therefore Book 2 of a planned three-book series.

Book 3 is titled "Brothers" and is the sequel to both Books 1 and 2. The story is set in mid-twentieth century Dallas. Look for it in bookstores or your favorite online retailer in 2023.

Jim Cole
Victoria, Texas
April 2020

About the Author

JIM COLE is a retired civil/structural engineer. While traveling around the world on various engineering projects, he always dreamed of becoming a writer. When he retired after 42 years as a consulting engineer, he saw his chance to fulfill that dream. He attended Rice University's Glasscock School of Continuing Studies in Houston, taking classes in creative writing. Later, he joined the Houston Writer's Guild and was fortunate to be under contract for several years to the Houston Chronicle for stories for their Sunday supplement magazine, Texas.

Today, Jim and his wife Marian live quietly in their hometown, Victoria, Texas, where Jim continues his interests in writing and studies Victoria's rich history and heritage. Jim currently authors a monthly newspaper column for

Victoria Preservation, Inc., where he is a member of the Board of Directors. His well-received column, 'Vanished from Victoria', published in The Victoria Advocate, documents Victoria's vanishing nineteenth and early twentieth-century architectural heritage.

Never Cry Again was the then 80-year old Jim's debut novel. His second, completed by Jim four years later, is Run With the Wind, a story of World War II and Galveston, Texas.

The two novels are planned as Books 1 and 2 of a three-part series. Book 3, Brothers, focuses on the Neilan and Burkhardt families in Dallas, Texas during the middle years of the twentieth century.